Terroir

Michael Myette

Also By Michael Myette

Free Radical

Terroir is a work of fiction. All names, characters, places, and incidents are a product of the author's imagination. Any resemblance to actual current events, living persons, or locales is entirely coincidental.

DEDICATION

This book is dedicated, to my spouse, Thao, my children, Annie, Maylee, and Wakee, and my parents, Mike and Anita. The support of my family defies reason and exceeds all of my expectations. I am truly the luckiest man alive.

ACKNOWLEDGMENTS

I wish to thank all of those who supported this endeavor. Thanks to Christopher Koehler for early editing and advice. Thanks to Dan McNamara for constructive criticism and for making legal aspects of the story more plausible. Thanks to Dr. Jamie Sherman, Dr. Natasha Fine, and Dr. Han Vu for wine education and character inspiration. Thanks to Dr. Thao Doan for disproportionately taking on all of the unspoken burdens of our shared life while letting me continue to joust windmills.

Terroir/Myette

ter·roir [ter-**wahr**; *Fr.* ter-**war**]

The environmental conditions, especially soil and climate, in which grapes are grown and that give a wine its unique flavor and aroma.

Chapter 1:

They were coming for him again, soon. He was certain. There were no warnings, no alerts, save for the ache between his thumb and index finger. Strange as it was, that ache was almost always reliable. Matthew Quinn didn't smell trouble; he felt it, right in his hands.

The whole damned situation started a year ago with threatening phone calls. Unsatisfied with the results, they began the menacing, unexpected visits. Home invasions were a better description. But these were nothing compared to what happened next. The "abductions," forced trips down to the bay area for coercive interrogation, were an experience beyond terrible. They felt a lot like the time he was kidnapped several years back. Only this time it wasn't organized crime, it was the feds. He wasn't sure which federal agency it was. Everything was so vague, no Miranda, no lawyers, no witnesses. This was all on purpose, the *modus operandi* of a new, clandestine federal agency, so much for the Bill of Rights.

Quinn was a man with a history. He was a scientist, once a national-class runner, an inventor, a millionaire, and most recently a winery owner and winemaker. Today he was out on a run. Despite his age and the busy life he led, he was still in remarkable condition. He wasn't out to race, that part of his life was over. Quinn ran to reduce the stress caused by his present circumstances and to prove to himself that even in his early forties he wasn't over the hill. He also needed to reassure himself that the feds were not getting the best of him, and that even without ingesting the age-reversing drug he invented, patented, and then sold, he could beat back Father Time. For several weeks now, that pain between his thumb and index finger warned him that the clock on his freedom was ticking.

So was the clock on his life.

Quinn knew he was in trouble when the dark Chrysler approached. He slowed, casting about for an escape route. Screeching rubber on asphalt alerted him to the second car behind him. Six men efficiently surrounded him, guns drawn. Quinn's eyes darted up and down the road, looking for a witness, an escape route, anything.

"Don't be stupid. Get into the car Quinn," a linebacker-sized federal agent with a flattop haircut, pasty skin, dark sunglasses and a black suit said. His name was Walker Dunn, and he was the only one Quinn recognized. He had been present at the previous encounters, the previous abductions.

Quinn hated him.

Quinn envisioned bolting toward Dunn. He thought about how he could hurt him, bad. It was an uncharacteristic thought for Quinn, who despite his black-belt in judo and experience in kung fu and tae-kwon-do, was docile by nature, and about half the size of the ample federal agent.

It was just a thought.

Dunn's size and strength didn't scare Quinn, but he wasn't stupid either. There were too many of them. He'd have six bullets in him before he reached his target.

Defeated, Quinn did as he was told. An instant after climbing into the back seat of the sedan he felt the sting of a hypodermic needle and the burn of concentrated medicine in his deltoid. An unfamiliar agent entered and sat to his left as Dunn capped the syringe, sitting to his right. In a show of defiance, Quinn's elbow slammed Dunn hard in his muscular midsection. The agent let out a grunt. A second later, the butt of Dunn's gun crashed across the bridge of Quinn's nose, Quinn's reflexive forearm block only partially deflected the blow. Blood erupted in alarming quantities.

As the car pulled away, the pain in his nose drifted away too. Quinn felt the effects of whatever cocktail was in the syringe. His face felt like molding clay, and his shoulders slumped as the tension in his muscles melted. His mind struggled to stay alert and his heart quickened, even as his body wilted under the effects of the drug.

"Feel like telling us the truth this time?" Dunn asked.

"I told you the truth the last time," Quinn mumbled, more to himself than anyone else. His neck was flexed, eyes cast down into his lap, watching the blood drip off the end of his nose and soaking into his running shorts.

"Right, so how is it that we can detect the polymer in wastewater on Martha's Vineyard, in Napa, Aspen, Sedona, and other places where rich people go?" he asked.

"I don't know," Quinn said, looking up and holding pressure over the bridge of his nose.

Dunn was silent. He looked Quinn over, and Quinn sensed he was going to change tactics. "How's the winery?" he asked.

"I still haven't finished the cleanup after you and your goons tore it up," Quinn said. He felt drunk, not inebriated, but like he had consumed four glasses of wine. He also felt like none of the struggling was worth it anymore. He gave up a deep sigh and shook his head. Probably the drugs, but the fight just didn't seem worth it.

"I understand you sold it," he said.

"Selling, present tense, but yeah," Quinn acknowledged.

"Must be a heartbreaker," Dunn said.

"Stop patronizing me," Quinn said, turning to face Dunn. "I can't run the winery with all my bank accounts frozen."

"Why not tap into some of that money you have off-shore?" Dunn asked. "I understand there's millions."

"Which money is that?" Quinn answered. He had nothing to hide. Well, almost nothing. But he was losing focus now, forgetting where he was.

"You know damn well what money, you little fuck. We know it, and you know it. When I can prove it, you'll be arrested for crimes against the United States," Dunn said.

"Like treason?" Quinn asked, confused. How had they arrived at that?

"Not treason, but like treason."

Quinn turned away, looking out the window at the passing hills. "I thought I was being investigated for patent infringement and possession and distribution of an illegal substance." The drugs were getting the better of him, and his tongue felt thick. He was dizzy, and embarrassed at his slurred speech, so he began to concentrate on speaking clearly, sounding sober. It seemed like the right thing to do.

"It'll be worse than that, believe me. I'll get you for tax evasion, too. Just like Al Capone. You know what they do to people like you?" Dunn asked.

"No."

"They lock them up and throw away the key," Dunn said with a smile. "You'll never see the light of day again if you don't cooperate with us."

Quinn felt his consciousness wax a little. He figured they gave him some sort of barbiturate mixed with an amphetamine to keep him awake, and to melt away any stubborn resolve they might think he had. A federal speedball, he thought to himself without any amusement. Looking out the window was making his head spin. He turned and tried to focus on his captor, but the focus in his eyes was shot. Dunn was now little more than two fuzzy blobs, partially superimposed on each other. "The funny thing is I don't want that drug out there any more than you do. When are you going to get it through your head that someone else is doing this, not me?"

"Tell me who else knows how to make the polymer, and none of this Vladimir Michinski bullshit. His body washed up on the beach in Pacifica more than three years ago and we know all his men are dead or in jail." Dunn said.

Quinn shrugged and was silent. Dunn had a point. Quinn had no idea who would be making the polymer. He had no idea who could make the polymer. As far as he knew, he was the only one left who knew how to produce it. But he wasn't making it. "I don't know, but it isn't me."

"Uh-huh," Dunn said, yawning.

"So how much blood are you going to take this time?" Quinn mumbled. "I couldn't run for two weeks after the last trip. My doctor checked my blood and my hemoglobin was down to seven. That means you took almost half my blood last time. Did you find anything?"

"Nope," Dunn said.

"How many more times are you going to check?" Quinn asked.

"As many as it takes. If I get a handle on where you keep your illegal money in the off-shore accounts, or if I detect that polymer in your blood, I'm putting you away. The accounts get you tax evasion, the blood gets you illegal production, distribution, and consumption."

"Swell," Quinn said.

"This time, Quinn, we're going to conduct our fact finding a little different," Dunn said, sounding smug.

Quinn didn't comment. Dunn was an ass. Drugs or no drugs, the conversation was useless, the answers, all of them true, were tired retreads. If Dunn wasn't going to believe him, then he wouldn't tell him a damn thing. He didn't say another word until after they arrived at the federal building in Oakland.

* * * * * *

Josephine Rodriguez was preparing to leave the library at her old law school. She had been up all night in the stacks, looking for a case precedent when she got a surprise text message and an odd request. She hadn't spoken to her older sister in two years, but despite her past troubles and the volatility of their relationship, Josephine desired to reconnect. She called her sister, Barbara immediately.

"What are you mixed up in?" Josephine asked and immediately regretted it. She was a criminal defense attorney, and knew it was sometimes better not to know, especially given her sister's colorful past.

"Mind your own business, and do this favor for me, please?" her sister said.

"Why don't we meet for coffee?"

"No, I need this to be taken care of now," her sister insisted. She sounded uncharacteristic, vulnerable. Josephine wondered what could make her usually self-assured older sister so unnerved, but Josephine was not going to give her something for nothing.

"Alright. There's nothing illegal about it. I'll run your 'rescue' errand for you, if you'll meet me for coffee in Berkeley." she said.

"Okay, meet me at Peet's near the University in an hour," her sister said after a long pause.

"Two hours."

"Why two hours? Where are you now?"

"I'm at the library at Hastings. But I'm going for a swim in the bay before I head over the bridge, so I'll meet you after the swim."

"A two hour swim? That's ridiculous," her sister said.

"No, just an hour, but it'll take time to dry off and get over to Berkeley, so we'll meet at seven-thirty."

"Damn, that might be too late. Why are you swimming for an hour in the freezing cold bay?" her sister asked.

"I'm getting ready for a triathlon."

There was silence. "That's a lofty goal: frivolous, but lofty. When did you set out to do that?" she asked.

"When I changed jobs. Working as a public defender didn't allow me the time to train."

"Oh, new job, eh?" her sister asked, though Josephine guessed she didn't care. "Tired of advocating for the slobs the public defender's office assigned you?"

Josephine sighed heavily, resting her forehead in her left hand. "You know I didn't see it quite like that."

"So how's the new job? I hope it pays better."

"Not exactly new, I've been with my firm for almost two years, but I guess it would be new to you, wouldn't it?" Josephine said.

"Has it been that long since we've spoken?"

"Yeah. I've missed you," Josephine said, trying to diffuse the tension between them.

"Well, fine, get your swim in, and then hustle over to Berkeley, take care of what I asked, and then we'll meet for coffee. But don't bother showing up if you're too late."

"I'll get there as quickly as I can," she said.

"You'd better," her sister said and hung up before Josephine could retort.

Barbara could hold her own with Josephine in a conversation. She was one of the few who could. She was scary-smart, and her mind was fast as hell. Josephine thought she'd have made a hell of a lawyer if she hadn't chosen a different path. She wondered if somewhere under her sister's arrogance and self-assurance she had any regrets about where she was in life.

After completing her swim Josephine felt refreshed. The cold salt water of the bay was invigorating and it shocked her into renewed wakefulness. She headed over the Bay Bridge enjoying the feeling of her sore, fatigued shoulders. She knew most wouldn't understand. She was also thinking about a shiatsu massage later that day and she was looking forward to seeing her sister.

Josephine exited where her sister told her to in Berkeley. She drove up the road in a light industrial part of town, inching along, looking from side to side of the road for her target when a man suddenly crawled out onto the street right in front of her car.

"Shit!" She was looking at the shoulder of the road and did not spot the filthy wisp of a man crawling across the street. She was on top of him in an instant. She slammed on her brakes, swerving left. The last thing she needed was to be involved in an auto-versus-pedestrian accident. She'd be taken apart by any plaintiff's lawyer, sleep deprived as she was. Exhausted or not, her reflexes were still sharp enough and her BMW M3 sport coupe was nimble enough to almost avoid the disheveled man crawling in the street.

Almost.

As her tires bit the pavement and screeched to a halt, there was the unmistakable bump of contact.

She gave a frustrated sigh before getting out of the car. "Damn it," she said, fumbling for her cell phone as she exited the vehicle, hoping she was not going to see a dead body mangled below her chassis. Adrenaline coursed through her veins. She was wide-awake now.

So much for meeting my sister.

The man gasped and grunted as she approached, but said nothing. He was breathless; his eyes squeezed shut as he held his leg. He was in a white bloodstained t-shirt and jogging shorts. He looked half-dead and the stink of stale sweat, blood, and adrenaline wafted up from him.

"What the hell are you doing? I might have killed you," Josephine said, alarm ringing in her gravelly voice. "You don't go crawling out into traffic like that!"

"Sorry," he whispered, wincing and breathless, his eyes squeezed shut. "I was trying to get your attention. I need help," the man gasped more than spoke.

That's obvious.

He opened one eye, giving her a pleading look. It looked like his arm was broken and he had blood oozing from his lower leg and knee. There was dried blood around his nose, which was swollen like a boxer's, and old bloodstains covered his filthy shirt and shorts.

"I think we both do," Josephine said, "I'm calling an ambulance." She dialed 911 on her cell phone. After a contentious conversation with the dispatcher she hung up. Somewhere far away, a siren sounded. She turned back to the man under the front bumper of her car, trying to remember something from the basic life support class she had taken in law school. He was a wreck of a human being, a reject, spit out of hell.

"What's your name?"

"Matthew Quinn," he whispered through chapped, parched lips.

Her belly did an involuntary lurch at the name. She wondered again what her sister was mixed up in. She studied his appearance, something she often did with her clients. She could find reliable data in appearances, like Sherlock Holmes.

He had three days of facial hair growth, and short-cropped steely gray hair, but he wasn't old. He was uncomfortably thin, but also looked fit. Clean him up and give him a few pounds of muscle and he could have been in her triathlon-training group. He looked like a cross between a refugee and a marathon runner. She noticed he had good skin and clean, soft appearing hands. He didn't look like someone from the streets, but someone who might be professional, or at least middle-class. But he also looked like he was dying.

"What on earth are you doing here?" she asked kneeling down next to him. They were on a deserted road amongst idle warehouses, closed on a Saturday morning. "Here, let's get this under your head," she said as she shoved a towel under his head. She hoped he didn't have a broken neck.

"I don't know," Quinn replied between short, raspy breaths. "I was out running, I think, and I don't remember what happened, or how I got here. Where are we?"

She could tell his strength was failing. He was breathing like he was in the final sprint of a race. His mouth was caked with dried saliva and his eyes were sunken, like he had been wandering the desert for days. He was starving for air and he shivered uncontrollably. He stopped talking and for an instant Josephine thought he might just up and die right there. She took off her hooded sweatshirt and placed it around him as rigors shook his body. She still did not know where she hit him, or whether his appearance was the result of some ominous internal injury.

“We’re in Berkeley. You’re close to a hospital,” she told him trying to sound reassuring. She was relieved by the sound of approaching sirens.

“Berkeley?” he said in little more than a whisper. “How did I get to Berkeley?” He then slipped into unconsciousness as the EMT’s arrived.

Chapter 2:

Strange sounds penetrated the darkness. There were beeps, bells, and voices. They were worlds away from Quinn. He didn't know where he was. It wasn't heaven. It wasn't hell. More like the bottom of the ocean.

Dark silence returned.

Quinn dreamed of a beautiful angel in a hooded sweatshirt with wet hair, floating above him, smiling a reassuring smile and trying to comfort him. Maybe it was heaven.

Later, chirps and mechanical sounds drifted back, pulling him from oblivion. He heard voices again, and this time fuzzy light and shadow danced before him. It was nothing he could identify, just light and dark, like looking through wax paper.

Once again darkness returned.

The third time that soundless oblivion gave way he seized his senses like a vice. If staying awake was an act of will, he would not drift off again.

Where was he and what was going on? His mind sharpened and he surveyed his available senses. He was recumbent and could not see. He felt air blowing into his lungs, but it wasn't him who had drawn breath. With a jolt of panic he felt the tube in his throat. He gagged immediately, attempted to yell, or cough, or…. something. An imperceptibly silent hhhhhhhhhhhhhhh was all that came out. He reflexively drew his hands up to his mouth to remove the object, but his wrists snapped back, held in place by limb restraints. He bent and contorted his body, trying desperately to get his hands on the breathing tube which was making him cough, gag, and retch violently, but in absolute silence. His bulging eyes opened and the startling face of a plump middle-aged woman dressed in nurse's scrubs was staring back at him.

"Relax Dr. Quinn," she said, placing a calming hand on his chest. "You've been through a lot. We were just waiting for you to wake up. You are in the hospital at Alta Bates, in the ICU."

Quinn calmed down, and wrestled back control of his gag reflex. He laid back into the bed, glancing down at his naked body: EKG leads on his torso, a catheter in his bladder, a large central IV line sutured into his shoulder, various bandages and wraps, and four point restraints on his limbs. He felt undignified and violated. What had landed him in the ICU?

Two hours later, a relieved Matthew Quinn was extubated. He still did not know what had happened. Dr. Monica Bikhram, a South-Asian intensivist and someone Quinn knew from his past life at the University of California, San Francisco and as a regular visitor to his winery, came by to see him later that afternoon.

"Close call Quinn," she said shaking her head as she sat at the end of the bed.

"What happened?" Quinn asked, still confused about how he had ended up in the ICU.

"What didn't happen? First was the trauma, though that turned out to be minor. You were in shock and cardiovascular collapse when the ambulance picked you up. If that weren't enough, you threw a huge clot into the pulmonary artery, shot up the pressures in your lungs, and ended up with a stroke," Bikhram said, arching her eyebrows. "You're lucky to be alive."

"Did you do thrombolysis on me?" Quinn said, looking at his hands as he opened and closed them. They both appeared to be working. He shuddered at the thought of the risky but often lifesaving and brain saving maneuver. They had given him a powerful clot dissolving medicine, which could save his life, but might have also made him bleed to death from his other injuries.

"You were a good candidate," she said. "Except for your other injuries, but we still felt like it was the right thing to do. It all started when you were found down on the mean streets of Berkeley. Out getting your kicks Quinn? There was quite a cocktail on your tox screen." Dr. Bikhram said, shooting a serious glance at him. "Fentanyl, barbiturates, dextroamphetamine, and some designer drug we can't even identify. What's a guy like you doing getting mixed up with garbage like that? You have to be more careful."

"I have no idea, honestly," Quinn said. "I'm not even clear on what it was that happened. I only have a vague memory of lying in the road."

"A car nearly ran you over, but it looks like the only contact was with your right arm and right leg. There's road rash on the leg and a broken ulna on the arm. But something else happened. When you arrived here you were in cold shock. We don't usually see that with drug addicts unless they're septic. You weren't septic. The trauma was too mild to cause it. You were in kidney failure from dehydration and blood loss, which we can't really explain. You were resuscitated and transfused, but you just kept trying to die."

"What happened next?"

"You threw a big clot from your leg. It lodged in your lungs. That pushed the pressure in your heart up and opened a hole between the right and left side of your heart."

"Oh, no," he muttered. This was a nightmare.

"Oh yeah," she retorted with a rueful smile. "Our cardiologist figured that out. The newly opened hole created the path for the next clot to pass into the arterial circulation, and up to your brain. We were right on top of it when it happened. You got the *Altepase* and flow was restored. You're lifestyle notwithstanding, Quinn, beware of dehydration, it can be a killer."

"Pulmonary embolism and stroke?" Quinn said in a faraway voice, contemplating the information he just received. Before his retirement and foray into winemaking he had been a pediatric critical-care specialist. He was an expert in such physiology. His area of research was pulmonary vascular hypertension, and the irony was not lost on him.

"Did someone do a cardiac catheterization on me?" he asked, feeling a bandage over his groin.

"Yes," Dr. Bikhram said, looking at Quinn hesitantly. "Your pulmonary pressures were more than twice systemic. There was a lot of strain on the heart. You were on inhaled nitric oxide for three days to keep down the pressure. After we treated the thrombus and the pulmonary emboli, the pressures retreated some. They are now a little over systemic pressure in your lungs, at least by echocardiogram."

"Son of a bitch," he said quietly, his spirits sinking. He *had* died. She just didn't realize it yet.

Or maybe she did.

There was a long pause while Dr. Bikhram looked at him sadly. "Matthew, I recommend rest. Change your lifestyle. You're too smart and too old to be doing whatever it is you were doing that got you into this mess. Keith Richards notwithstanding, there's no such thing as an old junkie. You of all people should understand. You nearly died of dehydration and hemorrhagic shock. I can't even explain how you survived. But there were clots in your calf, and also in your liver. We've restored flow, but it was a close call. You won't live though another episode like that."

"I'll be okay, Doc," he said, knowing it was a lie. He didn't want to explain the circumstances that were coming back to him. It was easier to let Dr. Bikhram think he was a junkie passed out on skid row.

"You've got holes all over both arms, Quinn. We tested you for HIV and hepatitis C. You're negative, but you won't be for long if you continue shooting up. If you were someplace more rural you'd almost certainly have died," she said. "As it is, you sustained permanent kidney and pulmonary vascular damage. I don't know what the implications of that are.

I do.

"How long have I been in here?" Quinn asked.

"Seven days," she replied. "At your worst, your creatinine went up to 4.5, but it's since normalized. Your BUN was 130. You know kidneys can only take so many hits like that."

"Yeah," he replied. The feds were going to kill him. They probably thought they had, and they were almost certainly correct. They were also destroying his reputation. He could see the headline: "Junkie Pediatrician found down on Skid Row in Berkeley, multiple drugs in his system…." The Medical Board would suspend his license, though he hadn't practiced medicine in four years anyway.

"We can offer you some help getting and staying sober, if you'd like," Dr. Bikhram said, passing a pamphlet to him.

Quinn smiled back innocently. "Doc, this is so much more complicated than you think. Trust me. I like wine, maybe a lot more than I should, but that's it. This other business, this is something else."

Dr. Bikhram looked confused. "You want to talk to the police?"

"No, they can't help. What's the plan for me here?" he asked.

"You'll stay here tonight, and spend some time on the floor tomorrow, and if things are going well, you can go home the day after as long as the cardiologist thinks it's okay," she said. "You'll need to be on a baby aspirin and some blood pressure meds. We also have you on a new pulmonary vascular dilator."

"Yeah, okay," he said his mind already far away.

Two days later, Matthew Quinn was discharged from the hospital. He had come within a whisper of death, and mortality was suffocating him. He was going to die, and soon.

He never thought about dying young, never thought he would. He felt like his dying had already started, he didn't feel like eating, exercising, or socializing. He felt only dread.

His real estate agent visited him at his home and reassured him that the escrow on his winery had closed on schedule. She hesitated before handing him a cashier's check. He looked down and his heart sank further.

"This was supposed to be for twenty one million dollars. Can you explain why it's less than a million?"

"When you weren't available, the money was put into an interest bearing account, per our policy. The feds have frozen it until their investigation of you is through," she said. "It was with the application of some obscure privacy laws which allowed us to retain that much for you. I am sorry, Dr. Quinn," she said with professional sincerity. "You still have a two week rent-back on your house." She struck a conciliatory tone before hastily leaving.

He buried his head in his hands. It was hopeless. They had almost everything. He couldn't practice medicine anymore. He had no money except for the check in his hand and the small weekly withdrawals they allowed him. His research career, his medical career, his winery, and his health, all of them were gone.

He sold the winery for a big loss, too. It was probably worth upwards of thirty million, but times were tough in Napa Valley, and it was a bad time to sell. Now the equity in it was gone too, disappeared into some federal black hole.

Quinn figured that the next trip downtown with the feds would be his last. How had things ended up here? He never pictured his life ending this way. He had no livelihood, nothing to give his life meaning, and the public thought he was a burnout and a junkie. Even if he weren't arrested or killed, what would he do with his precious remaining time? And how long did he have left before the right side of his heart failed from those pressures?

He sang "Bobby McGee" to himself as he lay in a near torpor on his couch. Freedom was a euphemism for 'nothing left to lose.' Janis Joplin was a great singer. Who had written that song? Was it Kris Kristopherson?

What could he do with himself now that he had nothing left to lose? Could he get off of the grid? Perhaps this was the time to find out. He needed to get out of Napa. He remembered when he left San Francisco under similar circumstances more than four years ago. Of course, back then he had millions of dollars, a thirst for wine, and his health.

He remembered some recent additions to his wine cellar, safely cared for by his best friends in the South Bay. Maybe that was something to live for? It might be pathetic but to Quinn, some bottles of wine were that good. He had always believed winemakers lived so long because there was always the next vintage to look forward to, and some bottle of wine that just wasn't ready yet. He was now a winemaker without a winery, but he still had some pretty good wine. All right, it was better than that; it was the kind of earth-shattering, life-changing wine that baffled the general public, but winos the world over dreamed about. He had collections of Lafite, Haut Brion, Cheval Blanc, and multiple years of Napa "cult" wines like Screaming Eagle, Scarecrow, Colgin, Schrader, Bryant, and others from stateside. It was wine to drink before you die, and it was the only thing he spent his money on, back when he had money to spend.

Mondavi drank wine every day and lived to be almost a hundred, Quinn mused. He had more than a few bottles to look forward to, and now the clock was ticking even more loudly in his ear. It's time to take a break from this, and get busy on the bucket list.

But where would he go? His heart sank again and Quinn slid back into apathy. He had no place to go and no one to go to. There was once someone special in his life, but like so many things, he let her slip away.

Tasha.

He was alone. He could not even muster any interest in drinking that great wine, and that was saying something. Quinn believed wine was something to be shared, not enjoyed alone. That was what alcoholics did, and Quinn was pretty sure he wasn't an alcoholic.

Pretty. Sure.

After a week at home, depression and sheer boredom evolved into anger and irritation. He cut off the fiberglass cast on his arm with a hacksaw. The ulna had a nice callus on it, and seemed to be healing fine.

Doctors make the worst patients.

He moved to his desk in his study and began going through his long neglected pile of mail. He found lots of junk, some medical literature, and bills. Several unopened editions of *Wine* magazine were in there, but he tossed them aside. He felt like he weighed a thousand pounds even though he had probably lost another fifteen pounds since being released from the hospital. He was past refugee status, approaching consumptive in appearance; his weight loss was muscle wasting as much as anything else.

His dying had begun to accelerate.

Near the bottom of the pile, he found a letter. There was no return address and the postmark was from a town called Fairplay, California. He hadn't a clue where it was, or whom it was from, though the writing was familiar. Curiosity tickled his brain so he shrugged and opened the letter.

Out fell a press release from the *Sacramento Bee* with Quinn's name underlined. Its headline read, "Drugged-Out Pediatrician crawls under moving car in Berkeley." With it was a brief letter from his old roommate in medical school.

Shawn Callihan and Matthew Quinn had been the best of friends for four years in medical school, but afterwards, Shawn had deferred his residency training indefinitely. He chose instead to live off of his trust fund, which Quinn recalled was substantial. Quinn went off to residency and ultimately his research career and they lost touch.

The letter explained that after leaving medical school, Shawn had purchased a twenty-acre vineyard and winery in a small town called Fairplay, and was making wine.

Wine?

Quinn laughed at the strange convergence in their lives. He recalled Shawn had an uncanny ability to drink vast quantities of beer and remain remarkably sober looking in medical school, but how had the Irishman gotten into wine? Quinn hadn't gotten into wine until his residency, after he and Shawn had parted ways. In the letter, Shawn inquired about the events in Berkeley, and acknowledged that Quinn was in Napa Valley and had just sold his winery. He explained that

Fairplay was only a three-hour drive from Napa, in the Sierra foothills southeast of Sacramento. Shawn invited Quinn to consider coming to spend a weekend at the winery to tell his side of the story and to catch up on old times.

Had this been any other time, Quinn would have tossed the letter aside. But his two-week rent-back was almost up. It seemed an odd coincidence that Quinn, who would never consider a vacation, was currently homeless, and had nothing to do. And his old buddy was a wine guy now.

Quinn felt a tinge of excitement for the first time in months. Could he get up there undetected? The Sierra foothills were rural, not the tourist destination that Napa was. The feds would never suspect he was in the foothills if he managed to get up there without being followed. How could he lose them? The same formidable mind that dissected complex scientific data in his former life was already at work. He had a winery to go and visit, to disappear into, even if just for a weekend.

"What the hell," he said out loud. For a moment he quit feeling sorry for himself. He looked at the phone number on the letter, and picked up the phone. Before dialing, he put it down; thought some more, picked it up again, and left a voicemail for his friend Minh Tran, who was taking care of his wine.

"Minh, I have one more shipment which is getting picked up tomorrow for delivery to your cellar later that day. They'll call you when it arrives, please do with it exactly what you've done with the others I've sent you," he told the recording. After he hung up he went to his car, leaving all his belongings behind in the sold house. He reached into the glove box, pulled out his cellular phone, and tossed it into the vineyard. He was going to do his best to disappear.

Off the grid, he thought, checking his ashtray for enough quarters to make his next call on a public phone. He chanced a glance at himself in the rearview mirror before pulling out and stopped short. He saw his gaunt and drawn face for the first time in two weeks. He was dirty and unshaven, an older version of that kid who got lost in the Alaskan wilderness.

He looked terrible, but also nearly unrecognizable. He adjusted his rear view mirror, and gazing backwards, realized that this was the last time he would see his beloved vineyards and home. He would have cried if he weren't so damn angry.

Quinn knew there was a GPS tracer the feds had placed in his car. He had a plan though. He drove south toward the freeway. When he reached Fairfield, he pulled off of the interstate into a gas station and fueled up. He reached behind the bumper and located the transponder. He disabled it by ripping the electronic guts out of it. He then disconnected it from the car and left it in the wastebasket of the gas station.

Chapter 3:

Henri Paradis walked with a purposeful gait into the meeting room intent on discussing his options. He had been dreading this situation for the past six months, but at least today there would be a solution. It would be a day of loss, but with any luck, he would have a recovery, the weather would improve, and Ronald Park of *Wine* magazine would again warm up to his style of Cabernet.

Marianne Duncan, his accountant, was seated to his left, his attorney Josephine Rodriguez was next to her. Also present was his vineyard manager, Raul Mendoza. On the right of the oblong meeting table was his daughter Gabrielle and her husband, winemaker Andrew Wooten. Paradis acknowledged everyone in the room with brief but sincere eye contact. He cast a longer look to his daughter, which offered empathy and reassurance, before sitting down. She was pale and obviously distressed by the situation.

Marianne called the meeting to order.

"Henri, you know our most pressing problem, lack of cash flow, has us teetering on bankruptcy. Sales are down, and we're faced with severe cash flow problems. Your charitable donation to the school of winemaking at Fresno State pulled ten million dollars from the coffers of the corporation last year. The failed venture in Tuscany cost us tens of millions more."

"What about the cork taint? How much did that cost us?" Wooten asked.

"Right, the trichloroanisole, T.C.A.," she said, shaking her head. "The cleanup and product loss from the T.C.A. contamination in the winery has cost the company over nineteen million dollars in the last three years. Coupled with a decrease in sales of 25% over the same three years, and the increasing dead weight of inventory in our caves, it was perhaps the costliest of the blows we've sustained. We're at a crisis point. Fifty million dollars in operating cash and leveraged loans are gone and were currently operating at a monthly net loss of over a hundred thousand dollars."

Paradis looked at his daughter, whose eyes were squeezed shut, as though that would keep out the bad news.

"Josephine, what are our options?" Paradis asked, though he had a pretty good idea what she'd say.

"There're a number of large corporate conglomerates which want your land, label and your name. They've discussed upwards of eighty million dollars for all of the vineyards the winery and all existing equipment and inventory, along with assumption of your debt if you walk away. You can bail out and retire, or you can liquidate your assets." Josephine looked at him as she finished, striking a perfect balance of empathy and professionalism.

She's amazing, Paradis thought to himself with the pride of a surrogate father. He loved her as much as he loved his own daughter.

Paradis sat quietly for a moment, taking the situation in. None of this was news to him. He took responsibility for his actions, stood by his commitment to Fresno State's winemaking program, and acknowledged the failed venture in Italy.

The T.C.A. problem was hard for him to understand, but these things happened from time to time in a winery. Even chlorinated water could lead to creation of the chemical contaminant, which made the wine taste like it had been wrung out of a wet newspaper. It was a vintage destroyer, a cruel contaminant, blamed on corks, but Henri knew it could come from many sources.

"My name is not for sale," Paradis said in a slow and even voice. His command of the room was indisputable. He spoke quietly, but with a soft clarity and intensity which made him easy to hear.

"There are few alternatives, Henri," Josephine said.

"This is not going to be a meeting about easy choices, but I remain thankful that we still have choices. We have assets, some in Italy, some in our caves, and," he paused, "some in the land we hold. What are our options outside of bankruptcy protection?"

"You have Cabernet based wines in your cellar and the caves, which total almost 22,000 cases," Duncan began. "Unfortunately, many of those cases are from the last two years we released, not old enough to be sold as library collectables, and not well rated by the major critics, especially Park, who's the only professional with an opinion that matters now.

"Park!" Wooten, Paradis's son-in-law and winemaker spat with ill-concealed frustration and hatred.

"Henri, we could discount the wine heavily, liquidating 15,000 cases, at say, forty dollars a bottle. That would give us over seven million dollars. Then we'd have to come up with another five million to get us paid up on our debts and through to the next harvest," Duncan said, turning to look at Paradis.

"What about Italy?" Henri asked.

"The land and winery in Tuscany are already maximally leveraged. We could sell, but we have next to nothing in equity. It wouldn't solve our problems," Duncan said.

Paradis closed his eyes for a moment. "The problem with dropping our prices on our inventory here is that it sends a message that we have dropped our quality, and that isn't true. We have neither increased case production, nor have we traded away our land for inferior vineyards. Those wines in our cellar are not the ones contaminated with T.C.A. We declassified those."

"It was Park who crucified us," Wooten said venomously. "No one from those years got great reviews. They were the most challenging three vintages in the last twenty-five. The rains never let up, and the grapes didn't ripen well. The other critics gave us decent marks on our wines. It was Park who gave us eighty-one points twice and then eighty-three, calling our wine chalky, green, and tart. Even the eighty-eight he just gave the newly released Reserve bottling was an insult."

"Park has more clout than all other critical reviewers, that's the problem. With all of the scandals, the bribes, and the kickbacks, now he's the only one anyone trusts. We need more critics in the industry with the reputation of Park, but who aren't so brutal. Park decides who lives and dies in Napa Valley as long as he is the sole critic with an intact reputation. If we can't impress him, we're finished," Josephine said.

"Park is a brutal bastard, no doubt about it," Paradis said. "I sent the magazine three extra cases of those wines, because what he said about our wine was just not what I tasted when I drank it, even blind. He sent me a letter stating that while there was significant bottle-to-bottle variation, which I dispute as well, the green, tannic, grittiness of the wine was consistent."

Marianne Duncan spoke up again. "So, we lose two vintages to T.C.A., we follow that up with three years of the worst weather in the valley in the last fifty years, a failed venture in Europe, and, forgive me Henri, an untimely ten-million dollar donation to Fresno-State. It's a perfect storm. Now, our latest release wine, our comeback wine, for which we dropped fruit and cut per acre production by another 30% to improve our quality at harvest, just got a whopping eighty-eight points from Park, another nail in our coffin."

"That's not a bloody eighty-eight point wine," Wooten said, shaking his head.

"I know it isn't," Paradis said, nodding supportively at his winemaker. "I taste a masterpiece, I've had it along side wines Park gave ninety five points to that year, and it stands up, I'm certain of it. We won't discount the wine. That tells the world that we have done something to drop our quality. Nor will we liquidate those cases."

"What other option do we have?" Marianne asked, turning to him.

"We sell some land." Paradis said quietly. The statement dropped like a brick.

Josephine looked at him in silence, a single eyebrow arched up.

"What?" Gabrielle gasped.

"The way I see it, it's the only way we can maintain our integrity and the integrity of our product. With the industry hit by real estate issues, the recovery of the dollar and the bargains coming out of Europe, and the spat of wet, storm filled springs, some fifteen wineries in Napa Valley by my count have gone belly-up. That has driven land prices down, but we have four separate fifty-acre vineyard parcels in the valley. I think we can get twenty million for one of the plots, my least extraordinary plot. That ought to give us another couple of years to recover, and we can concentrate on the remaining hundred and fifty acres, dropping our yields and further improving our quality," Paradis said.

"Downsize?" Josephine asked. "Have you had a change of heart, Henri?"

"Forty years ago, just before he died, my father told me that Napa was not going to evolve the way Bordeaux did," Henri said. "It looks like he was right."

"What do you mean, dad?" Gabrielle asked.

"When we had all that land, he said that Napa Valley would not be made up of large wineries like the Chateaux of Bordeaux, making twenty or thirty thousand cases a year of wine. He said the land would be divided and subdivided, making very small case productions, like in Burgundy. That's what's happened. I've been too stubborn to restructure, but maybe it's time."

"Henri, if you sell the land, you'll never get it back, you know that," Josephine said.

"If we cheapen our label, and destroy our reputation, we'll never get that back either," Paradis said. "I think it's the lesser of two evils."

"Someone needs to drive Ronald Park into retirement," Marianne said.

"Or drive a stake through his heart," muttered Wooten.

Marianne ignored the comment and turned to Paradis. "You already have in mind which plot you want to liquidate?"

"Yes, the plot which has my home on it. We can sell the plot and my house. Someone might build a winery and convert the house into a tasting room, like over at Beringer. It might make it more appealing," Paradis said, his broad shoulders slumping just slightly.

"Dad, I was born in that house! It's where I grew up. How can we get rid of it?" sobbed Gabrielle.

He turned a tender eye toward his daughter. "Sweetheart, it happens that the most common land is where the house is. That's why your grandfather chose it for the house. It was the least suited to great vines. I still have the bungalow in St. Helena. It's not like I'll be homeless, and besides, it's just me now, and that house is huge. I don't need it anymore. When we recover, we'll build another one on our remaining vineyard land. It'll be better, a new chapter for our family."

Gabrielle turned towards her husband and back to her father. Tears were streaming down her face. She silently wiped them away and nodded without speaking.

"The plot extends from the Silverado Trail east to the creek, and is bordered on the south by Allen Touchet's land. What is the northern border?" Marianne asked.

"An invisible line westwards from the southern edge of the disputed plot towards the Silverado Trail. It is slightly irregular, but will give the buyer almost fifty-one acres, by my calculation, forty-eight of which are planted to vine."

"Enough for several thousand cases of production," Wooten offered, "and half of that parcel is planted to Chardonnay, which we've been selling to Beaulieu."

Marianne thought for a moment, twisting her fountain pen between her fingers as she gathered her thoughts. "Henri, is there any chance you and your brother can agree to sell the disputed plot?"

Josephine Rodriguez shook her head as if she knew it was out of the question. Marianne shot her an angry look.

"My father is buried on that land," Henri said.

"If you sell that parcel instead of the one you want to sell, you lose nothing in production, and you retain the revenue stream from Beaulieu. That old plot of land has been dormant since the early seventies. It's worth more than any other parcel of land in the area. Even splitting the sale with your brother would give you more than the plot you mentioned. I know it is a hard decision emotionally, but it would be a better business decision," Marianne said.

"It isn't just a business decision," Josephine muttered.

"Alfonse would never agree to sell that land. He holds his stake in it over me to spite me, not out of reverence to our father. Besides, he owns half the case production in the central valley, and if you believe the business journals, he is the future of wine, not us," Henri said, shaking his head. "He doesn't need the money."

"He still hasn't forgiven you?" Marianne asked.

"What's to forgive?" Henri asked. "He deserved to get fired after the stunt he pulled. When our father was alive, Alfonse wouldn't have dared pull money from the business for such a lavish personal purchase. How he thought he would get away with it after our father died is still a mystery."

"If you'd of let it go, we'd still have four hundred acres, and the twenty-two acre plot where grandpa is buried over the mineral spring would still be producing the best wine in Napa Valley," Gabrielle said wistfully.

"No," Paradis said. "The breakup was bound to happen. Alfonse had no intention of staying with the family business or in partnership with me. The Alfa Romeo was just a convenient tool to incite a fight."

"I can't believe anyone would trade two hundred prime acres in St. Helena for a thousand acres in Modesto to make jug wine," Wooten said. "He unloads that garbage for less than ten dollars a magnum. What does he produce, twenty million cases a year? If he's the future of wine, I'll shoot myself."

"Is it worth a call, Henri?" Marianne asked. "Can you forgive him and see if he'll do the same?"

"No, it isn't, Marianne. He doesn't need the money, he doesn't want to help Henri, and even if he did, it will be a cold day in hell before Henri sells that land," Josephine said.

Marianne turned to Henri. "Does she speak for you?"

Henri smiled, and nodded. "She does in this case, Marianne. If Alfonse and I ever reconcile," he continued, "it will only be to make wine on that land. When we bought our land in the early fifties, the gypsy woman who owned it had all of it planted to fruit orchards except for that plot, which had vines. Her family believed that the land was magical, that the steam that came up from the spring below it made it unique, and that the wine from it was imbued with the divine. I've tasted wine from that land. Those gypsies understood its significance better than most modern viticultururalists. It's the most extraordinary plot of land in all of Napa Valley. I won't sell that land, ever. We sell the fifty acres with the house," Henri said.

"Okay, we get the point, no selling the mystical land, even though it's overgrown with brambles and prairie grass and hasn't produced a grape since 1973," Marianne said, conceding defeat.

"I'll speak with some of the land companies and Sotheby's. You ought to get 16-20 million for the fifty acres including the house," Josephine said, jotting down notes on a yellow legal pad.

Paradis nodded, steepling his hands. "I know you don't agree Marianne, and I respect your opinion. But the decision is final. I just hope we like our new neighbors."

Chapter 4:

Ronald Park, the most famous and successful wine critic in the world was in the passenger seat, Virginia Park, his wife and the financial workhorse behind much of Park's success, was driving the shiny black Maserati coupe. She was ten years younger than her husband, and even in her forties, could still turn heads. She was blonde, Nordic, and over six feet tall, with near perfect cream-colored skin, high cheekbones, and a slim, if not athletic build.

This was in contrast to her husband, who was in his fifties, six inches shorter, slightly overweight, with black hair, café colored skin, and facial features punctuated by deeply etched lines of a brow that was too often furrowed. The rest of his face had the features typical of his Korean heritage.

"Price of vineyards in Napa is under three-hundred thousand dollars an acre, even for the most prime land," Virginia said as they cruised up Highway 129, toward St Helena. "You know better than most how much difference the quality of the land makes."

"Irrelevant," muttered Park.

"Carneros is cheaper," she continued, undaunted. "I think you can get decent acreage there for half the price. With climate change, Carneros is going to be getting better and better for Cabernet. So will parts of Sonoma."

Park took a deep breath letting out a long sigh. "Gosh, Carneros? That sounds great," he said, his voice dripping with sarcasm. "A little climate change and it'll practically be the Left Bank in Bordeaux."

"Asshole," she muttered.

"What makes you think I would ever buy into this blood-thirsty, cut-throat, arrogance-ridden industry anyway?" The loathing in his voice was leaden.

"You don't think you'd fit right in?"

"I won't dignify that with an answer."

"Okay, now I am being serious. How about romance, working the earth, creating something incredible, even awe-inspiring. Doesn't that appeal to your softer side?" she asked.

"Wine, yes. The industry, not even a little bit."

"Look, no one on the planet knows more about wine than you do. We hire a great winemaker, one that has passed the test, making great wines in bad vintages and ethereal wines in great ones. We get the right plot of land and you go from being the foremost critic in the history of the industry to the brainchild behind the creation of the greatest wine in the new world, maybe the whole world. Why don't you leave being a wine critic behind? It just makes you miserable anyway."

"Why would you want me to stop doing what I do? I am the only one people trust," Park said, turning to her.

She paused, taken aback by his directness. "I just thought," she began.

"I have an obligation," he said, piercing her with a cold ebony stare, "to remain impartial, to render a verdict on wine, and keep those on both sides of the pond in check. If I buy into the industry, I lose the one thing I have which is truly my own, my objective voice."

"An objective voice in a completely subjective industry," she said, regaining her composure.

"Look at what's happened to the wine-review publishing industry. It's riddled with corruption. Subjective or not, I have the only voice anyone trusts. If I leave, there'll be a vacuum, and if I become involved in the industry, I'll be just as bad as those I have accused of corruption," he finished.

"You're accusations proved meritous," she acknowledged. "Those who use their ratings to sell advertising and create hype around vintages to drive up prices have rightly paid the price for their conflicts of interest. But it had an unintended consequence."

He looked at her, silent, waiting for the rest of it.

"Your damn wine ratings have become too important to the industry. The winemakers, the boutique shops, the trendy restaurants, and the cult-wine collectors waiting for the next big thing, they all hang on your every word. It's become surreal, even absurd. Whatever happened to drinking what you like?" she asked.

Park remained quiet. Virginia wondered if she had gone too far, and she waited for his ire to spill over.

When he spoke, his tone was measured. "When I started rating wines, I never envisioned that so much of the industry would live and die by my ratings. I never sought to be the most powerful man in the world of wine. It just happened," he sounded regretful, apologetic.

"I know," she said. "I just don't like what it does to you."

"If the others hadn't accepted the kickbacks, conspired to drive up prices, and create such a damn conflict of interest, I wouldn't have the weight of this damn industry on my shoulders. Do you think I like it when the press blames me for a winery going into bankruptcy?"

"No," she answered. "I understand that you're just being honest. I understand that you have the greatest sense of smell and taste in the industry. You're a reluctant demi-god."

"That's ridiculous," Park said.

"Is it?" she asked. "Name another person who destroyed the master sommelier's exam cold at the tender age of twenty-four. Name another man who can detect TCA at 0.3 parts per trillion in a wine. Name another man who can blindly taste any wine and state the vintage, the appellation, the varietal, and the winemaker with more than ninety percent accuracy. The movies notwithstanding, there's no one Ron. There is a reason you are the most powerful man in this industry. They're lucky you are so honest."

Park looked at his wife awkwardly, managed a half-smile and the slightest of nods. She understood that he did not do well with praise.

"The industry is in flux right now, the restructuring of it, new market realities, and the economy are more to blame for these failures than I am," Park said.

"Do you really believe that?" she asked.

Park shrugged and didn't answer.

"I just wish you could see the romance of it, working, growing, making something spectacular, instead of dissecting and cutting down everything out there that isn't," Virginia said. "When the sale of the magazine goes through, you'll be fifteen million dollars richer and you know we'd have enough capital to make it happen."

Park's smile disappeared. "I'm divesting my interest in the magazine, but I'm still the primary wine critic, or did you forget? I'm not going to make anything happen, and I am not going to give any son-of-a-bitch the chance to tell me how to improve my own wine, not ever," he said.

"Is that what this is?" she asked, "protecting your ego from the bruises you inflict on others all the time? Fine, then, it can be my winery. I'll look into it independently. How's that?"

"You can't. It'll be my winery by extension, and still my voice will be gone. I can never make wine, and neither can you," he said. "Don't you realize that I would critique my own wine? It would never live up to what I would want it to be. It would be my own personal hell."

Virginia sighed. "You're right. It would be hell for you. I hadn't thought of that."

"We could make beer," Park offered.

"No, thanks," she said. "That would be my personal hell."

"Fair enough," Park said. "Why don't you go downtown and do some research on the history book we've been putting together."

"Ah, the birth of the modern Napa Valley, farm to empire…." She said in mock reverence.

"If you don't want to help, I can write the damn thing myself. Most of our research is done anyway," he said.

"No, I'll help. Maybe tonight we can stop by the library after the tasting," she said.

They arrived at a small, single storey commercial building in a modern looking strip mall. It was just like any other strip mall in America, except for the tenants. There was an oak barrel outlet, a wine label making outlet, and a small office, which said, "Wine Magazine Napa Headquarters" etched onto the glass door. Virginia parked the car and both got out. They were buzzed into the locked door and Sylvia the receptionist took them into a room with two and a half cases of bottles. Park stepped out, and Virginia placed shrouds over each of the thirty bottles. That was it, thirty wines Park could taste before he began to get palate fatigue. A large spit bucket was nearby. Virginia glanced at each bottle before placing the shroud upon it, lining them up on one table. Once all the wines were shrouded, she removed all of the corks, and placed them into a black satchel where they could not be seen. To her right were thirty Reidel Sommelier series wine glasses, the greatest tasting glasses on the planet, she thought. They were clean, spotless, and with a satin cloth draped over them to prevent dust or anything else from getting into the glass. They were etched with a date and a number, from one to thirty. They would only be used once. Park had adopted this policy at the height of his paranoia, as the wine publications were going down, one by one. This was to prevent tasting glasses from being tainted by soap or another residue.

After preparing, Virginia motioned for Sylvia to introduce the third party. The third party was contracted to ensure there was no communication between Park and Virginia and no way Park was given knowledge of which wine he tasted. The addition of the third party had also been Park's idea.

The overseer placed the numbers on the shrouded wines in random order, so that even Virginia did not know what wine was being poured. Then, the shrouded, numbered wines were rearranged in numerical order for tasting. They were seated in witness chairs. Virginia called Park in and said, "We're pouring Napa Syrah today. Your reference is a 2006 Lewis Syrah to which you gave 94 points in the past." She poured the Lewis, which was not shrouded, and handed exactly four ounces of wine in the Reidel glass to Park.

Park spent nearly one minute with his nose at the edge of the glass, where the alcohol would not be the dominant aroma and the fruits, esters, and other polyphenols would be in greater concentration. After the requisite minute he took a large mouthful of the wine, drawing air in afterwards and making slurping sounds. He concentrated, eyes closed, shutting everything out but the wine, inhaling over and over again through his nose as he ran the wine over his tongue and throughout his entire mouth. Finally he spat, wiped his mouth with a linen napkin, and said, "94 points is an accurate score for this wine." He jotted notes on a yellow legal pad on the table next to the wineglasses.

For the non-wine person, the whole scene would have been laughably absurd, but everyone in the room took their jobs as seriously as if they were curing cancer.

The tasting continued over the next three hours, with Virginia pouring four ounces, handing the glass to her husband and stating only which numbered wine Park was tasting. Park did not say much out loud. He was slow and methodical, writing in utter silence. He spent an average of six minutes with each taste. Occasionally, he would mutter something identifying about the wine, such as, "This is mountain fruit," or "Hmmm, Stags Leap district," before returning to silence. Virginia did a yeoman's job of not responding to Park's comments, though everyone in the room knew that Park was almost never wrong.

At last they finished, and once the notes and scores were transcribed, the shrouds were removed and Park was able to see what wines he had rated, and what scores they had been given. Following this, Park and Virginia left and headed out to the library for some research before dinner. Virginia grabbed a dusty bottle of vintage Bordeaux from the cellar at the office, placed it in an insulated satchel to protect it from the heat, and took it with them to the library. They would drink it later at the restaurant with dinner.

Park never drank Napa wine in Napa when he was in public; it came too close to an endorsement. Of course, despite his best efforts, those in France soon heard what he was quaffing in the bistros of Yountville with surprising regularity, as did those around the rest of the world. He realized it is impossible to be the foremost wine taster in the world and not have some public record of what you drink in your off time. Those around the world of wine learned what their most influential critic liked. And subtly, over time, many began to make wine in an effort to please him.

He was aware of this on some level.

* * * * * *

Two weeks later, back at home in Monterey, Virginia put the second suitcase into the car. They had been fighting again, about money, about vineyards, and about their future. She felt increasingly closed in by her situation and was glad Park was leaving. She needed time away from him. She also needed to figure out where their relationship was going. She was obsessing about a way out of the marriage, and about vineyard land.

As she put the last suitcase in, Park came out of the house and shot a fiery look at her. "It's an hour and a half to the airport in San Jose, I do not want to hear a damn thing about this Napa bullshit. Do you hear?"

"No Napa bullshit, loud and clear," she said, and the two of them set off. The ride was one of silence, the noise of tire on road dominating. The tension was palpable, though both did their best to ignore it. She dropped Park off at the international terminal; he would be in Tuscany for the next two weeks.

After leaving the airport, Virginia continued north toward Napa. She was free of her spousal burden for the time being, and planned to spend a day or two gathering information and soaking in the atmosphere which she so desperately longed to be a part of. In addition to her own resources, she was connected to some dot-com money, and knew she could probably pull something off if she had the guts to try it.

With that in mind, Virginia decided to make a quick phone call to a gay couple she and Ron had become close to over the last several years. She needed some advice, and if she could coax it out of them, some financial support.

She called out the number on her Bluetooth voice activated dialer. A smooth voice answered the phone. "Joshua Mortensen here."

"Josh, it's Virginia, Ron Park's wife. How are you?"

"Hey Virginia," Joshua said. "What's going on? Minh and I were just talking about you two. Are you two going to be in the area any time soon?"

"Probably not before Christmas. I just passed through and dropped Ron off at the airport. He is on his way to Tuscany to do some barrel tasting. I was taking advantage of the down time and my pending retirement to take in some of Napa, you know, without persona-non-grata in tow."

"Aw, Virginia, you're not still carrying on about that winemaking business, are you?" Joshua asked.

"Well, maybe I am. What's the name of your friend up there?" Virginia asked.

"Matthew Quinn, but he's not there right now," Joshua said. "He's sold his winery and moved on."

"Damn, I was hoping to speak with him," Virginia said, "I want to know how he landed that property, and what he had to do to finance it."

Joshua was silent. Virginia wondered what she had said. "Is something wrong?" she asked.

"I think his financing was complicated," Joshua replied, sounding coy. "Virginia, you and I both know that Ron can't buy into the industry he's been critiquing all of his life. He'd be done as a critic."

"Maybe I won't stay with Ron," Virginia offered.

Joshua paused before responding. "Come on Virginia," he said, "this is nothing to do on an impulse."

"I'm not going to do anything impulsive," Virginia snapped. "All the same, isn't there a real estate guy up there you used to know?"

Joshua was silent again. She sensed tension.

"When I was an undergraduate at Cal, I briefly dated a guy named Todd Sandoval. We both majored in political science. Our breakup was tense, but we ran in the same circles, so remained amicable. Unfortunately, we both ended up at Stanford for law school. We stayed away from each other for the most part, and our relationship was almost cordial, until at a party he tried to pick up Minh."

"He tried to steal your husband from you?" Virginia asked, smiling to herself.

"Yeah. Afterwards he swore he didn't realize we were together, Minh was not the least bit interested, and afterward we distanced ourselves from that circle of friends. Now I understand that he's a broker for large real estate deals in wine country." Joshua said.

"He sounds like an inside player," Virginia said. "Do you know where he works?"

"I think he runs a firm up there called Terroir Unlimited," Joshua said. "Virginia, be careful with this guy, he's a predator. He's one of the most ruthless, charming, and seductive people in real estate up there."

"Devil in designer jeans, eh?" Virginia said.

"Something like that, but I wouldn't put it so nice," Joshua said. "Then again, he did help Matthew Quinn with his acquisition."

"Don't worry Joshua, I'm just heading there to learn," Virginia said.

"Be careful in Napa, Virginia. Don't do something you'll regret," Joshua said and hung up.

Virginia drove northwards through Oakland, making a couple of calls, and zeroing in on her mark for the afternoon. She thought about cultivating grapes, making wine, working in the barrel room, stressing out about harvest time decisions, and all of the things that go with being a winery owner in Napa Valley.

She thought about some of the other female giants in the industry: Helen Turley, Heidi Barrett, Kathryn Hall, and

Delia Viader. She sensed she was right for the job, part financial genius, part saleswoman, and full-blown lover of all things wine.

It was that love of wine that brought Park and her together in the first place. Before falling in love with Park she fell in love with his persona, his impeccable palate, his iconoclastic power in what she considered the most romantic of all the world's industries. Power was an aphrodisiac to her, and she knew it. It kept her close to Park long after the sexual attraction wore off.

Now with increasing ambivalence about their relationship, she had to admit that she was tempted to move on. He brought her tantalizingly close to the industry, but it was just out of her reach, both financially and because he was more intensely loved and hated than all others in the world of wine. If she broke the tie to Park, could she slip into the industry, or was she irrevocably associated with the foremost wine critic of the century?

Breaking the tie would also conveniently end another one of her problems. She had irresponsibly leveraged both her own and her husband's integrity already, and she felt guilty. She had to distance herself from Park's work one way or another. She suddenly felt disgusted with herself and willfully stifled the haunting memory of the treachery she had already committed.

As she turned up Highway 29 towards St. Helena, she felt her muscles relax. The vines were on both sides of her, dormant for the winter. The hazy winter sunshine softened the view of the hillsides. The smell of damp earth and burning firewood were in the air. Her attraction to the region was deep, visceral, and almost sexual. Again her heart longed to become a part of it.

She parked her car off of the main highway running north to south through St. Helena, and found herself wandering, eventually towards a small single storey brick office building off of the main street. A hunter-green awning shaded the entrance and contrasted with the burgundy colored bricks. There was no identification sign except for a small etching in the all glass door, a decorative "TU" etched in fancy writing, and in script underneath it, Terroir Unlimited. She found the door locked, and paused, wondering what in the hell she was getting herself into. But Virginia was impulsive by nature, and having come this far, she was not going to retreat. With a shrug, she pushed a door-buzzer, which rang in dissonant tones. She again asked herself what the hell she was doing as the door buzzed open and let her in.

After entering, she was greeted by a striking man about her age. He was dressed casually in pressed khaki pants and a white cotton button-down shirt, rolled up at the sleeves. He was blond, tanned, built almost perfectly, and devilishly handsome with an unnaturally perfect smile and teeth that were a shade too white. "Good afternoon, Ms. Robinson is it? I am Todd Sandoval. Come in and let's talk about how I might be able to help you."

An equally dashing woman with matching platinum blonde hair, dressed in a sharp business suit walked out of an adjoining office as they sat down.

"Todd I'm going to be gone for the rest of the day. I am meeting a client on Spring Mountain," she said. "He's interested in making an offer on the Chevalier property."

"That property's not for sale," he said. Sandoval glanced at her, his lips curving into a smile.

She stopped with her back to him, about five feet from the door. She turned her head over her right shoulder so that the two of them could just see the corner of her eye.

"Come on Todd, you know as well as I do…."

"Yes, yes, I know. Good luck," he said, waving her off.

"What did she mean, and what do you already know?" Virginia asked, confused by the conversation.

"Something everyone in the land acquisition business knows," Sandoval said, leaning forward and speaking in a low voice, "Everything's for sale. It's just a matter of price and leverage."

She wondered whether the scene had been staged just for her. "Listen, I'm not sure I'm ready to be talking specifically about anything. My interest in real estate here is complicated, to say the least." She forgot about her conversation with Joshua Mortensen. She was almost mesmerized by Sandoval's charm. She felt like he was familiar, like they had seen each other before.

"Complicated is not a problem," Todd answered reassuringly.

"Well, regardless, I can't just jump into a vineyard or the industry. It would present certain conflicts of interest," she said, trying to be delicate, and doing her best to remain above her own emotions, even as she found herself wondering what the man looked like naked.

Todd Sandoval motioned for her to sit down in a comfortable chair in front of his desk and sat behind his own desk, folding his arms upon it and leaning forward.

"I would guess that your," he paused, "association with someone connected to the industry makes breaking into the business somewhat problematic. Does that come close to describing your situation?"

Virginia was taken aback. She had given her maiden name when she called earlier, and she wasn't expecting to be recognized as Park's wife. She was partially frightened and partially aroused by Sandoval's surprising knowledge and innate ability to interpret. Her shock was only visible on her face for a trace of a second, before her composure recovered and she took the offensive.

"I represent myself and a couple of investors who need to remain anonymous during the scouting and contemplative phase of our acquisition, for many reasons, which I do not at this point wish to further discuss."

"I see," he said. "Well, I have represented several parties with similar situations. I can guarantee you the utmost discretion. I do require a retainer, just $50,000, if you are serious." He placed his arms back upon the desk, and leaned forward towards Virginia, radiating confidence and intensity which was beguiling. "I can work with you and those you represent. I can deliver what you want," he finished, staring at her with cobalt blue eyes.

Virginia stared back, willing herself not to be seduced.

He's queer for Christ sakes!

"You'll have to settle for working with me alone, and not knowing whom I represent. Will you be able to do that?"

Sandoval nodded silently, not breaking eye contact. "If that's your wish, and we have a way to verify the financial situation of your anonymous partners," he said pausing again, "then everything should be fine."

"I'll need some time to think this over," she said, standing up to announce that the meeting was over.

"Enjoy your stay in Napa Valley. I assume you're already familiar with our different appellations. Take some time to explore which regions you might be interested in."

Virginia nodded and smiled back. As she walked out of the small brick office, she was flushed. She wondered if she had the upper hand in this pending business relationship, or if she was being played.

* * * * * *

Todd Sandoval waited until Virginia Park left the building. Then, pursing his lips he picked up the phone and made a call. A husky voice answered the phone. "Hello Catherine. Want to hear an unbelievable coincidence? Guess who just walked into my office interested in acquiring real estate in Napa Valley?"

Chapter 5:

Matthew Quinn drove his Audi TT roadster into a long-term parking garage in Sacramento. The feds had become complacent with how easy he had been to track, and he was pretty sure he had successfully slipped away. With little more than a medium sized backpack, ratty, threadbare jeans, a faded sweatshirt, and a skullcap, he left the parking structure and took a taxicab to the train station. The cabbie made him show some cash before he let him in. Quinn understood what that meant, and was pleased as he flashed a twenty at the driver, who relented. He looked like a vagrant, a good disguise. At the train station, he purchased a ticket with cash and boarded a train headed east to Carson City, Nevada. Before departing, he furtively looked around the station. No one looked remotely like the feds who had been harassing him.

An hour later he disembarked in Placerville, small town in the Sierra Nevada foothills about halfway between Lake Tahoe and Sacramento. It was once called Hangtown, and like most other towns in the Sierra Foothills, it was rich in California Gold Rush history.

It was still forty miles to the township of Fairplay, another gold rush settlement due south. He did not dare rent a car or buy anything that needed to be registered. He got an idea when he passed a performance bicycle shop. He wandered in and was eyed warily by the staff. He paid no attention and settled on a lightweight road bike, mercifully second hand, and the only bicycle in the shop less than a thousand dollars. Again he paid cash. He departed on the bike, and headed south on Highway 49. He found that he tired easily on the bicycle. He hated being out of shape, but the shocks to his system were considerable. He wondered ruefully whether it was being half-starved and in pitiful physical condition, or whether this exercise intolerance represented early signs of heart failure.

Slowly and deliberately, he pedaled south, looking far more like a vagabond than an ex-physician and millionaire-inventor. He was huffing and puffing as he rode over the winding, hilly roads, and stopped twice to catch his breath. The watery sun was low in the sky when he reached Fairplay, sweaty and exhausted. He'd memorized his route, and soon came to the entrance to his friend's winery. A roughly hewn wooden sign read, "Callihan Vineyards."

On either side of the driveway were gnarled, freestanding, thick, old vines with trunks at least six inches in diameter. Quinn marveled at them, amazed that they stood without trellises. They looked like they were a hundred years old, so he guessed that they were Zinfandel vines. He took the undulating driveway, seeing little in front of him except vineyards. After cresting the third in a series of rolling hills, he took in a scene of splendor. Hills on three sides, all planted in vineyards, a large irrigation pond at the base of where two of the hills came to a small valley, and halfway up the third hill, a large, wooden lodge with an enormous outdoor deck, and below, built partly into the hillside, a second building, probably the winery. Right next to the winery building, built directly and recessed into the hillside were two large wooden doors enclosing what could only be the wine caves. The setting was idyllic, the isolation and splendor of the small valley and lodge were both rustic and gorgeous. Quinn was reminded of his loss again, and was deeply ambivalent about what he saw. He told himself he had no right to covet his friend's winery, but he was nostalgic for his own.

He rode up to the lodge and dismounted. It was very quiet as he got off his bicycle. He wondered if the place was occupied after it shut down for the night.

He walked up to the main door of the lodge, and knocked before letting himself in. He found himself alone in a moderate sized tasting area, distressed floors with years of wine spilt into them, dark wooden walls stretched from floor to ceiling, giving off a faint oaky smell. There were dozens of bottles behind the counter, and a sign, which read, "If you've come to taste, I'll be right back. If you've come to complain, go away."

Quinn smiled. He took a deep breath, inhaling the intoxicating and alluring scents of the old wood, spilt wine, and sanguine, happy people. He took his surroundings in again, this time noticing a black and white poster with Callihan Vineyards scrawled boldly across the top. On it was a picture of a plump old man with sparse gray hair, a deeply etched, weather-beaten face and a large, bulbous, bumpy nose ripe with gin blossoms, stuck deep into a glass of red wine. The whole picture was black and white except for the wine in the glass, which was inky-deep garnet. His eyes were closed and he appeared to be inhaling deeply into huge and frighteningly hairy nostrils. The man was ugly. The caption at the bottom of the poster said, "Nose-In" and below that was penned "Pronounced, 'No-Zin'." Quinn chuckled to himself. He and Shawn shared the same prejudice, it seemed. Maybe those large vines he saw weren't Zinfandel vines.

Growing inpatient, Quinn reached behind the counter, pulled a bottle of wine loosely stoppered with a cork and a clean glass. He looked at the label; it was a 2009 blend of Syrah, Grenache, and Mourvedre. Quinn shrugged again, pulled the cork, and smelled the wine. It smelled like an unlit cigar dipped in raspberry jam. He was intrigued enough to pour a small splash of wine into the glass. He swirled, and sniffed, and then drank the wine.

"Always just help yourself like that?"

Quinn jumped, nearly spilling the wine down his front. He spun around to the familiar voice, and saw his old med-school roommate, still pale skinned with strawberry blonde hair, sharp facial features, a goatee, and a lean, athletic build. He looked surprisingly like he had sixteen years ago when they parted company.

"Shawn, you're looking good," Quinn said, putting down the glass and holding out his hand.

"And you're looking skinny and tired, old buddy," Shawn replied, dodging the hand and hugging his old pal. "And you smell, too," he said, wrinkling his nose.

"Last few years have been tough on me, pal," Quinn said, embarrassed at his emaciated, unkempt, appearance. "Last few weeks even tougher. Sorry, I haven't showered in awhile and I cycled down here from Placerville."

"Jesus, pal, I hardly recognized you. You're skin and bones," Shawn said as his hands still wrapped around Quinn. "Were you just sprung from a prison in North Korea? Never mind, we have plenty of time to talk about the sad details of your post-medical school life. But first I need to help a large group of young ladies who are on their way here as part of their bachelorette party weekend." He arched an eyebrow and smiled a carnivorous smile.

Quinn gazed at his healthy, carefree friend. A sad, pained smile crossed his face. "The story's going to require a few hours, and maybe a few bottles of wine."

"As long as it doesn't involve narcotics," he said, smiling at Quinn.

"No smack, scout's honor. After you're done, let's sit down somewhere and talk."

"After I'm done? What the hell do you mean?" Shawn squawked. "You're pouring with me pal. Don't pass up an opportunity like this. Besides, I have been told that during these sorts of outings naked breasts occasionally appear. You wouldn't want to miss that. Go into the bathroom, splash some water on your face, clean up, and put some damn deodorant on."

Quinn obliged, and emerged from the bathroom just as the door swung open, and seven young, blonde women walked into the tasting room. All of them were blonde. What were the odds? Had they just come from Norway? One of them wore a wine-stained bridal veil.

"Are we too late for our appointment?" they giggled.

Shawn looked at them and smiled a disarming smile. "Never too late ladies, step right up." And with one fluid motion he placed seven tasting glasses on the counter of the tasting bar and poured a generous two ounces of a white wine he had on ice behind the bar, except for the presumed bride-to-be. For her he filled the glass all the way to the brim, to her wide-eyed astonishment.

"You're going to need that," he smiled and winked at her as she flushed. "This is one of two white wines we make here at Callihan Vineyards. It is a Marsanne-Roussanne blend, originally made like this in the southern Rhone region of France. Tell me what you think."

Quinn watched, as his friend exuded cool, and captivated all seven of the co-eds. Quinn busied himself behind the counter, casting an occasional furtive smile at the women, all of whom were ignoring him and engaging with his charismatic friend.

The ladies drank the white blend and expressed delight at its unique character. They were treated to a deluxe flight, which included every wine in current release. The second wine was a Viognier. Then they tasted a limited production Tempranillo, followed by a Syrah, a Barbera, and finally, the flagship wine of Callihan vineyards, the blend that Quinn had helped himself to earlier. Quinn was surprised to find that the most expensive of Shawn's wines was the flagship blend, which sold for a whopping twenty-six dollars.

There were no naked breasts, but the women bought a total of twenty-eight bottles of wine between the seven of them, and when they left, Shawn locked the tasting room door, glanced at his watch, and turned to Quinn.

"It's six o'clock. Let me grab a few things, and we can meet down in the cave. Why don't you wander down, it's unlocked," Shawn said.

Quinn strolled out towards the cave. The sun had long since set. The cool night air had a bite to it. The elevation was, he guessed, about two thousand feet. He walked out to the cave entrance and with some effort, unlatched and opened the large, eighteen-foot tall heavy oak door. He made his way into a dimly lit, cool, damp cave, which was according to the thermometer on the wall, 58 degrees, quite a bit warmer than it was outside. With the door closed behind him, he ambled down to a T in the cave, and looked right at the stacked barrels, and then looked left at more barrels, and at the end, beyond a wrought iron gate, was a long, roughly hewn heavy wooden table from another age. He made his way down to the gate, found it latched but not locked, and let himself in. He sat on a hard wooden bench which was surprisingly comfortable, and waited for his friend.

Five minutes later, Shawn arrived, a burlap carrying bag in one hand, and two bottles of wine in the other. He smiled, silently let himself in, and set the two bottles down. He reached into the bag and pulled out salami, some soft French cheese, a wedge of dried Italian cheese, some spiced hummus, an assortment of olives and cured vegetables, and a baguette.

"So I never had a chance to say, welcome to the Sierra foothills, and welcome to Callihan Vineyards, and now to Callihan's Cellar." He reached up to a shelf on the side of the cave, and pulled down two wine glasses and then reached for a wine bottle opener on the table. He corked a bottle of the wine, and poured two glasses.

"This tunnel, believe it or not, is the remnants of an old gold mine, from the forty-niner days here in the Sierra. It is now thankfully reinforced, sealed against the elements, and a nearly perfect place to store wine, and also drink it."

"Impressive," said Quinn, looking around.

"What shall we talk about first?" he asked with a smile, as he took a sniff, and then a large swallow of his estate wine.

"We can talk about my transition from medicine to wine, and my transition out of wine into nothing, or we can talk about yours. How is it that you became a wine guy when I remember you as a beer-guzzling bachelor-savant in medical school who drank wine only to woo women?" Quinn asked, sniffing his wine and feeling morose.

"Let's talk about you," Shawn said, cutting the bread, and helping himself to the cheese and salami. How'd you get the cash together to get a hundred and forty acres on Mt. Veeder anyway?"

"What have you read," Quinn asked warily.

"I seem to remember you were working on something big. Wasn't it some sort of pharmaceutical thing having to do with vascular mechanics or something? The media loves speculating. Then, just like that, everything disappeared. I would've thought U.C.S.F. would have rehired you and given you a deluxe lab with a view of the city, but next thing I hear, you're being rated in *Wine* Magazine. Ron Park seems to think you make pretty good wine, though a little austere for his taste. Try this wine," Shawn said, holding up his glass and taking another large swallow.

"More or less the story," Quinn said evasively. "Suffice it to say that I was given a large settlement to sell my patent, become anonymous, leave academic circles and research, and shut the hell up."

"Jesus, Quinn, hush money? How'd you let that happen? What could be so important?" Shawn asked with a mouth full of bread and cheese. "For God's sake eat something, you look like you're about to die. And please stop looking so damn depressed, it makes the cave colder."

"I could tell you, but then I'd have to kill you," Quinn said ruefully. "By the way, you've done well here. This wine is great." Quinn smiled in spite of himself.

"Thanks. So tell me, and then we'll duel to the death," Shawn said, persisting. "Martial arts or not, you're in no shape to whoop me, pal."

"Seriously Shawn, you don't want to get involved. I've been doing nothing for the last year except trying to get uninvolved, one step at a time," Quinn replied. He shrugged and took in some more of the wine, which seemed to be improving as it warmed up in his hand. He knew he wasn't ready for the conversation.

"Okay," Shawn said. "The answer is no, I will not not get involved. Why do medical people always speak in double negatives anyway? Tell me about it or I'll beat your ass."

Quinn shrugged. His buddy always did what he wanted, even in medical school. "Shawn, I am not ready to talk about it. You'll be the first to know when I am. The damnable misery of it is the more uninvolved I try to get, the more that the feds think I am involved in contraband drug production. That's why I had to sell the winery. They froze all my assets, well, almost all of them. I'm functionally broke."

"I read that you sold it, the winery that is. Wow, what a heartbreaker," Shawn said seriously. Then he cracked a grin and continued. "Well, here's to liquid assets my friend," he said, holding up his glass and then ceremoniously draining it. Quinn didn't think it was funny.

"I was thinking about a venture in Napa," Shawn continued. "I was thinking I might try to do something jointly with you. Guess I'm too late." Shawn stuffed his mouth with bread, Brie cheese and hard salami.

"That would have been nice," Quinn said distantly.

"You want to tell me a little bit about being found half-dead and stoned to the gills on the streets of Berkeley?" Shawn asked.

Quinn told the story of the feds and his close brush with death.

"Jesus, they almost killed you. Least they could do is explain why you were so doped up. Articles like that have to be rough on a guy's reputation."

"You have no idea," Quinn said, "but I think that was part of their plan."

"Lucky that lawyer woman found you. Did you get her phone number?" Shawn apparently still had a one track mind when it came to women.

"I think I have her card somewhere," Quinn said.

"So what about the pulmonary emboli? You're the expert on pulmonary vascular disease, what do they say about those elevated pressures in the pulmonary artery? Can your heart take that?" Shawn asked, "And the kidneys, they're okay right?"

"The kidneys have recovered, but don't have as much capacity. They hope the pressures in the lungs will go down. But Shawn, they're really high," he said shrugging.

"What about all that running you do? Won't that have conditioned the heart, make it able to tolerate those higher pressures?" Shawn asked.

"I think that's the reason I'm not already in heart failure," Quinn said, looking at his friend's empty wine glass. Some things never change, he thought to himself.

"Strong ticker," Shawn muttered.

"Make no mistake about it Shawn, I have a death sentence. Maybe it's one, three, five more years if I'm lucky, but the pulmonary hypertension is going to kill me. You're looking at a dead man."

Shawn looked at him without speaking, their eyes locked in silence. At last he spoke. His tone was measured. "Well, that makes each decision you make that much more important, doesn't it?" Quinn noted a subtle change in his tone. Shawn was being sincere.

"Yeah, time to start working on the bucket list," Quinn said.

"Do you think the feds know you're up here?" he asked.

"I jumped through a lot of hoops to make sure they didn't. I disabled the GPS locator they put on my car, which I left in Sacramento. I took a train up here, and biked down from Placerville. I look a lot different now than before being hospitalized, and I didn't notice anyone following me. I didn't pack anything either."

"You do look like shit. I'm going to call you Incognito-Man. It's good that you arrived unnoticed because it just so happens that I have an idea," Shawn said, filling his glass a third time, and taking the liberty of pouring more wine into Quinn's still half-full glass. Apparently he was not going to let Quinn's pulmonary hypertension ruin the evening. Quinn was hoping for a more sympathetic reaction from Shawn about his woes, but the brief moment of sincerity was apparently all he'd get. Shawn had never liked letting Quinn feel sorry for his self.

"What?" Quinn asked warily, "What's your idea?"

"Why don't you stay here, work at the winery with me?" he said looking serious. "That way you won't be homeless."

"What, pick grapes?" Quinn asked incredulously, though his heart leaped at the concept of staying at the winery.

"No," Shawn said, "I mean plant vines, tend to the irrigation system, pour wine in the tasting room, talk to customers, monitor the vines, do a little pruning and cluster dropping, flirt with drunk women, or dudes if that's your thing now, drink wine every day, eat good food, sleep for nine or ten hours every night, and let this place heal you." Shawn took a deep breath. "Wow! That was a mouthful."

"You got to be kidding me," Quinn said, laughing at the ridiculous thought of dawning overalls and doing manual labor. He'd done none of the manual labor at his own winery.

"The best part is, here you are totally anonymous and have no responsibility. You're Incognito-Man." Shawn explained. "Everything will happen whether you help or not. Being unimportant is a rare luxury, and I'm offering you the chance to be completely irrelevant. Help out if you want to, or stay in bed all day, I don't give a shit. It'll save your life."

"Well…" Quinn said, realizing that he did not have anywhere else to go. "Okay, I'll give it a shot. I wasn't going back to Napa anyway. I was thinking of hitting the road Bohemian style after I left here. Maybe like Jack Reacher in those novels. But no one knows I am here, and as long as it stays that way, I think I can hang out for a while."

"You'll be here longer than that, Incognito-Man," Shawn said, "so go buy a few pairs of jeans and some flannel shirts at the local hardware store. That's all you need, for now."

"For now?"

"You'll need more when it gets warmer," Shawn said.

"What makes you think I'll stay that long?"

"No one wants to leave after spending three weeks here," Shawn said, finishing up the last of the bottle. He began cutting the lead capsule on the second bottle of wine, preparing to uncork it as Quinn contemplated the next several weeks.

* * * * * *

Quinn awoke with a start, his body reacting to coming-to in unfamiliar surroundings. He was in a dark room with heavy, sueded leather window curtains letting in absolutely no light. His mind raced until he remembered where he was. He took a deep breath, relaxed, and fumbled for the bedside lamp. Looking at the black leather curtains, he wondered briefly if Shawn used the guest bedroom as some sort of bondage room. He stifled the thought and willed himself out of bed. He wondered what time it was. He was sore and tired from his bike ride. He felt a faint rumbling in his lungs as he breathed, but ignored it. He wandered out to the kitchen and saw that it was 11:00. There was no one in the tasting room. He ambled out onto the large outdoor deck to get another look at the property.

He located Shawn, down by the irrigation pond, using a compound longbow to fire arrows into a paper bulls-eye nailed to several bales of hay a hundred yards in front of him, Quinn watched in silence. Shawn was good. Quinn smiled to himself as he watched his friend hit bull's eye after bull's eye. Shawn was good at everything he did. That was just Shawn, and most of the time Quinn was okay with that.

* * * * * *

Quinn had been at the winery for less than two weeks when he realized Shawn had been right. The transition wasn't exactly smooth, but Quinn was settling in, and for the first time in a great while, he felt okay. Even the rumbling in his chest disappeared after the first few days.

Shawn could have been a hell of a bow hunter. He spent hours shooting his compound longbow and crossbow at targets near the irrigation pond. After watching this for several days without commenting, Quinn wandered down to the pond and engaged his friend about it.

"What's the deal with the bow and arrow? Fancy yourself a modern day Robin Hood?"

Shawn took aim, stood remarkably still and fired a shot squarely into the center of the bull's eye, one hundred yards away. He smiled and turned to his friend.

"When I bought the land, they told me that there was a problem with wild boar up here. I did this pretty well in high school, and my dad was an avid bow-hunter. So I bought a longbow and a crossbow, intent on defending my grapes from the beasts."

"I haven't seen any stuffed boar-heads on the wall," Quinn said. "No taxidermist?"

"Well, when it came down to it, I didn't have the heart to kill the damn things. So I had to invest in a perimeter high frequency virtual fence. It scares the bejesus out of them and keeps them out of the vineyard, but they aren't hurt by it."

"Well, for a non-hunting shooter, you're pretty good with that bow."

"Beats the hell out of a Judo hold, but thanks, Incognito-Man. Hey, if you're here, who's pouring wine in the tasting room?"

"Was I supposed to be doing that today?" Quinn asked.

"Or we could just keep it closed, but that's bad business."

"I'll go up and pour on one condition," he said.

"What's that?"

"Stop calling me Incognito-Man."

"I guess," Shawn said, clearly disappointed.

Quinn wandered up as the late morning sun was warming the earth below him. He smelled dry loam and limestone. This was a hell of a place all right. He opened the tasting room, then looked back down the hill to see Shawn, now backed up a full one hundred and twenty yards away from the target, hit another bull's eye.

An hour later, Shawn joined him in the deserted tasting room. He filled two glasses with Syrah and handed one to Quinn.

"How's this going for you?" he asked.

"Good. For the first couple of days I had trouble sleeping, but then I found the pool, and started doing laps," Quinn said.

"Yeah, how are those two a.m. swims anyway?"

"They've turned into seven a.m. swims now, I am sleeping better. Great idea to take the clock out of my room, Shawn," Quinn said.

"You seem to be keeping to yourself more than I remember," Shawn said.

Quinn shrugged. "I've lived alone since medical school, Shawn. I can socialize for a time, but I like my alone time."

"I noticed you are starting to eat more," Shawn remarked.

"The wine makes me hungry," Quinn said.

"Well, you need the calories, pal. You still look like a man-orexic."

"A what?"

"A man-orexic."

"Fuck you."

You're doing the manorexic's triathlon, pal, biking, swimming, and starving. I rest my case," Shawn said, taking a healthy pull on his wine glass, and looking pleased with himself.

"Touché," Quinn said, and abruptly walked out of the tasting room, leaving his still-full glass of Syrah behind.

One evening, in late February, just as it was starting to warm up, Shawn made the crucial mistake of opening a third bottle of wine during their almost nightly ritual in the cave. They were getting along better.

"Starting to like it here, aren't you?" he remarked.

"Shawn, you might've hit upon something here. There's something intensely satisfying about working all day, drinking wine all evening, and sleeping all night," Quinn said, looking fondly at the calluses forming on the palms of his doctor's hands.

"Have you looked in the mirror?" Shawn said.

"What?" Quinn said, reflexively feeling his face, bracing for more criticism.

"We ought to go out. You look as if you've gained about fifteen pounds of muscle, and you almost look your age. Next thing you know, your hair will start turning brown. You look a lot less like a refugee than you did when you first arrived. You might actually have a chance to score out there," Shawn said.

Quinn blushed reflexively. "Women," he said with a faraway look, "Sometimes you almost forget."

"No you don't," Shawn said, sounding disgusted. "But I'm glad to see that you weren't three steps beyond the grave. I can't imagine what would have happened if I'd have looked you up a few weeks later. You'd probably be dead."

Quinn stood up, ran his hands along his broader shoulders, and looked again at the calluses on his hands. He felt excellent. Maybe he was healthier, in spite of putting away a lot of red wine, or maybe because of it. Concentrating, he could feel his heart beating slowly in his chest. He took a deep breath and exhaled slowly. So far so good, he thought to himself. He wondered how long he could stay like this. He sat back down after inventorying himself, and looked at his friend.

"Shawn, I've been thinking."

"Then stop, for God's sake," Shawn said. He sounded irritated and his smile vanished.

"My heart was literally broken when I lost the winery. Everything I earned from medical school through my research career was taken. I was so depressed. When I came up here, I was angry that you had all this, and I didn't."

"Okay," Shawn said warily.

"I was never as involved with running things in Napa as I should have been, never as involved as you are here. I'm born to work, but I was completely hands-off with my winery. Why was I like that? I'm enjoying working here more than I enjoyed owning my own winery. Does that make any sense?" Quinn said, his eyes tearing up. The wine was still hitting him hard.

"Yeah, it does," Shawn said.

"We can't put together a joint venture like you had mentioned, but I'd really like to see what we could do down in Napa."

"You've been talking with Jose, my vineyard manager, haven't you? I better tell him he's not to speak with you. He doesn't understand how you get," Shawn said.

"Why are you up here in the Sierra? You're one of the best producers up here, and have even gotten some decent ratings on your Rhone blends. You're your own winemaker, and you've no formal education."

"I think you just answered your own question," Shawn said.

"This area is limited. You've gotten good scores up here. Why not go after the big prize?" Quinn said, fire in his bloodshot eyes.

"First of all, I take issue with your assertion that it's limited up here. It's not. We're just young still, as a wine region. And the second reason is because being down there and busting my ass and losing my shirt sounds like a shitty time," Shawn said.

"But Napa is where the masterpieces are made, not Fairplay," Quinn countered.

"Look at you. You come up here half-dead, and inside of three months, you're a workaholic again, which I guess is better than being a man-orexic. You see what happens to you Quinn?" Shawn asked.

"What?" Quinn was on the defensive.

"Your ambition gets totally out of control. You always have to run with the big dogs, go all-out. Now you can't, so you want me to do it for you. You're just like you were in medical school. You have the curse of the unforgiving minute."

"The what?" Quinn asked.

"Rudyard Kipling's curse."

"I didn't know he had a curse."

"I think it was in one of his poems," Shawn said.

"'If,'" Quinn said.

"What?"

"'If'," he repeated. "That's the name of the poem."

"So you know," Shawn said, pointing an accusing finger at Quinn. "Well, it's a cruel poem, pal. If you're cursed to fill an unforgiving minute with sixty seconds worth of distance run…."

"Mine is the Earth and everything that's in it?" Quinn asked.

"No, that's what he wants you to think," Shawn said. "But the truth is if you never take a second to relax, you don't get the world, you get exhausted, bitter, angry, or dead. Get it?"

Quinn paused, reflecting on Shawn's perspective. "On one level, you're right Shawn," he acknowledged. "And there's no question that before things started going so wrong for me I tried to fill every minute like that. It cost me the love of my life you know."

"I rest my case," Shawn said. "Was she hot?"

You have no idea.

Quinn didn't answer the question. "I haven't that much time left, Shawn. And I'm happiest when I'm working, when I'm creating something. Whether it is knowledge like in the laboratory, or wine like we're making here, it makes me happy, Shawn."

"What about the feds? Aren't they looking for you in Napa?"

Quinn considered this for a moment. "You're right. But I won't be able to hide here forever. Eventually I'll have to go down there and try to figure out how to clear my name.

That's on the bucket list too. Officially I couldn't be a partner to in anything we do together. I can be an employee, and maybe we can have a secret handshake deal."

"You're not going to let this go, are you?" Shawn said.

"Shawn, you were right about this place. I'm coming back to life, and you're the reason. You knew what it meant to bring me out of that funk. This train is rolling again. We have to give it a try."

"Give what a try?" Shawn asked.

"Hear me out," Quinn began.

"Don't fucking look at me like that! If this is about that medical school bullshit we used to argue about, don't start," Shawn said, appearing to brace for Quinn's imminent attack.

"You were the smartest person in our class, three classes above, and three classes below, too," Quinn said. "You had the makings of a great physician-scientist, maybe one of the best the school ever produced, and that was after finishing at the top of your class in law school."

"That's a load of shit and you know it," Shawn retorted, averting his eyes, though he seemed to appreciate the compliment.

"Let me finish," Quinn said, gathering a head of steam. "Motivation was your only issue. My success was based on sheer will, boundless energy, and mediocre talent, but you were born for greatness, only you never gave a damn." Quinn punctuated what he was saying by tapping loudly on the table with his index finger.

"That's not true," Shawn retorted though his tone suggested to Quinn that he was ceding ground.

"I understand that you didn't have to, with your trust fund and all, but there's more than that. Somewhere in there doesn't just a small part of you want to realize some modicum of your potential?"

"Nope," Shawn said.

"That's okay," Quinn said undaunted. "I have enough motivation for both of us. Don't you see? We need each other to make this work. I can't do it, especially not now. You have all the talent to do it better than I ever could, but you won't. You'll never get out the door without my foot in your butt. And you're my ticket back into what I love! Don't you see? You're the talent, and I'm the motivation. You get to own everything. Together we can do this," Quinn said. He was flushed and starting to sweat from the effort. His heart was pounding in his chest. He had to willfully calm himself.

"Do what?" Shawn asked.

"Go down there, team up on some land. Supplement your establishment here with a small premium plot of land down there, and make a kick-ass Cabernet blend, the best there is!"

"Napa's too damn expensive," Shawn said.

"You've got facilities up here if we can't get a turnkey place down there, and you can move most of this equipment to Napa if we get some land," Quinn said. "Besides, I still have some liquid assets. The feds didn't get everything from me. I had some gold, some cash, and quietly sold a large swath of my wine collection. I can bring something to this. It just has to be in your name."

"It's two or three hundred thousand dollars an acre down there." Shawn said. "Even with my trust and mortgaging this place, I'd never be able to afford it."

"Can you come up with a million?" Quinn asked point blank, his fierce, intense rusty-green eyes focused upon his friend.

Shawn stared at him, his slightly dilated pupils the only evidence that he was quite drunk.

"Yeah," he said a little slack jawed.

"Good, because that's what I have left. You can borrow the money for the balance. With two million down and your own equipment, you ought to be able to qualify for one hell of a loan. Besides, I have some friends, this gay couple, who are ridiculously rich, and big fans of the grape."

"Do they take their grape in pill form?" Shawn asked.

"No, they prefer the fermented liquid variety. They'd back us if I asked," Quinn said. "Shawn, I have nothing left, and little time. I need this. You aren't obliged, pal, but I'm struggling for meaning right now. This is something I can wrap the rest of my life around. Let my last minute be filled with sixty seconds worth of distance run."

"If we proceed with this madness, it wouldn't hurt to know that your rich friends would be there if we got into a financial pinch," Shawn said, stifling a hiccup.

"We'll talk about it more in the morning. What would we call a joint venture like this anyway, 'Callihan-Quinn Wine'?"

"No, we'd have to call it by our first names, S and M Wine," Shawn said meeting Matthew Quinn's eyes with a fierce stare of his own.

"Can we do that?" Quinn asked, wondering if Shawn was joking. His mind drifted back to the black sueded leather curtains in his room. He hoped Shawn regularly washed the sheets.

"I think we just did," Shawn said, the tone in his voice indicating at last, his commitment to the idea.

"So much for me being a silent partner," Quinn said, draining his glass and feeling better than he had in years.

Chapter 6:

Special Agent Walker Dunn was looking at the latest lab results when the call came in. He looked at his internal secure caller identification readout, which read only, "Field: 0161". He was glad it wasn't his wife. It was one of his agents, so he picked up the receiver on the third ring. The line would be scrambled and virtually impossible to intercept, as was the custom of his branch of Homeland Security.

"Walker Dunn here," he said.

"This is Agent Snow, calling from outside St. Helena," drawled a voice over the receiver. Dunn knew that Snow, a young and ambitious agent had recently transferred from Georgia and joined his team on the Matthew Quinn case.

"Go on Snow," Dunn said calmly.

"Quinn is gone," Snow reported.

"Gone?"

"The men covering him the last forty-eight hours lost him. He's been easy to track sir, never leaving the area except to see that gay couple in the South Bay or to go out for a run. They let him out of sight, and now his car is gone. We couldn't find it on any of the outbound freeway cameras, and now we can't find him."

"What about the GPS tracker?"

"Quinn managed to locate it. He destroyed it and left it on the side of the road in Fairfield. Do you think he was heading east?"

"Why east?"

"If he were heading west he'd have gone through Vallejo and not Fairfield."

"Snow, it means nothing. He could've done that to throw us off, or he could have headed east to Interstate Five and be heading north, or south."

"Fair enough, sir, but I was wondering…."

"Well, stop wondering and come into the office. How long will it take you to get to San Francisco?"

"I can be there in an hour," Snow said, and hung up.

Dunn sighed heavily, folding his powerful arms. This case was maddening. He knew Quinn was guilty, if of nothing else, of patent infringement, but he hated Quinn, who he thought was a smug, cocky little fucker. If he could get hard evidence linking him to the drug he was making, he'd lock him up. Quinn still had to slip up and reveal something to cinch the case. He was the one who thought to freeze all of Quinn's assets. He thought that by squeezing all of his domestic assets, Quinn would be forced to make a withdrawal from one of his offshore accounts. Once the accounts were uncovered, he could hit him for tax evasion.

D.H.S. wouldn't get front-end help from banks in Switzerland and the Cayman Islands. Their allegiance was to their clients, not the U.S. Government. But he could monitor any access to those banks by a specific citizen. He had been waiting for Quinn to make the move for some time. When he did, the money trail would be revealed.

But then Quinn went and sold his winery instead, which surprised Dunn. He received tip after tip on Quinn, and based on the information he received, he was sure that freezing his domestic assets would lead to an arrest. There couldn't be anyone else behind the scheme. A mountain of circumstantial evidence suggested that Quinn was the only man alive who had the knowledge and ability to pull it off. Even Quinn himself couldn't come up with a reasonable alternative.

Dunn hated that Quinn beat him on every interrogation. Dunn had never failed to get damning information from a coercive interrogation, before now. But Quinn, whether drugged, drained of blood, or made extremely uncomfortable, never gave anything up. He was nothing if not mentally tough. Maybe the toughest Dunn had ever come across. He accepted and endured what Dunn dished out too easily. That made his acrimony for Quinn that much more intense.

Dunn's anonymous source, by contrast, was a fountain of information. Catherine made his job easy, and this case foolproof. He didn't understand why she dismissed his idea to freeze Quinn's assets, but then again, she didn't have Dunn's experience.

He pushed his intercom to speak with his assistant.

"Wilma, please contact agent Peterson and tell him to monitor calls to and from the Mortensen-Tran residence, and inform me of any calls made to or from Quinn's cell phone."

"No problem, Mr. Dunn," Wilma said efficiently. "Is there anything else?"

"Not now, Wilma, but the wife and kids left town this morning. They'll be gone all weekend," he said.

"I'll see what I can do. Any place in particular you'd like to go?"

"Try to get us someplace up the coast, Bodega Bay, Fort Bragg, somewhere out there," he said.

"I'll let you know," she said.

Agent Snow came into his office less than an hour later. Dunn wondered how he could manage the trip from St. Helena in such a short time. But he wasn't going to ask Snow. He didn't want the young agent to start getting cocky.

"We can't find him anywhere," Snow said.

"We'll just have to wait for him to pop up on the grid," Dunn said.

"His cell phone number has been disconnected. We confirmed it with his carrier. All his credit cards have been discontinued as well," Snow said.

"What about his bank accounts?"

"You know they're all frozen, except one, where he gets his weekly thousand dollars wired from his frozen assets. We took a smidge over twenty million from his sale of the winery, but due to some regulations, he was able to retain about a million. I don't know where he has that."

"No question that the little fucker is dumping his money overseas. I have reason to believe most of his fortune is off-shore."

"How'd you get that information?" Snow asked.

"From my source. Listen, we have to make sure he doesn't get any more money out of the country. We have to make sure he doesn't get out either. If this goes international, we'll be in a world of hurt," Dunn said.

"Did you put him on the No-Fly list?"

"About six months ago. As far as low-level law enforcement is concerned, he's someone under suspicion for conspiracy to commit economic terrorism against the Government of the United States. If he tries to leave the country, he'll be arrested."

"Economic terrorism? That's more serious than I was led to believe."

"Yeah, we'll never make it stick, though. We'll get him for patent infringement, illegal production and distribution of a drug, trafficking, and tax evasion. That'll be enough," Dunn said.

"How long have we known he's been manufacturing this chemical?" Snow asked.

"The skinny little punk keeps denying it, but we've detected it in wastewater in Napa, in Sedona, Aspen and Vail, Cape Cod, and the Seattle area."

"Lord! How much is he manufacturing?"

"A fair amount, obviously. He has to have a plant up and running somewhere. We're talking at least a hundred kilos a month. We don't know where, though. In each of his interrogations he's mentioned that he thought someone in Napa Valley might be making the compound and selling it under-the-table at local health spas. But we haven't been able to confirm that. Personally, I think it's a dead end, a decoy. My source told me he might say that."

"Who's your source?" Snow asked.

"None of your damn business, but she has her pulse on this case, that's for sure," Dunn said smoothly.

"She a fed also?" Snow asked.

"That's on a need to know basis," Dunn remarked evasively. The truth was he didn't know who she was. What he did know was that her first name was Catherine, and all of her verifiable information had checked out. She was reliable, her help had led to his last promotion, and she made his job a hell of a lot easier.

"And Quinn is clean?" Snow asked.

"During his last interrogation, the one botched by the agent you replaced," Dunn said, "I personally interrogated him. "We gave him some strong drugs designed to loosen up his tongue and wear down his resolve. We also did a fair bit of coercive interrogation, but to no avail. I have a theory about long distance runners and coercive interrogation, but that is something else altogether."

"He didn't give anything up?" Snow asked.

"Nope, spoke about a dead mobster named Vladimir Michinski, said his people knew how to make the compound, but that's a dead end, we've already been over it," Dunn said, breaking eye contact. "There were no known survivors from that conglomerate, except a couple of thugs in prison. The whole family drowned off the Northern California coast."

"Did they find all of the bodies?" Snow asked.

"No. The car went off the road into the ocean at a tough to reach spot near Devil's Slide, but they're gone," Dunn said. "No one could have survived the drop. That was almost four years ago. And if by some miracle a survivor did pop up, we'd have known about it by now. Michinski had a son and a daughter, both of whom died with him at Devil's slide."

"So Quinn's clean? You didn't find the polymer in his system?" Snow asked.

"I thought that if I could get enough plasma from him, I'd be able to detect the drug, just from him inhaling it when he makes the shit," Dunn said. "So we nearly exsanguinated him. I took over a quart and a half of his blood. I told them to make sure he got IV rehydration before dumping him off, but my assistant didn't do it. He dumped Quinn off on the side of the road in shock and halfway to hell. He would have died if a motorist didn't find him shortly after he was dumped. Fortunately the local hospital was able to put him back together. But he nearly stroked out, and threw some clots into his lungs. It was a fucking disaster. That's why you replaced him."

"So what about the quart of plasma?" Snow asked.

"It's the fourth time we tried to isolate the compound from his blood, and even with all that blood, we found no trace. It amazes me that the little shit isn't taking his drug. Even more amazing that he manages not to inhale any of it when he makes it. He must wear a space suit when he makes the stuff. Hell, if I were him, I'd be making that shit and putting it in all my food."

"So he's just selling it?"

"He probably has hundreds of millions of dollars off-shore. And he hasn't paid a cent in taxes on it. We have a couple of leads, but I was really hoping that freezing his legitimate assets would force him to reveal one or more offshore accounts. He's disciplined as hell, and getting information from those banks is difficult. They handle these things with way too much discretion."

"What about the spas in Napa?" Snow asked. "Any leads as to which one?"

"During the first interrogation a year ago, Quinn mentioned The Silverado Springs Resort and Hot Springs."

"That's a hell of a nice place. Does he have a share in it?" Snow asked.

"That's just it. We can't figure out who owns it, or where the money goes. It looks like someone who deals out of Argentina has a controlling stake in the property, but the money trail seems to circle back on itself. The FBI has been trying to make sense of the money trail for three years, but we can't get names. Quinn denied owning it, or having anything to do with it, except staying there a few times before he moved to Napa Valley, but it doesn't matter. Any time you have a place where the owners have gone to such great lengths to protect their anonymity, there's probably a good reason why."

"Have you been able to get a hold of the illegal drug at the resort?"

"We sent two people in to try to buy it, but the people at the spa denied any knowledge of it. They tried to sell us some herbal crap instead."

"Did you look at the herbal crap?" Snow asked.

Dunn looked at him like he was an idiot and did not answer.

"What about Argentina? Has Quinn ever been there?"

"Quinn has been to Argentina, but only one time, about twelve years ago. He took a trip to Argentina and Chile when he was still in medicine. He told us he went to taste and buy wine."

"Guy is a god damn wino, that's about the only thing I know for certain. He has shipped more than two-thousand bottles of vino to that gay couple in Atherton since last October," Snow said. "But there's no question that the last trip nearly killed him. He looked like hell lying on his couch. You know he didn't get off the thing for nearly a week."

"Well, he's a smart wino and a dirty rat also," Dunn said. "He markets that stuff to enough people and the country doesn't have enough resources to deal with the consequences. He'll bankrupt the government."

"He makes everyone live so long that the federal government fails? It's a weak argument, don't you think?"

""It doesn't matter. What we'll get him on is tax evasion, unless we can isolate the compound and get him for illegal production and patent infringement. I just hate the little fucker. I'd like to label him a homegrown terrorist, just because he is such a smug asshole."

"Well, the tax evasion argument makes sense to me. But the economic terrorism argument doesn't wash. It seems to me he's just trying to help people live longer, like any doctor would," Snow said. "We don't arrest cardiac surgeons for keeping people alive."

"Cardiac surgeons don't make people live to be a hundred and fifty years old," Dunn said. "How'd it be if every blue-hair in the country suddenly got an extra seventy years to suck on the tits of Medicare and Social Security?"

"Quinn's polymer can do that? How do we know?" Snow asked.

"We don't, but we've seen what it does in animals, and we have statistics showing that in the areas where we are seeing high consumption of his drug, we are seeing lower all-cause mortality over the last four years. His shit works."

"Why not just make actuarial adjustments to our government benefits structure?" Snow asked.

"An attitude like that will get you reassigned, Junior," Dunn said. "Don't be seduced by the fucking fountain of youth, okay? It's illegal! He sold the patent, sold it to us. He has no legal right to make the drug. He has even less right selling the drug and keeping all the royalties, tax-free. The fucker is a crook."

Snow backed off. "I'll get the guys in the field to comb the state. We'll find him, especially if he can't get on an airplane. We have people also watching all airports in Mexico and Canada, even if he manages to get across the border."

Snow got up and made to leave Dunn's office. Having forgotten about the tension between them, Dunn said, "Get them all out there. We need to find that bastard." After Snow left the office, Dunn hit his intercom. "Wilma?" he asked.

"How's the Pelican Inn in Bodega Bay?" she said seductively.

"Perfect," Dunn said, smiling. "Listen sweetheart, I have a few more phone calls to make, and then let's get out of here." He hung up the phone, and let out a cathartic sigh.

"Son-of-a-bitch," he muttered to himself as he dialed the number. "Catherine, we have a problem," he said when the phone was answered.

"What is it?"

"Quinn is gone."

"Did you intercept the money when his winery closed?" she asked.

"Most of it, he got a cashier's check for a little over a million, though."

"When you've definitively traced the drug to him, you'll need to find him to arrest him," she said with a razor sharp edge to her voice.

"I know how to do my job," Dunn said. "And the information you've given me has really tightened up the case. We'll have the little fucker arrested in the next couple of months."

"You better, with the information I am giving you. That bastard destroyed my family, and he is going to bleed. Find him, and figure out how to lock him up, forever," she said.

"What's your angle here? Did he fuck up and kill your kid when he took care of him back in his doctoring days?" Dunn asked.

"Something like that," she replied. "He's bad news. He has to hurt."

"I understand how you feel. We'll put a case together soon," he said. "We can even hold him for a few years without trial if we want to," he offered.

"That'd be nice," she said, "Lock him up until he dies." She hung up.

Dunn hung up, looked at his watch, grabbed his coat, and headed to his car and his weekend on the North Coast.

Chapter 7:

Alfonse Paradis leaned back in his leather chair, resting his arms on his more than substantial belly. There was fat, and then there was Alfonse. He tipped the scale somewhere close to four hundred pounds.

He stared at the magazine with a mixture of curiosity and loathing. He chuckled to himself and then swiftly leaned forward, picked up the magazine, and thrust it into the garbage can next to his desk.

"So our Chardonnay got 81 points," his administrative assistant Barbara said, poking her head into his office smirking. She was the third one in the last four years. He smiled and she came into the office and sat down facing him. She was of Mexican descent, with shiny, long black hair tied up tight in a single braid. She had a dazzling figure, both graceful and athletic. She dressed in khaki slacks and a silver colored silk shirt, fitting snug around her waist. With three buttons undone, a substantial V revealed café colored, perfectly sized, firm breasts. She sported retro-stylish black-rimmed glasses, which Alfonse thought gave her that slutty-librarian look. Sexy as it was, her look might have been too casual except that Paradis himself was in custom tailored blue jeans and a massively oversized polo shirt. He looked at her lasciviously, imagining himself in various sexual positions with her.

"I think that is the first time you've broken 80 with Park. I guess congratulations are in order," she said.

Paradis looked over at the periodical sitting in his wastebasket. It had a picture of an idyllic scene in Tuscany, with the caption, 'Brunello shines despite challenging weather.'

"Barbara, you and I both know that someone like Ronald Park is only useful to me when he torches one of the so-called premium labels over in Napa Valley. The people who buy my wine don't read magazines about wine. They drink it with dinner in front of the television, mix it with 7-up, use it to get drunk, or serve it at parties where they don't know the guests very well. Whether Ronald Park thinks my wine is art or swill doesn't matter to me at all. But he makes my day every time his ratings close up another winery."

"Speaking of closing up wineries, word has it that your brother is close to financial ruin. How does that make you feel?" she asked, seeming intent on his reaction.

Alfonse looked over at her, his enormous chin resting on his chest.

"Henri's pig-headed stupidity epitomizes the arrogance of the industry. When he fails, it'll be a good day for wine. It'll also be a great day for me. The land we have in dispute is worth a fortune, and when he goes belly up, I'll be able to leverage it from him. By that time, he'll have no choice. How does his ruin make you feel?" he asked her. "After all, you have an emotional stake in it also."

"I don't give a damn either way," Barbara said, looking away. Then, cocking her head, she looked at him and asked, "Alfonse, you're not thinking about making wine in Napa Valley again, are you?"

"Barbara, I'd die before I became neighbors with those snobby bourgeois Napa Valley people. No, in fact the only land in the valley I'm interested in is that little plot of land with the old man buried on it. In addition to his carcass, there is gold in it, a lot of gold."

"I remember," she replied. "Did you see that Henri has put up a fifty acre parcel off of the Silverado Trail for sale with Sotheby's?"

"Yeah," Alfonse said.

"You're not interested, though, are you?" she said, more than asked, "Since you have no intention of growing wine in Napa Valley."

"To see the look on his face would almost be worth it," Alfonse said. "To witness his horror as he realizes that he lost the house we grew up in to me, and then to see the horror, as I unload it onto someone else, someone he'll be sure to hate. That would be fun. But no, the market is soft right now, and I don't want to hold onto a piece of land I have no interest in growing grapes on. I'll wait for that last plot, the priceless one that I still have a legitimate claim on. It's worth several times as much. As time goes on, he's going to get more desperate."

"You're such an evil man," she said studying his face and smiling.

"Yeah, but I am good at it," Alfonse said.

"Speaking of which, do you want to go to the Gala event celebrating the 1976 Paris tasting and the Auction in Napa Valley in May?"

"Yeah, how much is a table for eight?"

"You can sponsor a table for twelve thousand," she said.

"Reserve two of them for us," he said. "I'm looking forward to seeing my brother."

"I'm sure he'll be glad to see you too," she said. "I'll be unable to accompany you. I have a previous engagement."

"That's fine sweetheart," he said. "But I'm going to have the time of my life, and that's going to needle my brother something fierce."

When Barbara returned to her desk, closing his door, Alfonse turned to the window, thinking a long time. Finally he turned back, picked up his phone and hit speed dial number six.

"Richard," he asked, "how much can I get in collateral for the Modesto properties and our holdings in the Sierra? It'll just be short term, eighteen months max." He paused, listening. "Really? That much? Okay, let's meet for lunch tomorrow."

* * * * * *

Barbara returned to her desk and booked two tables under the corporate account for the Gala event in Napa commemorating the 1976 Paris tasting. After she hung up she shook her head and smiled. She picked up her phone and made another call.

"Hello Catherine. We're sponsoring two tables at the celebration in Napa in May. It looks like things are coming together perfectly. Quinn has sold his winery to our subsidiary. The game is on and the pieces are set."

"Excellent work. What about our friend in accounting?" Catherine asked.

"He just gave his notice, as per our plans. The books are cooked, and the money is being wired into the accounts you specified."

"Perfect, this is going to be easier than I thought," Catherine said. "All thanks to you, sweetheart. Keep your eye on the prize, and we'll get what we're after, as long as those federal dolts can find Quinn."

"They lost him? Bunch of rocket scientists over there," Barbara said, disgusted, "Christ almighty, do we have to do everything?"

"They'll find him. They have to, he's the centerpiece," she said.

"Catherine, do you really think he'll put it up, I mean Henri, not Alfonse. I'm just not sure we'll get it," Barbara said.

"The feds are already looking for Quinn, and you've done your job perfectly over there. Let me worry about the rest of it. It doesn't matter if it's Henri or Alfonse. We'll get what we need. Stop worrying."

"Yes, sorry," Barbara said, flushing slightly.

"In any case, our success here depends only on leverage. We'll have plenty of it, I'll see to that, darling," Catherine said and hung up.

Chapter 8:

The boardroom felt large and empty as Henri sat with Marianne Duncan and Josephine Rodriguez. She reached inside her briefcase and pulled out several packets of paper.

"We have three realistic offers, all lower than I had hoped. There's been a lot of real estate in Napa for sale in a relatively short period of time. Demand is slack right now, and it's a buyer's market."

"I understand the dynamics of the market," Paradis said. "So what've we got, and is it enough to keep us afloat?"

"The first offer is from a doctor. He owns a successful winery up in the Sierra. He has just over two million to put down, and is backed by a loan secured on the property he would acquire here, and by his property in the Sierra. He proposes eighteen million dollars total for the transaction," she said, looking at Paradis, whose pained look told her that the sum was too low.

"That's less than \$360,000 an acre. Are you telling me that we've already lost 10% of the land's value because of the current market?" he asked, exasperated.

"Five to ten percent, Henri, that's just the business. We don't have the luxury of waiting right now, or I'd say wait until the market recovers. The advantage of this offer is that you have a pretty transparent view of who will be your neighbors. This guy looks like he wants to make wine, and doesn't have any corporate ties."

"It's too low," he said finally. "What other offers have we got?"

"Well, there are two higher offers, but both of them are from anonymous buyers, and I can't get any more information from the lead over at Terroir Unlimited, or from Sotheby's," she said.

"Tell me about the one at Terroir Unlimited," he requested.

"Okay," she began, pulling out the paper outlining the offer. "This one offers three million dollars down, with the balance of nineteen million being given twelve months after close of escrow. There's no financial institution involved, and all backing is from an anonymous trust, funds verified and insured by Terroir Unlimited."

"Twenty-two million, but nineteen million held back for twelve months. That's a shrewd offer. Someone has a hunch we're in financial trouble," Henri said, contemplating the offer.

"Henri, we are in financial trouble," Marianne said. "And this offer doesn't solve our problems. We need that capital at the close of the transaction, not twelve months later."

"We can leverage it, we can borrow on the promised funds if we want to," Paradis said. "It might send out the message that we aren't in as bad a shape as everyone thinks."

"Only if you can borrow against the nineteen million owed without anyone knowing. If they find out about that it'll make it look like you are in worse shape than you actually are, and trying to cover it up," Josephine said.

Paradis was silent. He knew that Josephine was right, that was why she was his advisor. That and he owed a debt to her late father. This was not an ideal offer for him either, though at least it was better than the first offer. "What about the third offer?"

"This one is a cash purchase," she said. "Sotheby's has verified the available funds, and the offer is twenty-one million dollars."

"Sounds corporate," Paradis said.

"It certainly does," Josephine said.

"I like the buyer in the first offer the best, there's no doubt, but it is not enough money for the property. The second offer ultimately gives the most money, but holding it back complicates things. It is unlikely that I will be able to borrow more than eighty percent of the residual, and that puts us in a pinch, and complicates things more than I would like. The third is straightforward enough, and frankly, makes the best business sense. I just wish I knew who was behind it," Paradis said.

"Me, too, but that is a luxury we don't have, Henri. So which is it going to be?" Marianne asked.

"My gut says to take the first offer and give the land to that doctor, but my head says I have to accept the third offer. It stands the best chance of keeping us afloat," Paradis said.

"So take the third offer," Marianne said. "And Henri, make damn sure that you get a flawless product into your pipeline."

"We have to. If the scores aren't there, and we can't sell the product, we're finished."

"I'll inform Sotheby's that we accept the offer, and let the other two know we've passed. The transaction will close in thirty days, unless there is a problem," she said, handing the contract to Josephine and then turning to look at Henri, whose face showed the strain of losing a quarter of his land, the same land his father had worked a lifetime to obtain.

"$420,000 an acre," Paradis said. "It's a premium on the land, anyway. In the end, the new owner is irrelevant. We have to make this decision based on the health of our own organization, not who our neighbors will be," Paradis said, sounding as if he were trying to convince himself. "Whoever they are, it is still one of the best parcels in The Valley."

* * * * * *

The news was frustrating for Todd Sandoval. He had anticipated that given the current climate in Napa real estate that his offer was going to be the only one and therefore accepted. He was not looking forward to the conversation he was about to have with Catherine. He had made guarantees based upon his extensive experience within the vineyard real estate industry, and this is the first time he had ever blundered. He wondered who the idiot was that paid twenty-one million dollars in cash for the property, but it was considerably more than the property was worth in the present market.

Sandoval did not blame Paradis for taking the cash. He would have done the same thing. It was a better deal. The issue was not that he had taken an inferior deal. The issue was that someone with deep pockets was competing for Paradis' land. Todd needed to find out who it was, and what his or her ultimate objective was.

With a sigh, he picked up the phone, and made the call he had been dreading since hearing the news.

"This is Todd, over at Terroir Unlimited. We have a small problem," he said when the phone was answered.

Catherine was silent for ten excruciating seconds. "What kind of problem?" she asked.

"There was a better offer on the land," Sandoval said.

"How can that be? You said the plot was not worth more than eighteen million in the current climate, and we offered twenty-two million, more than a twenty percent premium on the land. Someone offered more than that?" she asked with icy calm.

"Not exactly, the offer he took was for twenty-one million, but it was a cash offer, up front," Sandoval explained. "Your gimmicks backfired."

"Who bought it?" she asked.

"I don't know. It was an anonymous buyer, represented by Sotheby's," Sandoval said.

"You need to find out right away. I need to know who bought it, and whom we're competing with," she demanded with quiet intensity.

"I should be able to figure that out in the next few weeks. There is a bright side to all of this," Sandoval said in a conciliatory tone.

"Yes, there is. The fact that he took a cash offer tells me that he really is in trouble. Keep the screws to him. This wasn't the big prize, just a step toward it."

"Our plans go forward. By the end of June, we'll be where we need to be." Sandoval tried to sound reassuring, though he was unnerved by the presence of this other anonymous buyer.

"Any chance Park's wife could be the one we're competing with?"

"I doubt it," Sandoval said. "She hasn't been back here since we last spoke. She said she had some strong backing, dot-com I think, but I don't think she was quite ready to go behind Park's back on this."

"Wouldn't it be convenient if she were, though?" she asked.

"Maybe. It certainly would be another distraction," Sandoval offered.

"Maybe she's got more chutzpah than you think, Todd," Catherine said and hung up.

Todd stared at the phone after hanging up. When the idea was hatched, it seemed a once in a lifetime offer. He was now up to his neck in it, and dealing with people he knew were dangerous. Catherine frightened him. She was as cold-blooded as anyone he had ever met.

As Sandoval contemplated his next move, the door opened and Arianna Richardson walked in wearing a sharp business suit. She shot him a glance with topaz eyes before returning to her desk. She was smokin' hot and Sandoval, even as a gay man, appreciated her charisma. She was perfectly suited to the job and an apt pupil.

"Arianna, were you able to get the Chevalier property for your buyer?" he asked, though he guessed, based on her facial expression that she had not.

"Park keeps making love to the winemakers up on Spring Mountain. As long as their releases stay in the ninety-plus point range, they remain strong and I can't touch them. What I need is a spat of bad ratings and some financial turmoil," she said.

"Don't we all," Sandoval replied.

"I've been thinking, and despite my failure up on Spring Mountain, I like the idea of becoming an independent contractor with Terroir Unlimited. I just think that twelve percent of my land commission plus office rental is a little too high. Would you consider eight percent plus office rental and upkeep?" Richardson said.

Sandoval looked at her. He knew twelve percent was steep, and she had proven her abilities in the vineyard and winery real estate business. He did not want her going to Sotheby's or anywhere else where she would compete directly with him.

"How about we split the difference, and ten percent of the land commission goes to the corporation, and you're free to pursue whatever and whomever you want," he offered.

She looked at him shrewdly, and was silent for a time. He wondered what she was thinking. "Okay," she said, "but the contract is good only for one year, and then we renegotiate."

"Starting when?"

"How about now?" she offered.

"Deal," he said. "What've you got cooking Arianna?"

"We'll see," she said, continuing toward her office. She disappeared behind the entrance and a lock clicked into place.

Chapter 9:

Torrential rains were due in the Sierra after what had been an unusually warm spring. The storms threatened to wash away the pollen and interfere with the flowering and health of the vines. The storm might ruin an otherwise promising start to the growing season. The plan was to cover as many of the fledgling bud-breaks and flowers as possible.

Quinn was up early. He was already in the vineyard for an hour when Shawn emerged from his bedroom. As usual he had slept late. Once again, waltzing out behind him was a knockout twenty-something lady wearing an oversized man's white button down shirt, open with a bra underneath it, a pair of jeans-shorts that revealed bronze skin on beautiful legs. She made her way to her black sports car and left, and Shawn joined Quinn.

"You're still a man-whore," Quinn remarked.

"And why aren't you?" Shawn asked.

"Never my style," Quinn said. "I can't even date a girl unless I can picture her as Mrs. Quinn."

"So why are you forty-something and single?" Shawn asked.

"I let too many other things get in the way of my relationships," Quinn said. "And now, who would want to marry a destitute guy who'll be dead in a couple of years?"

"Maybe you should forget this marriage thing and concentrate on the one-night-stand," Shawn offered.

Wishing to change the subject, Quinn said, "Man I can't believe we lost that land. It was tiny compared to my Mt. Veeder estate, and we offered nearly as much as I paid for my land."

"Premium land is going to cost more, especially land with a pedigree like that. Besides, there's always more where that came from," Shawn said. He seemed to take the news in stride, shrugging it off like a bottle of TCA-tainted wine.

"Not land like that," Quinn said. "That was a once in a lifetime opportunity. Maybe I should call my friends in the South Bay, see if we can put some bigger muscle behind our next effort."

"Not a bad idea, but something will come our way," Shawn said.

"We need to get down there, and scout around," Quinn said, loosely tying the garbage bag around a young vine. "Maybe another opportunity will present itself."

"I have a plan," Shawn said, walking up a row of vines parallel to Quinn, and no longer tying down bags. "As long as you promise that the proximity will not drive you further into old habits."

"Are you going to keep it to yourself, or are you going to tell me about it so I can stop stewing?" Quinn asked.

"Well, another time I would've let you stew. But seeing as how you've have had a device closure, have pulmonary hypertension, are in pending heart failure, and you are on a baby aspirin, I think I'll tell you." Shawn said.

"How thoughtful," Quinn said.

"There's a large event in Napa every spring. It's a charity auction, and this year it is in conjunction with a celebration of the anniversary of the 1976 Paris tasting. It is a big deal."

"Of course! The Napa Spring Auction! It raises money for the medical clinic for workers who don't have insurance. I've been invited to that in the past, but have never gone," Quinn said.

"I have two tickets. Being a winery owner, even one up here in the foothills, affords some privileges," Shawn explained. "It's on May 24th, but I figure we head down there a week early, leave things up here to Jose and the boys, find us some land, a couple of ladies who're into wine, and hang out with the Napa elite."

"Sounds like a bad movie I once saw," Quinn said.

"It'll be much better than that," Shawn said.

"Well Shawn, that sounds about perfect. I think my friends will be there. They go most years. They have a lot of contacts in the business in Napa. They're the ones who might help us with the land. There's also this group called Terroir Unlimited. They're headhunters for vineyard land. I got my property up on the mountain through them. They'll know what's going on down on the valley floor," Quinn said. Looking at his watch, he said, "We better get up to the tasting room, it'll be opening time soon."

Shawn yawned. "I'll be there in a few minutes, why don't you go and open things up. It's a Tuesday, it'll be slow anyway."

Quinn looked at Shawn and knew he was heading back to bed. "Lazy bastard, or were you up all night?" he muttered just loud enough for Shawn to hear.

"She was hot, from out of town, and does not wish to see me again. How perfect is that?" Shawn retorted, "and who were you with last night?"

"Fine," Quinn said. "Go back to bed. I'll take care of it."

Quinn walked up to the tasting room, eager to smell the oak, the spilt wine, the open bottles and the scent of drunk wine and happy people. The tasting room was Quinn's favorite place on the whole compound. Why hadn't he spent more time with the nuts and bolts operation at his own winery?

He smiled as he entered and set up the tasting room. Maybe a bunch of cute college co-eds would skip class today and come up for a sorority group tasting. That would be just excellent.

Quinn sat quietly for a couple of hours, with only two small groups of tasters coming in. He ate a light lunch of smoked turkey and Gouda on a baguette, with figs, persimmons, and sliced carrots, marveling at how his diet had changed since leaving home. He couldn't even remember when he last ate a hamburger. He hoped his new habits were keeping heart failure at arm's length.

At about 2:30, the promised rain was just starting to fall, making weekday customers even less likely. With no sign of Shawn emerging from his bedroom, Quinn was about to pour himself a glass of the estate Rhone blend when a large dark colored Chrysler sedan, which screamed “Federal Government” pulled up.

Deja-vu.

Quinn’s stomach gave a lurch. His yet-to-be-filled wineglass crashed to the floor. How had they found him? Where was Shawn? Would he be taken, and would this be the last time? Quinn’s mind was racing, trying to think of how he could escape when surprisingly, a solitary man Quinn didn’t recognize got out of the car wearing a gray suit and dark sunglasses. Quinn took a deep breath.

The federal agent walked up to the tasting room and entered. Quinn decided not to make a break for it. Maybe he could overpower him. What kind of an idiot comes alone? When he saw Quinn he took off his sunglasses and smiled at him.

“Dr. Quinn, you’ve been a difficult man to find.” He had a thick southern accent and almost sounded friendly.

“I don’t recognize you, though no doubt you’re a fed,” Quinn said. “It’s gutsy of you to come up here alone.” He made an inventory of things he might use as a weapon, including the broken stem of the glass he just dropped.

The man sat down on a stool and leaned forward onto the tasting bar.

“I’m not taking you in, Quinn,” he said matter-of-factly. “I was just assigned to this case a few months ago, after the last encounter with you.”

“The one that left me for dead in Berkeley?” Quinn asked, an eyebrow raised. He was deciding how much damage he could inflict with a wine bottle as the man replied.

“Yeah, I replaced the guy who botched the last interrogation. I’ve never met you, or seen you in action, but you’ve quite a reputation, Dr. Quinn,” he said in a Georgia drawl. He spoke so slowly that Quinn had the urge to physically pull the words out of his mouth.

"You work for Walker Dunn, the senior agent, in, whatever agency you all work for?" Quinn asked.

The man nodded.

"What do you want?" Quinn asked.

"Beyond re-establishing your whereabouts?"

Quinn nodded.

"I want to understand what's happening here. I know that after the sale of your winery you still had close to a million dollars even after we froze most of it. I know you allegedly have hundreds of millions of dollars off shore somewhere from your illegal manufacturing operation. And I am impressed that you've never taken your own polymer. But now, with the damage to your lungs and kidneys after the last interrogation, there's got to be a temptation." He looked intently at Quinn.

"You want to know if I've started taking it after the misadventure in Berkeley?"

The federal agent nodded.

"Dunn told you how it works?"

"No, just that it does work," the agent said. "How good could it be, though?"

Quinn leaned forward. "Listen agent, what's your name?"

"Snow," the man replied. "But you can call me Marty."

"Okay, listen Marty, the story is, I invented a drug so good that the feds didn't want it to get out into public. See, if we doctors do our job too well, everyone has to rethink every actuarial assumption upon which our society relies: social security, Medicare, pensions, retirement, life insurance, all of it. Easier to bury it, I guess, than deal with it, especially with the debt crisis the politicians have created. They bought my patent. They paid a hundred and fifty million for it. After all is said and done, you assholes have frozen about fifty million dollars of my money and I have somewhere around a million of my own. What does that say?"

Snow shrugged, but continued to pay attention.

"It says that I haven't made a penny since I retired to Napa. As a matter of fact, I've lost money. Your federal pals have drained my whole blood volume looking for the fucking polymer, and they haven't found it. If I was making it somewhere, do you think I'd be pouring wine in my buddy's tasting room in the damn Sierra?" Quinn asked.

Snow considered what Quinn said. "Is there money off-shore?"

"No, but I can't prove that there isn't. What do they say about trying to prove a negative?"

"It's practically impossible," Snow conceded.

"How is it that you are so sure that there is money hidden somewhere? What is the source of your information?"

Snow was silent.

"What, you don't have a source?" Quinn asked.

"I don't know where the information is coming from. It is not my source. It's Dunn's," he said at last.

"Are you certain of its veracity?" Quinn asked. "Think about it. You want me to prove I'm innocent. Isn't that turning American justice on its head?"

"You make a valid point," he said. "I want you to know, as far as I'm concerned, you're innocent until proven guilty. But if half of what I hear is true, you'll still have a lot of explaining to do."

"I have to hand it to you, Agent Snow," Quinn retorted. "You appear to use your brain more than most of your colleagues."

"I have to hand it to you Dr. Quinn, You sure know how to lose yourself, and us for that matter. I finally found your car in the garage in Sacramento. My friends at the NSA traced some shipments and a couple of calls made by Minh Tran, your friend and former business partner in the South Bay to this area. We can do that thanks to the Patriot Act. I've been up here looking around for over a week. Looks like I finally found you."

"Looks like you did. But this town's not that big. Are you and your buddies going to tear this place apart too, looking for a secret laboratory?" Quinn asked.

"No. Do you own the Silverado?" Snow asked.

"No," Quinn replied. "But I told your boss some time back that they're selling my polymer there, disguised in an herbal supplement."

"Dunn?"

"Yeah."

"So, if the polymer is there, and you aren't making it, who is?" Snow asked sounding sincere.

"I don't know. Someone from Michinski's inner circle might have the ability to manufacture it."

"I was told they're all dead or in prison," Snow said.

"Well then, it beats the hell out of me," Quinn said. "But it isn't my job. The polymer patent belongs to your people now, so I guess it's your problem. Remember, I don't need to solve this case, you do."

Snow was silent for a moment, scrutinizing Quinn's face it appeared.

"Funny, either you're a great liar, or else…." he said, shaking his head. He sounded impressed.

"Or else I'm telling you the truth," Quinn finished for him.

"Consider yourself back on the grid, Dr. Quinn. Will I be seeing you in Napa again?"

"Likely. We're going down there for the auction in May." Quinn said. What was the point in lying?

"We'll see you there. And Dr. Quinn, we will get to the bottom of this, no matter where that leads," Snow said, handing him a card which gave his name and a phone number in the San Francisco area code, but no agency. Quinn looked at it for a second before watching the man leave the tasting room.

"I hope you do, and then you and your federal goons can give me my money back and leave me the hell alone," Quinn said.

"Nothing would make me happier, Dr. Quinn," he said. Snow closed the door behind him, not looking back as he entered his car and accelerated down the gravel driveway, the dust plume behind his wheels settling fast in the increasingly aggressive rainstorm.

As he was pulling out of sight, a black Maserati coupe pulled into the parking lot and a beautiful blonde woman in a designer dress and heels got out of the driver's seat.

"That's more like it," Quinn said to himself, wiping his sweaty brow on his sleeve and attempting to compose himself.

She circled to the trunk pulling out a large box as a shorter, older Asian man got out of the passenger seat, carrying a smaller box. Quinn realized that both of them looked grumpy, but the blonde also looked harried as they opened umbrellas and hurried toward the tasting room. Quinn was still composing himself as the two approached.

They entered with a purposeful gait, and Quinn stepped in front of the counter to open the door for them. "Welcome to Callihan Vineyards, have you come to taste today?" he asked, still a noticeable tremor in his voice.

"In a manner of speaking," the Asian man said curtly, putting the box on the tasting counter before looking Quinn in the face. "Matthew Quinn, what are you doing in the foothills? Have you purchased this facility?"

"No, I um…." Quinn said and turned to the blonde woman, who looked apologetic before speaking.

"We had an unfortunate mix-up today. We were supposed to taste in the back office of Granite-Top Vineyards, but for some reason our calendars were off. They didn't expect us until next week, and have some sort of private party going on at the vineyard. This sort of thing never happened to us before, but the magazine has new owners right now, and is in transition, so there is a lot of chaos. I was wondering if you would be able to host us for a tasting of a handful of new and current releases from some of the local estates. We have all the wines we need, and would be willing to taste whatever wines you would like to have us taste today, up to five wines."

Quinn stared dumbly at them, unsure of what they were asking, when the identity of the Asian man dawned upon him.

"Holy shit! You're Ronald Park!" he gasped.

"Holy shit I am," Park answered, deadpan as he brushed raindrops off of his coat. "This is my wife, Virginia. And you, Dr. Quinn are not the proprietor up here," he said. "So who is?"

"Ummm, Shawn Callihan, an old friend of mine is the owner. He's…." Quinn paused, not wanting to finish the sentence with 'sleeping' at nearly three in the afternoon. "…he's indisposed at the moment. But I would be delighted to help you any way I can." Quinn blushed as he finished.

Park didn't seem to notice. He looked at him with a confused look, as though he were trying to remember something.

"Sold your winery but unable to leave the wine business behind?" he asked. "I recall reading something about you being ill and in the hospital, but never any follow-up. Is this some sort of rehab for you or something?"

Quinn blushed again. "Rehab?" he asked. "No, just some rest, recreation, and reeducation," he said turning a full crimson at his absurd alliteration.

This is going well.

"I see," said Park, smiling for the first time. "Have you got a table we can use to set things up?" His wife disappeared to the car to retrieve a second case of wine.

"Yes, I can get that set up for you. Do you need glasses?" Quinn asked rushing to make sure he had enough clean wine glasses.

"No, we'll use our own," Park said, opening the box he carried in as his wife returned.

"You see," Virginia said as the door closed behind her, "we have a policy, developed by Mr. Park himself, that each wine is tasted in a new, clean, unwashed glass, which is etched with only the date and a number. It prevents outside tampering. It further ensures our integrity."

"Integrity?" Quinn asked.

"You must know about the troubles in the industry," she sighed.

Quinn nodded. He wished desperately that Shawn would get his butt out of bed and deal with the situation. Quinn set the table, and watched as Park pulled thirty clean, unused Reidel glasses were set up each etched with the date and a number.

Virginia turned to Quinn and asked, "What do you have that you would like evaluated today?" Quinn scrambled. He figured Shawn would want his best wines evaluated, but they were also the smallest of his productions. He gave her Shawn's Syrah, the Rhone blend, the white Rhone blend, the Viognier, and the Tempranillo. Virginia graciously accepted the wines. Park stood up and walked out onto the deck as Virginia placed the wines in shrouds.

"Can you place the numbers on these wines, as you see fit?" she asked.

"Sure, but why me?" Quinn asked.

"That ensures I don't know what I'm pouring. I'll need you to monitor the tasting to make sure it is blinded per the custom of the industry," Virginia stated more than requested.

"Sure," Quinn said. Virginia turned away from the bottles as Quinn placed the numbers on the shrouded bottles. He then went behind the counter and grabbed a barstool, sitting down to watch as Park returned and the ritual of tasting began. Virginia handed him a reference glass.

"This is the 2008 Jackson and Jones Amador County Bandit. It is a blend of forty five percent Syrah, forty percent Grenache, and fifteen percent Zinfandel. You rated this wine 91 points last year."

Park took the wine and began looking and smelling the wine in the manner to which he was accustomed. Virginia stole a look at Quinn and silently motioned for him to close the tasting room to customers. Quinn looked around again, desperately wishing Shawn would emerge. He wondered briefly whether Shawn would be mad if Quinn turned away customers. Shawn was apparently not going to emerge, so

Quinn made an executive decision, locking the tasting room door by placing a sign up which said, "Private Event, No Tasting Today."

Park muttered something about the wine, and then continued the tasting. Quinn watched in silence, entranced by the process. His wines had been reviewed at least seven times in the last three years, but he had never seen Park do it. He watched carefully as Virginia poured the same amount from the shrouded bottles into each glass, inspected the wine herself for a moment, and then handed the wine to Park stating only a number. Park then did his evaluation of the wine, spending a few minutes writing notes on a yellow legal pad after each taste. It was a simple but fascinating process. After a little more than a half case of wine, Park got up silently and went to the restroom.

"Dr. Quinn, I understand you know some friends of ours, Joshua Mortensen and Minh Tran," she said.

"Ah, the boys. Yes, they are two of my closest friends," Quinn said, smiling. "How do you know them?"

"We've been friends for a number of years," she said. "I'd love to spend some time talking with you about your winery in Napa." Park emerged from the bathroom and shot a furious glance at Virginia. Virginia flushed, then shrugged an apology to Quinn and returned her attention to the tasting table. The ritual continued.

They were nearly finished tasting when Shawn emerged, his hair a spectacular mess, bed-head brought to a new level of chaos. He saw Park and Virginia seated, and immediately deduced the situation.

He looked at Quinn and mouthed, "What the hell?"

Quinn looked back apologetically. Park finished, and Virginia unshrouded the wines, writing the identity of each wine next to the corresponding number. Shawn walked up to Ron Park, and shook his hands, as Virginia packaged up the dirty tasting glasses into the same box with which she brought them in.

"I'm Shawn Callihan, proprietor and winemaker here. It's a pleasure to have you here, Mr. Park."

Park spent a moment gazing at Shawn's hair, and then settled on him without smiling. "Your assistant here, Dr. Quinn, was most hospitable. We're in debt to you for hosting us. Thank you."

"If you two need a place to stay, we have a bed and breakfast here. We can host you as long as you need. How many days are you going to be tasting up here?" Shawn asked.

"We're done," Park said, his mouth twisting into a tight smile. "Your hospitality has been wonderful. Good afternoon."

He turned to leave. Virginia produced a form. She approached Quinn and asked him to sign it.

"What is it?" Quinn asked, looking over the legal-looking form.

"It's the attestation that I didn't know the identity of the wines and their corresponding numbers, and that I didn't communicate or compromise the blind nature of our tasting today in any way," she said.

"Okay," Quinn said, "I was here and watched. There was no communication. I numbered the shrouded wines in random fashion without you observing." He signed the form.

"Thanks again, to both of you," Virginia said, handing Quinn a card with her number on it before she made to join Park, already outside waiting by the locked car. "Call me," she whispered before leaving. There was a handwritten phone number scrawled on it.

"Okay then," Shawn said. "Drive safely."

She smiled and walked out, bringing with her the yellow legal pad, and leaving behind, thirty bottles of wine, each minus four ounces.

"What are we going to do with all of this leftover wine?" Quinn asked.

"One guess," Shawn said.

"Okay," Quinn said, smiling at his friend. They sat down, each with a clean glass, and prepared to begin tasting the wine.

Shawn rummaged through the bottles, until he saw which of his own wines had been tasted. "Thank God you didn't give them the Barbera."

"You hate the Barbera."

"He would've too. The residual sugar, the volatile acids, it's just crap," Shawn said. "I really shouldn't be selling it."

"It's no '47 Cheval Blanc, that's for sure." Quinn said.

"You're a smart ass," Shawn said cocking his head. "And how the hell do you know what a '47 Cheval Blanc tastes like anyway?"

"I don't know, but the scientist in me says we need to find out," Quinn said.

"You get a hold of one, and let me know when you got it," Shawn said flippantly.

"I got it."

A stony silence followed, as Shawn stared at his friend, looking incredulous. Quinn returned a smug, broad grin.

"Where?" Shawn asked, his tone suggesting he hadn't yet decided whether Quinn was telling the truth.

"Down in the cave, where else?" Quinn said.

Without another word, the two men rose and made a beeline through the rainy evening to the entrance of the wine cave, leaving the two and a half cases of Sierra Foothills wine behind. They entered, making their way to the cozy table where they spent most evenings. Quinn went to a wall racked with bottles of wine and pulled a dusty bottle, handing it to Shawn. The label was lightly soiled, but the lead capsule, which covered the cork, appeared intact, and the fill was very-top-shoulder.

"I've been reading about that wine, and how different it was than anything else that was created at that time," Quinn began.

Shawn reached into a cupboard and pulled two tall, open-mouthed Bordeaux glasses down, nodding. “I think it was a case of a blind squirrel finding a nut,” he said. “Most people, even today, wouldn’t tolerate a wine like this, I’ve heard.”

“One way to find out,” Quinn said, handing the bottle over to Shawn, who was ready with a sharp knife and an “Ah-So” wine opener. “Good choice. This cork is too old for a corkscrew.”

“This isn’t my first bottle of old wine, pal,” Shawn said.

“But it’s your first 1947 Cheval Blanc,” Quinn retorted.

One less thing to do before I die.

Shawn carefully cut the capsule, examined the cork and with surgical precision, extracted it. “Where did you find this anyway, it looks like it’s in great condition. There’s no sign of seepage. Do you want to share what prompted you to make such a purchase?”

“I found it a year ago at an online auction. You don’t want to know how much,” Quinn said. “And I pulled the trigger because this is one of many things I need to do before all is said and done.”

“Tax deductable, you know, education,” he said, ignoring the death reference and winking at Quinn as he poured the wine carefully into the large leaded crystal glasses.

“I’m sure that would fly in an audit,” Quinn said, “as if I want trouble with the IRS too.”

“On about the feds again?” Shawn said sounding dismissive.

“The feds found me this afternoon, while you were sleeping. One of them came into the tasting room. We talked, nothing more, and then he left. But they know I’m here now,” Quinn said. “It doesn’t seem to be a problem yet, and I kind of liked this guy. He struck me as a thinking man’s fed. But enough of that, we have more important things to do. I don’t want anything to distract us from the greatest wine in the history of the world.”

The two then immersed themselves in the evaluation of the sixty-plus year old bottle of Bordeaux that Quinn knew some consider the greatest wine ever produced. They looked, sniffed, smelled, swirled, smelled again, looked again, and warmed the wine in their hands, the time they took increasing the tension as the anticipation of the wine built.

"What'd Park give this wine, anyway?" Quinn asked out loud.

"Ninety-nine points."

"Not a hundred?"

"He's never given a wine a hundred points." Shawn replied.

"Never?"

"Never."

"What an asshole," Quinn said.

"That bastard is the sole man in the game right now. He is the only internationally recognized person rating the world's wines. If he says it's great, it commands a huge price, if he says it's schlock, it sits on the shelf," Shawn said.

"Kind of a vacuum now," Quinn said, more than asked. "I never paid much attention, but then again I guess I didn't have to," he added. "You know, I really regret that. I wish I'd been more engaged in the whole process."

Shawn nodded silently.

They drank the intoxicating nectar.

"This is different from any wine I have ever tasted," Shawn said.

"It's ridiculously soft, almost unnaturally so," Quinn added puzzled at how different the wine was than, well, wine.

"It's odd. Can you taste the residual sugar?"

"No, but it's there. I read that this wine was the product of a stuck fermentation. It's supposed to be high in alcohol, but I can't taste that either," Quinn said.

"I catch a whiff of volatile acid, but only for a moment, and then it is gone," Shawn said.

"I can't detect that, but Jesus, Shawn, this is fuckin-omenal!" Quinn said, as proud of his profane neologism as he was impressed with the wine in his glass. "My ex-girlfriend once gave me a bottle of wine she said was life-changing. I still have it. But if this wine, right here in our glass, is not the most surreal, spectacular wine I have ever tasted, I don't know what is."

"True art," Shawn said agreeing with Quinn as he stared into his wine glass. "It tastes as if it were made in the last ten years, like it could age forever."

They fell into silence, experiencing and puzzling on the wine, forgetting the thirty bottles of open wine upstairs.

"How did this wine manage to be so different from every other wine on the planet?" Shawn asked.

"I don't know, Shawn. Perhaps striving for perfection is an imperfect way to approach wine," Quinn said.

"Like medicine, winemaking isn't a pure science," Shawn said. "It's the artful application of scientific principles to a complex multivariate system in the hopes of influencing the outcome in a positive way."

Quinn looked at his friend with astonishment. "That's a mouthful. But it's a brilliant description of medicine," Quinn said.

"And winemaking," Shawn said.

"Maybe that's why so many doctors end up in the business," Quinn said.

"I think lots of doctors are romantics," Shawn said. "They go into medicine with a specific notion of what it means to wear a white coat, do research, save lives, whatever. And then they get disenchanted with the real picture of it, the bureaucracy, inefficiency, finances, difficult patients and so forth. So they either become bitter, develop a sense of entitlement, or they go looking elsewhere for a romantic notion of life."

"You think they come into the wine business with the same notion?" Quinn asked.

"Yes, I do. Then they realize that it is actually hard work being a winemaker. They either end up aloof to the business, or working their ass off. A lot of them end up miserable again."

"Like me," Quinn said, with some dejection.

"Like you," Shawn agreed. "But now you're here, rediscovering what you liked about it in the first place. Besides, I don't think it was the winemaking but other stuff going on which made you so miserable."

"Yeah, definitely," Quinn said. "So, what about you?"

"Me? I think I was exactly like that. I went to law school because it seemed like the thing to do, and then I discovered I hated lawyers, so I went to medical school thinking I'd like those people more. I did it because I could, not because I wanted to. I sure didn't want to take over the family business. I didn't like the lifestyle of a contractor. Then I got tired of medicine even before I started. I didn't need to do anything, but I guess I had to do something."

Quinn laughed and Shawn smiled at the ridiculous honesty of his explanation.

"So, did you like docs more than lawyers, Shawn?" he asked.

"Yeah, it turned out I did. Then I learned about the wine trade shortly after leaving medical school, and got this idea that I could buy a winery, make wine, and immerse myself in this industry. It was a romantic notion. I always imagined myself hosting, whether in the wine room, at a party, at the bed and breakfast, or whatever. It was a notion of partying with people all the time. Reality is different, but in spite of working harder than I ever thought I would…"

"Though still not very hard," Quinn interrupted.

"In spite of working hard," Shawn repeated, "I realized I like winemaking. Up here in the Sierra, there's potential, but not too many great winemakers yet. I think a lot of them are farmers more than winemakers. It's like Napa in the sixties and seventies. But there's great potential here, once the region discovers its best grapes beyond bloody Zinfandel."

"Beyond Zinfandel," Quinn said, raising his glass and nodding in agreement.

"Not that Zinfandel is so awful, but I think it is limited. Tempranillo and Rhone grapes, those are what're best suited to this area. We're just starting to discover that, and you watch, in ten, twenty years, we'll be huge."

"Maybe you'll be in Napa by then," Quinn said.

"I'll never give up making wine here, even if we have success in Napa. I like the atmosphere in the Sierra," Shawn explained.

"Yeah, it's not too bad." Quinn said, contemplating the last glass in the bottle of legendary Bordeaux in front of him.

"I think it saved your life," Shawn said to Quinn. "And you're even opening up again. I like the social Quinn better than the brooding, silent one."

"I think you're right," Quinn acknowledged. "About saving my life, I mean. I really like the way you view winemaking. I like that mistakes can make a masterpiece," he said, nodding at the Cheval Blanc, "and I like that you can go into this, work your ass off, and still lose your shirt. But most of all, I like the smell of the tasting room. I like talking about wine with people. I like eating fresh food, and I really like the taste of great wine. I had everything, so how could I have been missing this down in Napa?"

"I don't know," Shawn said. "But I agree the taste of great wine is better than almost anything in the world. What if we could make a wine like this '47? I'd like to be able to do that."

Quinn nodded in agreement. "I also like that before today I hadn't seen a federal agent in nearly four months."

"Sooner or later you'll have to explain the details to me, you know," Shawn said.

Quinn nodded. "Soon," he said, "because you've earned it pal."

Chapter 10:

Virginia's cell phone chirped. The caller ID was blocked. Upstairs, Ron was finishing packing his suitcases. She had to make a quick decision. She hoped it was Quinn and she could ask him a few questions about his winery in Napa. She took a quick breath and answered. "This is Virginia."

It wasn't Quinn. In the next forty-five seconds she sat down silent, listening intently at her kitchen table. The jugular veins were bulging out of her neck as she listened, her muscles taught from her scalp to her toes.

Not again, you promised yourself, Virginia.

"If this ever gets out, it would ruin me, my husband, and the magazine," she said with just an audible tremor to her voice, her brow furrowed in deep concentration. "Not to mention the damage to the industry as a whole. I can't let you continue to hold that over me. I need an out. What's the alternative?"

She listened some more, feeling a trickle of sweat on the back of her neck. What had she gotten herself into? "When do you want me to do this?" she asked quietly. "How much are we talking about?" she asked, her eyebrows jumping in surprise. She tried to remain calm. She gasped into the phone, her heart racing as she heard the offer. She took another deep breath before continuing. "Okay, if you can do the transaction without it being traceable, and if you can guarantee you'll keep it secret, I'll do it, but this is the last time," she said, screwing up as much courage as she could, "and I want a cashier's check for the rest mailed to my P.O. box in San Francisco."

Virginia finished the conversation feeling a curious mixture of dread and excitement. She dreaded what she had to do, but she realized that after she was done, she'd be able to get what she'd waited a lifetime for. She looked up to see Park stopped in the doorway staring at her.

How long has he been there?

"You look like you've seen a ghost. What was that all about?" Park asked.

"I don't want to talk about it right now. Are you ready to go?"

"Yeah, the suitcases are in the car," Park said, looking at his wife warily.

"Good, then we'll go. Do you have your speech ready?" she asked, regaining her composure.

"I still need to revise it, but the outline is done, and I already know what I'm going to say," he said. "I just need to retaste the wines. I have them packed away."

"The Paris tasting was quite a moment for Napa," she said.

"The single most important day in the history of Napa Valley," Park acknowledged.

Virginia forced a smile, and by the time they were in the car, she had relaxed some. She knew what she had to do to protect herself and the integrity of the industry she loved more than anything. She knew she was also protecting her husband, no matter how she felt about him now. Two turns to freedom, she told herself as she entered the freeway, heading north to Napa Valley as she contemplated a divorce lawyer.

They arrived three hours later to an unseasonably warm May evening, Napa Valley's vines in full bloom, creating a shocking green blanket all up and down the valley floor. They crossed to the Silverado Trail and the Silverado Springs Resort and Hot Springs, just up the Eastern slopes of the valley, north of St. Helena. It was the place they usually stayed. Virginia checked in under her maiden name, as was their custom. She paid with cash, and left a cashier's check for the deposit. This was all to maintain as low a profile as possible for her husband who remained in the car. They went to great lengths to ensure that few knew where they were staying. The Silverado Springs Resort respected the privacy of their guests, and allowed them this discretion.

"We'll have to be out the door by eight am tomorrow," Park said to Virginia. "Barrel samples will be rushed to the facility after they're bottled under argon gas, but we best have them tasted within thirty minutes of arrival. How many runners are there going to be?"

"The magazine will have ten people running, so it'll be a three ring circus, but we have to get this information into the page setters in forty-eight hours, so the release of the magazine coincides with the event," Virginia explained.

"It's this kind of stunt which cheapens the magazine. It looks like the magazine favors Napa above Bordeaux. It destroys objectivity," Park muttered.

"Over eighty percent of the magazine's subscriptions come from the United States. It's a good marketing decision," Virginia offered.

"For the magazine, or for the readers?" Park retorted. "Remember, if the readers think there's bias, they'll stop reading."

"You don't own the magazine, anymore. This decision came from higher up," Virginia said.

Park was silent.

The two spent the afternoon in their room, reading and passing time in what Virginia thought was an uncomfortable silence. There was still tension, though they had not had any talks about real estate. She was also tense about her phone call before they left. Her die was cast.

The next morning, they were at the magazine headquarters in downtown Napa, arriving as three of the first barrel samples arrived. The samples arrived in unlabeled bottles, called 'shiners' corked, and with a sealed tape over the cork with each winemaker's signature over the tape. A removable tag identified the wine. The bottle was examined by Virginia, who made a note of the winemaker and wine, and then removed the sealed tape and cork, and poured the familiar four ounce pour into Reidel glasses and handed the glass to Park, stating only a numeral. The process was a mild departure from the usual tasting, but was still witnessed by impartial observers.

Park was immersed in the wine, with intense concentration upon all his senses, shutting out the rest of the world. Virginia was sweating some and feeling anxious as she looked at each wine, not knowing which wine was coming next. The two impartial observers, making sure that the unorthodox tasting remained blinded, did not seem to pay much attention to Virginia, as long as she was not communicating with Park.

After wine nineteen, Park had an almost violent reaction. "This is awful. Sherry, smoke, yeast, and barnyard," he said, returning the glass to Virginia. Virginia turned to the monitors, who looked back at her with interest, watching to see how she would react.

"It…. it could be contamination of the bottle," Virginia said, stammering. "I'll get the backup. They're in the next room aren't they?" The observers nodded, and pointed to an adjoining office. Virginia set the bottle down, and disappeared into the room, one of the observers followed her. They emerged a few moments later with the bottle already open, smelling the bottle and the cork herself. "Must've been a bad bottle. This one smells okay to me."

"No talking to Mr. Park," one of the observers snapped.

Virginia, visibly flushed, embarrassed, and sweating, nodded and took a fresh glass, filling it with four ounces of the second bottle, her hands shaking. "Er, number nineteen," she said, handing the glass to Park, who took the glass, sniffed deeply, shook his head and tasted. He did not have a repeat of the violent reaction to the first bottle, and spent what seemed like an inordinate amount of time evaluating the wine. Finally with a deeply furrowed brow, he scratched some notes onto the paper, and moved on.

After thirty tastings of barrel samples from the previous Cabernet vintage, now just eight months old and still in barrels, they concluded the tasting. Park handed his notes over to the assistant editor, who promised him he would have typed transcriptions for review tomorrow. Since the wines were unlabeled, Park did not know the identities of the wines he tasted as he left.

Virginia looked particularly relieved that the tasting was over. She offered to take Park to an off-the-beaten-track bistro in St. Helena for dinner.

"Yes, that'd be fine," Park said stiffly. She knew he was never comfortable in Napa.

"I've been thinking," Virginia said as they drove through the city of Napa toward St. Helena, "that maybe stepping down from the advertising executive job at the magazine wasn't enough."

Park abruptly turned to face her, shocked.

"I've been pouring for you for almost fifteen years. I think it would actually be best if I stepped away from the magazine completely," she finished.

"For the sake of perceived objectivity?" Park asked.

"Yes, exactly. And besides, I think I want to pursue something completely different."

"Please tell me that this is not about winemaking," Park said.

"No, it isn't," Virginia said, and glanced furtively at Park.

Park took a moment to digest the information. "I don't see why you have to stop pouring for me, you do it perfectly most of the time, and we'd have to train someone else to do it. What do you have in mind?"

"I was thinking of doing something with the Internet," Virginia said, "pouring is not that big a deal Ron, anyone can do it."

"Whatever you do, I'll support you. I'll miss having you at the tastings, though."

"You'll support anything I decide to do?" she asked incredulously.

"Don't push it," Park said.

"Well, Minh and Joshua have invited us to the Bounty Hunter for dinner and wine the day after tomorrow. I can discuss it with them then. Do you think you'd be willing to join them there?" Virginia asked.

"Yeah, that sounds fine." Park said.

Chapter 11:

Henri had been in a state of depression since the deal closed. It was hard to acknowledge it, but he worried that he was near the end of his family's run in Napa Valley. He contemplated what he would do if he were faced with selling his family name to a large beverage company interested in marketing and not at all interested in maintaining quality. Would he take the money? How desperate would he have to be to sell his name and watch as it was placed on a mediocre product deemed "good enough" for public consumption?

The phone at his desk jarred him back to reality. "Henri Paradis," he said reflexively into the phone.

"Mr. Paradis, sorry to bother you, but it looks like someone broke into the supply shed," Raul Mendoza, his vineyard manager said.

"What's in there?" Paradis asked, his hands running through his fine, wispy hair. "It's just a bunch of old tools, and chemicals, right? Did they take anything?"

"I don't think so," Mendoza said. "It was probably some kids, looking for a place to get high. Some tools and stakes were knocked over and the padlock was destroyed. We found some spilt fungicide and fertilizer, nothing else. We'll get it cleaned up. Do you want me to call the police?"

"Damn kids," he said shaking his head. "No, it'll just be a waste of everyone's time. Get it cleaned up and put a better lock on the door. I don't want that shed turning into their clubhouse."

"I'll get it taken care of right away," Mendoza said and hung up.

Paradis was in the process of forgetting the incident, and remembering his previous train of thought, when the phone rang a second time. He contemplated letting it switch over to voicemail, the news seemed to be bad every time he picked it up. After the third ring, he acquiesced.

"Henri Paradis," he said.

"Henri, I just got off the phone with our insider at *Wine* magazine," said Andrew Wooten.

Paradis could tell be the tension in his winemaker's voice that the news was going to be bad.

"What'd our barrel sample get?"

"Park hasn't done his final edits, but my friend does the transcription for them, and he gave me the rough version." Wooten read him the review over the phone.

(Notes from alternate bottle as first bottle was contaminated.) This wine was clunky, with lots of residue, and deep garnet color. Nose was of black currant and smoke. The mouth feel was disjointed, tannins were dominant, overwhelming the cassis, green pepper, dark berry, and grapey fruit. There were overwhelming presence of smoke, and waves of oak dominated the midpalate. Experience tells me that the tannin structure will remain long after the fruit has faded. 82-84 points.
-Park

"There's got to be some mistake. It's a barrel sample, how could it be tainted? That is not our wine, what he described there. It is absolutely not our wine," Paradis said, confused and crestfallen.

"No, it isn't. I smell a rat here," Wooten said venomously.

"Were both bottles pulled from the same barrel?" Paradis asked.

"Yeah, but we tasted it right before we filled the bottles. It was fine."

"Could there have been something which was in the first bottle, something to contaminate it?"

"I… I don't know. No, there couldn't have been, we'd have seen it." Wooten said, sounding unsure.

"We can't be absolutely certain, though, can we?" Paradis said.

"Not absolutely, no," Wooten said with dejection.

"Then we have nothing."

"Henri, there's something not right here, I just know it."

"I know, Andrew. There is no one to check him right now." Paradis felt defeated. "Until someone picks up one of the defunct publications, he's it. That man just has too much power."

"Someone has to stop him. He's killing us!"

"This might finish us," Paradis said with a touch of finality. "That is a review for some central valley swill, not our reserve Cabernet."

"Park has to be after us. We can't be that out of touch with our wines."

"No, we aren't," Paradis said, "but Park tastes blind. He can't be going after us. I used to trust him. He picked up our TCA problem when the other publications failed to. He was right, the others were wrong. He has always been honest. I don't understand what's going on now."

"That man is trying to do us in, and do you really think he tastes truly blind? He has the most acute sense of taste and smell on the planet. He can taste a wine and know what year, what appellation, and usually who the winemaker is. Blind my ass!" Wooten said.

Paradis shrugged, acknowledging Park's rare gift.

"What has he got to gain by killing my winery?" he asked out loud.

"I think it's an ego thing. The guy is drunk on his power. He gets off on being a giant killer, and right now you might be one of the most vulnerable giants in Napa Valley." Wooten said.

"Well, we're not dead quite yet," Paradis said, and hung up.

Paradis looked down at his desk for several minutes, contemplating what to do next. He thought about the disputed plot again, and thought about his brother. Was he fighting to prolong the life of his beloved winery, or to prolong its death? He looked across his office at a painted portrait of his father, the old patriarch's gnarled hands and weather-beaten face showcasing the life of tremendous physical labor that went into building the Paradis Empire. What would the old man have done? Paradis wondered, himself an old man, growing older it seemed, by the minute.

Chapter 12:

At last the week in Napa came. Quinn had been looking forward to it ever since Shawn hatched the plan. The two eager ex-medical professionals headed a hundred miles west to Napa Valley, staying at the Silverado Springs Resort, now the most popular resort in Napa Valley. Quinn was initially hesitant, asking Shawn to find different lodging, but Shawn had made the reservations several weeks in advance and now all lodging in Napa Valley was booked. The suite was booked under Shawn's name, so no one would officially know Quinn was there. Could that be an advantage?

Quinn surmised that he was done hiding, and his strength and spirit was renewed. It was time to get to work clearing his name. Maybe it was a good thing he was there. Maybe it was sleuth time. He planned to search for information on the illicit sale of the polymer, to find out more about the ownership of the resort, and to uncover something to clear his name at the resort.

They arrived late morning only to learn that they were unable to check into their room until three in the afternoon. They decided to head up the valley to look at the different areas, and see if they had a region or sub-appellation within the valley that they wanted to focus upon. Initially they did a great arc, driving up the Silverado Trail to Calistoga, where the valley narrowed significantly, and then down Highway 29, into St. Helena.

After taking in the topography in silence, Shawn turned to Quinn. "Have you ever been up Spring Mountain?"

"Yep," Quinn said, "last time was with my ex. I think you'll meet her this week. She's one of the most beautiful women on the planet."

"Nice," Shawn answered. "The mountain wines are more austere than on the valley floor, but the character of the mountain fruit is just excellent." Shawn said. "That's what I like about them, but then again, you know all about that, don't you? How come I never knew you had a winery down here?"

"I didn't have anything in the name identifying me as the owner. The last owner referred to it as 'Wildhorse Ranch Winery and Vineyards.' I liked the name and kept it. When I sold it, the conglomerate that bought it kept the name. One of their representatives assured me that they'd maintain the standards that had brought the winery to prominence. We'll see," Quinn sounded doubtful. "But let's not talk about that. I think we should get you something on the valley floor, Rutherford, St. Helena, Yountville, Oakville, you know."

"Maybe we should visit those folks at Terroir Unlimited. Did you say they're in St. Helena?" Shawn asked.

"You want to drop in on them?" Quinn offered.

"Couldn't hurt, we got twenty million dollars to spend," Shawn said.

"Most of it is borrowed," Quinn said sounding cautious.

"As long as the funding is secured, they don't give a damn," Shawn said.

The two of them wandered around the small town, abuzz with events in anticipation of the celebration of the anniversary 1976 Paris Tasting. They eventually found the etched glass door in a single storey brick building under a hunter-green awning, which said in script, "TU" and underneath that, "Terroir Unlimited." The door was locked, so they hit a call button. The door buzzed mechanically, and they stepped inside.

"Good afternoon, is there something I can help you with?" asked a striking blonde woman with cobalt-blue eyes. She was in a business pants suit with an athletic cut, which hugged her slim body, revealing no inefficient curves. "My name is Arianna Richardson, I'm one of the contractors with Terroir Unlimited."

"Shawn Callihan, and this is my buddy, Matthew Quinn," Shawn said smoothly. He was like velvet when dealing with women, Quinn thought.

Arianna smiled in a way that managed to be knowing and disarming at the same time. "Proprietor of Callihan

Vineyards in the Sierra Foothills, I presume? Thinking of jumping into the valley and pairing up with one of our quietest and most discreet owners?" she asked, cocking an eyebrow at Quinn.

"Ex-owners," Quinn corrected her.

"Thinking about it," Shawn said, not betraying any surprise at being instantly recognized.

She's good.

"Looking to reenter the game, Dr. Quinn?" she asked. "You two are contemplating some sort of joint venture in Napa, grape growing and winemaking?"

"I'm just a friend and a cellar rat," Quinn said.

"We're interested in about forty or fifty acres," Shawn said. "Something on the valley floor if you have it."

"What about Spring Mountain, Pope Valley, or Atlas Peak?" she asked.

"We'd consider it, if the terroir is right," Shawn said.

"What sort of price range are you looking at, and who is backing you?"

"We are, that is, I am backed by a commercial bank in Sacramento. I'm footing two million of my own money, and am looking in the fifteen to twenty million dollar range," Shawn said. Quinn winced as Shawn mentioned the dollar figure.

Arianna smiled. "Don't worry, you'll decide what to offer, and I won't squeeze you, it's not my style. The more information you give me, the better I can narrow things down, and get you what you're looking for. There are rumors of a few parcels coming up on the valley floor very soon. I think they might interest you."

"They aren't up yet?" Quinn asked.

"Not yet, but it looks like it's just a matter of time. Things are tough in the valley for anyone cash strapped, what with the resurgence of the dollar, and the string of challenging vintages, coupled with the excellent weather and banking crisis across the pond, weakening the Euro."

"We've heard that explanation a number of times," Shawn said.

"Well, there's truth to it. We've lost a lot of weaker wineries, and some icons have fallen. Another one is close to that."

"Who?" Quinn and Shawn asked simultaneously.

She paused, giving them a scrutinizing look. "Are we going to be working together?" she asked, holding her secret as collateral.

"We'll need to see your fees and commission schedule," Shawn said.

"Here it is," Arianna said, moving efficiently to her office and returning with a paper. Quinn and Shawn studied it, talking quietly to each other.

"Dr. Quinn, you worked with my colleague, Todd Sandoval in the acquisition of your land on Mt. Veeder. I trust you were happy?"

"I was happy, my selling the vineyard had nothing to do with my happiness," Quinn said, distracted as he read the commission schedule.

"We'll work with you, but if you haven't anything we're interested in, we reserve the right to move on. The retainer isn't a problem." Shawn said.

"I'll take you at your word, and I look forward to finding you your land," Arianna said.

"So who is it, who's in so much trouble here that they're going to liquidate their land?" Shawn said, his curiosity getting the best of him.

"Henri Paradis," Arianna said. The words fell like bricks in the small office.

Quinn and Shawn stared at her in disbelief, and she smiled back.

As they drove back towards the Silverado Springs Resort, they were still shocked at the thought that an icon, some might say, *the* icon of Napa Valley was close to liquidating more of his land holdings. "How does that happen to a guy like Paradis?" Quinn asked. "He has been the biggest player in Napa for a generation. I thought he was just downsizing with the first sale, but now he's selling another one. What does that mean?"

"It means he's near the end. Some people, when they get older, lose the ability to adapt to a dynamic environment. Maybe he's one of them," Shawn offered.

"Terrible luck," Quinn said. "I've always liked his persona. I've always loved his wine. When I started getting into wine, his was the first Napa label I remember drinking and thinking, 'this is terrific!'"

"Yeah, you hate to see someone like that go down. I'd almost feel guilty buying his land from him. But the problem is, well…." Shawn paused.

"It's great land," Quinn finished.

Shawn nodded in agreement. "Do you feel like an early dinner and wine tonight?" he asked.

"As if we'd do anything else," Quinn said. "You know, I think my friends are here. They're the ones who might be interested in helping us with the land purchase. Maybe I'll call them to see if they want to meet us somewhere."

"The gay couple?" Shawn asked.

"Yeah."

"Give 'em a call," Shawn said.

Quinn called Minh Tran, who encouraged Quinn and Shawn to meet them at the Bounty Hunter.

They drove in silence into the city of Napa and toward the Bounty Hunter, a local bistro and wine bar, and a favorite among winemakers and locals in Napa. They arrived early, a little after five in the afternoon, and were able to easily get a table. Judging by the number of staff present, though, it appeared that they were expecting to be busy.

Quinn elected to start the afternoon with a fifteen year old bottle of Leoville Las Cases, a wine from Bordeaux, which was just entering its drinking window, according to Park. Quinn wondered if it was obnoxious to drink Bordeaux in Napa. He guessed not. Good wine was good wine. They had just poured the second glass of the brooding Bordeaux when

Quinn's friends Joshua Mortensen and Minh Tran entered the restaurant, with a woman of Eurasian descent whose presence made Quinn's heart nearly leap out of his chest.

Tasha, even more beautiful than the last time I saw her.

Minh saw Quinn and smiled, his perfect, shockingly-white teeth a contrast to his smooth, dark Vietnamese features. Looks ran in that family. He and his life-partner Joshua were dressed gay-casual, which meant that they were in expensive but wrinkled designer shirts and tattered jeans that probably cost north of $200 and came off the rack complete with rips and distressed material. Their avant-garde fashion sense aside, Quinn marveled at the couple's amazing vitality. They looked the picture of polished health. But they were nothing compared to Tasha. Shoulder length shiny ebony hair that fell perfectly, framing impossibly green eyes, runway bone structure, an understated nose and perfect lips, parted into a smile that rivaled her brother's. In short, it was a face that could launch a thousand ships. But it didn't stop there. Her neckline showed graceful lines, efficient musculature, and soft sculpted curves and shadow. A stylish cream-colored blouse and black pants, well tailored and cinched tight around her narrow waist showed the gorgeous figure and completed the understated elegance that Tasha always exuded. Minh introduced his partner, Joshua and his sister Tasha as they took their seats.

Joshua glanced at their table and asked, "Do the two of you mind if we switch to a larger table? We're going to be joined tonight by two more."

"Who?" Shawn asked.

"Virginia and Ronald Park," Joshua said, motioning them over to a larger table.

Shawn and Quinn stared at the other two, as they moved their wine and glasses, trying to discern if they were joking or not. "Really?" Shawn asked.

"Yeah," Joshua said, smiling at their reaction.

"I met them a month ago when they were tasting in the Sierra Foothills. Ron's wife mentioned that they knew you.

How did you two get to be friends with them?" Quinn asked.

"We've been friends for a number of years. We met them when Minh was doing some freelance work on Park's Wine-Online website, which accompanies his magazine. What was that, eight years ago, Minh?"

"Yes, indeed. The two of them aren't comfortable here. The locals have a love-hate relationship with Park. Familiar faces out of the industry are a welcome distraction," Minh explained.

"Yeah, well, we're not exactly out of the industry," Quinn reminded them.

"I run a winery up in the Sierra foothills," Shawn explained.

"Which one?" Tasha asked.

"Callihan Vineyards," Shawn said.

"I like your Tempranillo," she said and smiled at him.

That smile.

"Thanks," Shawn said, smiling back. Quinn watched the electricity between Shawn and Tasha with a sinking feeling in his gut. "So you and Minh are brother and sister?"

"Yes. He's my punk-ass little computer-nerd brother," Tasha said lightly.

Minh smiled. Quinn wondered what it would be like to smile so damn much.

"But, forgive me," Shawn said. "You look very Eurasian to me, but you," he said turning to Minh, "look pure '*nguoi Viet*' or am I wrong?"

Quinn felt all the air leaving his lungs as Shawn spoke two perfect Vietnamese words and Tasha lit up.

"Nice accent, and very astute," Minh said.

"I picked it up while traveling in college," Shawn said.

"Technically, we are half-siblings, but in Vietnamese culture, a half-sibling is treated the same as a full sibling. Tasha's father, my mother's first husband, was a major in the United States army. He was killed during the Tet Offensive in Hue. He died helping my mother and much of our family escape. I guess he was an amazing man." Tasha nodded, quietly agreeing with her brother. "That was shortly after Tasha was born. My mother came to America in 1975 with only Tasha, but met my father after they arrived. I was born here, in the late seventies."

"My billionaire baby brother is a bit of a brat," Tasha said, teasing. "Born in America, never had a tough day in his life."

"Tasha stop exaggerating. I'm not a billionaire, and I've had at least two or three tough days," Minh said.

"Okay, he's had a few challenges. I'm not being completely fair," Tasha acknowledged.

"I am sorry to hear about your father," Shawn said. "I bet you have some amazing stories to tell."

Tasha smiled at Shawn and the five of them settled into the table for eight as the restaurant filled up. They ordered dinner and Joshua asked for a magnum of Henri Paradis' reserve Cabernet from 1999, a cool year with a long growing season, he explained, which made some terrific and age-worthy wines. Quinn leaned over to Shawn interrupting his conversation with Tasha. Shawn shot him a dirty look.

"Chill out and try this Cabernet. This was grown on what might be your land someday," Quinn whispered so no one else would hear.

Quinn knew Shawn would never turn down a glass of wine. His look softened, and he accepted the pour, tasted it and nodded at Quinn before returning to his conversation with Tasha, who was fully engaged with him.

Tasha glanced at Quinn with an apologetic look, and Quinn nodded at her ever so slightly. A big part of him hadn't accepted the end of their relationship, but he stifled it, an act of will. It had, after all, been more than three years since they broke up. And now he was a dead man, not exactly relationship material, he told himself. But she looked absolutely amazing. She and her brother had some amazing genetics, Quinn had to acknowledge.

Minh shot a serious glance at Quinn before saying, "What the hell happened in Berkeley, Quinn?"

Quinn looked ruefully at his friend and old business partners before answering. “Unexpected and somewhat unfortunate coincidence has put me in the place of my old patients back in the PICU. But I got it under control now.”

“Explain that,” Tasha said, her head snapping out of the conversation she was having with Shawn. “What do you mean, in the place of my old patients?”

Quinn shrugged as he looked at Tasha. “Irony of ironies: I was picked up by the feds again. I don’t remember anything after passing out.” Quinn told the story of his ordeal. “Shitty luck eh?” he said, smiling in spite of himself.

“You could always try Viagra,” Minh said before getting a hard elbow in the shoulder by Joshua and a fierce glare from Tasha.

“Jesus, Quinn, nothing happens to you half-way does it?” Tasha said, turning back to him.

Quinn shrugged at Tasha. “When I got out of the hospital, the feds had frozen the last of my assets. I couldn’t run the winery, so I had to sell it. I was half dead and had nothing.”

“God, Quinn, that’s awful,” Minh said.

“Then what did you do?” Tasha asked.

“I went to the Foothills, became a cellar rat for Shawn, got my hands all dirty, and have had the best five months I can ever remember. I bet those pressures are a little lower now. Great wine, eh?” Quinn said, drinking the wine.

A moment later his smile disappeared and he put his glass down, his eyes drawn to two men who were sitting at the bar.

“God damn it,” he whispered.

“Quinn, what else is wrong?” Tasha asked.

Quinn looked at her and then leaned in to the table, keeping his voice low.

“See those two men at the bar drinking coffee?” he motioned to two men in suits who looked out of place in the bistro where almost everyone was dressed casually.

"Are they feds?" she asked. Shawn looked at Tasha and then at Quinn.

"Yeah. The one on the left found me up at Shawn's place. When I went up to Shawn's place, I lost them for awhile. The time up there gave me a long period of respite. They didn't find me until they located my car in Sacramento and traced a package Minh sent me."

"Jesus, Quinn," Minh said, "I'm sorry. I mailed those things out as discreetly as I could."

"They're tailing you and Joshua also," Quinn said, holding a glass up to agent Snow, who nodded slightly back at him.

The restaurant was getting busier, the noise building toward a crescendo. Minh flagged down the server and ordered a magnum of Joseph Phelps Insignia, also from 1999, as the last drops of the Paradis Cabernet were poured. As Minh turned back to his friends at the table a hush fell over the restaurant. Quinn looked around and saw that all eyes were on the door. He turned to see Ronald Park and his wife, the blonde woman who accompanied him at Shawn's winery, enter the restaurant.

Joshua waved them over across the crowded room, and they approached, but halfway across the crowded bistro, Park stopped and whispered something in Virginia's ear. She stopped and looked over at the table. They engaged in an intense, hushed conversation. Virginia looked over at a puzzled Joshua and Minh and gave a defeated shrug. She turned and spoke with the hostess at the front of the bistro and the two were seated in a corner table for two.

Quinn looked at Joshua, who appeared unconcerned.

"I thought that something like that might happen," Joshua said. He nodded at Minh who got up and walked over to the couple, engaging them in a brief conversation before returning to the table with a smile.

"Ron and Virginia send their apologies, and they'd like to meet up with us later at the Silverado. Ron is uncomfortable sitting with winemakers and owners in public. That feeling is heightened right now given the recent scandals."

"Sorry," Shawn and Quinn said simultaneously, and then shot a puzzled glance at each other. Tasha laughed silently over her glass of Insignia.

"Don't worry about it," Joshua said. "He's kind of funny that way. He's held hostage by his integrity, which he guards zealously, and with all the scandals, you can understand why. Anyway, he's given some good reviews to Quinn's Cab and Syrah, and I heard you got a ninety-one with your Rhone blend," he said looking at Shawn.

"I did?" Shawn said. He looked at Tasha who smiled a look of approval.

"Yeah, it was featured in his Quality-To-Price Best Buys section. So, if he came over here and had dinner with us, and was having fun, and if we picked up the check, well, some people who saw the blunt end of his pen, well, they might just take a swipe at him, and he isn't going to give them the satisfaction. You can kind of understand his dilemma," Joshua said.

"Congratulations on the QTP," Minh said, on the edge of a chuckle.

"Fair enough," Shawn said, "I just wanted to meet him again. I didn't even know about the scores."

"There'll be time for that," Joshua said, gazing around the restaurant. "Boy, the valley's abuzz right now, with the auction coming up, there're a lot of people out."

The bistro and tasting bar were now jammed with both revelers and insiders. Minh slapped Joshua on the back as the door opened again, and nodded towards it.

"Look who decided to come in for dinner," he said.

"I'll be damned," Joshua said, as an older gentleman, dressed in Levi's, a flannel shirt, and work boots ambled in with sturdy shoulders and a steady gait, his movement much younger and more spry appearing than his sun-damaged face and long wisps of white hair suggested. "Folks, that's none other than Henri Paradis, the long-standing king of the valley.

You have to give him credit, no matter what the rumors about his pending demise, he's here for dinner to tell all the vultures around here that the old man is still alive." Joshua and Minh looked at Paradis reverently, and Quinn and Shawn made rueful eye contact.

"Who's that young lady he came with?" Shawn asked, "His girlfriend?"

"He's not the kind of guy who would date someone forty years younger," Minh said. "That's his daughter. Her husband is Henri's winemaker. He's a good winemaker, too."

"Imagine that," Quinn said, hoping that the conversation was going to drift away from that particular patriarch of Napa winemaking. He watched the older gentleman walk past the table where Virginia and Ronald Park were drinking a bottle of Australian Shiraz and keeping to themselves. Paradis paused for just a moment looking at Park.

Park looked back with what Quinn thought was a perfect poker face, absolutely expressionless. The two stood there in the corner of the restaurant, suspended in time, it seemed, while tension built. The whole bistro stared, wondering what would happen next. In a split second, Paradis gave a curt nod to Park, and continued to his table.

"Interesting moment there," Joshua said. "Rumor has it that Park just lambasted Paradis's reserve Cabernet during the barrel tasting, in what was supposed to be his comeback vintage. No one knows how many more punches the old man can take, but I don't think it's too many."

"I hope he's not done, yet," Tasha said looking at Paradis and sounding sympathetic. "His father built that winery and both of them poured their blood and sweat into the land and the wine. No one deserves to be ground into oblivion like that. How did it happen? I mean, how did such an icon become so vulnerable all of the sudden anyway?"

Shawn shrank visibly in silence. Quinn winced, too.

Her brother Minh spoke up with a soft demeanor, his face flushed and his normally perfect white teeth stained by the wine. "Perfect storm, as the cliché goes." He told the story, adding, "After Paradis was contaminated by TCA several years ago, he declassified three vintages, selling the juice, which was supposed to be recycled into something different, but instead it was picked up by none other than his rich, bombastic bastard of a brother, who makes jug wine in the central valley. His brother made the label look like he was doing a joint venture with his brother, so that Henri was made a scapegoat for the flawed juice, which garnered a score in the low sixties. Then this year he sold off fifty acres, about a quarter of his land. Those are really good acres, too. People know that once you sell land, you never get it back, so that seemed like the beginning of the end for him, and now that Park has crushed his comeback, it seems like he's past the point of no return. It's a shame too, he has always been upstanding, and was a true believer in his wine, his land, his practice, and Napa Valley in general."

"Wasn't there some sort of a row between him and his brother some time back?" Tasha asked.

"Yeah, about a car I think," Joshua said.

"Well, no matter what, I hope he makes it through this. That '99 was fantastic," Tasha said.

"I know how he could get out of the funk he's in," Joshua said.

"How?" Quinn asked.

"Well, apparently there's this plot of about twenty acres, owned jointly by Paradis and his brother. It was left to them by their father, and supposedly became a center point of contention when they had their fight and split. It's supposed to be over some sort of mineral spring or something. Their father said that it was the best twenty acres in the entire valley, maybe the best twenty acres in the New World," Joshua explained.

"Better than Screaming Eagle?" Shawn asked.

"Better than Scarecrow?" Tasha asked.

A plot of legend? Quinn thought.

"Better than anything. Produces ageless Cabernet blends, like the best vintages of Bordeaux. It is rumored to be the best wine ever produced outside of France. The terroir is absolutely unique. The last year it was harvested was in 1972, they say. Paradis is rumored to have a few bottles left of those old vintages, which are legendary, were never released, and if they exist at all, are absolutely impossible to get your hands on," Joshua said. "We know because we've tried."

"Wait a minute," Quinn said, looking at Minh and Joshua. "I've seen your cellar, Screaming Eagle, DRC, Petrus, Le Pin, century old D'Yquem, Lafite verticles, and maybe some relics out of a certain founding father's personal wine cellar. You can get those, and you can't get one of these?"

"People know about the Jefferson wines. The wines Joshua is talking about aren't even confirmed, they're just alleged," Minh said. "For all we know the whole damn thing is nothing but a valley legend."

"That's one hell of a legend," Quinn said. "Why wouldn't he release those wines, or put them up for auction? It seems to me that would get him out of debt, or at least enough capital to keep going for awhile."

"Maybe he will. Or maybe he doesn't have any. Who the hell knows? This is all just hearsay," Minh said.

"Maybe he's waiting for the right moment," Tasha offered.

Quinn contemplated Tasha's comment as the door opened again, and in walked a middle-aged, toad-shaped man in enormous khaki shorts and a massively oversized, garish Hawaiian shirt. Out of the corner of his eye, Quinn saw a stretch Hummer limousine pulling away. The man was with a surgically augmented young lady of about thirty. Her breasts were too big for the rest of her body, barely contained by the silken material of her expensive looking Italian evening gown, and her lips were in a perfect pout. Her hair was one shade beyond natural auburn, and she had a necklace that sparkled with an array of diamonds worthy of aristocracy. While she was unmistakably striking, her beauty was as artificial as Tasha's was natural.

"You got to be kidding me," Minh said. "This just keeps getting better and better."

The fat man was shown to a seat in the center of the restaurant by a reluctant host as locals, winemakers, vineyard owners, and tourists in the know stared in shocked disbelief. Quinn looked over at Minh and Joshua, insiders of Napa Valley gossip. "Who is that?" he asked.

"Alfonse Paradis, Henri's brother," Joshua explained.

"The one he had the fight with?" Shawn asked.

"Yep. He's thumbed his nose at Napa Valley for years, making millions of cases of jug wine in the central valley. He's made a fortune, and has said that no wine is worth more than ten bucks a bottle, no matter what. His disdain for the winemakers here is no secret."

"I think the feelings are mutual," Minh added.

"He might be the one person in this valley who's more hated than Ronald Park," Joshua said.

The entire table watched as the fat man produced a magnum of central valley Zinfandel, and set it up for corkage with the Sommelier.

"Is that General Zin?" Minh asked sounding a mixture of shocked and disgusted.

"You can get a magnum of that stuff at the supermarket for nine bucks, and he brings it in here for corkage. You got to hand it to him. He knows how to thumb his nose at the establishment. Bombastic is right," Shawn said, shaking his head.

The fat man appeared to be relishing the spectacle he was creating. After the Sommelier opened the bottle, which it turned out was a screw top, and poured a glass for Alfonse and his buxom lady-friend, Alfonse Paradis, realizing that he was still the center of attention stood up, as if to make a speech.

"Here we go," Minh said.

"Never a dull moment in Napa Valley," Quinn said, taking a large swallow of his Insignia and helping himself to the last of the magnum, as the Sommelier brought over a magnum of Caymus Vineyards Cabernet. They were drinking well tonight. Quinn always drank well, but especially so with Tasha and his gay friends.

"Ladies and gentleman of Napa Valley," Alfonse Paradis began, tapping loudly on his glass with his fork as Henri got up and walked calmly over to his estranged brother's table.

"What are you doing here, Alfonse?" Henri asked with quiet intensity.

"Making an announcement, older brother. Listen up because this concerns you," he said and continued. "Thirty-five years ago I sold off my land holdings here, and moved east to the central valley, where I pursued a different course of wine production than most of you. As I've become more and more wealthy, I've watched with sadness as my brother, like so many of you, has struggled to make money in the so-called 'premium' wine market. While I think such a market is ridiculous, I have to acknowledge that as stupid as it seems to me, the market does in fact exist. So as I come here to see my brother in what I expect will be one of his last seasons in Napa Valley before he joins so many others like him in bankruptcy…."

Whispers permeated the restaurant, which was at a near dead stop, hanging on his every word.

"You haven't changed a bit," Henri Paradis said just audibly.

"Ahem," Alfonse Paradis continued, "as I see my brother making his last stand so valiantly here at the Bounty Hunter, I wish to raise a toast to all those responsible: my brother, the legendary Henri Paradis, his would be slayer, Ronald Park," he said turning to Park, who managed a return stare of cold hate, as Virginia quickly put a hand on his shoulder. Alfonse turned back to his now crimson-faced brother and continued. "And I wish to toast the third player, the one who is now your neighbor. Here's to me," he said, holding up his glass of Zinfandel for a moment before tipping the glass back and draining the central valley swill.

Henri Paradis was apoplectic. He staggered two steps backward. "You? You bought the land? But, why?" he said.

There was utter silence in the restaurant, as though it were a theatre building to a climax.

"To see the look on your face tonight," Alfonse said. "Looks like I got the house after all," he said his face twisted into a wicked smile.

Henri Paradis leaped at his portly younger brother with speed, agility, and ferocity that belied his age. He had punched his brother squarely across the jaw and was working his fingers around his surprisingly large gullet when Henri was reluctantly pulled off by one of the wait staff and the Sommelier, both of whom looked as if they wanted nothing more than to watch him tear his younger brother apart. The manager approached and stared Alfonse Paradis down, getting right into his face. "Get out of my restaurant, Mr. Paradis. And don't ever come back." The threat in his voice was as compelling as his balled fists and his fierce body language.

Alfonse met the man's gaze for just a moment, and then shrugged and turned to his lady friend who appeared to Quinn to have had too much Botox injected into her face. She had absolutely no expression in response to the events.

"Come on, dear, we're going. I hear the food here, like the wine, is vastly overrated, anyway." The two of them turned to leave.

"Terribly sorry Mr. Paradis," the manager said to Henri Paradis, who had just been released by the staff. Henri Paradis was too riled up to respond. With his face still fiery red, he turned, and without a word, his daughter got up, and the two of them exited, just as the oversized Hummer Limousine sped away.

"I guess we know who outbid us for that land," Shawn said quietly.

Quinn nodded as the others at the table met them with perplexed stares.

Chapter 13:

Virginia felt nauseous as she and Park left the Bounty Hunter. By the time they reached their car, she handed the keys to Park.

"I can't drive, Ron," she said weakly, doubling over and holding her stomach as she rested one arm against the side of the car. She was losing her vision; she felt like she was going to pass out.

"You haven't drunk much," Park said, looking confused. "You're just angry that we didn't sit with Minh and Joshua."

"That's not it at all. There's something going on, Ron, I'm sick," she muttered. "I haven't felt this awful in years. What in the world?" She stopped speaking suddenly, and began to retch and vomit on the sidewalk.

"Super," Park said. "How convenient."

"Ron, I think I need to go to the emergency room," she said, clutching her belly further. She vomited a second time. "Oh, God!"

"We're not going anywhere until you are finished. I'm not cleaning vomit out of the car," Park said.

"You son-of-a-bitch! Can't you think of anyone but yourself?" she spat.

Park looked at her, still doubled over in pain, and his look softened.

"I'll take you back to the hotel. I think you just need to rest. Maybe you have the flu," he said and then added, hesitating, "I'm sorry."

Virginia nodded in silence, and crawled into the passenger seat wiping her flushed face. Ron started the car and pulled out into traffic, narrowly missing a passing car. Virginia figured he was hoping to avoid being seen with his vomiting wife.

"No one saw it," she said.

"I know. Everything will be fine," Park said.

He pulled up to the valet who met him as he opened the door. He got out and went to help his wife, who swung her car door open with great effort. She smiled weakly at him, and his look turned to alarm.

"Jesus, Virginia, you look terrible!"

She shrugged, and tried to stand, her legs buckled slightly and Park caught her. The two of them staggered inside, Virginia leaning onto Park as they made their way to the room.

She continued to lean heavily on Park, her eyes closed as Park fumbled for the electronic pass-key. She heard more than saw two people approach them.

"Excuse me," one of them said, "are you okay?"

Park was silent. Virginia opened her eyes and saw the two people she recognized from the restaurant.

"Quinn, aren't you a doctor?" she asked weakly. Park was staring at Quinn and Shawn, apparently unsure of what to say.

"Yeah, I'm a pediatrician, actually," Quinn said. "What's wrong? You two looked fine at dinner."

"She began getting sick about an hour after dinner," Park said. "Maybe it's the flu."

"Flu season should be over," Quinn said, looking puzzled. "Did you have a lot to drink?"

"Just one glass of Shiraz," she gasped, putting a hand to her forehead. Virginia groaned, and felt the blood draining from her face, as a cold sweat forced itself out of every pore.

"Oh, no," she said weakly, and then retched so ferociously that a stream of bright red blood came out both her mouth and nose.

"Oh my God!" Park said, his look turning instantly from disgust to shock and fear.

"I feel awful," she said, slinking down to the ground.

"You need to go to the hospital," Quinn said calmly. Shawn nodded in agreement.

Virginia nodded, too, as Park looked on in silence.

"I'm sorry about this Ron," she said.

"I'm going to call an ambulance, I think she has a Mallory-Weiss tear," Shawn said as Ron bent over and tried to comfort his wife.

"Not bad, for a rookie," Quinn said.

"Fuck you," Shawn muttered, calling 911 on his cellular phone. After the brief call, they made their way into Park's room and made Virginia comfortable on the bed.

"What's a Mallory-Weiss tear?" Park asked.

"A tear at the junction of the esophagus and the stomach which happens when someone retches really hard," Shawn said.

"You haven't got any liver problems, have you?" Quinn asked.

"No, at least none I've ever known of," Virginia responded, attempting to smile, but it was more of a grimace.

"They'll take care of you, it's probably food poisoning or something," Shawn said.

"What did you have for dinner?"

"Steak, medium rare, asparagus, and roasted potatoes," Virginia said.

"What about lunch?" Shawn asked.

"I had a mushroom risotto here at the resort, and also ate some of Ron's salad," Virginia replied.

"Did you eat any of her meal?" Shawn asked.

"No, I hate risotto," Park said, his face almost a sneer.

"Hmmm, neither of those sound like slam dunks, maybe it's viral," Shawn asked.

"It really doesn't matter," Quinn said trying to sound reassuring. "Either way, it's rest, IV fluids, and hydration, with a slow return to eating."

"Superb timing," Virginia said.

"We owe you a debt of gratitude," Park said, "and…I apologize for not being able to sit with you at the restaurant."

"Our mutual friends explained your predicament. You have nothing to explain to us," Quinn said, "and we'd enjoy your company even if you crucified us on the ratings."

"Well, if you crucified us, well, that would just be awkward," Shawn said.

Park held up his hand shaking his head.

Shawn gave him a look that seemed to say: *Are you freakin' serious?* Quinn was worried the two were going to start shouting at each other right over Park's ill wife. Mercifully, they were distracted from one another as two paramedics arrived in the room.

"You'll be in good hands over at Queen of the Valley," Quinn said as Virginia was wheeled out. Park again thanked them, and ushered Quinn and Shawn out of the room as he followed the paramedics and his wife out to the ambulance.

"Thanks, Dr. Quinn," Virginia said weakly as they wheeled her down the hall.

* * * * * *

"What the hell happened there?" Quinn asked as Shawn and he wandered back to their room.

"I don't know, but she looked shitty, don't you think?" Shawn asked.

"She had that horrible color about her skin, I can't tell if it was jaundice or just looking sick-as-shit," Quinn said, buzzing from the evening of wine and theatre. "You want to open a bottle of something in the room? I brought some good bottles,"

"Actually, I think I'm going over to Tasha's room for a visit, she invited me over there," Shawn said, looking ashamed.

Quinn was silent for a moment, his buzz instantly squelched. "Shawn, it's been years since she and I broke up. I can't blame you for pursuing her. But so help me if you treat her the way you've treated all the other women in your life, you will have me to answer to, and as tough as you think you are, I have nothing to lose," he said with great effort. "Fear a man who has nothing to lose!" Quinn's index finger tapped hard on his friend's sternum as he glared into Shawn' eyes.

Quinn was ashamed of himself and the jealousy he was feeling. But he was also afraid. He didn't know if he was more fearful that Shawn would hurt her, or more fearful that Shawn would succeed where he had failed.

"Easy, pal," Shawn said, pausing for just a second before turning to leave. "I get it, loud and clear."

"You fucking better," Quinn muttered, turning away from his friend, feeling a mixture of guilt and dread.

As Shawn wandered down the hall, Quinn retired to the suite he was sharing with Shawn. He walked over to the mirror and saw his reflection. He could see the jugular veins in his neck. They were just a little too full. It was starting to happen. He shook his head in disbelief. Five minutes after he closed the door there was a knock. Quinn answered the door to find his friends, Joshua and Minh Tran in the hallway. They walked past him and into the room.

"Where's Shawn?" Joshua asked.

"He's over in Tasha's room," Quinn hesitated.

"Sorry, Quinn," Minh said, "I know how you must feel."

No you don't.

Quinn shrugged feeling despondent.

"I thought that might happen. There was definite electricity between them at dinner tonight," Minh said still sounding apologetic.

"The whole restaurant was full of electricity, I don't think I've ever been somewhere where so much seemed to be happening," Quinn said. "By the way, Park's wife just got taken away by an ambulance."

"She did? What for?" Joshua asked.

"Intractable puking. Probably food poisoning or viral gastroenteritis, I don't think it's anything to worry about," Quinn reassured.

Joshua relaxed.

"What have you got to drink in this place?" Minh asked.

"Sit down," Quinn said, pointing to a table and chairs. There's a bottle of Two Hands, Ares we were going to drink tonight. Sound good? So, gentlemen, tell me, what are you into?" he asked with the concern of an older brother, as he opened the bottle of Australian Shiraz and poured three glasses.

"You said the feds have been following and harassing you," Minh said. "And that they're following us, too. What else has been happening?"

"I told you they drew my blood. The last time I think they drew more than half my blood volume. I arrived at the hospital with shock and a hemoglobin below the survival threshold. I got six transfusions. They're looking for the polymer in my blood.

"What can we do to help? We know a guy who might be able to figure out who's behind the manufacture, if you'll let us."

"Is that Tuan Nguyen, the cop who helped us during the Michinski affair?" Quinn asked.

"No, he's with DEA now, and last we heard, he was transferred somewhere down south, LA, San Diego, or something," Joshua said.

"Well, who is it then?"

"Someone I know from way back," Joshua said.

"Not yet," Quinn said. "I want to try to get some answers for myself. I don't want you two, or any of your people to get into any trouble on my account."

"Our friend is suited to just this sort of thing," Joshua said.

Minh nodded seriously. "He's good."

"Well, the stakes are high. They think I'm making the drug, and evading taxes with the profits I am supposedly making. It's enough to put me away for the rest of my life if they manage to make it stick."

"Tax evasion? Jesus, how do they get from making your polymer to that?"

"It makes sense, if I was making the polymer and selling it, I couldn't pay taxes on the profit, especially if I couldn't explain where it came from. They think the money is hidden somewhere. I can't prove it isn't. But the fact that they haven't found it is why I haven't been arrested yet."

"Do they know that the drug is for sale here?" Minh asked.

"I think so," Quinn said. "I told them, but they don't know who owns the Silverado. They're under the impression that I might be a silent partner here. They think the polymer is available lots of places, but they haven't traced it to anyone yet, so they think it must be me," Quinn said.

"Our guy could figure this out for you, Quinn, he's the best there is," Minh said, "Both of us would trust him with our lives."

"Is this why we've been putting your assets into euros and gold?" Joshua asked.

Quinn looked at his old business partners and smiled.

"Thanks for storing my remaining fortunes in your basement vault. I owe you guys. Yes, I earned that money, legitimately, and someone wants to make it look like I'm breaking my contract, and illegally manufacturing this stuff somewhere. The feds keep trying to pin this on me, and if they do, I'm toast. They have almost everything already. I just want to make sure that there's a little bit of money somewhere for me to reclaim if I ever get the chance." Quinn said. "Who the hell is behind this?"

"I don't have any idea," Minh said.

"We've done what you asked, a thousand dollars a week in cash. We converted the money from selling your wine collection into gold bullion certificates. I take it you think it is just a matter of time before they come after you with an arrest warrant?" Joshua said.

"Yeah, I think it'll be soon. They've refused to renew my passport, which is a pretty good sign that they consider me a flight risk. I bet that means I am on the 'No Fly' list. The feds always seem flummoxed that they can't find any evidence directly linking me to the polymer. They figured I'd be taking the stuff and that's how they'd get me, but of course I'm not taking the drug. They intimated that they froze the assets to force me to delve into one of these phantom accounts where the unlaundered money supposedly sits. Where do they get these ideas?"

"It's like someone's setting you up," Minh said.

"Not like, someone is. I just haven't any idea who," Quinn said.

"Tasha told us that you are going to die in the next year or so unless you get a heart-lung transplant," Minh said.

"Maybe," Quinn said, thinking about his jugular veins. "If I only have a few more years, I sure as hell don't want to spend any of them in prison. Shawn and I were talking about a venture down here, all in his name, but with the backing of my remaining assets. I figure I can sink a million into it, and if I'm caught the feds can't touch that either, because it's all in Shawn's name."

"You trust him that much?" Minh asked.

"As much as I trust you guys," Quinn said.

But not with Tasha.

"What a bad scene that was tonight," Joshua said, changing the subject.

Quinn nodded in agreement. "What a world we live in. Makes you thankful for the friends you got."

They touched glasses and drank in silence for a time.

"We got your six, Quinn. You know that, right?" Minh asked.

"Yeah, I know Minh. You boys need to be getting back home. I'm going to get some sleep tonight. I want to be fresh for the festivities of the next few days, and also any negotiating that we end up doing. I sure as hell don't want to catch that bug Park's wife has."

Minh and Joshua got up to leave.

"Quinn, about Tasha, I'm really sorry that things didn't work out the way they should have," Minh said.

"Minh, who says this isn't exactly the way things should have worked out?" Quinn said. Minh paused at the door nodded, smiled his toothy, and ridiculously perfect smile, and disappeared into the hallway. Quinn turned and poured the last glass of the Ares into his glass, contemplating it for a moment before setting it down without drinking it.

He looked at his bed, waited another five minutes for Minh and Joshua to get back to their suite, and then he grabbed his coat, a pair of leather driving gloves, and an Ah-So wine opener. He stole out the door, alcohol in his brain, but purpose in his gait.

He walked the halls, careful not to make eye contact with anyone. The resort was busy that evening. He briefly entertained going to Tasha's room, but thought better of it. He went to the spa. It would be closed at this hour.

He checked his watch; it was nearly midnight. Of course the door to the spa was locked, but mercifully there was no deadbolt. He slipped on the gloves and produced the Ah-So. The wine opener had two narrow strips of flexible metal which slid between the cork and the inside of the neck of a wine bottle to pull out a cork without "screwing" into it. Quinn also knew it could be used to jimmy open a locked door. He worked it into the latched door at a ninety-degree angle above the latch. Once he was through the side of the door jam, he worked the opener down at a forty-five degree angle, inching it back and forth, until the latch and the door popped open. He winced in anticipation of an alarm, but none was heard. He couldn't believe that the Silverado wouldn't have the spa alarmed, especially if they sold illegal drugs in it. But, fueled in part by the wine, and in part by an intense desire to exonerate himself from his legal quagmire, he continued inside.

The spa smelt of fresh linen, aromatherapy, and ozone.

Quinn advanced with silent determination. He saw several cases of vitamins for sale.

What were they marketing it as? Peruvian resveratrol?

Yes, that was it. But nothing there was labeled Peruvian resveratrol. He continued past the massage suites. Near the back there were two doors. One of them read "Spa Supervisor" and the other read "storage." Both were locked. He again pulled out the Ah-So, this time going to work on the storage door. As he worked on it, he felt a jolt of panic as the front door opened.

Was it security? He frantically worked on the lock as footsteps came at him, echoing on the travertine floors. It was someone in high heels, by the sound of it. If he couldn't get the door open in the next few seconds, he would have to overpower the person approaching, and then take off. Mercifully, the storage door opened, and Quinn disappeared into the storage room, closing the door with a faint click, which was nonetheless, too loud.

Quinn winced, hiding behind some boxes, ducking down as the door swung open and a flashlight swept the room. Quinn held his breath, aware that the smell of wine emanating from his pores might give him away if his clumsy movements had not. His heart quickened and sweat trickled down his brow as he waited in gut-wrenching silence.

The flashlight swept the storage room a second time, but whoever it was did not turn on the light. Quinn stayed crouched behind the boxes. At last the flashlight switched off, and Quinn stole a glance at the person holding the flashlight. The darkened silhouette he saw was unmistakably the shape of a woman, a perfectly shaped, athletic woman. Quinn wondered why, if she suspected someone, she didn't turn on the lights. He contemplated that as he opened the door a crack to see if she had gone. He saw the door across the hall ajar, with the lights on. Quinn guessed she was the spa manager.

Then he heard her speak, was she with someone? Quinn again panicked. As he strained to listen, he realized he could only hear one side of the conversation.

She was on the phone.

He relaxed and tuned into the conversation.

"Catherine, as I look at our inventory, we have about six hundred cases left here at the Silverado, and another fourteen hundred cases at our other spas. The shutdown has caused us to burn through a large chunk of our inventory. The warehouse has been nearly emptied of finished product, as you requested."

She paused, and Quinn, struggling to hear her, chanced moving out into the hallway, hiding just beside her door, listening to her conversation. Catherine? His memory was jarred. Where had he heard that name before?

"I know. I know we're phasing it out. But darling, we have just twenty million dollars in inventory, and you're still not sure if you can get it made that way. What if it doesn't grow as well as we need it to?"

Again there was another pause. What is growing? Quinn wondered.

"Listen, you are the science expert, but I've never trusted genetic engineering. There are too many variables. Even you can't control them all, Catherine. What if it doesn't produce the monomers like we hope?" There was silence as the woman listened to the person on the other line.

Quinn was thinking about whether and where he knew anyone named Catherine, and what sort of genetic engineering they were talking about. He inched closer. He had to see the woman, even if just for a second. The door was open a crack, and he aligned his eye to it. He could only get a partially obscured view of the woman. She was facing away from him, but she was dark skinned, South Asian or Latina, and had black high heels and nylons on, her legs draped over the side of the desk. What a pair of legs! She had flowing raven colored hair landing below her shoulders, but he couldn't get a good look at her face, which was obscured by a lamp on the desk. She sat upon her desk, turned sideways at her computer screen while talking on the phone, twirling a pencil absentmindedly in her right hand. Quinn returned to her legs. They were million dollar legs, and her hips had perfect lines, and he had seen some good ones in his time.

"Yes, I know where to plant the remaining product. No, I haven't had the chance to slip it to him. He hasn't eaten at the restaurant here. I'll make it happen, and then he'll be cooked. In any case, I have made all the transactions we talked about earlier, and you have the paperwork we need to close the loop on this. I'll see to it things are taken care of here, but I need to make sure I don't run into Alfonse."

There was another pause, and the woman turned and glanced at her door. Quinn backed away from the crack.

Did she see me?

"No, I don't think you should risk another evening in the kitchen, Catherine. Several of the chefs are still muttering about you and the risotto. It's time for you to show some patience. We'll get it to him some other way."

Quinn's heart pounded. His mind was dull from the wine he consumed all evening, but adrenaline helped. He had to remember everything. He began writing on his wrist.

Inventory.

Warehouse.

Product, growing.

Genetic engineering.

Plant the product.

Slip something to someone at the restaurant.

Kitchen.

Risotto.

Suddenly Quinn realized that there was silence. The conversation must have ended. He moved, quick and quiet, back to the storage room as the light turned off in the office and chanced leaving the door open a crack, to try to get a look at the woman's face.

He peered through the crack as she closed and locked her door, and then, turned in the dark towards the storage door. Quinn backed up a step, realizing with horror that she was moving towards it.

Why did he have to try to see her face?

Again he held his breath creeping to one side, hoping, praying, that she might miss him again in the dark.

With a swift click, the door was pulled closed by the woman, and a relieved Matthew Quinn exhaled.

Chapter 14:

Virginia was discharged the next afternoon from Queen of the Valley Hospital. She was diagnosed with viral gastroenteritis and a small Mallory-Weiss tear. She had recovered nicely after three liters of IV fluids and some intravenous anti-emetics. Though she still felt weak, Virginia was relieved to be out of the hospital. When she and Park approached their room at the Silverado Springs Resort late that morning, Shawn was returning from somewhere down the corridor. He was wrinkled and disheveled, like he had just gotten up.

"Good morning, feeling a little better this morning?" Shawn asked jovially. He was certainly in a good mood, Virginia thought.

"Quite a bit. Amazing what some IV fluids and nausea medication can do," Virginia said.

"Think it was something undercooked, or just a bug?" Shawn asked.

"Does it matter? Anyway, I am over it, and just need to get my strength back," Virginia said.

"Well, keep up with the fluids, I'd hate to see you get dehydrated and get sick again," Shawn said.

"Are you a doctor, too?" Virginia asked.

"Yep, but not trained beyond medical school," Shawn said and disappeared into his room.

"What did he mean by that?" Park asked.

"No idea. Let's get into the room, I need some more rest, you should stay away, in case this is something infectious," Virginia said her husband.

"Where am I going to go?" Park asked.

"I don't care, take a drive somewhere," Virginia offered. "Go and see Minh and Joshua."

Park elected to go for a drive, giving Virginia her needed rest. She slept for four hours before awakening overcome with nausea. She got up and vomited blood a second time. She staggered to the bathroom, was shocked at what he saw in the mirror. She sat and passed bloody urine into the toilet. She felt short of breath and called Park on his cell phone.

"Ron, I feel terrible," Virginia said, starting to cry. "I'm getting really sick. I just peed blood, and I can't catch my breath. I'm jaundiced all over."

"I'm on my way back, but maybe you should have one of the doctors look at you," he said. "Give them a call, now."

* * * * * *

"Hello?" Quinn answered the phone.

"Dr. Quinn, this is Virginia, the woman across the hall, the one who went to the hospital," she began.

"Yeah, Ron Park's wife, Jesus, you sound awful."

"I think I am getting worse. I'm passing a lot of blood."

"Bloody diarrhea?" Quinn asked.

"Urine, and yeah, how'd you know?" Virginia answered.

"Just trying to put this together. Do you have petechiae?" Quinn asked.

"What's that?" Virginia asked.

"A rash, red dots, do you have a rash?" Quinn asked.

"No, but I'm jaundiced all over, why?"

"I think you might have hemolytic-uremic-syndrome: bloody diarrhea, gastroenteritis and bleeding. You need to go back to the hospital," Quinn said. "I'm coming over, are you in your room?"

"Yeah. Come over, please," Virginia begged. "I've left the door ajar."

Quinn found Virginia lying on the floor next to the bathroom. He called the front desk and asked them to get an ambulance as soon as possible. He examined the stricken woman. He felt her swollen liver edge down near her pelvis.

"Are you sure you don't have any liver problems?" Quinn asked sounding grim.

"Yeah, I've never had problems, why?" Virginia asked, alarm ringing in her voice.

"Because your liver is really enlarged, maybe two or three times its normal size, which means you've got something bad going on," Quinn explained, realizing how lousy his bedside manner was with embarrassment.

"How bad?" Virginia asked, looking more frightened.

"I don't know, but you're going to need to stay in the hospital until this situation is figured out. This is not garden-variety food poisoning. It looks more complicated than hemolytic-uremic-syndrome, which is usually caused by E.coli, and doesn't usually cause jaundice this severe or a swollen liver. You have something else," Quinn finished.

"What will they do?" Virginia asked as the paramedics arrived at his room.

"Run some tests, and figure out what in the world is causing this," Quinn said.

As Virginia was taken to the hospital a second time, Quinn returned to his room. He told Shawn about the unexpected turn of Virginia Park. Shawn listened without comment, and then changed the subject. He explained that Tasha would to drop by soon, and they'd meet Minh and Joshua for dinner again. Shawn looked excited.

"Apparently we are sharing a table at the auction with Henri Paradis," Shawn said.

"Who else will be at the table?" Quinn asked.

"The two of us, Tasha, Minh and Joshua, Paradis, his daughter and her husband." Shawn said.

There was a knock at the door, and Shawn let Tasha in. Quinn gazed at her only briefly, and forced a smile.

"Whoa!" Shawn said as she walked in with a big grin and a confident gait. Under one arm was a bottle of red wine, and there were three glasses in the other.

Was that for me or for the wine?" she said, flirting with him. Shawn looked as if he were about to burst forth from his skin.

"You're so hot!" he said to her without a trace of self-consciousness.

"Thanks, and you're not too bad either," she said.

"Will you two please cut it out," Quinn snarled.

"Sorry, pal, just slipped out. It won't happen again," Shawn said.

"I have a little pre-treat for the three of us before we go out to dinner," she said turning to Quinn. "Matthew, what do you think of Barolo?" She set the bottle of Italian wine on the table. "This wine is a really small production, but as 2000 was the best year in the last couple of decades, this wine turned out to be one of the best Barolo's I have ever had. They only made about a hundred and fifty cases of the stuff."

"Sounds excellent Tasha, this will be exciting," Quinn said without a trace of excitement. He looked at Shawn who appeared apprehensive about showing any more enthusiasm for Tasha. At least he felt guilty, Quinn thought spitefully.

"That's an understatement," Tasha said, smiling.

"What the hell happened to this?" Shawn asked, looking at the Ah-So wine opener, which was twisted and bent out of shape, making it unusable.

"Sorry, little accident," Quinn said, flushing. "There's another one over there near the dresser."

"My lady," Shawn said, after picking up and handing her the Waiter's Friend corkscrew.

"Thank you Shawn," Tasha said, cutting the foil and opening the wine. "This might be a little young still, Barolo takes so long to soften and open up. We'll have to see. It should develop up in the glass."

They tasted the wine, which was intense and earthy, and, Quinn thought, layered with dark fruits and complex woody notes. He sniffed and took another drink of the wine. She was right, though young, and a little angular, it was really excellent wine.

Really. Excellent.

"It's something, isn't it?" Tasha said, raising an eyebrow. "We'll have a glass here, and then head out to dinner. We'll let the bottle stay open for a few hours, and then we'll come back and finish it. That way it has time to soften up."

The three of them savored their glass of the Barolo and fifteen minutes later left to join Joshua and Minh at a new small Bistro in St. Helena, where they were assured, it would be quieter than it was at the Bounty Hunter.

When they walked into the restaurant, called 'New World Red' they were greeted by a young lady who looked to be scarcely out of high school.

"The first two of your party have already arrived. Welcome to New World Red. You'll notice our wine list has only American, Chilean, Argentinian, Australian, and New Zealand wines on it. We are a strictly new-world establishment. We even have a policy of refusing to cork European wines," she said with a smile.

"Seems kind of protectionist, don't you think," Shawn said.

The young lady shrugged and smiled.

"Maybe it is reverse snobbery," Quinn offered.

Her smile vanished and she turned cold as they approached the table.

"Here you are," she said, almost tossing the menus onto the table before they had even sat down.

"Was it something I said," Quinn called after her as she left. She ignored him. Tasha and Shawn fought back laughter. Quinn felt himself loosening up.

"Nice call," Shawn said. "It seems like some of these people are getting drunk on their own success."

"Literally, I think," Tasha added.

"Why are you three pissing off the help?" Minh asked in mock annoyance.

They ordered and enjoyed their meal among idle chatter and light, humorous conversation. They ordered a magnum of

Quilceda Creek Cabernet from Washington State, which won rave reviews from all. Tasha spoke about the wine.

"I don't know if you guys know this but this wine, even though it is a Columbia Valley product, is a child of Napa Valley. The winemaker is related to The Maestro of Napa Valley, Andre Tchelistcheff. I think this is one of the best wines ever from the state of Washington."

"It's incredible," Quinn said.

"We've been drinking this for years, and there hasn't been a bad vintage in the last ten years. It's always good," Minh said, enjoying the wine.

When the wine was finished, each looked around, wondering what the next bottle would be. That is when Shawn reached under the table, as he said, "Excuse me while I whip this out."

Quinn rolled his eyes as Joshua and Minh looked at him apprehensively. At last there was a muffled "pop" of a cork, and Shawn produced a bottle of single vineyard Cayuse Syrah from Walla Walla, Washington.

Quinn rolled his eyes and drained his last swallow of the Quilceda Creek.

"Better pour me a glass before the staff sees you didn't pay corkage. At least you didn't pull out a Bordeaux." The bottle went around, each of them getting a full pour of the French-styled Syrah from the Walla Walla valley. The last drops were out of it when the waiter approached. Shawn held up the empty bottle for him to see. "We owe you corkage."

The waiter nodded and smiled. "We'll wave it since you bought the Quilceda Creek. Is there anything else I can do for you?"

"We're doing fantastic," Quinn said, and meant it. He couldn't have been happier at the moment. He was with friends who were like family, and there were no feds in sight.

As they finished the last of their wine, Quinn told Joshua and Minh that Virginia had been taken back to the hospital, feeling worse. Quinn said he feared it was something more serious. Joshua and Minh appeared appropriately concerned.

"Maybe we should go and see her at the hospital," Minh said.

"We should at least call," Joshua said, pulling out his phone and getting the number for the hospital.

"Virginia Park's room, please," he spoke clearly. After a short pause he said, "Hello? Ron? This is Joshua, how is she," he paused, "I see. Do they think she needs to be transferred?" He listened again. "Well, what about Stanford or UCSF? Okay, but if anything changes, let us know." He hung up and turned soberly to the rest of the table.

"Ron said her liver enzymes are up really high, but she isn't in liver failure. Does that make sense?"

Quinn, Shawn, and Tasha all nodded.

"Well, the folks at the hospital think it might be some sort of food borne hepatitis, and they are testing for it. But she sounds really sick. Ron said her kidneys are not working well, but that they are not doing any dialysis yet, just something called CVD or something." Joshua said.

"CVVH-D," Quinn said. "It's a way to remove fluid and evil humors from the blood when someone is sick."

"Evil humors?" Shawn asked.

"Cytokines, inflammatory mediators, and stuff," Tasha explained. "It's state-of-the-art medicine. Good to hear that they're doing it at Queen of the Valley."

"I think she should be transferred. Ron wants her to stay at Queen of the Valley as long as it's safe, until after he gives his speech, and then he'll request transfer down to Stanford, which is closer to where they live," Joshua explained.

"Do you think she has hepato-renal syndrome, Quinn?" Tasha asked. "It sounds like fulminant hepatitis. She could need a liver transplant," she said. "What kind of food borne poisoning causes that?"

Quinn shrugged. "Hepatitis A and hepatitis E can do it on rare occasions. But I have to admit that it sounds odd."

"Do you two think she'll be all right?" Minh asked.

"Nothing will happen too quickly, and they said she is not in liver failure, despite the high enzyme levels, right? But, yeah, this sounds pretty serious. I don't know if she'll be all right," Quinn said.

"We have to tell Ron. He should cancel his talk and stay with Virginia," Minh said.

"You know as well as I do that Ron won't cancel his engagement. He'll just worry more, Minh. We'll speak to him as soon as it's over. God, this is awful," Joshua said.

"What's Ron like?" Shawn asked Minh. "He's seemed like an ass to me. He's antisocial, obsequious and compulsive, from what I've observed. He even seems arrogant when addressing his wife. What's the matter with him?"

Minh shrugged, and Joshua spoke.

"He and his wife have been struggling with some issues," he said. "At one point they were talking divorce, but I think they've worked through it. He really isn't mean, just awkward. He doesn't express his emotions well and only understands empathy on an intellectual level."

"He understands, but doesn't feel what others are going through, even his wife," Minh said, trying to further elucidate Joshua's explanation.

"Fair enough," Shawn said. Quinn had been wondering the same thing.

The five of them left the restaurant and returned to the Silverado. Minh and Joshua returned to their room, and Quinn returned to his room alone. Shawn and Tasha decided to go for a moonlight walk through the vineyards. No one touched the remainder of the Italian wine on the table. Quinn ignored it and lay down on the bed. As soon as his head hit the pillow he was asleep.

Chapter 15:

Todd Sandoval screwed up his strength and dialed her number, taking a deep breath. He decided it was time to grow a pair and remind her that he was an integral part of their plan. When she answered, his heart jerked up into his throat, and his courage vanished. He began with the spine of a jellyfish. "Hello Catherine, I, I want to discuss the plan some more. I mean, it's just that there are some things I want to get clear in my head before we go to the next step." He cursed himself and his cowardice in silence.

"Todd, you aren't getting cold feet, are you?" Catherine asked, condescension thick in her voice.

"I'm just not sure this is going to work in the time frame you want," he said. "The barrel tasting went as you said it would. I don't understand how you got her to do it, but it worked."

"You're ongoing doubt is irritating, and frankly, a bit insulting," she said.

"Paradis has enough capital though. I think he can continue to limp along. What if she talks? That'd end things really quick."

"Todd, why don't you worry about your end of the deal? Terroir Unlimited is solvent again, and so are you, or are you forgetting that? Mrs. Park is already taken care of. Even if she weren't, going public about fixing ratings would destroy them both, not to mention the only wine publication left with any credibility. She has nothing to gain, and everything to lose."

Sandoval swallowed hard, and said nothing for a moment. He could never get any traction speaking with Catherine, and it was destroying his otherwise inflated self-image. Working to gain his composure, he continued. "What happens when Park tastes it again, when it's been bottled, and he realizes that it isn't consistent with his previous tasting? What'll we do then?"

"Park isn't going to taste it again, and very soon, Henri Paradis is going to be even more desperate for money. His brother wants to unload the land in question, and soon he too will have desperate motivation. Henri will soon have no choice at all."

"Catherine, I am beginning to wonder if all of this is worth it. Ten million really sounded good when we first started, but now…." Todd said.

"This is all part of the plan, Todd. You gave your unwavering commitment. The only one that can ruin this is you. And if it implodes, you know where you'll end up."

"You mean where we'll end up," Todd said.

"I didn't misspeak. Have patience, Todd, this is going perfectly." She hung up the phone. When she said his name, it was as if she were describing a filthy, decomposing vermiform corpse, forgotten in the cellar.

How on earth did I get myself into this?

He walked outside to get some air. He went into his daily routine, picking up the local paper. He scanned the headlines as he wandered back to his office. On page two was a small article with the headline: "Park plans to give keynote speech despite wife's condition." His throat clenched involuntarily and he went into a fit of coughing. He looked around to see if anyone saw his reaction. It was just mid-morning in the sleepy town, and the streets were empty. He retreated into his office and read the headline a second time, just to be sure. He scanned the article, learning about Virginia's hospitalization. The article said Park had inquired about canceling his appearance, but had decided to go on with the speech.

Sandoval was relieved that Virginia was ill. He didn't give a damn about her. He shuddered, though, at the realization that the illness was no accident. Catherine had shown again that she was as dangerous as she was ruthless, and she was in complete control of the situation. It seemed that nothing and no one was beyond her wicked reach, which made him wonder about his own safety.

He was distracted by vibration of his personal cellular phone. The identification was blocked and taking a chance, he answered the phone, "Todd Sandoval here."

"Todd, this is Arianna. Have you ever heard the lore of the disputed plot owned by the Paradis brothers? The one with all of these remarkable properties?" she asked.

Todd's belly did another involuntary lurch. He felt his face flush. He took a deep breath and tried to compose himself. "Arianna," he began, "the folklore surrounding that plot is as old as Napa Valley itself. It was started by a bunch of gypsies who settled the land after World War II. There is nothing special about it, and it'll never be for sale anyway. The Paradis family has owned it since sometime in the early fifties, and the brothers can't agree on anything, especially what to do with that land. But in spite of its supposed legendary status, it's just a piece of dirt, like any other in the valley. What I hear is that actually, it is one of the least desirable portions of the Paradis land. It's swampy and sulfuric. Who wants to know about it?"

"Some clients of mine asked about it in an off-hand manner, and I realized the only thing I knew is that it is jointly owned by the Paradis Brothers, that the old man is supposedly buried there, and that neither brother wants the other to have it. Henri Paradis once said about thirty years ago, that it'd be a cold day in hell before he sold it."

"Well, there it is. The fairy-tale that has developed around that land's magical properties, that's all bullshit. Who's your client?" he asked. He knew it couldn't be Paradis's brother Alfonse.

"They want to remain anonymous," she said. "Thanks for the information, though. I'll pass along what you said."

"No problem." Sandoval said, and hung up the phone. He took a deep breath, sighed heavily, and got up, grabbed his keys and looked at his watch. How could someone else in Napa be suddenly interested in the land? It made him uneasy. The ground was shifting under his feet and it was time to do something about it.

He called his friend over at *Wine Magazine*. "Hey, can I meet you at magazine headquarters? I have something I want to ask you about," he said. After pausing, he continued, "Great. I am on my way."

He had something he needed to get hold of. Now was the time to take an active role in ensuring his own safety, and he knew just how to do it.

* * * * * *

Shawn and Quinn spent the morning exercising, and had a simple lunch at a Gott's Roadside, a burger stand in St. Helena. They discussed their conversation with Arianna and their next move in real estate acquisition. Amid the noise, Quinn looked about. He didn't see anyone he could pin as a fed, and no one in particular seemed to be paying attention to them. He engaged his friend, beginning the long overdue conversation.

"Shawn, you are my very good friend and I trust you implicitly," he began.

"Quinn, if this is about Tasha," Shawn said.

"Shawn, I told you, that ship sailed for me a long time ago. You and Tasha are adults. I'd just appreciate it if you didn't slam it in my face."

"Fair enough, pal," Shawn said.

"The bottom line is with my health, I probably have no more than two or three years left anyway. I don't want to burden someone like Tasha, or anyone else with that. She deserves better. But I meant what I said, you treat her like all those other women, and you and I will have a problem."

"That's the reason you aren't trying with Tasha?" he asked.

"No, Shawn, it's not. I just don't think I can ever be what she wants. I'm too hard wired, too ADHD. I get too distracted, too wrapped up into whatever it is I am doing, and that won't work for her. She needs a partner who is present for her, and I just wasn't. In fact, you might be a better fit with her."

"You better not be just saying that, because I am crazy about her. I'm fantasizing long term for the first time. So speak now, friend…." Shawn said.

Quinn shook his head in silence.

"All right, you have my interest peaked," Shawn said. "Tell me your secrets, pal, and I am not referring to Tasha. I want to know about your life before the winery."

"You've already heard about my struggles with the feds," he began.

"The invention, the issues with the law, and the hush money, yes, I heard all of that," Shawn said. "What else is there to know?"

"A lot. I never told you about all the business before the hush money, and the feds."

"There's more?" Shawn asked.

"A lot more. Let's move over to those empty tables under the trees," Quinn said.

Shawn nodded and they moved, sitting down at a vacant picnic table under a large oak tree, out of earshot of anyone else.

"When I was getting my Ph.D. I had a failed project. I was trying to make an antimetabolite cancer drug," Quinn began.

"Chemotherapy?"

"Exactly. A common one in use is called L-asparaginase."

"Yeah, it destroys the amino acid asparagine, I remember," Shawn said.

"Right, the bottom line is normal cells can make their own asparagine, or do without, but since cancer cells grow so fast, if an amino acid is not immediately available to them…."

"They die, I get it, Quinn."

"Good, so I tried to invent a long polymer which bound up another amino acid, in this case Arginine. I had hoped it would work similar to L-asparaginase."

"Sounds good, why didn't it work?" Shawn asked.

"I made a mistake with my design of the active site. Instead of binding arginine, it bound a common biological waste product, called asymmetric dimethyl arginine, or ADMA," he explained.

"Too bad," Shawn said.

"Not really. I mothballed the stuff until after medical school when I learned that ADMA is associated with heart disease, kidney disease, senile dementia, and stroke."

"Holy shit," Shawn said. So your polymer binds and rids the body of this naturally occurring poison?"

"Yeah, more or less. Here's where it gets weird. An old mobster named Vladimir Michinski, a figure in the Russian Mafia, wanted to steal my drug. See, I didn't have it patented, because I thought it was useless," Quinn explained. "He heard about it, kidnapped me and tortured me to give him the formula."

"Did you?" Shawn asked.

"No, I escaped, but later he managed to steal it and start making it anyway. I got the patent secured, and made it impossible for him to pass it off as his own. To get back at me he kidnapped Tasha. I managed to rescue her with help from Minh, Joshua, and another friend of ours, but he escaped," Quinn said.

"Tasha was kidnapped?"

Quinn nodded silently.

"So he's still out there?"

"No, he and his adult kids were wounded in the fight to get Tasha back, but they got away. For some reason, they lost control of their getaway car and drove off of Highway One near Devil's Slide into the Pacific. All his henchmen were either arrested or killed. So it seems like a dead end."

"Why are you telling me this?" Shawn asked.

"Because the feds are right about one thing. There is no one else out there that could be doing this. And I'm not making the stuff. I've ruled out every possibility, which leaves only one."

"You think one of his men is still alive?" Shawn asked.

"Maybe," Quinn said, "or he was able to pass the production process on to someone else before he died."

"Quinn, you don't want to be messing with anyone with connections to organized crime," Shawn warned. Quinn saw apprehension in his face, which was uncommon for Shawn.

"You don't have to tell me," Quinn said, holding up his right hand. Half of his pinkie digit was missing.

Shawn was silent. "I saw that one day, when we were pouring wine together, but didn't think I should ask. The feds didn't do that, did they?"

"No. Simulated drowning, drugs, exsanguination, and sleep deprivation, yes, cutting off appendages, no," Quinn said. "That was done by Michinski's goons."

"Since you're in full-disclosure mode," Shawn said, "you never go anywhere without a shirt on, but I saw you getting out of the pool one morning. There's a round scar on your back by your shoulder blade, and one on your chest. Are those bullet wounds?"

"Also Michinski and his men."

"Boy, you've been through it, pal," Shawn said.

"The bottom line is that I may have a lot more than the feds to worry about," Quinn said.

"So what does that have to do with us?" Shawn asked.

"If some offshoot of the Michinski crime syndicate is after me, they might come after you too, the way they went after Tasha."

"Because we make wine together?" Shawn asked. "I'm not your lover, pal. Organized crime doesn't kidnap people's friends for leverage. Haven't you seen 'The Sopranos?'"

"Shawn, I don't know," Quinn said. "If you are going to associate with me, you have to know that's a risk. If you want to turn around and hightail it back to the Sierra, I'll understand."

"It'll take more than tales of the boogeyman to get me out of here, pal," Shawn said. "But I have another question.

What happens if they haul you off to prison? Do I lose my shirt to the feds?"

"You went to law school, you tell me. If you don't know, you can ask my friend Joshua, he's a corporate attorney, but I don't think they'll come after you."

Shawn nodded.

"As far as anyone can prove, I'll just be an employee. What I give to you will be negotiable, either cash, or gold. It's all in Minh and Joshua's safe now. So I think you're fine. If I go to jail or into some federal black hole, you can continue with the venture as your own, and if I clear my name once and for all, I can become an official partner, as long as I am still alive. After I'm dead, its all yours."

"Quinn, why are you bothering with this? You've got issues here that are way beyond making wine," Shawn said.

"Shawn, I need this, especially after my collapse and stroke last year. Learning that I have a pending cardiovascular disaster has made it all more urgent to me. You've proven to me that winemaking gives me more joy than anything else right now. I want to be a part of it again. If you're comfortable having the whole thing in your name, then we can proceed. I obviously trust you, I just need you to trust me as much," Quinn said.

Shawn seemed lost in thought about the situation. They sat in silence, Shawn looking around, seeming deep in thought. Quinn fidgeted incessantly. After ten minutes, Shawn turned to his friend and spoke.

"It has taken a toll on you, losing Tasha, and then seeing her take an interest in me. That can't have been easy."

"It hasn't been easy," Quinn admitted.

"That's honest," Shawn said. "Still, I think I owe you for that, and frankly, the closer we get to starting an operation down here, the more interesting it all seems to me. The wine from here can be absolutely breathtaking, and there is so much drama down here. It would be pretty damn cool to become a part of this surreal scene, and I just bet that you and I can add to the drama, both in the valley, and in our own lives. Maybe we already have. When you came up to the foothills, I never could have dreamed that this would be where we'd end up in six months, but look around." Shawn waved his arms at the perfect spring day in Napa they were experiencing. "We're about to come storming into this valley, at a time when the electricity in the air is so high it might reanimate the dead!"

Quinn smiled at his friend and said, "Let's go taste some wine on the Silverado side of St. Helena. Tomorrow night is the Auction, and soon I hope, our opportunity will present itself."

Late in the afternoon, as they left their fourth winery, and headed back towards the Silverado Springs Resort, Shawn received a call from Arianna Richardson, indicating that she was relatively certain that Paradis was going to be offering up another parcel within the next month.

"Are you going to be spending the evening with Tasha tonight?" Quinn asked Shawn as they returned to the Silverado.

"Actually, pal, I am free all night. Tasha is involved in some preparation for an event tomorrow which will coincide with the auction and celebration, something to do with a charity she works with."

"Wishmakers?" Quinn asked.

"How'd you know?" Shawn asked.

"I missed a big event that she helped organize. I was too wrapped up in my work. That was the last straw for her," Quinn explained. "Are you supposed to be at it tonight?"

"No it is just the organizers, but she did invite me to a lunch thing tomorrow, I better make sure I don't screw it up."

"You get to that lunch no matter what happens," Quinn said. "Okay, boys night out, let's hit the Silverado's restaurant and have some wine."

"I can't think of anything I'd rather do," Shawn said as the two of them set off towards the restaurant. They sprung for a bottle of Araujo Cabernet, a cult wine which both found inspiring.

"Jesus," Quinn said flushing as he consumed the wine, "this is just what I would hope we might be able to make if we get the kind of land we're looking for."

"Jesus is right. This wine makes me want to believe in God," Shawn said, his comment the only thing besides his stained teeth suggesting he was intoxicated. He seemed to be able to hide the fact much better than Quinn, who was flushed, floppy, and more relaxed than any conscious person should be.

Minh and Joshua entered the restaurant, looking sober and subdued. They approached and agreed to sit at the table. As Quinn and Shawn engaged them, they could sense tension, even in their impaired state.

"What's wrong?" Shawn asked.

"We just got back from the hospital. Virginia has been intubated. They have her on a ventilator and have put a pressure monitoring system in her skull. They are worried about brain swelling. They are talking about a liver transplant, and are awaiting a bed at UCSF right now."

Quinn and Shawn looked at each other ruefully. "How many plasma transfusions did she need before they could put the EVD in?" Quinn asked.

"The what?" Minh answered.

"The drain," Shawn explained. "He's talking about the tube the neurosurgeon placed in her skull, you can't do that if your blood is not clotting properly, and if you are in liver failure, the first thing to go is your ability to clot your blood."

"He's right. So how many units did it take to correct her?" Quinn asked.

"She didn't need any transfusions," Joshua said. "We're sure of it because afterwards they asked Ron to sign the consent in case they needed to do any transfusions on her later, and he asked all sorts of questions about directed donation." Both Joshua and Minh looked puzzled.

"So then why do they think she is in liver failure?" Quinn asked.

"Because her liver enzymes are over twenty thousand," Minh said.

Quinn was silent, trying to reason out her situation even as he dealt with his considerable blood alcohol level.

"Wow, that's really high. If she has hepato-renal syndrome, that would explain the intubation and the pressure drain in her head, but if her clotting ability remains, and they placed a drain without a transfusion, that means her liver synthetic function must still be okay. That just doesn't add up," Quinn said. "There must be a mistake."

"What kind of mistake?" Joshua asked.

"You're telling me that Virginia has hepato-renal syndrome and has brain swelling. That sounds like someone who needs a liver transplant. But then you say she is clotting her blood fine, and hasn't had any transfusions. That is someone who does not need a liver transplant. Are they transferring her to UCSF tonight?" Quinn asked.

"Park thought they would, but one of the intensivists, who also seemed confused, mentioned something about bed availability, and Virginia not meeting criteria yet, and having to observe her awhile to see what happens." Minh said.

"There's something weird going on with your friend." Quinn said. "So, where's Park now?"

"He's pretty down. He didn't want to be in public tonight. We briefly accompanied him to a pre-party over in Yountville that he was contractually obligated to attend, but left after about a half an hour. He didn't want to join us here. He said something about going over his speech and presentation tomorrow," Joshua said. "He just walked back to his room when we came here."

Minh and Joshua passed on the wine, and remained subdued throughout the dinner. As Quinn and Shawn finished their bottle, a woman with black hair, tanned but European facial features, straight hips and a masculine, purposeful gait approached the table. She was powerful looking and stocky, though not overweight. She reminded Quinn of a college softball player. "Are you Dr. Quinn," she asked in a husky voice that exuded confidence.

"As a matter of fact I am," Quinn said. Do I know you?"

"I don't think so. I thought I recognized you. Sorry to hear you sold your winery," she said with a disarming smile. "You had great land up there, and I really enjoyed the Syrah you made."

"Thanks. And you're name is…." Quinn asked.

"Veronica Thompson. I just wanted to put a face with your name. I have been something of a fan of yours for some time. Have a nice night, Dr. Quinn." She turned and left.

Quinn's forehead wrinkled as he strained to remember something.

"What is it?" Minh asked.

"I don't know. There was something familiar about her. I can't quite put my finger on it," he said, wishing he were not so drunk. She was too stocky to be the one in the Spa, and her hair wasn't right, but he still felt like he knew her.

As they finished their bottle and prepared to leave, a server came over with a bottle of wine. This is with complements of one of our other guests. It is a gift for you, Dr. Quinn. Shall I open it?"

Quinn looked at the wine. It was a bottle of Orin Swift's 2004 'The Prisoner.' Quinn looked up at the server and then around the restaurant.

"Who bought that for us?" he asked, looking for federal agents.

"The woman over…." the waiter turned to identify the woman, looked around puzzled, and then turned back to Quinn. "She must have left. Sorry, sir. Shall I open the wine?"

"I don't usually go in for Zinfandel blends, but by all means, open it." Quinn slurred, now quite drunk. "Was her name Veronica?" he asked the server.

"No. I don't remember her name, but it isn't Veronica. Maybe Candice or something. She comes around here from time to time. I've seen her helping out in the kitchen."

"What does she look like?"

"She has dark hair, strong, stocky, kind of butch."

"Okay, thanks." Quinn shrugged and tasted the wine and indicated it was fine. As the waiter poured the inky dark wine into each of their glasses, Shawn looked at Quinn seriously.

"Coincidence, or sick joke?" he asked. "Is she with the feds?"

"I don't know, and I don't think so." Quinn said. "I don't know who the hell she is, or what this means, if anything," he said looking at the bottle of peculiarly named wine. "I definitely don't know anyone named Veronica, or Candice, assuming it is the same woman, but I just can't say for certain I've never seen that woman before tonight."

Terroir/Myette

Chapter 16:

Ronald Park returned to his hotel room. He and Virginia had not been getting along for some time, but he had hoped they were over the worst of it. She was still his wife and closest friend. He couldn't bear to spend the night at the hospital, especially with her totally unresponsive.

He felt isolated and was ashamed of his selfishness. Weeks ago he had been contemplating a divorce, now he was petrified he'd lose her. He felt guilty for leaving the hospital, as though he had abandoned his wife, but he also felt abandoned by her.

The animosity towards him and the events at the Bounty Hunter made him feel even more isolated. Everywhere he walked, restaurants, the hospital, that damn pre-party, there was a cone of silence around him. His presence hushed everyone within a ten-foot radius. How had it all come to this? He cursed as he entered his suite and locked the door. He felt like he was half-celebrity and half-pariah.

Park's speech was in less than twenty-four hours, at the beginning of the auction. He was asked to comment on the famed red wine winner of the Paris Tasting, the 1973 Stag's Leap Wine cellars Cabernet Sauvignon, and a second great wine from that era, the 1974 Heitz Martha's Vineyard Cabernet Sauvignon, a benchmark wine, and a wine which he had in the past rated at ninety-nine points, the highest score he had ever given, and a benchmark he had only dolled-out four other times.

With a heavy heart, he recalled his last interaction with Virginia. Before being intubated she had begun hallucinating, mumbling about tainted wine, and stating over and over again that she was sorry and that it would never happen again. Ron had no idea what she was talking about, but had tried to reassure his confused and agitated spouse. Comforting and reassuring did not come naturally to him, and he felt like a fish out of water at the hospital.

The doctor explained that it was toxins caused by the liver failure and kidney involvement that sometimes caused swelling in the brain, which in turn caused altered mental status and hallucinations. As alarming as it sounded, the young doctor continued to reassure. Park didn't interrogate the young physician, but wondered if his rosy prognosis was disingenuous.

After Virginia was placed in a pharmaceutical coma, Park made the obligatory appearance at the pre-party with Minh and Joshua, mingled uncomfortably for about fifteen minutes and then returned to the resort. He was so worried about Virginia that he couldn't eat, but he was unable, or at least unwilling to cancel his appearance. His ego carried more weight than his empathy, and even he knew that he was one of the most stubbornly compulsive people in the world.

Virginia had always provided a buffer between him and the people whose wine he judged, and much as he liked Minh and Joshua, they didn't cut it like Virginia. He knew it was her affection for the romantic ideal of winemaking that allowed her to engage and distract the industry's elite, shielding Park. Without her, he felt naked.

Park decided to get down to the business of his speech tomorrow. Tonight, in preparation, he would retaste the two award winning wines, the Heitz pulled from his cellar at his home in Monterey, and the Stag's Leap Cabernet, donated to him for the tasting four months ago. He planned to taste the wines to refresh his memory and give updated scores on both of them. He would release the scores during his speech the next evening.

It felt awkward tasting without Virginia, who always accompanied him on tastings. But with her stepping down, he realized he would have to get used to it.

First he took the Heitz Martha's Vineyard Cabernet. He slowly and deliberately examined the intact capsule, removed it, wiped the neck with a fine cloth, examined the top of the cork, which was intact and without signs of seepage. He then uncorked the bottle and poured four ounces into a large

Bordeaux style glass. He examined the hue, holding it up to the light, marveling at the bright orange rim of senescence at the edge of the wine. He swirled gently, sticking his nose into the glass and inhaling the cedar, menthol, and baking-spice aromas. There was also sage, and could he detect a little bit of toasted almond?

What's that?

Park was puzzled. He examined the cork again to see if he could smell TCA or other off-odors. He could not, and since his hyper acute nose was able to smell TCA at homeopathic concentrations, he knew it was not present.

Shrugging off the curiosity as bottle-to-bottle variation, he tasted, noting the mature flavors and subtle sherry-like taste of a wine that was past its prime. He concentrated on the cassis, menthol, oak, and licorice tastes.

"Maybe ninety-two points non-blind," he said out loud. "Not outstanding, but for a Napa Cabernet close to forty years old, not too bad." He wrote his notes, shrugged, and tasted again, closing his eyes, concentrating intensely upon the sensations in his mouth and nose. He was unable to discern any almond taste and even now, could barely register the scent. He gurgled and swallowed an imperceptibly small amount of the wine.

He jotted down another brief note, and then, alone in the room, he did something unexpected. He decided to swallow the rest of the wine in his glass before turning to the second bottle.

Park sighed deeply, knowing that the second wine was not nearly as age worthy as the Heitz he had just tasted, and knew he would not be able to say anything truly outstanding about it in its present condition. Nevertheless, he had agreed to do the review and speech, was being paid for it, and he would do a thorough and honest job. That's what everyone expected, and that's what he would deliver. He examined the capsule, this time noting a faint wrinkle in the lead capsule that protected the cork. He frowned, his brow furrowed as he strained to remember whether that defect was present prior to this.

Some hotel guests ambled by his door, obviously drunk, talking too loud. He turned towards the door, distracted for a moment, before returning to the wine. He then cut the foil to examine the cork. He found no signs of seepage. He examined the neck, impressed with the amount of sediment. It looked as though some of the base of the cork had disintegrated. He decided he would have to decant the wine. He prepared a filter and pulled the cork from the bottle, decanting it through the ultrafine, chemical-free filter and into a decanter he brought from home. He checked the clarity of the wine in the decanter, to make sure all of the sediment had been filtered out.

He poured the wine into a new glass, again looking at the clarity of the wine under the light, turning the glass to see the colors, garnet, then brick, and finally a ring of orange senescence at the lip. He swirled the wine, noting the sharp and raw oxidized smell of old wine, the faint scent of cedar resin, and hints of loamy earth. He drank the wine, tasting sherry, burnt earth, coffee, and oak. The wine was intensely bitter, more so than he had remembered from his last tasting and notes, some twenty years earlier. There was no fruit left, and the tannins were harsh. He swallowed hard.

Park was disappointed. It was out of balance, and not nearly the wine that had beguiled the French tasters more than thirty years ago in Paris.

Park looked at the bottle, a piece of wine history, and sighed sadly. He couldn't stand another taste. He shrugged and returned to the Heitz. Feeling lonely and sorry for himself, Park poured the wine into his glass and began consuming it. His lips grew faintly numb and his senses dulled.

Was it wine on an empty stomach?

He vaguely registered that wine was hitting him unusually hard. His anxiety over where he was and by whom he was surrounded subsided. In less than an hour he polished off the bottle.

He smiled a defeated sort of smile. He was relaxed enough to resign himself to his situation. So many people hated him here. He understood why, but it still made him sad. He was not rooting for anyone, save the consumer. He was honest, too, and clearly that couldn't be said by some of the other reviewers. Maybe his honesty and the lack of control that the industry wielded over him was what made their feelings about him so strong. As far as he was concerned, if consumers were paying a hefty sum for a bottle of wine, they deserved to know if it was truly excellent or common swill, regardless of whether the producer was a venture capitalist with deep pockets or a farmer breaking his back and depending on the success of the vintage to stay alive.

A little more drunk than he thought he'd be after one bottle, he looked at his bed, wishing he were not alone. He was light headed more than buzzed, but felt euphoric, his senses dulled and his skin ruddy, although his nose itched terribly.

He turned back to the Stag's Leap Cabernet, thinking, maybe it had softened up. He decided to retry it. His palate was dull and he could no longer clearly discern good from awful, which would make drinking it easier.

Park had one glass of the wine, during which the euphoria gave way to inebriation, nausea, and exhaustion. He wondered if he was catching that virus which had so severely affected Virginia the last couple of nights. He drifted into unconsciousness.

In a vague, half-stupor he heard the phone ring. He fumbled for it.

"Yes?"

"Is this Ronald Park?" a woman's voice asked.

"Yes."

"Mr. Park, I am one of the nurses in the ICU over at Queen of the Valley. There has been a sudden deterioration in your wife's condition, we think you should get here as fast as you safely can," she said.

"What, what's happened?" he said, his vision going in and out of focus as he spoke.

"Her heart has stopped and the doctors are doing CPR on her as we speak, I really think you need to get here as soon as possible," she said.

"Okay," he said in a moment of clarity. Adrenaline coursed through his impaired body, waxing his consciousness. He hung up and made to stand, but the room spun mercilessly, forcing him to lean against a wall. He sat back down on the bed and closed his eyes. His consciousness faded.

Some moments later, he heard the phone ring again. It seemed like it was miles away. He did not have the strength to move or to answer it. He did not have sense to care either. He was feeling more disconnected from his environment by the minute, his impaired brain having already forgotten about the phone call from the hospital.

The phone rang a second time, but Park was now too disoriented to locate it. He got out of bed and collapsed on the floor, knocking the side table over as he fell.

A moment later, in a stupor, he heard a knock at the door. He tried to call for help, but something else altogether came from his mouth, a torrent of vomit spilled out of his nose and mouth, all over himself and the floor of his suite. At once he felt rapid heart palpitations followed by an ominous feeling in his chest. The next moment he collapsed, unconscious.

Chapter 17:

Quinn and Shawn started back to their room. They were quite drunk, and their friends were subdued with the hospitalization of Virginia. As they were heading back to their room, Shawn asked what was available in the room.

"You know, they aren't our friends, we don't have to mourn that poor woman's liver problems. We ought to create some liver problems of our own."

Quinn smiled and nodded in agreement, even though they really didn't need any more wine. As he pulled out his key to the room, he heard a crash and a loud "thump" from the room across the hall. Quinn motioned towards the room.

"That's Park's room isn't it? Knock at the door," he said as he opened their door.

Shawn knocked, and a moment later heard a guttural noise that sounded like it might have come from a fraternity bathroom on a Saturday night.

"Jesus do you think he's getting sick too?" Shawn asked.

Quinn looked more alarmed than his friend as he felt that familiar tingle between his thumb and index finger. His level of awareness increased instantaneously as the shot of adrenaline rocketed him into the present moment. Someone was in trouble. He suddenly felt sober.

"Something's weird here," he said coming to the door. "Ron, Ron answer the door, now!" he shouted, banging his fist on the door. There was only silence from inside the room. Shawn looked at him expectantly.

"I'm going to regret this," Quinn said, and took a single step backwards, and with a swift and ferocious kick placed immediately adjacent to the door handle, the door splintered open revealing an overturned table, and Ronald Park, still dressed in slacks and a button-down shirt, lying face down in a pool of his own vomit, which was the color of either blood or red wine.

"Jesus Quinn! You and your fuckin' martial arts," Shawn said as he ran towards the unconscious Park. "I'll stabilize the neck. Help me log-roll him over."

"Is he breathing?" Quinn said, frantically feeling for a pulse.

"No! I'm going to do a blind sweep of the mouth," Shawn said.

"There's no pulse," Quinn said, "I'm going to get the defibrillator in the hall, start chest compressions. We need 911!"

"I'll start compressions," Shawn said, starting compressions, about two every second.

Quinn returned with the defibrillator, and set it up. Shawn was silently singing a Bee Gee's tune as he pounded on the heart. Quinn laughed, remembering that the song *Stayin' Alive* had about 109 beats per minute when played, just the right tempo for chest compressions. It was better than singing *Another One Bites The Dust*, he thought to himself.

"Alright, don't stop compressions until I say clear," Quinn said. "Ready, clear!"

Shawn backed away from Park, and Quinn activated the Automated External Defibrillator, Park stiffened as the electricity passed through his chest, and then relaxed.

"I feel a pulse, but it is weak," Quinn said.

"I am going to give two rescue breaths, you call 911!" Shawn said, leaning near Park's airway.

"Careful," Quinn said, dialing the phone, "You don't have a mask and we don't know what caused this."

"I hope whatever it is it isn't contagious," he muttered to himself and gave two large breaths to Park.

Park responded with a torrent of red wine vomit. Shawn ducked out of the way almost in time as Quinn explained the situation over the phone to emergency dispatchers.

"Jesus Christ!" Shawn said, having been only partially successful at avoiding the torrent of vomit. Swiftly he log-rolled Park on his side and cleared his mouth. He rolled him back and had the courage to try two more rescue breaths. These were not followed by more vomit.

"EMT's are on their way, pulses are still there, but thready," Quinn said returning to Park.

"What's happened here?" Shawn asked, between rescue breaths.

"I don't know, this guy has been drinking wine since he was in diapers. How could he get so drunk on two bottles of wine?" Quinn asked motioning to the two bottles of wine on the one upright table.

"Something's not right," Shawn said.

"Shawn you're doing a great job with the rescue breaths! His color is great!"

Shawn took a deep breath and gave two more rescue breaths.

"Jesus this stinks! He smells like wine and an almond factory," he said. Then he turned to the table. "One bottle, Quinn, the other one's still three-quarters full."

"Is he waking up?" Quinn asked.

"No, and not breathing spontaneously either." Shawn said. "I need a friggin' mask!" he said as he leaned in to give two more rescue breaths.

"Shawn, I think his pulses are getting better," Quinn said. "Keep doing what you're doing."

"There's puke everywhere!" Shawn said. "We need to secure this airway right now!"

As if on cue, two EMT's entered the room, with the resort manager right behind them.

"Good heavens," the manager said. "What happened?"

The two EMT's kneeled beside Quinn and Shawn. One was a twenty-something with bulging muscles and a pony-tail. The other was a skinny older woman with a deeply etched and sun damaged face suggesting too many cigarettes and more than a lifetime of tough experience. Quinn thought he recognized the woman.

"Good job boys. EMT's. We'll take over," the man with the pony-tail said, dismissing Quinn and Shawn.

"I'm Matthew Quinn. This is Dr. Callihan. We need to secure this airway immediately," he said making eye contact with the young EMT. "He was in a pulseless rhythm when we got here. Looked like wide v-tach on the AED's monitor. We shocked him into a perfusing rhythm. He has a pulse, but it's thready and rapid, and there's no spontaneous breathing."

"Thank you gentlemen, we'll handle it," the young man responded.

At that moment the woman stepped between pony-tail man and Quinn. She placed a firm hand on pony-tail man's shoulder, shot him a look but said nothing.

"Dr. Quinn, we're here to help, you direct the show," she said.

"First, get Dr. Callihan an ambu bag. The poor fellow's been doing mouth-to-mouth. Then get a pulse oximeter on this patient, and get out some tools to secure his airway. Ma'am, if you're comfortable securing the airway, by all means, do it, if not, I am happy to help. And we need a blood pressure right now."

"Pulse ox is 100%," pony-tail man said to Quinn. Then he reached for a blood pressure cuff.

"I'll take a shot if that's okay," she said. "Thanks Dr. Quinn." Pony-tail man, hoping to save face, opened the bag with equipment to secure the airway.

"Poor drunk, looks like he drank himself nearly to death," he said, looking at all of the wine stained vomit.

The female EMT efficiently placed an endotracheal tube below Ronald Park's vocal cords, effectively securing his airway.

"By the look of things he is going to have one hell of an aspiration pneumonia," she said. "There's purple puke everywhere down there."

"75/30," Pony-tail man said, and turned to Quinn.

"It's bitter," Shawn said quietly, ensconced in thought. "Really bitter."

"We need two large bore IV's as soon as you can get them, then wide open with Saline. Have you got norepinephrine in your kit?" he asked, ignoring Shawn.

"Epinephrine only," pony-tail man said.

"Give 1:1000 Epinephrine, 3cc, down the tube," Quinn said. He bagged in the epinephrine, a synthetic form of adrenaline, which did not seem to be doing much.

"His puke, his saliva, his mouth, it's bitter," Shawn repeated as the man placed the epinephrine down the endotracheal tube and bagged the liquid into the lungs. The pulse on the defibrillator's cardiac readout quickened, but Park otherwise did not respond.

"What are you talking about Shawn?"

"Excuse me ma'am, but do you carry naloxone?" Shawn asked.

She nodded silently.

"Give him some, IV or down the tube," he said.

"Okay, Dr. Callihan," she said, reaching into her kit, pulling out two vials of naloxone, breaking them open, and drawing them up with a 5cc syringe. She did the same thing that pony-tail man had done with the epinephrine. This time the response was different.

Park let out a violent retch, sitting up and nearly dislodging his breathing tube. Still more vomitus came up. His response was as if a thousand bees stung him simultaneously. He began flailing in panicked, if not quite purposeful movements, communicating nothing except mortal distress.

"Holy cow!" pony-tail man said. "What a response. It looks like this fellow likes his Oxycontin, too."

Shawn looked at Quinn and then at the bottles of wine.

"Maybe he's been poisoned!" he said.

Quinn looked at him incredulously, and then at the manager, who was standing in the corner, slack-jawed and speechless.

"Call the police, and have this room secured, in case this is due to foul play," he said with authority. "Guys, I really need those IVs," he said. "If we haven't got one in the next ninety seconds, place an intra-osseus line. The EMT's responded by looking for suitable sights on either arm. Shawn took over squeezing the ambu-bag, giving breaths to Park.

"If it was a narcotic ingestion wouldn't reversing it also reverse the hypotension?" pony-tail man asked, stopping what he was doing and checking the blood pressure again.

"Opiates won't lower blood pressure that much. They lower it if they relieve pain that is causing high blood pressure, but they don't affect the heart that much. They won't tank the pressure, like what's happened here. His blood pressure issue is due to something else." Quinn said.

"80/20, in spite of the epi. I guess you're right," pony-tail man said.

Park was continuing to flail, making bagging him difficult. The female EMT placed an eighteen gauge IV in Park's right arm, and started him on a bag of IV fluids, letting gravity deliver it is as fast as it would go.

"Good, we got to get him to an ER and get him something to stabilize his blood pressure. Give him saline as fast as you can," Quinn said.

The police arrived as the EMTs, Quinn and Shawn had gotten Park secured onto a traveling gurney. They immediately began taking stock of the scene. Quinn and Shawn spoke briefly with the officers, before being allowed to travel with the EMTs to the hospital. The officers told them that they would have someone meet them at the hospital to ask them questions, since they were the first two people on the scene.

In the back of the ambulance, Park continued to flail about. Pony-tail man drove the rig while his partner stayed back with Park, Quinn and Shawn. Shawn seemed deep in thought as the EMT spoke.

"Lucky for him you guys arrived when you did. Which one of you destroyed the door, or was it like that when you got there?"

Quinn looked at her and flushed. "That was me. We knew our friends were calling him and he wasn't answering. We heard a crash and," he paused, "sounds of distress." We banged on the door and sensed something was really wrong. So I kicked it in."

"Most people don't know how to do that," she said. "But I guess you aren't one of them."

"Bitter almonds, Quinn!" Shawn burst out.

"What the hell are you talking about?" Quinn looked at him dumbly.

"Bitter almonds, and he was pink really quickly, never really dusky. Do you think he was poisoned with cyanide?" Shawn asked.

Quinn thought for a moment before responding. "Shawn, what are the chances? I've never seen cyanide poisoning before, never even heard cases of it, except in smoke inhalation where there's burning particle board and in reading old murder mysteries."

"But it fits perfectly," Shawn said.

"While I vaguely remember what you are talking about, if he had been given cyanide we never would have been able to resuscitate him. He'd be long since dead."

"Damn, I thought I was onto something," Shawn said.

"I think you might have been on to something with the opiate though. He definitely responded to the naloxone. I haven't a clue what's wrong, but I wouldn't jump to cyanide as a conclusion." Quinn said, "But it was more than just an opiate. If it was opiate overdose alone, the naloxone would have been enough to bring him back."

Shawn shrugged. "I just remember a great toxicology lecture we had back in medical school. I thought I might have found a match for the smell and his pink skin."

"You did great, Shawn. You might've saved his life with the naloxone," Quinn said in a conciliatory tone.

They arrived at the hospital and brought Park into one of the trauma bays, where the ER staff, docs, nurses, and respiratory therapists descended upon him and began a rapid assessment. Quinn and Shawn backed away and watched as the doctors went to work immediately.

"Blood gas shows pH of 6.82 with a CO2 of 31, oxygen of 300, bicarb of 3 and a base deficit of 25," one of the nurses called out.

"He's got a metabolic acidosis, send off a lactate level," shouted one of the doctors, whose tag said he was Dr. Garcia. "We need a central line fast. Get some bicarb into him now! Two amps STAT please," he called out. Quinn was silent.

"Isn't his wife upstairs?" one of the nurses asked. There was a murmur of acknowledgment.

"Quinn, metabolic acidosis! He wasn't down that long. It fits so well with cyanide!"

Quinn looked at his friend. He did not want to insult him, but thought that it was a medical student mistake.

"Remember when you hear hoof prints in the hallway…"

"I know, think of horses, not zebras." Shawn said.

"And cyanide is a three-legged albino-Zebra," Quinn said.

"Just the same, what if we told them it was a possibility? What's the treatment for cyanide toxicity?" Shawn asked.

"IV sodium nitrite, I think," Quinn said. "I guess it probably wouldn't hurt."

Shawn went over and spoke with the ER doc, who listened to what he had to say, and then shrugged, and spoke with one of the nurses. Five minutes later, a bag of saline with sodium nitrite was hung.

The two watched the resuscitation for some time, marveling at how the emergency staff seemed to get so much done so fast in what appeared from the outside as utter chaos. After the bicarb was infused and support with intravenous norepinephrine, Park appeared to stabilize some more. He was given some sedation, and finally stopped flailing about. As they were preparing to move him up into an ICU, one of the police arrived at the scene came in and spoke with them.

"Deputy Donald Hooper. I work for the Napa County Sherriff's Department."

"Excellent," Shawn said, shaking his hand. "I'm Shawn Callihan and this is Matthew Quinn."

"Are you two still needed for anything here?" he asked.

"No, the doctors here have it under control. I don't think we have much more to offer," Quinn said.

"Good. Let's go over to the station so you two can give me some statements about the night's events, and maybe some statements about anything else you might know of leading up to this."

"Sure," Quinn said.

"Have you two been drinking?"

"We've been drinking wine all day, and happened upon this scene by accident. We were just trying to help…" Shawn said, sounding like a teenager caught skipping class.

"Couple of drunk Samaritans eh," the deputy said.

Quinn and Shawn exchanged glances, and turned back to the policeman.

"Can you give us a ride down there, and then drop us off at the Silverado afterwards?" Quinn asked.

"Yeah, no problem," he said. "In spite of your successful resuscitation, it looks like neither of you are fit to drive anyway." He shook his head and motioned for the two men to follow him. He led them out into the cool night air.

"We really stepped in it, didn't we? Maybe we shouldn't have helped given our blood alcohol levels," Shawn said ruefully.

"We're covered by Good Samaritan law under this circumstance," Quinn whispered into Shawn' ear, "and besides, two drunk doctors are usually better than two sober untrained people." Shawn nodded back as the two got into the police car.

Chapter 18:

When Shawn and Quinn arrived at the station, the deputy showed them into a cramped office and left. They sipped coffee, trying to shake the cobwebs spun from their earlier partying. After an excruciating and sobering two hours Sherriff Robert Hernandez came in to meet them.

Sherriff Hernandez was a lanky and tall man in his forties with an acne-scarred face and a silvery tinge to his otherwise black crew-cut hair. Despite his severe appearance, he had a friendly demeanor.

"Gentlemen," he said as he sat down across from them, shuffling papers. "What happened tonight?"

"We're down here for the celebration, and are also looking at property, but we were wine tasting in the valley today, and came back for dinner with some friends," Quinn began. "After dinner and some more wine, we returned to our room. We don't know Mr. Park very well, but the friends we were dining with are close to him. We knew he had been distraught about his wife's illness."

"Right, his wife was in the hospital with some sort of liver problem I understand," Hernandez said. "She died tonight. Did you two know that?"

"No, we didn't," Quinn gasped. "What happened?"

"I don't think the doctors know what killed her," Hernandez said. "It was unexpected, and very sudden."

"That's terrible," Quinn said. "Our friends, they know them both. They knew Park was in his room, having returned to the resort with him. They were calling him on the phone as we went back to our room. We heard a crash in there, and asked if he needed help. There was no answer, so we went in and saw him in trouble." Quinn then told him the details of their attempted resuscitation.

"You think he tried to off himself because of what was going on with his wife?" Hernandez asked.

"I don't know him that well, but I doubt it," Shawn said. "He had a speech to give tomorrow, and wasn't going to cancel it even though his wife was so ill. Don't you think this is more likely some sort of foul play?" Shawn asked.

Hernandez looked at Shawn. "Giving a speech at a wine auction while his wife is in the ICU makes him sound like an asshole. Maybe he is, maybe he isn't, but it would seem, gentlemen," he said, "that there is no shortage of people in the valley who have plenty of disdain for Mr. Park and more specifically, for the credence given to his reviews, both good and bad. With the current economic situation, there are all sorts of reasons for me to believe that this was not a suicide attempt. I am not even sure it looks like that. I was just wondering what you two thought."

"We gave him naloxone, a reversal agent for narcotics," Shawn said. "Because when we resuscitated him, I tasted something very bitter."

"What, did you give him mouth-to-mouth or something?" Hernandez asked.

"Yes," Shawn said.

"You're a brave man."

"Anyway, I wondered whether he might have been given a narcotic," Shawn continued. "We reversed him with naloxone, and there was a definite response. That doesn't mean for sure that there were narcotics on board, but it supports my theory some."

"Gentlemen, Mr. Park is positive for a derivative of fentanyl. We have reason to believe that one of the bottles he was drinking was in fact, infused with a high concentration of it. It seems to me, though to be an odd way of trying to kill someone. It's obvious, and would show up on any toxicology screen. The hospital is sending quantitative blood levels to UC Davis Medical Center for confirmation. So it seems that someone decided to slip him opiates, and it turns out, something else."

"Not cyanide?" Shawn asked.

"How did you know that?" Hernandez looked at him seriously, perhaps with a hint of accusation, Quinn thought.

Shawn slapped his hand on the table.

"Ha! I was right. Bitter almonds, Quinn, bitter almonds and metabolic acidosis! What was his lactate level?" he asked Hernandez.

"I don't know anything about a lactate level, but the antidote is still going into him still at this hour. The doctors and the toxicologist, who came in from Travis Air Force Base in Fairfield, are certain that he has been poisoned with cyanide."

"Obviously they didn't give him a lethal amount," Quinn said. "Did someone think that the cyanide would kill him slowly, and that drugging him with the opiate would give the cyanide time to work or something? I mean, this seems really amateur, cyanide and opiates, come on! What is this, an Agatha Christie novel?"

"On the contrary, Dr. Quinn, a preliminary test run by the toxicologist suggests that the levels of cyanide and in Mr. Park's blood are astronomically high. Unless Captain Williams is incorrect in her math, Mr. Park has ingested at least four times the lethal dose of potassium cyanide."

Shawn and Quinn stared silently at Hernandez.

"So how the hell is he still alive?" Quinn asked.

"Indeed, how?" Hernandez answered. "He isn't exactly doing well at the moment. He is in a coma, with multi-organ failure, and they expect fatal brain swelling is imminent. They're worried about something called 'irreversible shock' and aren't optimistic that he'll survive."

"Jesus, that's terrible," Shawn said, slumping. "I thought we did a hell of a job of saving him." Quinn shrugged and turned a sad eye to his friend.

"You two did fine, especially considering your state of mind. If he has half a chance in hell, you two gave it to him. I heard you two suggested the cyanide antidote before it crossed anyone's mind in the Emergency Department. Nevertheless, it doesn't look good right now," Hernandez explained.

"Damn," Shawn muttered.

"No one over there, least of all the toxicologist can believe he's not dead. So you two have exceeded everyone's expectations. For now, there's someone in Napa Valley who's guilty of attempted murder. In two days he'll be brain-dead, and it's likely to be murder, straight up."

The Sherriff paused, looking uncomfortable for a moment before changing his tone.

"Forgive me for changing subjects gentlemen, but did either of you hear about the fire?"

"The what?" Quinn asked.

"Someone set off an explosive after soaking *Wine Magazine's* Napa headquarters with gasoline," Hernandez said. "It's a total loss. We were trying to see if that is somehow tied in with the attempt on Park or the death of his wife."

"That's a strange coincidence, but how could it be tied to the attack on Park?" Quinn asked. "When did it happen?"

"Just a few hours ago," Hernandez said. "Destroyed the building and everything in it, but it no one was there."

"It doesn't seem like a good way to commit murder," Quinn said.

"Yeah, but it might be a hell of a way to get rid of evidence," Hernandez said, sounding frustrated.

Quinn nodded, acknowledging the point.

"Any leads?" Shawn asked.

"Well, I don't have any reason to suspect you two wanted him dead, or the magazine torched, if that's what you're asking. Without you two, he'd be dead for sure. Besides, it looks like both of you received favorable ratings from him in the past, and neither of you appear dependent upon his opinions to keep afloat. But any number of people in the valley might be better off with Mr. Park and his magazine up in smoke. We might be able to get a signature on the sort of cyanide he was given, and that might point us in the right direction. We got a tip tonight that we are checking up on. Maybe it was someone else working at the magazine."

"Wow, that was fast," Shawn said.

"What was fast?" Hernandez asked.

"Park goes down just a couple of hours ago, and no one knows it was cyanide, but you got a tip that the cyanide might have come from somewhere?"

"Yeah, it's a little fresh, but it might have been an accomplice who got cold feet. It was an anonymous tip," he explained. "We see this from time to time."

"Is there anything else?" Quinn asked.

"As a matter of fact there is," Hernandez said. "Did one of you break the door down to Park's room, or was it destroyed when you got there?"

"Sorry, that was me. He sounded like he was in trouble and I acted instinctively," Quinn said, trying to sound more contrite than he was.

Hernandez nodded slowly, taking in what he heard. "Dr. Quinn, do you want to talk about the reason that there are federal agents crawling all around Napa following you? Can you shed some light onto why my men have been instructed to report your whereabouts and any suspicious activity?" Hernandez asked. "And why you are on the terror watch list?"

"The terror watch list?"

"Yeah," Hernandez said. "You don't strike me as the Timothy McVeigh type."

"Didn't they tell you? They think I am making illegal drugs," Quinn answered matter-of-factly.

"And are you, Dr. Quinn?" he asked leaning forward.

"No," Quinn answered. "But despite multiple negative blood tests, and no evidence that I have touched this drug since I left my research career five years ago, they just don't believe me."

"What kind of drug are we talking about?" Hernandez asked, "designer ecstasy or some other street drug?"

"No. It's a polymer which reverses the aging process," Quinn said.

Hernandez looked at him incredulously. "Hardly a steet drug. Why would a drug like that be illegal?"

"I don't own the patent," Quinn said, "at least, not anymore."

"What about the terror watch list?"

"I haven't a clue, you'd have to ask the feds," Quinn said.

Hernandez looked at him queerly, and then shrugged off the curiosity. "I was sorry to see you sell your winery. My wife and I have been up there a couple of times. You were making good wine," he said with sincerity.

"Thanks, Sherriff. I appreciate that." Quinn said. "And I give you my word, whatever it's worth, that I am no terrorist, and no criminal. I'm just neck deep in a bunch of crazy circumstances."

"I don't particularly care for the way the feds have dealt with me, and I want to give you the benefit of the doubt, Dr. Quinn. I do, however, expect you to behave yourself as long as you remain here in the Napa area," Hernandez said and then dismissed them. A deputy gave them a ride back to the spa and they went to sleep. It was after three am.

In the morning, Quinn awoke feeling fine, without a trace of a hangover. He puzzled over that for a moment and then shrugged the curiosity off. He called Minh and Joshua to see if they had any more information. They agreed to meet in the restaurant for breakfast.

When they saw the gay couple at the table, Minh and Joshua looked worn and aged, not their usual youthful selves. Minh had puffy, bloodshot eyes and Joshua had two days of stubbly growth and was wrinkled head to toe. As they sat down Quinn took a deep breath before speaking. "Were you two at the hospital all night?"

"No, Park is still in a coma and no one expects him to live," Minh explained, "You heard that Virginia passed last night?"

Quinn and Shawn nodded silently.

"And what's with the torching of *Wine Magazine's* Napa bureau that everyone is talking about? Boy someone really doesn't like Ron Park, that's for sure. I mean, why go after his wife? And he doesn't even own the magazine anymore. What's this about?" Joshua asked.

"Do they think his wife's death is foul play, too?" Shawn asked.

"We think it has to be," Minh said. "We're going to call our friend and see if he can independently get to the bottom of this."

"I don't have a clue about Virginia, but Sherriff Hernandez thinks whoever torched the magazine headquarters wasn't trying to kill anyone. They may have destroyed incriminating evidence." Quinn said.

"Let's get out of here," Joshua said to Minh. "We can't enjoy the Gala with this tragedy hanging over our heads, and we have some calls to make."

"We understand," Shawn said. "Has there been any change with Park?"

"Not as of this morning," Joshua said.

"We're going to get some sleep before leaving," Minh said. "What do you guys think? Who would kill our friends? I mean, why would they try to kill both of them?"

Quinn shrugged. "I don't know, but I agree they're both foul play. Park's definitely been poisoned. Now that we know that, it's a good bet that someone wanted to make sure Park was alone when he drank the poison. If Virginia had been there, Park might have been rescued sooner."

"No offense Matthew, but every time we get together with you, something awful seems to happen," Minh said.

"I hope this business with Park has nothing to do with me," Quinn said.

"Hardly seems like it could," Shawn said.

"Yeah, but what an awful coincidence," Joshua said.

"I understand how you two feel," Quinn said. "We didn't know them like you two did. So we're going to plan to go to the celebration and auction tonight. I hope you two aren't offended. If you need us for anything, information or whatever, just let us know. We'll keep our ears to the ground."

"Thanks," Minh said. Then he leaned in closer and spoke in a whisper. "Park was poisoned with the wine he was tasting, right? Do you think they poisoned Virginia with something else, or was she just given what was meant for Park by mistake?"

"Can you think of anything Virginia ate or drank which might have been meant for Park? It seems like a possibility, I guess." Shawn paused, holding up one finger while appearing deep in thought. The other three gazed at him silently while he thought. "What did they have to eat the other day? There was something…."

"I think they had steaks and Bordeaux at the Bounty Hunter," Minh said.

"No, before that. I was speaking with them before Virginia went to the hospital the first time. She mentioned something, something Park hated. Mushroom risotto, that's what she had for lunch, mushroom risotto."

"What's so important about that?" Minh asked.

"Yeah, Shawn, what is so important about mushroom risotto?" Quinn asked. As he asked, there was something stirring in the back of his own memory.

At that very moment, Tasha appeared in the restaurant, as if out of nowhere, startling all four of them. She sat down, making eye contact with Shawn.

"Mushroom risotto, if it were poisoned, might be poisoned by Amanita mushrooms. They would go down easily enough in a risotto. Then, six to twelve hours later, whoever ate them would get violently sick," she explained. "That would be followed by a honeymoon phase during which there would be massive destruction of the liver, and then later, signs of liver failure. Is that what happened to Virginia?"

"Exactly what I was thinking. God you are brilliant!" Shawn gushed. "Gentlemen, I present my girlfriend, Dr. Tasha Johansen, the smartest physician in the world!"

Quinn shrugged. "I'd say that you were both crazy, but after showing all of us up last night with the cyanide diagnosis,

I'm not going to say a damn thing. But that's hard to prove, right?"

"If they can find traces on the post-mortem, then they can nail the diagnosis," Tasha said. "What a random coincidence. I was just at a conference in Arizona, and one whole day was devoted to accidental and non-accidental poisonings. One of the lecturers told us about this family of Southeast Asian immigrants who collected mushrooms. They accidentally harvested a whole bunch of amanita and got really sick."

"What happened to them," Joshua asked.

"Well, two of them died. Two of them went on to get liver transplants. One of them recovered," she said.

"Good God, that sounds pretty lethal. Virginia didn't stand a chance," Minh said.

"How did that one survive?" Joshua asked.

"Milk thistle," Tasha said.

"Milk thistle, like the herb?" Joshua asked.

"Yeah, people take it for liver problems. One of the teenagers was born with hepatitis B and was getting interferon therapy. He was on the milk thistle to protect his liver. I guess it is a powerful antioxidant, and it bound up the toxin and saved his liver. This is described in the literature, and has been known by natives for centuries. If you ingest enough milk thistle with, or shortly after Amanita, you can survive it."

"Wait, antioxidant, like, free radicals?" Minh said, looking at Joshua, and then at Quinn.

"If that's what happened to her," Quinn said. "Shawn, we ought to call the police and tell them your and Tasha's theory. Maybe they can test for that on the post-mortem and get a diagnosis."

"Murder in Napa Valley, over wine," Tasha said shaking her head. "It seems so trivial, not at all worth someone's life."

"And it's all so damn theatrical. Cyanide, opiates, poison mushrooms. It's like someone wants us to figure out what happened," Shawn said.

Quinn called the police on his cell phone, while Minh and Joshua got up and left a little too quickly, with expressions of what Quinn thought was a mixture of awe and dread. He wondered what had been said to set them off.

* * * * * *

Quinn stayed at the hotel resting and exercising. His stamina, which had continued to diminish, seemed to have improved slightly. He was still able to run an easy 4 miles on the treadmill, while far less than prior to his 'accident' it was the best he had done in a couple of months. Tasha and Shawn went to the Wishmakers fundraiser and then took off to do some mid-afternoon wine tasting.

At about 2 pm, alone, bored, and overcome with curiosity, Quinn made his way to Queen of the Valley Medical Center. He once had privileges there for emergency calls when he first retired to Napa Valley and he figured he'd try to get the scoop on Park. When he let himself into the ICU, he saw that a critical care team was packaging up Ron Park, who was still sedated and on a ventilator.

"Where's he going?" Quinn asked.

"Down to the Air Force base for some experimental hyperbaric treatment, and then to Stanford. We've paralyzed and cooled him and have kept him in a barbiturate coma. We did a double exchange transfusion. Now we're going to try hyperbaric oxygen. His lactate is still over forty."

"Forty?" Quinn said, impressed. He had heard of lactates over ten and that was ridiculously high. A lactate over two was associated with increased risk of mortality, he knew. Forty would be absolutely lethal in his experience.

"How can he still be alive?"

"Timex syndrome," one of the internists said matter-of-factly.

Quinn smiled. "Takes a lickin'…."

"You get the picture. In the end it's all probably window dressing, but the guy's heart's still beating, and the last two CT scans have failed to show the signs of brain swelling we've been expecting. Pupils still react, so we thought, what the hell. Let's do a full-court press."

"Did someone make a mistake on the cyanide assay?" Quinn asked.

"I didn't hear anything like that. They just think this guy's like Keith Richards, with some super-human metabolism or something," the internist explained.

Quinn was dumbfounded by the strange events as he made his way back to the Silverado. He agreed with Shawn. The whole thing was surreal, overly artistic, and dramatic. It was something out of a soap opera, not reality. He recalled his break-in at the spa earlier, and tried to place the beautiful Latina woman. She seemed familiar to him, though he had to admit that he sort of had a thing for dark-skinned women in general. Still there was something.... What had she been talking on the phone about? He was drunk at the time, and despite his note scrawling, he couldn't get his head around the things that she was saying.

Someone named Catherine was growing something, and perhaps it was the two of them who were making his polymer. What did they say? Their inventory was low? In an instant, Quinn thought he had part of the story. The woman and her friend Catherine were making his polymer. They were going to grow something to take its place sometime in the near future. What else did they say, something about risotto?

Risotto!

Quinn lurched. That woman and someone named Catherine had been talking about risotto! Shawn was right. Virginia must have been poisoned. Quinn's heart skipped a beat as he pieced together the parts of the story. There was something about slipping something to someone else, too? Were they talking about Park? Or was it someone else? They hadn't done it yet, but it was clear that Park's wine had been compromised perhaps days, weeks, or even months before the day of his poisoning. No, someone else was going to be slipped some sort of poison that weekend. Quinn felt panicked.

Then he remembered the wine that had been given them and became physically sick. A stranger had given all of them a bottle of The Prisoner. Had that been Catherine? Did she poison them? Or was there going to be another murder?

Quinn wasn't dead, didn't feel ill at all. As a matter of fact, he felt fine.

He had to figure it out. Was he poisoned? Was it someone else? Was it Park? Who were these people, and what was the connection between his polymer and the murder of Ron and Virginia Park?

Quinn still felt like they were familiar to him, the Latina woman, and Veronica or Catherine. Who were they? Quinn tried desperately to remember the events around the death of Vladimir Michinski. He decided to go to the Internet. He scanned the newspaper archives of the days after that event, almost four years ago.

When he came to the article, he froze. At once he understood who she was and what he was up against. Michinski and his son's bullet ridden bodies were found in the car that was pulled from the depths off of Devil's Slide. Catherine Michinski's DNA and fingerprints were found in the car, in the driver's seat and on the steering wheel, but her body was never recovered. It was presumed to have washed out to sea.

Quinn sensed that she was alive, she was here, and she was hell-bent on revenge. The pain in his hands began, deep and dull. At that moment he was more frightened than he had been in years.

Chapter 19:

The call came to Quinn just two hours before the dinner and auction were to start. Minh Tran unusually severe in his demeanor. He asked Quinn to meet in the courtyard outside Minh and Joshua's suite at the Silverado. Confused about Minh and Joshua's return to the resort, he asked what turned them around. They told him they would explain.

Minh opened the gate, and seemed hesitant when he saw Tasha and Shawn also, but let all three pass. They entered the courtyard which was beautifully landscaped, and had three water features, a central fountain, a waterfall spilling out of a stone wall abutting one of the fences, and a koi pond with a three-terraced splashing cascade into one corner of it. The babbling water was at once peaceful, and provided enough background noise to prevent any meaningful eavesdropping. There was a third man there who Quinn didn't recognize. He set down what looked like a portable radio on the table and turned it on.

"What's this all about," Quinn asked looking at the machine the man appeared to be tuning. "I thought you two were going home. Was there some sort of change of plans?"

"In a manner of speaking," Joshua said. "We need to speak with you. Quinn this is Jeff McLeod, an old friend of mine, and someone who is going to be helping us here."

Jeff stopped tuning the machine and turned to Quinn. They shook hands in silence. Jeff had a marine-style buzz cut and coal-black eyes. His nose was slightly crooked with an ugly scar along the bridge. Adorning his sinewy and powerful looking arms were several military tattoos. Where he wasn't inked, his skin was tanned and leathery, and his eyes had deep lines around them. He had other scars on his face and forearms, from what, Quinn didn't know. Quinn immediately sized Jeff up as someone you don't screw with. He trusted Joshua and Minh more than anyone else, so if they trusted him, he must be okay. "What is that thing on the table?" he asked.

"It's a jammer. It will disrupt any electronic surveillance. Just a precaution," Jeff said.

Quinn considered this. "How do you know Minh and Joshua?"

"I went to school with Joshua. We were doubles partners on the tennis team. He went off to Stanford, and I went back east, but we kept in touch," Jeff explained.

"Quinn, Jeff's ex-military, he's a West Point graduate. He is going to be watching over Ron Park. If Ron survives, we think whoever poisoned him is going to try to finish the job."

"Good thinking, guys. He's probably still in danger," Quinn said ruefully. He glanced at Jeff, wondering for a moment if the ex-soldier knew exactly what he was getting himself into. Quinn just as quickly decided that Jeff probably did, and was a guy who could take care of himself in most situations.

"Quinn, you have to know something else," Minh began. "We've believed in you from the beginning. A few years back, when Tasha was approached here at the Silverado with the herbal supplement that had your polymer in it, we knew people would start benefiting from it. We wanted to be among those people. Joshua and I have been taking the supplements since shortly after that weekend at harvest a few years ago."

"Why am I not surprised," Quinn said flatly.

"You selfish little shit," Tasha said.

"You might or might not know that Shawn and Tasha were right again. Virginia was poisoned with mushrooms."

"Really, from Amanita," Quinn said. "But what does that have to do with…."

"That's not what killed her. She had a massive air embolus in the hospital. Someone injected air into her veins and killed her. Virginia and Ron were also on the supplement. We talked about it once. They told us about it, and we knew it was your stuff. They started shortly after we did. Probably every wealthy wine lover who has ever stayed at the Silverado is on those pills. Who knows how big this operation is. Anyway, someone is making millions off this stuff."

"Swell," Quinn said. "The feds have a good reason to be suspicious. The polymer is enjoying wider use than I thought. No wonder they are so desperate to find out who's behind this."

"Who else knows how to manufacture it?" Jeff said.

Quinn looked ruefully at him.

"You can trust Jeff," Joshua said. "I would trust him with my life."

Quinn shrugged. "Anyone with ties to Belmont Biogenetics might know. Vladimir Michinski and his men stole the formula before I had patented it. But I thought all of them were dead or in jail. Then I remembered something and this afternoon I Googled the news articles from that night we rescued Tasha. They found two bodies in the car that went into the ocean at Devil's Slide. Neither one of them was in the car. The authorities thought it was lucky that they found two, and there was residual DNA in the car of three people, one female. They assumed Michinski's daughter was also in the car, her body washed out to sea, or eaten by scavengers."

"A body was never found?" Shawn asked.

"No, but there was nothing to suggest she had escaped either," Quinn said, "So I never gave it much thought. But now I wonder if she survived."

"What was her name?" Minh asked.

"Catherine Michinski," he answered. "But I think she was that Veronica woman who gave us the wine. We probably shouldn't have drunk it," he said.

"Well, we all drank it, and we are all okay," Minh said, "So it couldn't have been poisoned."

"Unless it was with my polymer," Quinn said, thinking about how he woke up feeling better, had run 4 miles, and had no hangover despite drinking way too much wine the night before.

"How much do you two pay for the polymer," Shawn asked.

"Six hundred bucks a month," Minh said.

"Each," Joshua added.

"So if there are ten-thousand regular takers of this stuff, then whoever is making it is grossing 6 million a month. Over the last four years, that's more than 200 million dollars." Tasha said.

"And the Feds think there are more people on it than that," Quinn said. "If I'm going to stay out of prison, I need to figure out who really is behind this back-door marketing scheme. I'm starting with this Catherine woman."

"And you think she's a surviving member of the Michinski crime syndicate?" Jeff asked. He didn't appear to be intimidated.

"I think so," Quinn said. "Jeff these guys are really dangerous."

"Quinn, there's something else," Minh said.

"What?"

"Virginia never went into liver failure. And Park had enough cyanide in him to kill four people. They both should have died right away. They aren't superheroes. When Tasha mentioned that milk thistle, and it helping free radicals, Joshua and I made the connection. Quinn, could it be that… I mean don't you think that their survival had something to do with your polymer?"

"You think the polymer allowed them to get through the poisoning, the way it allowed my mice to survive free radical loads a thousand times normal," Quinn finished the thought for Minh.

"A thousand times normal free radical loads? Holy shit!" Shawn exclaimed.

"I suppose it is theoretically possible," Quinn said answering Minh's question, "depending on how pure the supplements are and how much someone has been taking and for how long, but Park must have anoxic brain injury, even with our prompt and thorough resuscitation. Cyanide kills by preventing oxygen from getting into cells and tissues. Shawn knew that and remembered that Park looked pink, almost rosy when we resuscitated him. That's because all the oxygen stays in the blood, and none of it gets into the cells, tissues, and organs. He might as well have drowned. I don't see how he can survive."

"My God, Quinn! He should never have made it to the hospital," Tasha said. "Your polymer is more powerful than I realized."

"And it's illegal, understand?" Quinn snapped. "Everyone who takes it puts me one step closer to federal prison."

"None of us wants you to be blamed for this, Quinn," Joshua said. "Ironically you, Tasha, and Shawn are the only ones around here who are innocent. Yet you're the one that the feds are harassing."

"We have to figure out how to prove that this Catherine woman is behind this," Shawn said.

"They have her DNA, We could see if we can get a hold of that," Quinn said.

"What?" Tasha asked.

"DNA," Quinn said. "They have her DNA footprint from the car."

"How in the hell are we going to get that?" Tasha asked.

"I don't know, but there is something more than this Catherine making my polymer and framing me for it," Quinn explained. "I think the attempt on Ron and the murder of his wife were orchestrated by the same people making my polymer, but I don't understand the connection."

"Why do you think that?" Joshua asked. "And why would it matter?"

"We have to find out, or I am finished," Quinn said. "I overheard a conversation between Catherine, who I am guessing is also Veronica, the woman who gave us the wine, and another lady, a very good looking Latina."

Shawn perked up when he heard 'very good looking Latina' but recovered so that Tasha barely noticed.

"What did you learn?" Tasha asked.

"I didn't understand it at the time, but they spoke about poisoning the risotto, poisoning someone else at the restaurant, and phasing out the distribution of the polymer at the Silverado and some other places they didn't mention by name."

"They must have access to the kitchen. Either they are the owners, management, or they work in the kitchen," Shawn said.

Quinn nodded. "They also talked about genetic engineering, and some other stuff I can't remember," he looked down, upset that his judgment and memory were clouded that night by too much wine.

"It is amazing that Ron is hanging on, even if by a thread," Joshua said. "Both of them would be dead if they hadn't benefited from your timely diagnosis, Shawn, and your invention Quinn. You have to admit, that stuff is miraculous."

"Sometimes I wish it didn't work so well, but I am glad your friend is still alive," Quinn said.

"Well, we need to find out the connection between the manufacture of your polymer and the attack on Ron and Virginia, so that you don't get blamed for a crime you didn't commit. It's crazy, but if these two weird events are linked, we need to find out how," Minh said.

"And we need to figure out a way to get Catherine's DNA," Joshua said. "We have to prove that she's Catherine Michinski and she didn't die in that accident at Devil's Slide."

"And we have a party to go to right now," Shawn said, looking at both Quinn and Tasha. "Quinn, you and I have some real estate to buy. And we need to start drinking wine like that '47 Cheval Blanc. Quinn has to taste all of the titans, and I have to taste them all with him. So let's go to the Gala and taste some great wine tonight. First thing tomorrow, we'll start to solve these problems."

"I couldn't agree with you more," Tasha said. "Will you go over to the auction with Quinn? I'll join you over there. I have something important to discuss with my brother before he heads back to Atherton."

Minh looked ruefully at Joshua and then dropped his gaze.

"If you all will excuse me, I am going down to Stanford Medical Center to watch over Mr. Park," Jeff said.

"Sure Tasha. We'll see you there. Don't be late," Shawn said.

Shawn and Quinn left the courtyard and headed towards the front of the resort. Shawn handed a ticket to the valet and waited for his car to be brought around.

"You and I have something else to talk about also," he said, looking seriously at Quinn.

"What?" Quinn asked.

"As soon as we're in the car," Shawn said.

The valet came around with the car. Shawn got in the driver's side, and Quinn got into the passenger's side after placing the half case of wine for later consumption into the trunk.

"All right, what has you so uptight?" Quinn asked. "That's my job, remember?"

"Actually, I just have one thing to tell you. You need to make your drug, and start taking it, period," Shawn said.

"If I do that I am toast," Quinn said. "Didn't I tell you they've interrogated me four times and have taken blood samples? They nearly killed me last time, the stupid bastards. If they see that I am taking it, they'll assume for sure that it is me who is making it. I am the last person in the world who should be taking that stuff. Besides, as it turns out, I think this Catherine slipped us some in that bottle of wine she bought for us. I may be toast already. The next time the feds take me will be my last, unless I can clear my name before then."

Shawn looked puzzled for a second, but ignored the comment.

"If you don't take it, you'll die. That polymer reverses vascular pathology and got that couple through Amanita poisoning and cyanide poisoning, who's to say it won't mitigate or even reverse pulmonary hypertension?"

"Scylla and Charybdis," Quinn said. "If I take it, I go to prison, if I don't, I die. But I felt it Shawn, today I felt better than I should have, more energy, just better. If one dose slipped into a bottle of wine can do that…."

"Take the meds, formulate an escape plan, fuck the feds, and save yourself. We'll do our thing, and when it looks like they'll come and harass you again, you get out, go somewhere where they can't extradite you."

"I have no idea where I could go and not be extraditable. At least no place where I would like to be," Quinn said.

"Yeah, Damascus, Yemen, Nigeria, no places for an American ex-pat. I think you could go to Dubai. At least that place is civilized. But I don't think they sell a lot of wine there. You're right. We'll do some homework. Maybe you can go to Argentina or something. They make good wine there," Shawn said.

"I don't know. I have managed to do the right thing since this whole thing went down a few years ago, and don't want to break my word."

"Quinn, the feds are treating you like a criminal, at least you can earn that right by saving your own life. For Christ's sake, you have the tools to undo what that blood clot and the feds did to you! Do it!"

"Not yet," Quinn said, looking out the window at the vines growing in the vineyards they were passing. "If we manage to get Catherine, and she goes to jail, and the feds get off my back, maybe I'll try."

Shawn nodded in understanding. "Have your cake and eat it too," he said. "To hell with the feds. You deserve to get old and fat like the rest of us."

"We're almost there," Quinn said with a touch of optimism in his voice. He was frightened to be dealing with the remnants of the Michinski family, but for the first time since the harassment started, he felt like he was starting to dig himself out of the hole he was in. He was on to her now, he was certain. He just needed to know why Park and his wife were targeted.

Chapter 20:

Quinn and Shawn arrived at the Auction and registered. It was in an outdoor venue, and it was a perfect night with clear skies and comfortable temperatures. They picked up their numeric flags for bidding, and were assigned to Table #29, close to the front of the auction and right in the middle of the action.

They sat down alone at the table and Shawn immediately opened a bottle of Bryant Family Cabernet, pouring a generous for Quinn and himself. After about half a glass, Quinn excused himself to go to the men's room, and as he returned, he ran smack into a beautiful and shockingly fit Latina woman, dressed in a black evening gown. She had shoulder length black hair, flawless skin, and perfect proportioned features. Her body was trim, but not the emaciated look of a model that starved for the look. There was strength and sinew to her, and she pulled it off with out a trace of masculinity. She was something beyond gorgeous, and she was vaguely familiar to Quinn and that gave him an uneasy feeling. Was this the woman he saw at the Spa?

"Excuse me ma'am," he said, looking intently at her, trying to see if he recognized her. She was familiar, but from that night? He found himself so absolutely taken with her beauty that he almost forgot his foreboding. As she turned to answer, her look of surprise suggested she recognized him.

"Dr. Quinn, oh my gosh!" she gushed.

"Ma'am, have we met?" Quinn asked.

"Dr. Quinn," she said awkwardly, tilting her head with a puzzled expression, before returning to her smile. "I guess it isn't a surprise you don't remember. My goodness you look better than the last time I saw you."

"And when was that?" Quinn asked. "Forgive me, you are so familiar, but I can't place you. And you look so absolutely smashing tonight. What's your name?"

"Thank you." Her smile was disarming, and Quinn's heart nearly jolted out of his chest. She was perhaps the most striking woman he had ever seen. In addition to her spectacular fitness, she looked graceful and light on her feet. Quinn hadn't physically reacted to a woman this way since Tasha.

"I am the one who hit you when you crawled onto the street in Berkeley. I am Josephine Rodriguez, and I am delighted to see you have recovered so well."

Quinn realized that she was the angel he saw in Berkeley. It would be too much of a coincidence for her to also be the one at the spa, he told himself, and he wanted to believe it. He smiled at her, suffocating in her radiance.

"If you hadn't stopped and helped me, I'd have died out there on the street. I owe you a debt of gratitude. What is your connection to wine country?"

"I'm glad you see it that way, I'm here with my law partners, but my connection to wine country is with Henri Paradis. Our families go way back, and I grew up here. Now I get to do some work for him from time to time."

"I see, we're sharing a table with him tonight," Quinn said.

"You'll have to excuse me for beating the subject to death, but I'm sometimes just the worst damn driver," she said. "All I've been able to think about is that if I wasn't so tired, if I had stopped a little better, if I hadn't agreed to meet my sister for coffee, I wouldn't have hit you."

"Josephine, you bumped my lower leg and foot. It gave me a scrape and a bruise, I barely even broke a bone."

"But the clot…."

"How can you be responsible for a clot which was already there? I mean no insult by it, but lawyers have funny notions about responsibility sometimes," Quinn said, trying to be disarming.

"Maybe we do. You're sitting with Henri tonight," Josephine said, looking at Quinn with respect, and was there something else? He felt all of his viscera churning inside him.

"Yes, we're at table #29," Quinn said speaking a little too fast. "Where are you?"

"We have a table in the corner, #41," she said. "I'll be over later tonight to say hello."

"Well," Quinn said smiling at her as he told himself to slow down and calm down. "If you promise to come and have a glass of wine with me tonight, I promise not to file any lawsuits about my scraped leg."

"Okay," she replied. "I'll come over, but can I have that in writing?"

"You can have whatever you want," Quinn said and cursed himself for the enthusiasm and desperation in his voice.

She smiled a genuine smile at him and returned to her seat. Quinn went back to sit down to Shawn's interrogating expression.

"Who was that?" he asked.

"That striking lady was the young attorney who ran me over in Berkeley," Quinn replied. "Quite a looker, don't you think?"

"She's not the same woman from the spa, is she?"

"Couldn't be," Quinn said, trying to sound certain. "Definitely not."

"You sound like you're trying to sound certain. But I have to agree with you, pal. She's welcome to run me over any time." Shawn said. "How come you got so lucky? If a car hit me, it would be a senile ninety year-old man. But Quinn, you should be careful with lawyers."

"If I'm given half the chance, I will be," Quinn said. "…careful, that is. Now pour me some more of that wine."

A moment later Tasha walked in, waved amicably, and joined them.

"Quinn, you look relaxed for maybe the first time since I saw you here. And you're not even drunk," she said teasing him.

"Thanks, Tasha" he said, smiling back. "How was the meeting with Minh?"

"How do you think it was?" Tasha snapped.

"If I were him, I probably would have done the same thing," Quinn said.

"At least you'd have an excuse," Tasha said. "They're off to Atherton, and Jeff is off to guard Ron. I wasn't too hard on him. I understand that after the hyperbaric treatment, they claim to have seen Park reaching for his breathing tube. Purposeful movements, like his brain might still be partially intact. What do you think about that?"

Quinn shrugged but said nothing.

"Tasha, I don't want to butt in where I am not welcome, but go easy on your brother. Minh and Joshua aren't Quinn's enemy, Catherine and her Latina henchwoman are," Shawn said glancing over at Josephine, "And maybe the feds too."

Tasha raised her eyebrows, giving him the look Quinn remembered with a sinking feeling. "I don't wish to discuss it, Shawn." He nodded to her, and smiled. It was water off of a duck's back.

Quinn saw Henri Paradis, his daughter and her husband walk in. Henri briefly spoke with someone in registration.

He smiled and hugged one of the hostesses before walking with the square shoulders of unshakeable dignity toward them. He had a satchel in one hand. Quinn watched in silence as Paradis sat down at the table with them, wondering what was in the satchel as Paradis turned immediately to him.

"Dr. Quinn, correct? You're the former owner of Wildhorse up on the ridge?"

Quinn nodded silently.

"I think you made some great wine. I hope the new owners take the same care in managing that place as you did."

"That's a very nice thing to say, Mr. Paradis," Quinn said. "And it means a lot coming from you. I look forward to your speech tonight."

"Please, it's Henri. Mr. Paradis is my father, God rest his soul," Paradis said with a smile.

They eased into a conversation, as though they had known each other for a long time. Quinn marveled at how relaxed Paradis was. He remained a champion and a cheerleader for Napa Valley, even as it evolved away from his vision. He still exuded class, quality and quiet strength. There was a youthfulness and warmth about him which belied the troubles he had suffered in recent years, and which were splashed all about the local and national wine publications like tabloid gossip. He found himself captivated by the man in a very short time.

Soon the lights dimmed and the Master of Ceremonies came to the microphone. He gave a brief and subdued speech announcing the death of Virginia Park, and said Ronald Park remained in critical condition, unconscious at Stanford University. There was icy silence in the audience as he spoke.

Quinn leaned in toward Shawn. "I bet half the crowd is worried about Park, and the other half…."

"Hopes he dies?" Shawn offered.

"I bet they only regret that it happened in such an ugly way, disrupting the idyllic setting here," Quinn said.

"Yeah," Shawn said quietly. "Murder doesn't really fit the scene here, does it?"

"Do you think she'll be here tonight?" Quinn asked.

"Who?"

"Catherine, or Veronica, or whatever her name is now," Quinn said.

"Not if she's smart," Shawn said.

"We're going to get her," Quinn said to himself.

After the MC finished his acknowledgment and there was a moment of silence for Park and his late wife, he announced Henri Paradis, who was to give the speech tonight in Park's stead.

Henri walked up to the microphone deftly, but without hurrying. He smiled before he began speaking, making eye contact with numerous people in the crowd. He began his speech as if he were in front of a group of close friends. He had no notes, but told a story of Napa Valley as though he had told it a thousand times. He spoke about the humble beginnings of Napa Valley, the cowboy and farmer days.

Paradis was charismatic, and the audience was drawn to his every word. The only person clearly ignoring the speech championing the pioneers of the Napa wine industry and early culture was his younger brother, who was talking loudly at his table to, Quinn figured, a bunch of cronies and yes-men. He noticed with a chuckle that they were again drinking central valley Zinfandel. Quinn shook his head.

Paradis spoke of the years leading up to the famed 1976 Paris tasting, told of the frequent impromptu blind tastes done in fine restaurants for patrons in the likes of New York, London, Los Angeles, and Chicago where those Napa pioneers and Paradis himself would often go and purchase high-end Bordeaux bottlings for the patrons and invite them to taste it against their own bottlings.

It was clear by the speech that he was as much a vital part of the valley today as he had always been, and the audience demonstrated a reverence for him that was touching.

Quinn was listening to Paradis when there was a nudge at his side. He turned to see Josephine Rodriguez smiling back at him.

"Here I am. What are you pouring?" Her eyes sparkled, and her smile was utterly infectious.

Quinn looked around seeing only empty bottles, but Shawn was lightening fast into his satchel and pulled out a 25 year-old bottle of Chateau Margaux.

"Ms. Rodriquez, I presume? This is drinking just fantastic right now. I think you two will enjoy it." Swiftly and gracefully, he cut the capsule and corked the wine. Quinn shrugged at her and smiled, and she returned his gaze as a fresh glass was poured for her, and Quinn refilled his empty glass to a large grin from Shawn and a wary look from Tasha. Josephine knelt down at the table beside Quinn, managing to do it with grace, and Quinn deferred introducing her, giving proper respect to the speaker, to whom they were all primarily engaged.

The thirty-minute speech drew to a close and there was enthusiastic applause. Quinn noticed that Paradis managed to avoid saying anything about Park.

Paradis seemed at ease, and turned to Quinn, and acknowledged the presence of Josephine Rodriguez. With a wave of his hand, she was given a chair.

"Josephine, you are more beautiful by the day," Henri began. "I understand that congratulations are in order. No one deserves partnership as much as you do. I've never been more pleased to have such a counselor available to me," he said with genuine warmth.

"Partner, Josephine? I am so happy for you," Quinn said, raising his glass.

"How's your sister?" Paradis asked.

"She's well, thank you for asking," Josephine said. "I saw her just recently. And I must say it is wonderful to see you here tonight. I loved your speech. It's important for the newcomers to realize what it took for Napa Valley to get where it is today."

"Your late father played a big role here during that time, my father said there was never a finer vineyard manager in the entire New World."

"Your family treated him well, when most others wouldn't even look him in the eye," she said, "undocumented as he was."

"He earned our respect, Josephine, just as you have. I believe in merit more than imaginary and arbitrary borders, and I saw merit in your father immediately, just as my father did."

"You have an amazing perspective," she said.

"I see you are acquainted with Dr. Quinn."

"Henri," Quinn said. "If you insist on Henri, than I must insist on either 'Matthew' or 'Quinn' but none of this Dr. Quinn business. It makes me sound like the medicine woman."

"Fair enough," Paradis smiled. He introduced those at the table that they did not know: his daughter, his current vineyard manager, his winemaker and son-in-law, and a long-time patron of his establishment.

There was a bustling as the first item for the live-auction was moved onto the stage. Wine and merrymaking became the order of things, and auction paddles began waving. Paradis turned to Shawn and spoke.

"You aren't the doctor who bid on the plot I recently sold, the one off of the Silverado Trail, are you?"

Shawn turned crimson, which given his pale skin was a spectacular sight. "Jesus, I am sorry, I meant no disrespect by it. We're just looking around for great land, and Mr. Paradis, you have no shortage of that."

"I am sorry, too," Paradis said. "Sorry I did not sell the land to you. The other offer was for three million more, but was an anonymous bidder, who turned out to be none other than my brother, trying to fan the flames of our feud. It would have been much better to have you as a neighbor."

"Well, I am honored, and if you decide to sell any more land, I'm still interested," he said with a disarming smile.

"Hopefully not, but if it comes to it, I'll look you up," Paradis said with a smile of his own. "Now, ladies and gentlemen," he said, motioning everyone to come into the center of the table so he might speak more softly. "I have a surprise for all of you. This is something from my own personal cellar. You won't find this at any of the national auction houses."

He presented a magnum of red wine that appeared very old, had a wax capsule and a slightly stained handwritten label. Quinn heard frantic whispering between people at an adjoining table. Paradis looked at them and smiled.

"Some know the folklore of the valley, I see," Paradis said with a sparkle in his eye.

"Is that, I mean, is that from the plot that is currently under ummm…." Josephine spoke with absolute shock on her face.

"Dispute. Yes it is. This is from 1968, my father labeled it 'Blend, Plot 1'. It's a funny story. He had some peculiar ideas about that land. But the results are, well, I'll let you decide for yourselves." He used a pocket-knife to peel away the wax, and an Ah-So opener to preserve the integrity of the cork. He opened the bottle, and poured a glass for everyone at the table.

Quinn looked at Josephine who had her eyes glued upon Paradis. "Henri, I remember hearing my father speak of this wine and that land, but I didn't realize that there was anything left."

Quinn leaned over to Tasha. "I bet Minh and Joshua won't be too happy when they hear about this!"

"Serves him right!" she said, and Quinn was pretty sure she meant it.

Quinn smelled the wine, and felt a sense of *deja-vu.* The smell was something old-world. He tasted the wine, which unlike most Napa cabs more than 40 years old, was absolutely ageless. Quinn savored the taste, which was sweet, fragrant, and at once brand new. It was hands down better than the Margaux, or any other wine they had had since arriving in Napa Valley.

"My God, Henri!" Quinn stammered. "This is… this is perfection in a bottle!"

"There's about 2% residual sugar in it, but you wouldn't know that by tasting it, the acid makes it taste dry as a bone," Henri explained.

The others at the table were speechless. After an inordinately long silence, Shawn turned to Quinn.

"Quinn, this reminds me a little bit of the '47 Cheval Blanc."

"Shawn, nothing reminds anyone of the '47 Cheval. That was a once in a thousand year fluke," Tasha said.

Gabrielle Wooten, Henri's daughter spoke up.

"I think I have to agree with Shawn. I once had a bottle of the '47 Cheval, at my wedding," she said smiling and turning to kiss her husband Andrew on the cheek. He smiled sheepishly.

"I can't believe you corked and drank that bottle! What was the occasion?" Tasha asked Quinn.

Quinn shrugged. "You never know what day will be your last day on earth."

"It's funny that you mention the '47 Cheval. It's just what my father said," Paradis said to Shawn. "If course it is not a dead-ringer, but year in and year out, it seems to taste similar to this. I think there is also a unique yeast profile and terroir in that parcel of land which influences the wine. Being over a mineral spring, I think the sulfur in the groundwater produces a unique mix of native yeasts. It also keeps fungus and other rot it in check. We've never added yeast, just letting the natural yeast on the grapes do the fermentation."

"That's taking a chance," Shawn said. "Can't you get Brettanomyces and other bad yeast or off-flavors if you do that?"

"There're chemicals in the mineral spring which prevent the overgrowth of some strains of yeast. At least, that's our guess," Henri said.

"I think I could talk myself into believing that," Shawn said, tasting the wine again. "This is absolutely unbelievable wine, Henri. Absolutely. Unbelievable."

The auction was now in full swing, and the tables took time to listen to the Master of Ceremonies introduce the second item. A ten-year Vertical of Magnums from the Chevalier property on Spring Mountain and a trip to Switzerland with the winemaker was up. The item was going for nearly $110,000, when Alfonse held his card up and shouted, "$150,000!"

Henri rolled his eyes, as his brother won the lot.

"Arrogant son-of-a-bitch!" Quinn heard Paradis's daughter say just audibly.

"At least it's for a good cause," Paradis whispered to her.

The evening continued, with more wine and more misbehavior from Alfonse Paradis, who made a spectacle of himself lobbing lavish bids upon absurd prizes he could not possibly have wanted. On a number of occasions Quinn looked to Henri Paradis who seemed to be the target of such behavior. A few times he saw a subtle twitch and a just perceptible head shake, but for the most part, Henri seemed to enjoy the auction, doing his best to ignore his brother.

Quinn spent the next two hours engaged with Josephine. "How long have you done pro-bono work in the valley for the immigrant field-hands?" he asked.

"Just since moving up here from San Francisco," she said. "Before that I was a public defender and had no time."

"What is your connection to that, I mean why them? Is it your family, your heritage, or is there another reason?"

"My father was one of the thousands of undocumented immigrants who worked in Napa Valley before it became what it is today. My sister and I grew up on Paradis's land, and Henri helped me pay for college and law school. It was out of respect for my father, who rose from a field hand to be his father's and later his vineyard manager."

"Tell me about the rest of your family," Quinn asked.

"There's not much to say, my mother died back in the early eighties, when we were just girls, my father died of cancer twelve years ago, my sister left Napa for the Bay area after high school and we didn't keep in touch. I don't know any of my relatives in Mexico."

They continued their small talk for most of the evening.

Of the fifty lots in the Auction, Henri's brother took seven of them, and was the big winner for the year, proclaimed by the Master of Ceremonies. As the night was drawing to a close, the MC smiled the sort of smile that suggested a juicy secret. An unpublished lot was becoming something of a tradition at the auction, so no one had yet left for the night. Shawn had apparently seen the same thing.

"This should be interesting," Shawn said.

Quinn nodded silently.

"Ladies and gentlemen," The Master of Ceremonies began. "We have a surprise, a bonus lot donated at the last minute. This deserves your attention, Ladies and Gentlemen, because like the Paris Tasting of 1976, it goes right to the heart of Napa Valley legend."

The murmur in the crowd grew in intensity.

"I am speaking of a wine so special its very existence has been the subject of rumor, innuendo, and plausible deniability. But we have solicited an expert from Christy's Auction House who has verified its authenticity, both by micro aspiration of the contents, and by extensive MRI analysis. I am speaking of these two beautiful double magnums of personal family wine from the legendary family plot of Paradis vineyards, known only as Plot One. This is a 1968 vintage of the wine, and has been deep in the Paradis Cellar since it was made more than 40 years ago.

"They do MRI on wine?" Shawn asked, sounding incredulous. "And how do they do micro aspiration without spoiling the wine?"

"If it's priceless, they do," Tasha whispered. "You can learn a lot from an MRI. I learned about it when I took some wine courses at UC Davis. With micro aspiration they use a long slender needle that passes between the cork and the bottle, it is so small it can pass without breaking the seal. They can sample the wine and use gas chromatography or other tests to see if it is spoiled."

"You are brilliant!" Shawn said, and then he turned to Quinn. "Think a tool like that could have tainted the wine that poisoned Park?"

Quinn considered this, acknowledging that it was possible before turning back to Josephine.

There was a profound gasp from the audience as the MC finished his introduction of the final lot. Henri Paradis smiled a knowing smile, and glanced over at his brother, who shot a furious glance at him. Alfonse looked off-balance for the first time all evening.

"And the old man strikes back," Quinn heard Shawn whisper sounding triumphant.

"Ladies and gentlemen," the Master of Ceremonies continued, "for two such legendary and priceless large format bottles of wine, I am going to open the bidding at $150,000.

A moment later, the frenzy began. Quinn looked at Henri Paradis who appeared very smug. It was clear that his daughter and her husband did not know that he had planned this.

"What would you give to be able to make wine from that plot of land?" Shawn whispered.

"It sounds like the wine practically makes itself on that plot," Quinn said.

He looked at a very wealthy couple, guessing that they were tycoons of some Dot-Com venture in the roaring 90's. They bid $600,000.00. A bidder, a brooding man of South-Asian descent across the aisle raised his paddle and bid $620,000.00. The man holding the paddle for the power couple nodded silently at his wife, waiting for an imperceptible okay, and raised the bid to $640,000.00. The audience gasped. The man across the aisle was not finished yet, though. He raised his paddle indicating a bid of $660,000.00. The man looked at him shrewdly, narrowed her gaze. He took a deep breath and waited for approval from his wife. She gave it, and he raised her paddle, bringing the total to $680,000.00. Their competition shrugged, ceding the bottles. At the close of the last lot, there was a resounding standing ovation for the plot, and talk of the legendary wine began buzzing though the crowd immediately.

Quinn saw, out of the corner of his eye, Henri's brother, get up quietly and move toward the exit. As Quinn saw him exit, he saw two men in suits enter. Feds? They made their way toward his table.

Here we go again.

Quinn felt both trapped and panicked. He thought about the wine he had drunk at the Silverado, and immediately began looking for an escape.

In the next moment, he was shocked to see the men approach Henri Paradis. Henri looked surprised. There was a hushed conversation between them. One of the agents pulled out a pair of handcuffs, but the other one shook his head decisively and the first agent put the cuffs back in his pocket. Henri managed to maintain his dignity as they escorted him out of the auction area, right in the midst of his triumph. The looks of alarm were visible on the faces of his daughter and her husband. Josephine Rodriguez saw the men leaving with Henri Paradis and turned to Quinn.

"Please excuse me, Matthew, I have to leave now. It has been a real pleasure getting to know you. Here is my card again, and my cell phone number, I hope we can get together soon, please call me. I'm sorry. This, whatever it is, needs my attention right now," she said quickly and hurried off before Quinn could answer her.

Quinn was relieved that the men were not after him as he was so accustomed to, but was curious about why they had arrested Henri Paradis.

"There she goes," he said, watching her exit.

"Boy you just can't get a break can you, buddy?" Shawn said.

Chapter 21:

Quinn awoke in his room at the Silverado Springs. Shawn had not made it back to the room. For once he didn't care. Especially since he felt, for the first time in years, a strong and immediate attraction to Josephine Rodriguez, "the lawyer chick," as Shawn referred to her.

He was still wondering what had caused the authorities to arrest Henri Paradis, making her rush off the night before when Shawn marched into the room with a copy of the *Napa Valley Register.*

"Take a look at this," he said, throwing a second copy of the paper at Quinn.

"They say gasoline and dynamite were used, old fashioned dynamite! Pretty low tech, don't you think?" Quinn asked.

"No, below that," Shawn said, pointing to the article.

"I'll be damned," Quinn said, the fog on his hangover starting to lift. "They think Henri Paradis tried to kill Ronald Park?"

"Read the article," Shawn said. "The bottle of '74 Martha's Vineyard was laced with potassium cyanide." At some point in the past that stuff was used to make cupric cyanide, which was used as an anti-pest agent in vineyards. They were able to match the cyanide in the wine with cyanide stored on Paradis's land.

"What about the dynamite?" Quinn asked. "Did he do that too?"

"Well, dynamite is commonly used to clear stumps out when planting a vineyard. That wasn't what they traced, though. They found the cyanide in Paradis's work shed."

"Shawn, it's only been what, two days? How'd they get on this so quick?" Quinn asked.

"I guess they had another tip. Besides, it isn't news that Park had single handedly destroyed the reputation of Paradis. Paradis is in deep financial trouble, and was depending on good scores to market his wine. He not only didn't get them, he was crucified by Park's reviews, and they figure this is the only way the Paradis was going to stop the bleeding and hold onto his empire."

Quinn read the article quickly, and then put it down. "Boy, that guy we had dinner and wine with last night just doesn't seem the type to do such a thing."

"I agree, he seems too classy to go after someone like that, but the cyanide is his, and remember the way he attacked his brother at the Bounty Hunter? The guy has a temper."

"It'd be easier to believe that he killed his brother than it would to believe he killed Ron Park," Quinn muttered. "But you're right about his temper."

"What do you think about his motive?"

"Revenge?" Quinn asked. "It's something everyone understands, but it doesn't suit him. Preserving what is left of his legacy is more plausible, but the whole thing is way too theatrical."

"We don't really know him Quinn," Shawn cautioned. "With Park out of the way, the other critics might embrace his product, and then he would recover."

"Shawn, you're forgetting a few things. This is all too easy, and too pretty. The methods used to try and kill Park, they were obvious and easy to trace. This thing has to be a frame job. Remember that conversation about the risotto?" Quinn asked.

"Right, but that was the murder of Virginia, not Ron Park," Shawn said.

"Do you think that both she and Park were targeted for murder, and the two murders aren't related?" Quinn asked rhetorically, "*Lex parsimoniae*, Shawn."

"Well, the odds are against it," Shawn conceded.

"And the odds are our instincts are also right. Paradis is being framed for this murder by the same people who are making my polymer," Quinn said, his adrenaline-fueled mind sharpening. "Remember that tip Sherriff Hernandez was talking about? It was strange how quick that came in.

Someone is manipulating law enforcement, the feds, everyone!"

"Someone?" Shawn asked.

"Catherine," Quinn said.

"So what do we do?" Shawn asked.

"We have to tell someone about that conversation I overheard in the spa, which suggests Henri Paradis is innocent."

"How does it do that," Shawn asked.

"Whoever killed Virginia has to be the same person who poisoned Park. And we know it was Catherine and the Latina woman."

"Why don't I go and find out who the hottie is that works in the spa, and you go out and speak with Josephine Rodriguez, let her know what you know about what you heard, and that we think Paradis is innocent," Shawn said. "I assume that her leaving last night means that she is representing him."

"Yeah, Josephine seems like a level-headed person," Quinn said. "I'll explain to her what I know, maybe she can help Henri, and maybe by doing so, she can also help me."

"But then again, you don't know her that well, either," Shawn said hesitating, wrinkling his forehead. "You're sure she wasn't the one at the spa?"

"Again, what are the odds that she is the one who hits me in Berkeley, then finds me again here, and that she is stealing my polymer and killing Virginia, and trying to kill Park?"

Shawn looked back at Quinn with a smug expression. "Not as long as you think, Quinn. Maybe she knew where you were going to be dumped off and was conveniently there, in Berkeley. Maybe she tailed you here, and 'accidentally' bumped into you again, and maybe she is the one manufacturing your polymer, and is close enough to Paradis and so able to frame him. Her father managed his vineyards, she might know where chemicals are kept. I just don't know the motive for framing him, and killing Park and his wife. But

Quinn, you have to admit, she matches your description, I mean, she's gorgeous."

"Framed Paradis and is now representing him?" Quinn asked, looking hurt. "Jesus Christ, Shawn, I like this girl!"

Shawn looked apologetically at Quinn. "I am sorry, man. Look, I hope she's not involved either. I just think you should be careful. Maybe you should go to the Napa police, and not directly to her."

"If I went to Napa police, they'd relay any information I had to Josephine if she's representing him. It would look suspicious if she knew I didn't want to give that information directly to her. Besides, I am certain she wasn't the woman in the spa."

"Okay, pal. It's your call. I'd just be careful giving her too much information about your situation unless you think she can help you," Shawn said. "Tasha had a wary feeling about her, and her motivation with respect to you," Shawn said.

Quinn felt a surge of anger. "For Christ's sake, Shawn, I don't date anyone for more than four years, and the first person I am interested in since my ex-girlfriend, who is carrying on with my best friend, gives her a moral crisis about my well-being? That's bullshit!"

"Maybe you're right. I was out of line for bringing it up," Shawn said.

"I'll consider it," Quinn said.

"Consider what?" Shawn asked.

"Consider being careful what I say to Josephine, though I doubt that she's involved in stealing my polymer and framing the man who gave her father a job when no one in the valley would touch undocumented immigrants, and paid for her college. That would make her a monster."

"Fair enough, and I did not get that impression from her in the least. She really seemed to like you," Shawn offered.

"What in the world do the people who are making my polymer have against Henri Paradis and Ronald Park? Why frame Henri for the murder of Park, and why try to kill Park in the first place?"

"Who hates Park?" Shawn asked.

"Half the valley hates him, and everyone thinks he has too much power," Quinn said. "Unless you are sitting on a pile of money, what he writes dictates your fortunes if you are in the industry. Even if you do have a pile of money, what he writes dictates whether that pile gets bigger or smaller. I'd say a lot of people would be threatened by that power."

"Especially someone stretched to the end of his financial leverage," Shawn acknowledged.

"The man was selling land, and you don't get that back in Napa Valley. He was near the end, all right," Quinn said, sadly reflecting on the recent sale of his own land.

"It is really convenient that Henri had a reason to kill Park, but we know that someone else killed Virginia. That someone is Catherine, if the risotto is where the poisonous mushrooms came from," Shawn said.

"Is there a chance that Park killed his wife, or hired someone to do it for him?" Quinn asked.

"Maybe. Didn't Minh or Joshua say that the two had been fighting?" Shawn asked.

"I think they mentioned marital problems, but I just can't convince myself that the murder of Virginia is not related to the attempt on Park's life. It makes no sense that the two would coincide like this, but not be related," Quinn said.

"What about the second question?" Shawn asked.

"Second question?"

"If Paradis didn't do it, someone's framed him. Either it was Catherine, or someone else. If Catherine framed Paradis, why? And if she didn't, who did?"

"Well, the only other person I can think of is his brother," Quinn said, scratching his head. "It would be strange to have him connected to this scheme, though."

"I agree," Shawn said. "But maybe Alfonse wants Henri so leveraged he has to sell that disputed plot. If so, then Henri played right into his hands by auctioning that wine off. Now the legend of that tract of land is the buzz of the valley.

The ultra-rich will be knocking each other over for a chance to bid on that land."

"So this thing with Paradis might be about land, and Paradis's brother stands to gain the most?" Quinn asked. "You think the murder attempt and frame job is about a land grab?"

"It's possible, but it's weird, because if Alfonse tried to kill Park and framed his brother, he has offed the goose who, from his standpoint, has laid the golden eggs. I mean, Alfonse liked how Park was such an iconoclast. He celebrated each failure in Napa. Why kill the dragon slayer?" Shawn said. "Besides, he looked like he'd seen a ghost when Henri auctioned off those two double-magnums, bringing all the attention to the disputed plot."

"Right," Quinn said. "It's almost too easy."

"Then again, maybe we're over thinking it," Shawn said.

"Wouldn't be the first time," Quinn acknowledged. "But if that theory is right, he should have been happy about the last auction item, and he clearly wasn't. Maybe he's a really good actor."

Shawn nodded. "Give Josephine a call and meet with her, and I'll wander over to the kitchen here at the restaurant and see if I can get a handle on Catherine and her link to the Silverado. I'll see whether she was around the day Virginia ate the risotto. Then I'll go over to the spa and find out if there are any hot Latina chicks who work there."

"All right, I'll get cleaned up and go," Quinn said. "You also need to see if there is any connection between Catherine and Alfonse Paradis." Shawn nodded his assent.

Shawn left the room and Quinn jumped in the shower, shaved, and cleaned himself up. He called Josephine and arranged to meet her for lunch. Initially she told him she was too busy organizing a defense for Henri Paradis, but she acquiesced after Quinn told her he had some information that might be relevant.

He waited outside the Spa where she picked him up in her BMW. They drove off to a small locals-only restaurant in an out of the way place in the Napa city limits. They sat down at a corner table of the not-too-busy restaurant. The city still seemed to be in a hazy slumber from the festivities the night before. When Quinn made to talk about Henri, she demurred asking him to wait until they got back to her office. When lunch was done, she drove him to her office in downtown Napa. He sat in a comfortable chair facing her as she sat down behind her desk.

"Matthew, how could it be that you have information which is relevant to my case. I thought you met Henri just yesterday?"

Quinn took a deep breath. "Josephine," he began.

"You can call me Josie," she said. "Just don't call me J-Rod."

"Okay, Josie, I am in hot water with the federal government because they think I am making an illegal polymer drug for which they hold the patent. I invented the polymer several years ago when I was a researcher, and sold it to them when I retired from research."

Josephine looked at him confused. Sensing the confusion, Quinn explained. "It's relevant, just bare with me."

"Okay," she said, looking at him intently.

"So they think I am making it and marketing it in several places as an herbal concoction. One of the marketing places is at the Silverado Resort here in Napa. I am not making the polymer, but someone is."

"Who?" she asked.

"A dead mob-boss's daughter, I think. I'll tell you more about her later. Suffice to say that knowing that the Silverado is one of the places peddling my polymer, I went sniffing around in the spa after hours. That's where they sell the stuff."

"Quinn, that's trespassing," she said, a sharp edge to her voice. "I am not your lawyer. The information you're giving me isn't privileged, I can make you testify to it, and I will if it clears Henri."

"I don't give a damn, you can be my lawyer if you want, but it won't matter because I am not going to be around long enough to go on trial."

She looked at him incredulously, but said nothing.

"Here's where it gets interesting, I overheard a conversation acknowledging that in addition to making my polymer and marketing it, two women, a Catherine somebody and a thirty-something Latina woman whose name I don't know, have plans to do something else. They want to grow it or manufacture it with genetic engineering. I couldn't fully understand, just hearing one side of a phone conversation."

"Matthew, while I am sympathetic to your problems, what does this have to do with Henri?" she demanded.

"Well, it sounds like one of these women, the Catherine woman, was meddling with a dish of mushroom risotto eaten by Virginia Park, at least we think she was, and that was specifically mentioned in the conversation."

Josephine's confusion seemed to be growing.

"Josephine, we're waiting for the autopsy results, but we believe that Virginia's death was due to intentional poisoning with amanita mushrooms, and that the mushrooms were given to her in the risotto."

"And this Catherine person did it?" Josephine asked.

"Yeah."

"Well, what does that have to do with Park's poisoning?" she asked.

"We haven't definitely linked the two, but we think that the murders can't be separate events with nothing to unify them. Someone kills Virginia and tries to kill Park on the same weekend; they have to be related, don't you think?"

Josephine was silent, her hands steepled, and her eyes closed. She appeared deep in thought. Quinn waited in deafening silence for her to process what he said. He wondered what she was having such a difficult time with. When her eyes opened, it was as if her entire face had changed.

She seemed older, more sober, more reserved. When she finally spoke, her tone was measured. "A Latina woman, and another woman, named Catherine, you say?"

"Yes."

"I agree. It seems far-fetched to think two separate plots are at play here if Virginia's death was in fact a homicide. Any idea who these ladies are?" Josephine asked, "And more importantly, do either of them have a reason to want Park dead?"

"I don't have any idea who the Latina woman is. And as for Catherine, I don't know for sure, but I think she is the missing and presumed dead daughter of Vladimir Michinski. I suppose you don't know who that is," Quinn said.

Josephine was silent again, as if she were trying to piece together the puzzle herself. Quinn waited for her to process what he had said.

"No, I know exactly who he was," she said at last. "I was a public defender in San Francisco, and I knew of the Michinski family. Jesus, Quinn, what are you doing mixed up with the Russian Mafia?"

Quinn told her his story.

After he finished she looked at him with a mixture of incredulity and, he thought, increased respect. "There's a lot more to you than meets the eye Matthew Quinn, that's for sure," she said, taking a deep breath. "No wonder," she dropped her gaze and shook her head.

"No wonder what?" Quinn said.

"Nothing," Josephine said, maybe too quickly. "It's all so incredible, that's all." She looked at the ceiling, then the wall, anyplace, it seemed but at Quinn, who was staring at her.

"We don't know who this person is who was at the spa. But she was Latina and very good-looking. I never got a good look at her face."

"I know Henri would never be involved in anything like this, but whether this information is or isn't relevant, it sounds like it is a lot more complicated than a simple revenge murder," she said. "Thanks for coming to me with this."

"Josephine, I don't know why the people who are manufacturing my polymer would want to frame Henri, but there must be a reason. I just don't know what it is yet. The only other player who stands to gain is his brother, Alfonse. Maybe he's in on it too," Quinn offered.

"Alfonse is an arrogant and mean-spirited person, but I don't think his vitriol for his brother would go to the point of killing Park and framing Henri for murder," Josephine said. She sounded professional, distant, almost cold.

"What if it was worth tens of millions of dollars, meaning the sale of this disputed, legendary plot of vineyard land?" Quinn asked.

"I suppose theoretically you might have a point. He is one who stands to gain. But is there anyone else who might also stand to gain?"

Quinn shrugged. "Has Henri posted bail?"

"He was denied bail this morning. The judge thinks his international connections make him a flight risk. But I will try again this afternoon to convince the judge to let him go. Henri won't run, he'll work to clear his name," she said.

"I believe you. I also believe that this Catherine woman and her accomplice are behind manipulating the police, the feds, and the rest of it. Somehow the murder, the poisoning, the frame-job on Paradis, and the illegal production of my polymer are all related," Quinn said.

"Quite a situation you find yourself in, Quinn," she said. "You should retain a lawyer."

"I'm going to try," he said, smiling at her.

She smiled back. Her warmth seemed to return instantly. "Matthew, thanks for confiding in me. Thanks for all of this. If you need a lawyer, one of my partners would be an outstanding advocate for you. I can't represent you, and I will need to take an official statement from you about what you overheard."

"Too busy with the Paradis case? I told you they might be related," Quinn said.

"No, I have a conflict of interest," she said.

"Oh," Quinn said, not totally sure of what she meant.

She got up and circled behind him, placing her hands on his shoulders.

"You are damn near irresistible," she whispered in his ear, kneading his flesh as he melted in her arms.

"That feels so good," he muttered, closing his eyes.

She worked his shoulders for about five minutes, and then crossed to his front. His eyes opened, sensing her presence. His heart was thundering in his chest.

"Josephine, you have to know, I have been hurt," he said.

"I won't hurt you," she said.

"No, the day you found me, I was hurt. I had a clot, and it caused permanent changes to my heart and lungs. I'm damaged goods, Josephine. I'll be dead in a couple of years, maybe sooner," he said to her as her hands made their way down his front.

"Right now, Matthew, I can feel that you are very much alive," she said, a lascivious look in her eyes.

In what appeared to be a single move, she got her heels off, and hoisted her slim athletic frame onto his lap, straddling his midsection as she faced him. Before he could speak she locked her lips onto his. He felt her slight but powerful muscles clench around him as she pulled him hungrily toward her. He resisted only for a second before surrendering. He let his arms slide around her waist, and up onto the middle of her back. He fussed with her blazer for a moment before she released her arms, letting it slide off. His hands found their way up her loosened blouse.

He could feel her heart too, a strong athlete's heart, powerful and slow, as she pressed her chest against his. He drank her in, smelling her intoxicating scent, feeling her attacking him with the same abandon with which he wanted her. He stood, her legs still wrapped around his waist, and silently, his lips still locked onto hers, carried her to the leather couch against the wall. They sunk into it burying themselves in each other.

* * * * * *

Once outside her office, Quinn realized he had no way home. Not wanting to go back in and disturb her, he hailed a cab and returned to the resort. When he went to his room, he found Shawn and Tasha sitting at the table, a bottle of Chateau de Beaucastel Chateaneuf du Pape open and more than half empty.

"Well, you've got a glow about you," Tasha said. "Things went well, I take it?"

"Yeah," Quinn said, not making eye contact with Tasha.

Why do I feel guilty?

"Quinn," Shawn said jovially. "I went into the kitchen with an air of someone who belonged there, and asked about that woman who bought you the bottle of Orin Swift. They know her as Veronica. She hasn't been seen in the kitchen since the day we were at the Bounty Hunter, the same day Virginia had the Risotto. She's been in there a number of times before. No one really knows how she's tied to the Silverado, but they know she's in the ownership or management hierarchy. She's rumored to be dating someone who works there. Whenever she shows up, the other managers never seem to be around. Weird coincidence eh?"

"Yeah, weird," Quinn said, wrinkling his forehead in thought, trying to concentrate on what Shawn was saying. Guilt made no logical sense, but then again, guilt itself was not logical, Quinn thought. But he still felt guilty.

Shawn continued. "So then I marched right into the spa, made an appointment, and began asking about hot Latina women who work there. I thought it might be a good way to get right to the chase."

"You're audacious, Shawn, I'll give you that," Quinn said, shaking his head and smiling.

Shawn smiled. "They are currently in between managers at the spa. They don't have any hot Latina women who provide massages, but they did acknowledge a woman named Barbara Garcia. She's a health and wellness consultant who drops in and out. But she's not a regular, and apparently she only sees private clients. It is some sort of agreement with the upper management."

Quinn looked appreciatively at his friend. "Thanks, Shawn. I am going to call agent Snow from the Mystery Man division of the Federal Government."

"That guy who found you up in Fairplay while I was," Shawn broke off his conversation suddenly, as Tasha looked at him thoughtfully and he looked ruefully at Quinn.

"Sleeping it off, yes, the same day that we hosted Park," Quinn finished for Shawn.

Shawn looked relieved and said nothing more. Tasha looked at Shawn and then turned to Quinn.

"Do you think you can trust this guy?" she asked.

"I think so," Quinn replied. "He seemed like he was interested in the truth, at least, more so than the other agents I've encountered, plus he has a deep southern accent. You can't have a deep southern accent and be untrustworthy, can you?" Quinn asked half-joking.

"And you are sure you can trust Josephine?" Tasha asked. Her expression told Quinn she did not like Josephine.

"Absolutely," Quinn said.

"Absolutely?" she repeated.

"Tasha, what business is it of yours?" Quinn asked and immediately regretted it.

She was silent, eyes locked on Quinn. She shot a glance to Shawn, and then back to Quinn. "You're right. It's none of my business. But Matthew, I love you like a brother, and I don't want to see you hurt."

Quinn nodded.

"So give him a call," she said.

"Who?"

"Agent Snow," Tasha said. "Get the feds on your side."

"This guy has to give me a break," Quinn said.

Tasha smiled. "I hope he does. You deserve it after all of this."

"I know," Quinn said. He picked up the phone and called Snow's cell phone number. It clicked over to voicemail, and Quinn spoke clearly. "Agent Snow, this is Matthew Quinn. I have some information, which I believe might help you in your investigation into the illegal polymer production at the Silverado. Please give me a call at your earliest convenience. I am staying at the Silverado, room 218."

The three of them sat down to a final glass of the excellent beverage from the southern Rhone River region of France and enjoyed the fragrant earthy wine, which reminded Quinn of Autumn in a cornfield. Suddenly the phone rang. Quinn jumped up to answer it.

"Matthew Quinn," he said.

"Agent Snow. Dr. Quinn, I must admit my surprise here. I didn't expect that you would be contacting me," he said.

"Well, Agent Snow, I have some interesting information I have managed to uncover here," Quinn said. "I have some names which might be of interest in the case about the polymer I sold to the federal government some years back."

"I am listening," Snow said.

"First, there is a woman, her first name is Catherine, but she also goes by Veronica, and I can give you a description. She is somehow connected to the Silverado Springs Resort here in Napa. She's a major player in this. I don't know if she owns the resort, but she is connected. She seems to come and go, but no one at the resort knows what her role is. I believe that she is the daughter of Vladimir Michinski."

"That's impossible, Catherine Michinski was killed at Devil's Slide almost five years ago."

"Look at the reports. The news releases say her body was never found," Quinn said.

"That happens all the time in vehicles submerged for a long time. And her DNA was found in the car. She was in there," Snow said.

"But she could have gotten out, and this woman here, if she is a Michinski, would explain how she knew how my polymer was made," Quinn said.

"Have you looked over the cliff at Devil's Slide? It would be impossible to survive," Snow said.

"Unless she got out before the car went over the cliff," Quinn said, thinking on his feet.

"All right, so you're suggesting that she killed her father and brother and dumped them over the cliff, faking her own death then? How do you know the woman at the spa is familiar with the polymer?" he asked.

"She was talking with her friend, another woman, named Barbara Garcia. I overheard half the conversation. Catherine was the name identified on the other side of the phone. They spoke about the polymer, and were discussing a plan which utilized genetic engineering as some kind of alternate way of making the polymer."

"You only heard half the conversation?" Snow asked.

"Yes, but the bottom line is I was able to follow it. They were talking about the polymer, I am sure of it," Quinn said.

"What else?" Snow asked.

"They spoke about Catherine having poisoned someone at the Silverado, I think it was Ron Park's wife, Virginia."

"Ron Park, the wine critic?"

"Yeah, I think so," Quinn said.

"Why would they want to kill Park's wife?"

"I don't know that yet," Quinn said. "But I think they poisoned Ron Park, too."

"This sounds like bullshit, Dr. Quinn. They've got a suspect in custody for that crime. Did you know that?"

"Yeah, I know, but Henri Paradis is innocent," Quinn said.

"If you say so. Is that all you've got?" Snow asked.

"They spoke about someplace they referred to as 'Belmont.' It might be a coincidence, but when I was harassed several years ago by Vladimir Michinski and his men, they were working out of a physical plant called ‘Belmont Biogenetics.’ I wonder if this is the same plant, or at least the same physical setup.”

“Dr. Quinn, that lab was shut down and the equipment was auctioned off. There’s no such thing as Belmont Biogenetics,” he said.

Quinn was silent. He hoped he was going to end the conversation feeling cleared of any wrongdoing, but it did not seem that that would be the case. But he was determined. At last he spoke. “We think Henri Paradis was framed for the attempt on Park, and that this woman is somehow involved. I just don’t know what the connection between Paradis, Ron Park, these two women, and my polymer is, but they are all connected. And Henri’s brother, Alfonse, he might also be involved somehow.”

“Let me see if I get what you’re saying,” Snow said after a big sigh. “There is a woman named Catherine, who is presumed to be the dead daughter of Vladimir Michinski. She survived the plunge into the Pacific Ocean off of Devil’s Slide by jumping out of the car and sending her father and brother to a watery grave. She and her friend named Barbara Garcia, both of whom are connected to the Silverado, but you’re not sure how, are making your polymer, planning some sort of genetic engineering to enhance or change the product. They are also involved in the attempted murder of Ron Park and the murder of his wife, and they have framed Henri Paradis for those murders. And they are using, or at least referring to the old physical plant of Vladimir Michinski’s in Burlingame to make the polymer. They are framing you for the production of the polymer and framing Henri Paradis for the murder of the wine critic and also his wife?”

“And they plan on poisoning someone else at the Silverado,” Quinn blurted out, immediately regretting it. Listening to Snow’s tone made him feel stupid. He realized he sounded both desperate and pathetic.

“This is incoherent, Quinn,” Snow said. “What am I supposed to do with this?”

"I don't know, nothing maybe," Quinn said. "I just think I finally have a break in my case, the first break since I discovered that they were selling my polymer at the Silverado several years ago. I just want to be out of trouble and be able to go on with my life."

"You need a lot more than this to get your life back. I think we're done here," Snow said.

"At least go out and check out the old plant in Burlingame," Quinn requested.

"Our conversation's over, Quinn," he said and hung up.

"Great," Quinn said and hung up the phone. "That went well. I was hoping we were going to get Snow to check some of this out, but I guess we need to do some more homework before we talk with him again."

"Maybe we should go down to this Belmont place, and check out that old physical plant ourselves," Shawn offered.

Chapter 22:

Quinn and Shawn drove to the San Francisco Peninsula the next morning. Quinn had never been to Vladimir Michinski's pharmaceutical company, but he knew it was south of the city. Going through Internet news archives before leaving, Shawn was able to locate the old address. He discovered that the current tenant called itself "Infinite Wellness Natural Cosmetics and Herbs."

"That's got to be it, Shawn," Quinn said.

"Let's go down and see if we can't sneak in and look around," Shawn said.

"What kind of security would they have at a natural cosmetics plant?" Quinn wondered out loud.

"We're going to find out, but this might take more than an Ah-So and liquid courage to get us in," Shawn said. "But I've got everything we'll need."

"What if we get caught?" Quinn asked.

"Then they'll investigate, discover your polymer being made there, and they'll arrest the owner, Catherine Michinski, or whatever her name is. Remember Quinn, we want the feds to discover this operation. It exonerates you," Shawn said.

"How are we going to do this? I'm no cat burglar, Shawn," Quinn said.

"Confidence, my friend," Shawn said sounding more confident than Quinn felt.

"You'll have to give me more than that, pal," Quinn said.

"We're going in as contractors from PETA. Did you see their website? These people claim to do no animal testing, and to repudiate such practice. So we're going to make sure that they aren't doing experiments on animals. I have our props, and already made a call to them, to feel them out. I'll let you know what we'll do when we get there. Just follow my lead."

"Shawn, have you done something like this before?" Quinn asked.

"Not really, no. But if anything goes wrong, we want the police to come in and arrest us, right? It's foolproof, Quinn."

Quinn waited nervously until they arrived. He hadn't committed any major breaches of the law, but he had been arrested several times. He dreaded having to justify his behavior to the police or the feds, especially if this proved to be a wild-goose chase. He realized with a jolt of panic that if the affair was a remnant of the Michinski Empire, he might have to deal with thugs like the ones who took him hostage, cut off his finger, and beat him to within an inch of his life several years ago.

"Remember, you and I are contractors with PETA and we're checking out the claims of this natural cosmetics and herbal supplement producer. We verify that they don't experiment on animals, and we endorse them. They have to show us their entire warehouse. We have an appointment in thirty minutes."

"You've got to be kidding me," Quinn said.

Shawn smiled. "Not bad eh?"

"How do we dress, should we put on wigs, or something?" Quinn asked.

"No, don't overplay it," Shawn explained. "We're just writing a report. We explain that to them. That way we can walk in there looking like ourselves, and we don't have to pretend we're anyone other than who we are."

"Brilliant," Quinn said, impressed with his friend's audacious ingenuity.

"I know," Shawn said, still looking smug. "Make sure you aren't wearing any leather."

The two parked Quinn's old roadster. They staked out the building as people were entering and leaving. The operation looked to be medium sized, with maybe twenty employees.

"Damn, this is smaller than I thought. I'd hoped it was a bigger operation than this," Shawn said.

"Does that change anything?" Quinn asked.

"Nah," Shawn squawked. "Remember to act like you know what you're doing. Here's your identification."

"Jim McGowan? How the hell did you get this together so fast?" Quinn asked.

"I'm resourceful, and so is your friend, Minh Tran." Shawn said. That guy can counterfeit anything, it seems. Good thing he's a venture capitalist. He could have been a hell of a criminal."

"Right, here goes nothing," Quinn said, swallowing his dread as he felt the warm tickle of sweat dripping down the small of his back.

Shawn led Quinn into the lobby of the warehouse, marched right up to a receptionist, flanked by security guards. Quinn swallowed hard as Shawn began flirting with the receptionist.

"We have an appointment to look through the facilities. I'm Dr. Shawn Callihan and this is Dr. Jim McGowan," he said. "We are representing People for the Ethical Treatment of Animals. We're scientists working as independent contractors with PETA."

The receptionist seemed uninterested in Shawn' flirting.

"PETA has come through here before, but they've never outsourced their evaluations. Is this something new?" she asked, chewing gum as she spoke.

"They're growing. There've been staffing issues. We're new, and temporary, I suspect, based on the length of our contract," Shawn said, with absolutely no hesitation.

"Hmmm," she said, looking at their identification. "Well, go ahead, then. Is there any area you'd like to focus on?"

"I understand that the people we represent are most interested in the Research and Development wing of your physical plant," Quinn said, his voice just breaking. Shawn glanced over at him without expression, but Quinn knew he nearly blew their cover.

"That'll be fine. Ramsey, one of our security guards, will take you wherever you want to go," she said, nodding to the man on her right, who stepped forward.

"Right this way," Ramsey said, leading them through locked doors he accessed with a swipe of his key card. He was south Asian by the look of him, and was the size of a refrigerator. Shawn shot a nervous glance at Quinn.

A moment later they marched through the locked doors behind Ramsey. Shawn turned and flashed a smile at Quinn, who was nearly doubled over with anxiety.

He thought about when a group of animal rights activists infiltrated and destroyed his laboratory several years back. Now, he had come full-circle, and was in fact impersonating an animal rights activist to break into someone else's laboratory. For a moment he forgot his anxiety, chuckling in silence at the turn of events.

"Gentlemen, this is the research and development division," Ramsey said. "As you can see, there are no animals here. We do not use any toxic substances, and therefore do not require animal testing. Everything at our plant is naturally derived.

Shawn looked at the guard, who at the moment sounded much more like an apologist.

"Heroin and cocaine are perfectly natural also. So is lead and asbestos. You think they aren't toxic? Natural and non-toxic aren't the same thing," Shawn said.

Ramsey appeared taken aback by the comment. "I'm sorry," he said. "Perhaps it would be easier if I left you two to your work."

Shawn turned to the guard and softened some. "I don't mean to be rude, I just prefer that everyone concerned, whether PETA or any manufacturing or marketing group, leave the science to the scientists. Why don't you wait here, we'll get some samples and make some observations, and then we'll move on."

"Samples?" Ramsey asked, looking uncomfortable. "We don't usually allow...."

"Please!" Shawn shouted, startling both Quinn and the guard.

Quinn worried he was overplaying his hand, but bit his lip and said nothing.

"Damn it! Do you want to go on record as obstructing our investigation?" Shawn barked.

The guard looked at his side, and put his hand on his cell-phone, attached to his belt. But then he released his grip, and smiled.

"No, sir. I'll wait here at the door, you two go about your business, get what you need. Let me know when you are finished collecting whatever you plan to collect, and we'll move to the main manufacturing area."

"Thank you," Shawn said, looking pleased. "We won't be but a few minutes." He motioned a relieved Quinn to follow him.

How does he do that?

The two of them worked their way through the rows of laboratory benches, looking more like a college chemistry laboratory than a manufacturing plant. They found cultures of yeast, fungal cultures, and empty bottles of wine. Quinn scowled.

"Look at this," he said. "They were talking about growing it in the vineyard. I wonder if they were thinking of genetically modifying a fungus from a vineyard. Could they do that?"

"That would be something," Shawn said, taking some empty vials from a station and labeling them with a black Sharpie pen 'fungus'. He took several samples from plates, and some dried powdery substance. "I don't know who we can get to analyze this, but maybe we can contact someone at the department of Viticulture and Enology at UC Davis."

"We better get moving," Quinn said, "let's go to the main production facility." They pocketed the samples, and returned to the guard, who was on his phone, as they approached.

"Uh, oh," Quinn said ruefully.

Ramsey, the security guard smiled at them as they approached.

"Find everything you were looking for?" he asked a bit too cheerfully.

"We are satisfied with what is going on here," Shawn said seriously. "We just need to go to your main pharmaceutical production plant, and take some samples. We need to verify that there are no detectible animal products in your supplement products."

"Of course, you do," Ramsey said. He led them to the main production facility. Quinn looked around, trying to imagine what industrial production of the polymer, might look like. He had made batches of five hundred grams at a time. This was going to be thousands of times that level of synthesis. He wandered the plant, looking for the necessary equipment. At last a pattern emerged. It was the final two dissolutions, the polyethylene glycol double dissolution and supersaturation with resveratrol at 39 degrees centigrade with a platinum catalyst, which caught his eye. It appeared that the production had been shut down recently.

"This is it, Shawn," he said under his breath. "This is my stuff."

Shawn nonchalantly collected some of the residual finished product where it came out like thick, jelly-like goo, which was then placed into pharmaceutical capsules. The equipment was covered with dried residue. He turned to Quinn and smiled.

"Our work here is done, my friend."

Quinn was relieved that they were leaving. He felt a sense of guilt trespassing in the warehouse, though he acknowledged that the feeling made no sense. As Ramsey led them to the lobby, they emerged to find two other guards waiting for them and the receptionist facing them, her arms folded with an accusing look on her face.

"I called PETA, and not only have they never heard of you two, they haven't begun outsourcing their inspections. Who the hell are you, and what sort of industrial espionage do you think you're getting away with?"

Quinn and Shawn froze. Shawn looked over at Quinn. Quinn returned the look, trying to gauge his friend's ability to react to a bad situation. Quinn then looked at each of the guards. They had long metal flashlights, mace canisters, but no guns.

"We were concerned that these gelatin capsules might contain material from horse hooves," Quinn said.

There was a moment of stunned silence as the guards looked at them in confusion. Before anyone could reply Quinn bolted forward, dodging a swing from the butt of a flashlight, and catching one of the guards in an arm-bar. He lunged forward, head butting the startled guard who began to fall backwards. The giant guard named Ramsey moved toward him, pepper spray out. As the noxious aerosol was sprayed at Quinn, he kept his face a hundred and eighty degrees from the spray, and bent forward, his left leg coming up in a swift kick. Though facing away, he had visualized the trajectory of the oncoming guard before protecting his face. The kick landed somewhere solid. There was the unmistakable crack of breaking bone and cartilage. Quinn chanced a look at the refrigerator-sized Ramsey falling to the ground with a badly broken and bloody nose. Some of the mist of pepper spray caught Quinn in the face, and he felt the pain of a thousand needles stabbing his eyes and nose.

He heard a barrage of flesh-on-flesh impacts, but only muffled grunts. As he reeled, trying to regain control of his free-flowing eyes and nose, and deal with the pain of the pepper spray, he caught a vision of Shawn, in perfect old-school boxing pose, pummeling another of the guards. Ramsey was lying unconscious, a trickle of blood coming from each nostril, his nose bent at a horrendous angle. Shawn ducked a swing of the flashlight and connected with an uppercut, which knocked four of the teeth of the guard out with a spray of blood. Quinn turned and saw the receptionist talking with someone on the phone. A quick half-turn and an outstretched side-kick connected perfectly with the edge of the phone, missing the head of the woman, but sending the wireless phone receiver across the room. The startled woman yelped, then backed away as Quinn turned to help his friend. He approached to get a second faceful of pepper spray, which nearly paralyzed him in a fit of coughing, wheezing, and uncontrollable burning of his eyes and nose. He again heard the sound of flesh repeatedly pounding against flesh, and the next thing he knew Shawn grabbed his arm.

"Let's go buddy! I'll drive."

Quinn fished for his keys as Shawn led him by the arm out of the building. They were in the roadster in a flash. Ramsey, up again but still bleeding, and two new guards followed a few seconds later.

"Shit! Drive, Shawn!" Quinn yelled, as the blurry objects approached the car. He heard the engine of another car roar to life as Shawn engaged the engine of the little Audi TT. In the blink of an eye Quinn heard the high-pitched screech of his tires not quite catching the pavement as blue-white smoke bellowed up from the wheel wells.

"Hold on," Shawn said, burning the clutch to gain traction. "Sorry about your car buddy," he said to Quinn whose vision was just coming into focus.

"What?" Quinn said, his burning eyes catching Shawn's swift turn away from a closing chain link gate.

"Get the fuck out of the way!" Shawn yelled as the security guards peeled onto each side of the oncoming car. The small roadster bounced over a curb, nearly leaving the front axle behind, and met with an auxiliary chain-link gate at the side of the parking lot, which was locked with a chain and padlock. The front end of the TT smashed into the metal, which bent but didn't give. The tires screeched, leaving burned rubber and plumes of smoke behind. The fence bent some more, the Audi lurching forward in fits and starts until at last the hinges gave way to the momentum of the car. The gate collapsed onto the hood, and bounced over the ragtop of the coupe, shredding the canvas and destroying the hood. The TT screeched away from the locked compound, gathering speed.

"Nice driving," Quinn said, half grateful, half angry at his friend.

"Sorry, pal," Shawn said, "it was our only way out. Is anyone following us?"

"I don't see anyone," Quinn said as they drove north towards San Francisco.

* * * * * *

Bob Windsong, head of security at the warehouse was in his Dodge Challenger and ready to pursue. He radioed in to the receptionist.

"I'm going after them. Call the police. They're heading toward the city,"

A husky woman's voice answered him with a tone of absolute authority. It was a voice he did not recognize.

"You will not pursue them and no one is calling the police."

Bob was incredulous. "Who is this and what are you talking about?" Not waiting for an answer, he continued, "Those sons-of-bitches broke in under false pretenses, stole proprietary material, assaulted guards, and damaged property when they destroyed the fence! We have 'em nailed!"

"Bob, there's something you don't understand. You can't go after them and you can't detain them."

"What don't I understand?" Bob asked.

"One of them owns this plant," she said, as Bob sat slack jawed in his muscle car, trying to comprehend the meaning of what he heard.

Chapter 23:

Forty-five minutes later, a stressed Quinn and a noticeably less-stressed Shawn Callihan dropped off the samples with a friend at UCSF with whom Quinn used to work. David Rosenblum and Quinn had not always gotten along, but his old lab manager, now working in one of the primate labs and doing a pretty good job of running things, had said he felt bad that Quinn got such a "raw deal," as he put it, from UCSF so he agreed to run some tests for Quinn.

"Sure, hell I'll do some chromatography work for you. That's easy, Quinn," David said, sounding grateful to be able to do him a favor. "So some asshole is making money off of our sweat, huh?" he asked. "If you want to crucify him, I'll be glad to help."

"Actually, the him is a her, David," Quinn said, "How long until you can have some results?"

"A woman, huh?" David said, considering this carefully. "Well, it'll take me about two hours to prime the machine, but after it's calibrated, I should be able to identify it in forty-five minutes to an hour. I'll give you a call this evening."

"What about the yeast? Will you be able to tell if the yeast is producing any polymer?"

"That might take longer, I'll culture it, grow it out, give it plenty to eat, and see what sorts of products I can detect," David said. "Unless you have a better idea?"

"That sounds perfect. Thanks, David, this means a lot," Quinn said, giving Shawn's phone number to him.

As they drove back to the Silverado, Shawn's phone rang. He answered it squawking, "Callihan here."

Shawn was silent, his brow furrowed as he appeared to be concentrating on whatever was said on the other end of the line. Quinn looked at him expectantly. Slowly, a smile appeared on his face.

"You got it. We'll be there in half an hour," he said and hung up.

"Matthew my friend, that was the smokin'-hot Arianna Richardson," Shawn continued, turning to Quinn. "She says she thinks she has an inside track on a plot of land which has our name written all over it."

"Sounds pretty good," Quinn said, still feeling disconnected from anything that was not immediately tied to his getting out of trouble with the feds.

"We got a lot going on here, don't we Quinn?" Shawn said, his tone that of a concerned older brother.

Quinn turned to look at his friend who appeared quite sincere.

"Do you want me to go there without you while you sort the rest of this out?"

Quinn thought about that for some time. He had to wait on David Rosenblum, who more than likely wouldn't get back to him before five o'clock. He needed a distraction. "No, Shawn, I think it'll be better for me if I am distracted until I get those results. I'll try to exist in the present for a while."

"Excellent, except you sound like someone on a twelve-step program," Shawn said lightly. "Let's go and get some land and make the best wine in the New World."

"I like the sound of that, Shawn," Quinn said.

An hour later they arrived at Terroir Unlimited. As they approached the door Arianna met them, walking out and closing the door behind her.

"Let's go, I don't want to talk in here," she said, walking briskly past them.

"Why not?" Shawn asked.

"Ears of the competition, and I know that I'm not the only one interested in selling this piece of land," she said.

The two of them followed her down the street, and through some shopping areas, to a small clearing, behind which were some small vineyard plots. St. Helena was full of such small plots.

"I have reason to believe," she began when they were clearly out of earshot of anyone, "that the Northeastern plot of Henri Paradis is coming up for sale in the next day or so. It includes forty-two acres, and is some of his better remaining land."

Quinn looked at Shawn curiously. "Shawn, what do you think about taking this land from Henri Paradis," he asked. "It seems terrible to be taking advantage of his situation, especially since he is innocent, and we know that."

Shawn took a deep breath. If he were feeling any emotion about the possible transaction, he was not letting on to Quinn. But he was silent for a while. At last he spoke. "Why don't you call Josephine, explain our situation to her, and see if she thinks a meeting, face to face with Henri would be a good idea. But remember, Quinn, Henri Paradis knew we were unsuccessful bidders in the first land sale he had. He told us he regretted not selling the land to us. Now he has to sell some more land, and I bet he doesn't want to make the same mistake. This is a free country, Quinn, he decides if he is going to sell his land, not us. And he ultimately decides if picking his neighbors is as important to him as whatever premium he might get from selling the land to someone he doesn't like."

"I just feel like a carpet-bagger, that's all," Quinn said. "And I get a sense that before long, I will be able to be an actual official partner in this, if we can close the net on Catherine."

Quinn saw Arianna shoot a quick glance at him as he spoke, before recovering just as quickly.

"Then let's talk with Josephine, and if he's willing, directly to Henri. We can make this as ethical as you'd like," Shawn said.

"Would you consider a clause in the contract for him to buy back the land at the same price, covering only the commissions, if his finances unexpectedly improve?" Quinn asked.

Shawn looked shrewdly at Quinn. "You and your damn conscience, Quinn. How long of a window do you want to give him? I don't want to lose the land after we've put something of ourselves into it."

"How about three months?" he asked.

Shawn contemplated the number for a few seconds before nodding his assent. Quinn was satisfied with this as he called Josephine to explain their plans to make the offer and to hear her reaction. She was not opposed to the idea, especially when she heard that Quinn and Shawn wanted to give Henri a buy-back clause essentially penalty-free. She set up a meeting with Henri Paradis for that afternoon at the county jail.

"Shawn, twenty million for forty-two acres is a big premium to pay. Are you sure?" Quinn asked.

"Hey this is not just any forty-two acre plot, this is some of the best vineyard land in Napa Valley. It has made some of the best wine in the New World. It's worth it," Shawn said.

The ride to the jail was uneventful.

As they met Josephine, dressed smartly in a well-tailored pants suit, she led them, with a business-like expression and little small talk, to a room with Henri Paradis. She sat in silence at his side, working as his counsel. She did not make eye contact with Quinn, seemed to be avoiding it. Quinn's heart sank.

Arianna Richardson did the talking with Shawn and Quinn sitting silent at her side. When she finished, as she had coached, she turned to Shawn, who explained the idea for a buyback clause at cost, with the only additional cost being for Henri to pay back the closing costs and commission to Shawn.

Quinn watched Henri, stealing occasional glances at Josephine who did not let her professional demeanor disappear for even a second. Henri's face looked pained at the beginning of the offer, but began to soften as Arianna finished, and even brighten as Shawn spoke about the buyback clause. The spry septuagenarian had a piercingly sharp gaze, and his expression suggested he was ready to make a decision. As Shawn finished, Henri turned towards Josephine, smiled, and nodded. He turned back toward Shawn and spoke.

"I have seventy-two hours to accept or reject your offer, but the nature of this offer tells me that my instincts about you were correct. It's an honorable offer, and to me worth more than a twenty percent premium on the land. I accept your offer of twenty million, and will exercise the buyback if I am able in the next ninety days. If I am unable, I trust that you and whomever you work with," he said glancing over at Quinn, "will be excellent stewards of the land."

"Henri, there are two other offers on the land set to come in, are you sure that you want to take their offer? Shall we at least see what the other ones look like?" Josephine said.

"One is from Alfonse, and I don't know which one it is. These gentlemen are not hiding behind an anonymous offer. I don't give a damn what the other offers are," Henri said. "I've made up my mind, Josephine. Let's draw up the papers, and close the escrow account as soon as possible."

"Mr. Paradis," Arianna said. "We can close escrow in thirty days, I might be able to drop it to fifteen days if you need to close sooner."

"Arianna, I know your father," Henri began. "He taught math at the local high school, and taught my daughter. He is a good man. I hope he is proud of his daughter. A thirty-day close will be fine. I have a relationship with the bank, which will allow me to borrow against the proceeds of the land at a low interest rate. I can use the bridge loan to make my bail."

"So this is about you making bail, sir? If you don't mind me asking, how much did he set it at?" Shawn asked.

"It was a she, and she's tough as hell," Paradis began. "She initially denied bail, but after Josephine wore her down, she acquiesced and set bail at fifteen million dollars."

"Henri," Josephine said, "I'll be able to get you out of here in the morning as soon as the bank reopens."

"Thanks Josephine," Henri said. "I'm lucky to have you here with me." He turned to Quinn and spoke to him. "Dr. Quinn, I understand that you have been a staunch advocate for me as well, and have shared some information which strengthens my case. I also owe you a debt of gratitude. I think if the cyanide hadn't come from my supply shed, or if I had reported the damn break-in when it happened, I'd already be free of these charges, but your information is already paying dividends. It was a principle part of Josephine's argument, which got me from 'no-bail' to a fifteen million dollar bond. As ridiculous as it sounds, that's a hell of an improvement."

Quinn smiled and nodded at the thank-you.

Arianna Richardson got up and signaled that Shawn and Quinn do the same. She shook hands with Paradis and with Josephine before turning and leading Shawn and Quinn out of the room.

On the way back to the Silverado, David Rosenblum called Quinn. "Quinn, that's our stuff alright, but with the modification you made. It was bonded with the resveratrol, and carries the conformational change. There's no question about it."

"Thanks, David, I owe you one," Quinn said.

"Send me a case of your best wine, and we'll call it even," David said jovially.

The comment made Quinn's insides churn. The loss was still a memory that evoked pain that was close to physical. "Sorry, David, the winery is gone. I am just a collector now. But I have some great Marcassin's I can send you."

"That'll do, doc. I should have some information tomorrow about the yeast cultures. It'd be amazing if whoever is making this stuff got these little buggers to do all of the work for them. That'd change things quite a bit."

"You got that right," Quinn said.

"Hey Quinn, I was glad I could help you. You know, I uh, kind of miss you, and your lab," David said.

"That's nice of you to say. Take care, David," he said ending the call. "And a little hard to believe," he said to no one in particular after hanging up.

"Well?" Shawn said looking at Quinn.

"It's my polymer. That's where they're making it."

Shawn smiled, nodding his head. "Good work on that, pal, you're one step closer."

"Yeah, one step closer," Quinn said reflectively.

Closer to what?

The two had scarcely made it to the Silverado when Josephine called. Shawn answered the phone, said a few flirtatious words, and then handed the phone over to Quinn.

"Hello, Josephine," Quinn said, feeling relieved that she called.

"Can I come over and talk to you?" she said. She sounded upset to Quinn.

"Yeah, of course. We were going to have some champagne and celebrate the purchase of the vineyard. Shawn is going to invite Tasha. Why don't you join us?"

There was a long silence on the line. Quinn wondered what he had said. At last she spoke. "That sounds great, Matthew. I'll come over. Thanks," she said and hung up.

"She didn't sound too happy, I hope we didn't make a mistake," Quinn said to Shawn.

"It'll be fine, pal. Don't worry. I'm sure that whatever she is upset about has nothing to do with us. Maybe something went wrong with the judge, or something else. I am sure she'll tell us when she gets here."

Quinn relaxed as they made their way to their suite. Everything seemed to roll off Shawn. He was literally unflappable; Quinn enjoyed his presence, and despite the occasional spat, didn't realize how much he had missed him after medical school. Quinn lay down on his bed as Shawn excused himself to go and get Tasha. Quinn closed his eyes for a moment, and was instantly asleep.

He awoke with a start as Shawn and Tasha entered the room.

"Sorry, buddy, didn't expect you to be asleep just now," Shawn squawked. "We were only gone twenty minutes."

Shawn and Tasha had hauled in a magnum of Veuve Clicquot La Grande Dame champagne, chilling in a large bucket of ice. Quinn liked sparkling wine, though he rarely drank it. Shawn reached into a cupboard and pulled four champagne flutes as Tasha worked the cork out of the bottle, taking care to keep the cork from launching, and making sure to release the carbon dioxide as slowly and gently as possible. Shawn gazed at her with what Quinn figured was some sort of lusty, star-struck look.

"I love a woman who knows how to properly open a bottle of champagne."

"We wouldn't want to lose any of this great juice, and upset the Widow Clicquot. Besides, 1990 was one of my favorite vintages," she said.

They poured three glasses and settled into some small talk, much like three old friends. That was how Quinn's relationship with Tasha was evolving. With Josephine in his life now and obviously unconcerned that he was on borrowed time, it somehow seemed okay, even fitting, that Tasha was settling in with Shawn. She was just over forty, though you wouldn't know it by looking at her. She was as beautiful as ever. He wondered if she wanted children, and if Shawn would settle down with her.

After about ten minutes, there was a knock at the door. Quinn answered it and found Josephine, still in her business suit, smiling the sort of smile, which failed to conceal intense frustration. Quinn took her coat, offered her a seat and poured her some champagne. His heart accelerated then skipped a beat as he saw her, his mind drifting back to her office, to their brief time on the sofa. She accepted and took a drink of the sparkling wine as he sat down. She looked around, acknowledging everyone in the room before turning to Quinn.

"So you'll never guess what happened after you and Shawn left the county jail today."

"What?" Quinn and Shawn said simultaneously.

"Henri's brother showed up, demanding to see his brother," she began and then paused, looking around. "Everyone better top off their glass, because this is going to take a while."

Shawn got up, promptly pulling the chilled bottle of bubbly and topped off everyone's glass, including Josephine, who had managed to drain hers. She continued.

"Henri let Alfonse in to see him. He came in with this manic grin on his face, and sat down across from Henri. He just stared at him silently for about a minute before saying, 'You did it didn't you? You tried to kill Ronald Park.' Well, you can imagine, Henri is incredulous. Alfonse suggests he has plans to help get him out of jail. Henry tells Alfonse he already sold the Northeast plot to the two of you, and that's where it gets interesting. That's when Alfonse, I can't believe his audacity," she said pausing and shaking her head. "That's when Alfonse looked at his brother, and said, 'What about the plot sitting in the middle, doing nothing?' Henri said, 'you mean our family plot?' and Alfonse nodded. Then Alfonse pulled out a checkbook and made a check out for twenty five million dollars to Henri. He said it was for Henri relinquishing his claim on the family plot of land. He could have the money if he surrendered the twenty-one acre plot to his brother. It is more than two million dollars an acre, because Henri only owns half of it. At that point Henri looked at his brother, and asked him why he wanted it, what his angle was. Alfonse didn't say anything, but he hinted that he could unload the land to someone else, complete with his father's gravesite, for some huge amount of capital. Henri leaped up over the table, grabbed his brother by the necktie, pulled his face toward him and said, 'If you ever try to sell that land, I'll kill you!' He then released him before a guard had even approached, and demanded to be taken back to his cell. Alfonse recovered, but looked shaken up as he walked out of the jail." Josephine finished and drank her champagne.

"Did you talk with Henri afterwards?" Quinn asked.

"No, he was in no mood to talk with anyone. I think he is glad you two were interested in the property, though," she said.

"So Alfonse came in to harass his brother and then to offer him money for the land that grew the wine we tasted the other night at the auction," Shawn said. "I wonder if the auction lot he donated generated some interest in that plot of land."

"It certainly would make sense," Tasha said, eyeing Josephine warily.

"It's a weird play, though," Josephine said. "I would think Alfonse would go about it differently, at least wait until after the legal business was done."

Quinn looked thoughtfully at Josephine. "Well, it depends," he said. "What if he was trying to capitalize on Henri's desperation?"

Josephine nodded silently, looking like she was deep in thought. "That would make sense. What didn't make sense was that I got the feeling that Alfonse was more desperate than Henri."

"Do you wonder if perhaps someone else, someone who is manipulating a great many things, is trying to make sure that both of the Paradis brothers are desperate?" Quinn asked.

"Catherine," Tasha said.

Josephine shot a glance at Tasha but remained silent. Tasha's eyes burned into Josephine and did not waiver. Josephine looked away. Quinn watched in silence, as Josephine seemed at once sad, scared, and utterly deflated, a wounded gazelle, about to be devoured by a lioness.

And Tasha looked like a lioness.

Chapter 24:

Quinn and Shawn enjoyed rib eye steaks in their rooms with the ladies. They polished off another bottle of wine.

When it began to get late, Josephine, who had relaxed some and seemed to be having at least a passible, if not good time, unexpectedly decided that she would turn in early. Tasha got up and followed Josephine out.

"It's only about a mile up the Silverado trail to your new vineyard. Want to go and see it by moonlight?" Quinn asked after the women had left.

Shawn considered it. "In spite of the fact that taking a moonlight walk with you sounds kind of gay," he began, "it sounds like an intriguing night. Can we bring a bottle with us, and drink it old-west-whiskey-style? That'd make it seem more manly."

"Whatever assuages your fragile heterosexuality," Quinn said. "Sometimes night is the best time to see a vineyard, you can see fog belts, and more intensely feel the microclimes."

"That sounds like bullshit to me," Shawn said pushing himself to a stand, "but what the hell, a walk in the cool night air with a bottle of Mollydooker sounds pretty good right now."

"I'll get the Mollydooker," Quinn said to his friend, "but honestly, with a name like Mollydooker, will the wine really make you feel more masculine?"

"Fine, I'll get my bow," Shawn said.

Quinn went to the wine refrigerator in the room and fished out a bottle.

"Oh my God, you were serious?" Quinn asked as Shawn returned with his compound bow.

"You never know," he said, "when you will find yourself face to face with a ferocious wild-boar."

Quinn was incredulous, but said nothing. They ventured out into the night. It was close to midnight.

* * * * * *

Tasha moved swiftly after Josephine, catching up to her as she approached her BMW in the parking lot. "Josephine, can I have a word with you?" she said in a voice that was not quite threatening.

"Tasha," Josephine acknowledged. "What can I do for you?"

Tasha moved to the passenger side of the car, facing Josephine with the German sport coupe between them. "Don't take this the wrong way, but I care a great deal for Matthew. I need you to look me in the eyes and tell me that your intentions with him are honorable."

Josephine wore a business face as she gazed back at Tasha. "Why would they be anything else, Tasha?"

Tasha paused. "I don't like playing games, so I'll just spit it out. Quinn is dumped and left for dead by the feds in Berkeley, and you find him. That wasn't a coincidence, just a random occurrence, right Josephine?"

Josephine nodded but said nothing.

"And then he runs into you here. Now that's a coincidence."

"I grew up here and live here," Josephine said.

"And somehow Henri Paradis gets caught up in some parallel trouble which looks like it's also orchestrated by Catherine Michinski. And you conveniently grew up on his land, know him, and no doubt know the inner workings of his winery and vineyards better than most," Tasha said. "Now the coincidence starts to strain credulity."

"Where are you going with this, Tasha?" Josephine said, still professional, but steeling herself, not backing down, Tasha thought.

"And there's someone working with Catherine who loosely matches your description," Tasha said. "A fit Latina named Barbara Garcia that is in cahoots with the Catherine

Michinski. That is just too much, Josephine. If you are putting my friend in danger…."

"You mean your ex-lover?" Josephine shot back.

"Do you go by any other names, Josephine?" Tasha asked.

"You're suggesting I have an alias? What are your intentions, Tasha? You want me out of Quinn's life? Want to date your ex's best friend but keep Quinn on the back burner? Is that it?"

"You don't understand me, even a little bit," Tasha said, shaking her head.

"Let me state some things categorically to you, Tasha. First, I am not, have not, and never will work with, or for Catherine Michinski. I've never even met her. Second, I am unequivocally behind Henri Paradis and the resurrection of his winery, and would never do anything to harm him. Third, I am crazy about Matthew Quinn, and frightened for him, frightened for what he is up against."

Tasha looked at her trying to discern why she at once believed her, but still didn't trust her.

"Tasha, you and I should be allies, not adversaries," Josephine said, trying to diffuse the tension.

Tasha still sensed deception. "You didn't address the coincidences. There is something more here. You aren't telling me something; you aren't telling Matthew something."

"Tasha, I'm dealing with my own issues in this damn mess which is drawing all of us together. I can't say more about it now. But if you assume I don't have Matthew Quinn's best interests at heart, you're making a big mistake."

"I believe you, Josephine. But don't think for a minute I am going to take my eyes off of you. Not until I understand just how you fit into this puzzle," Tasha said.

Josephine did not reply as Tasha turned and marched back into the resort, leaving her alone in the parking lot.

* * * * * *

Quinn did not want to be seen walking up the shoulder of the Silverado Trail with an open container and a drunk buddy carrying a lethal weapon. He mused that his judgment, while impaired, was not that impaired. So Quinn and Shawn wandered through the back of the resort into the valley, trespassing through someone else's vineyards, they didn't know whose.

Quinn liked that Napa had few fences and that one could easily walk through someone else's land crossing territory rather easily on foot. The nearly full moon illuminated the vineyards, and the vines cast shadows on either side of them. From more than a few feet away, all one could see was the top of their heads above the vineyard canopy.

They walked through the vineyards for over an hour, passing the wine bottle back and forth, until it was gone. They definitely sensed random temperature changes, passing through cold, damp pockets, followed by warm, dry pockets of air.

They came upon a plot of land that was full of high growing prairie grass and wild brambles, surrounded on three sides by a creek. Damp heat radiated from the soil below them, and there was just a hint of sulfur in the air, as if there were a hot mineral spring somewhere deep below them. As they approached and prepared to slog across a five-meter wide creek, Quinn realized that there was a headstone ahead in a cleared area.

"Shawn, this is…." Quinn began.

"I know," he said. "And it's weird, not the sort of place one would think would grow the best wine in the New World."

Quinn and Shawn made their way to the edge of the plot, descended into the creek, which was surrounded on both sides by old, gnarled cottonwood trees. They waded across the creek, which was deeper than either had realized. They were nearly up to their hips in the water before getting to the shallows of the other side.

"Shawn, that water was warmer than I thought it'd be. There must be a spring nearby."

"You can smell it too, the sulfur. There are a lot of them in the valley," Shawn replied. "We both know that."

As they ascended the bank of the creek on the other side, they found themselves on Paradis' property, which was now in escrow to be Shawn Callihan's property.

"Here it is, Shawn. This land is unbelievable. It is many times better than my hilltop estate. You are in the realm of the Cult Wine down here!"

Shawn didn't say anything. They heard a car moving along the Silverado trail, which ran parallel to their path. It was about a quarter mile away on their right side.

"Hey Quinn, is that some sort of storage shed up there?"

Quinn strained his eyes, which apparently were not as good as Shawn's. After awhile, he could just barely make out the silhouette of a small storage shed, several hundred feet ahead of them and to their left.

"Do you think that's where someone stole the cyanide that killed Park?"

"Almost killed Park," Shawn corrected, "he's not dead yet, Quinn."

"You and I both know that he'll never recover, his brain has to be jello after all of that," Quinn said. "But yeah, maybe it is, you want to go and have a look?"

"Yeah, I do," Shawn said, moving toward it. They both approached. Even in the dark they could see the yellow tape surrounding the shed, which said, "Police Line, Do Not Cross" over and over.

"Fuck it, it's my property," Shawn said as he began removing the tape.

Quinn noticed some of the tape had already been broken, and some of the tape had been stretched.

"Shawn, look there. Someone's already been here. This thing's been broken into again."

Shawn stopped and looked to where Quinn was pointing.

"I wonder what they took," he said as he pulled open the unlocked door.

Both of them froze as they shined their light into the shed.

"Or left," Quinn said with quiet urgency.

"Uh-oh," Shawn said.

"Shawn we got to get the hell out of here, now!" Quinn said, panic in his voice, as he looked down at the blood stained corpse, laying face down in the shed in front of them. His hands began to ache.

"Hey, she looks like…." Shawn said reaching down and turning the head of the dead woman in front of him. One look at the face and both Quinn and Shawn recognized the pale dead face of Arianna Richardson. Her throat was slashed.

"Jesus, Shawn!" Quinn said. "Who the hell killed her and left her on your property?"

"It isn't my property yet, and I am not sure if her death does anything to the deal," Shawn said. "But this is Paradis's land until escrow closes."

"We need to get out of here and tell the police," Quinn said. Shawn nodded and the two of them backed away from the shed.

As they turned to go back the way that they came, a Silver Ford pickup truck sped down the dirt maintenance road towards them.

"Oh, shit," Shawn muttered. Quinn realized he still had the empty bottle of wine, but nothing else with which to defend himself. Suddenly the compound bow-and-arrow set Shawn had brought seemed positively brilliant.

The truck slowed for a time, and then, as it was less than a hundred feet from them, the engine whined and the truck accelerated hard, barreling toward them. The wine slowed their reflexes, but they dove to opposite sides as the truck nearly ran them over. There were two cracks of gunshots. Quinn rolled under some trellised vines as the shots rang out. He was not sure if the shots were fired at him or Shawn, or if either shot had hit its target. Quinn was up and running, still holding the empty bottle in his hand when he heard the crash of the truck hitting and destroying the storage shed. He looked around for Shawn, but couldn't see him anywhere. He ran parallel to the service road, between two rows of vines. He was thankful for the thick canopy forming on them, which obscured him from whoever was in the truck.

A moment later he heard the truck heading down the service road. Suddenly it veered to the right, crashing through the two rows of vines separating Quinn from the road. It accelerated hard at him. Quinn weighed his options before ducking under the row of vines, and then another and another, as the truck turned hard, going after him, creating a trail of destroyed vines behind it.

Quinn managed to get behind the truck, and head back toward the road, as fast as he could run in a drunken but adrenaline fueled state. The truck managed a wide circle and was heading back toward him. He knew he couldn't play chicken with a full sized pickup truck for long and was desperately seeking a way out when he heard the rush of something cutting through the night air at high velocity. The next moment, there was a loud explosion and the pickup truck appeared to sink on one side. The front passenger corner sunk to the soft ground, and the bumper caught some earth. The next thing Quinn knew, the truck had swerved and rolled over, landing on its top. It was about two hundred feet from them. Quinn saw Shawn emerge from behind a row of vines. "Get down!" he hissed as he drew another arrow and took aim.

Quinn watched as a lone figure got out of the truck. It was the silhouette of a man. They couldn't see him clearly, only his lean, athletic physique. He raised his gun and fired three shots at them. Shawn ducked down as the bullets flew past them. When Shawn recovered and took aim, the man was running away from them. He fired a second arrow. It connected. The man yelped and cursed, but kept going. A moment later, he disappeared behind some vines. Quinn and Shawn did not pursue him further.

"Where did you hit him?" Quinn asked.

"Right in the ass," Shawn said. "I was trying for the upper legs, to keep him from running. Apparently you can still run with an arrow in your ass."

"We have to get the hell out of here," Quinn said. "I don't want to be playing cat and mouse in a vineyard with someone who has a gun!"

"Go to the road. He won't follow us. He doesn't want to take a chance of getting another arrow in the ass," Shawn said sounding confident.

They ran to the Silverado Trail. There was no traffic at that time of night, and they jogged as fast as they could, given their state, back to the resort, where they called the police.

Chapter 25:

Sherriff Hernandez led Quinn and Shawn into his office. They had spoken briefly after the two had returned to the resort. After taking statements, he let them sleep off their wine, deferring more talk until the morning. He was troubled by the fact that wherever there seemed to be a body, Quinn and Shawn were close by, usually full of wine, but he stopped short of accusing them of anything. After he was able to check out their story he brought them in.

"Are you two ever sober?" he asked as they took their seats.

"Well, this is just the second time you've met us, and we are vacationing in Napa Valley. We're sober some of the time." Shawn said. "And we're sober this morning."

"You two were just wandering through the valley at midnight, trespassing on land you were purchasing, when you came upon the body of the woman brokering your deal, and then someone in a truck tried to run you down, shot at you, destroyed the storage building where her body is, and then fled when you, conveniently enough, shot him with a compound bow that you just happened to be carrying, hitting him in the rear-end."

"I know it sounds ridiculous," Quinn said, "but you saw the property, right?"

Hernandez had dispatched two officers to the Paradis property after their call, and was only mildly surprised that they found the truck, and enough evidence to corroborate Quinn and Shawn's story.

"I don't know why I doubted you two. The story is so idiotic that no one could make it up."

Quinn and Shawn looked at each other, unsure of how to respond. They said nothing.

Hernandez picked up his phone. "Darla, has Henri Paradis been released from County yet?" He paused. "Good. I assume that his attorney is not going to let us speak to him?

Tell her he is not suspected in anything else, and I have a green light from the DA's office to give him immunity for anything he says. See if she'll let us talk with him then. She can be present, of course." He hung up the phone and turned again to Shawn and Quinn.

"You know who the truck belongs to?"

"Who?" Quinn demanded.

"Alfonse Paradis. You'd of thought it was stolen or something, as it just seems too easy, but no theft has been reported. Any thoughts on how he or someone in his corporation might be involved in this whole set of shenanigans?" Hernandez asked.

Quinn couldn't think of anything, except that Josephine had said that Alfonse sounded desperate to sell the disputed plot of land. "I have no clue," he said. Shawn nodded his head, agreeing with Quinn.

"We received an anonymous tip that Alfonse Paradis wants the family's land back from his brother. There's a search warrant that has been issued to look through his house in Modesto. There may be reason to believe that he was involved in this murder as well as the attempted murder on Ronald Park and the murder of his wife."

"Was it a woman?" Quinn asked.

"How did you know?" Hernandez asked in return. Quinn said nothing, shrugging.

"Why would Alfonse Paradis be guilty of murdering Park and Arianna Richardson?" Shawn asked.

"We think he was trying to get his brother into a position where he would have to sell all of his land. We just found out he has been borrowing heavily against his land in the Central Valley, and of course everyone knows he just bought a quarter of his brother's holdings already. He approached his brother in jail not long ago and offered him money to drop the claim on the plot of land, which is disputed between them. The theory is that the whole thing is a family feud and a hostile takeover bid gone wrong," Hernandez explained.

"So what does Arianna Richardson have to do with it?" Shawn asked.

"We think he might have killed her to monkey-up the sale of the property to you, but we aren't sure. The transaction can be completed without her, so it's odd. Maybe she found out about what he was doing, somehow. The people at Terroir Unlimited have a reputation of being in tune with the pulse of the valley."

"What about Ron Park and Virginia?" Quinn asked.

"Well, Park is easy. Everyone knew that Park seemed to have it in for Paradis, what with the ratings Henri's been given over the last few years. Henri would be a suspect in the death of Park and despite his glowing reputation in Napa Valley. A lot of people would believe it. We have some ideas as to why Virginia might have been involved, but nothing definite. We're hoping to piece this together. It would be easier if our victim wasn't dead."

"Ron Park died?" Quinn asked.

"No, actually they say he's coming out of his coma now. Hard to tell how much brain damage might have been done, though. I was talking about Virginia and Arianna Richardson."

"Ron Park is waking up?" Shawn asked.

"Yeah, they're describing purposeful movements, and appropriate reactions to stimulation, but they haven't pulled his breathing tube yet. We'll see what kind of recovery he makes," Hernandez said, shrugging.

The phone on his desk rang. He picked it up, identified himself, and listened intently.

"Wait, fentanyl vials, cyanide, and dried mushrooms at his place? This is all a little too easy." He paused, listening to someone on the other line again. "I understand. He's still here in Napa Valley? We'll have him brought here for questioning. Good work," said Hernandez and hung up.

He looked at Shawn and Quinn and shrugged. "They found cyanide, fentanyl, and poison mushrooms stored in a shed on Alfonse Paradis' vineyards out in the Central Valley.

They'll see if it matches the stuff in Henri's shed, the stuff used to try to kill Park, but this sounds like a slam dunk,"

"Almost too much of a slam dunk," Shawn said. Quinn nodded silently.

"Yeah, it's awful easy. Might be a rat," Hernandez acknowledged. "We'll have to see what he says after he is brought in."

Hernandez's eyes moved away from Quinn and Shawn and towards his clear-glass door. Quinn turned to see Henri Paradis striding in, wearing his signature flannel button down over a t-shirt, and worn blue jeans.

"Gentlemen, if you'll excuse me, the DA and I have to speak with Mr. Paradis in private," Hernandez said.

"Of course," Quinn said, getting up to leave with Shawn. They walked right by Josephine, who was not smiling and avoided eye contact as she entered the room with Henri Paradis. He noticed Shawn and Quinn and stopped and smiled.

"I want to thank you two boys again for the company a few nights back, for buying my land, and for helping out with this case against me, which I hope is about to be dropped for good," Paradis said, glancing over at the Sherriff, whose face was noncommittal.

"We're the ones who should be thankful," Shawn said smiling at the Napa patriarch as he entered Hernandez' office. Quinn wondered why Josie gave him a cold shoulder, but chalked it up to her being in "professional mode." Quinn and Shawn returned to their room at the Silverado.

They opened a bottle of Clos De Papes from about twenty years ago. They discussed its earthy, leathery characteristics, and rich deep berry flavors, and were just about finished with the bottle when Josephine knocked at the door. Quinn let her in. She had a look of absolute incredulity on her face. She also looked as if she were about to burst.

"Did they drop the charges against Paradis?" Quinn was the first to ask.

"Yeah," Josephine said. "But this is where it gets really weird. They dropped the charges against Henri, and then they brought in his brother and charged him with the murder of Virginia, the attempted murder on Park, and the murder of Arianna Richardson. That's three murders if Park dies, and he could go from jug-wine mogul to death-row inmate like that if he's convicted."

"So they think Alfonse tried to frame his brother for murder to get him put away so he would have control of the land?" Quinn asked. He was not convinced.

"Wouldn't control of the land go to his daughter?" Shawn asked.

"Yes, but they think Alfonse would have been able to bully her, and her loyalty to her father would make her liquidate whatever she had to try to defend him. What the police really think is that this whole thing is about that disputed plot of land, which is worth a fortune."

"You'd think that bloody plot of land was the soul of the whole valley," Tasha said.

"It might be," Shawn said. "Quinn and I walked through it last night. It was a strange place. It's over some kind of mineral spring. There was warm damp sulfury radiation from the ground. And the creek surrounds it on three sides. Who knows what kind of stuff that creek has been depositing there for the last few centuries. And then there is the gravesite of Paradis's old man there. He would be part of the wine from that land, too. Maybe it is the seat of the soul of Napa Valley."

Tasha considered this. Quinn thought she would blow off the folklore and legend, but she seemed to take it in. "Was Paradis the first settler to own that land?"

"No, it was originally owned by the Church," Josephine explained. "They subdivided and sold most of the plots near that part of the valley after World War II. The land went to a European immigrant family. I think they were gypsies from Eastern Europe who came in as refugees and made some money in San Francisco after the war. They got discounted land from the Church. I guess the Pope felt guilty for looking the other way as the Nazis did their thing."

"They grow wine on it?" Quinn asked.

"They grew grapes on the area under dispute, and the rest of the land was orchards," Josephine said.

"When did Paradis acquire the land," Shawn asked.

"In 1955 they sold the land to Paradis' father, who worked the land with his two sons and settled on the property. When Paradis started, he was in Sonoma for a short time, but wasn't happy with the land. My father worked with him. My father and the elder Paradis scoped out the land in Napa and were able to procure a deal on it. When the elder Paradis died in 1971 the fighting began, and eventually the land west of the creek went to Alfonse, who sold it and moved to the Central Valley."

Shawn and Quinn listened without speaking.

"My father stayed with Henri and helped him with the land that remained. They built their reputation in the 70's and 80's. My father died a few years ago, but continued to manage the vineyard right up until he died."

"Wow," Quinn said focusing on Josephine. "Your family is as tied up in the valley as any of the patriarchs."

"Yeah," Josephine said. "Henri's father, and later Henri, treated my dad more like a partner than an employee, but he never owned anything," she explained. "Maybe that wasn't fair, but he was undocumented, and it was the time. I've moved beyond it."

"I'm not sure I would have," Shawn said. The others nodded.

"So that's it," Quinn said. "Alfonse is in jail and Henri is free."

"I guess he'll want to exercise the buyback option of his land, or cancel the transaction," Shawn said. "We're going to be back on the market buddy," he said to Quinn. "Did Alfonse mention Catherine?"

"Not so fast," Josephine said. "There's more to the story. Henri got his bond back after the charges are dropped. And then he paid the bond for his estranged brother, twelve million dollars. The judge set it late this afternoon. He still intends to sell the land to you, Shawn. He needs the money for operating costs, since he just dropped all of his operating money on getting his brother out of jail."

"He bailed out that asshole?" Shawn asked. "The guy who humiliated him at the Bounty Hunter the other day and was such a jack-ass at the auction? He's crazy. Why not use the opportunity to muscle back the disputed plot from him?"

"I think Henri wants to reconcile before he dies," Josephine said. "He told me that he believes the rift in the family is connected to his difficulties with the winery and the string of incredible bad luck he has had. He told me that mending his relationship with his brother is a necessary part of resurrecting his winery. It turns out that right now, Alfonse is apparently leveraged to the hilt. All that throwing around of money was for show. He couldn't come up with his own bail, the check to Henri for the disputed plot would have bounced, and he would have had to stay in jail until his trial. Most of his land appears to be heading into foreclosure in the Central Valley. Alfonse said something about someone at his company embezzling money, but an audit released Friday showed really sloppy bookkeeping. The whole company is riddled with debt, and there looks to be fraudulent transactions everywhere. Alfonse is financially in much worse shape than Henri. There's nearly a hundred million dollars he absolutely can't account for. So it was an opportunity for Henri to extend an olive branch, and he did."

"Well, he's a bigger man than I am," Shawn said. "Does Henri think Alfonse is innocent?"

Josephine nodded. "He told me that his brother was a bastard, but not a killer. Henri thought if he could bring his brother through this with his dignity, they might develop a joint venture, and start with the disputed family plot. And no, Alfonse did not mention anyone named Catherine."

"Well, if Henri knows he didn't do it, and he thinks his brother didn't do it, I would assume it was Catherine. Why would she do it?" Quinn asked.

"Someone hates the both of them," Josephine said. She took a deep breath and was about to continue when a melodic ringtone interrupted them.

Tasha reached for her cell phone reflexively and picked up. "Hello," she said. "Minh, how are you?" She fell into some silence, a coy smile crossing her face as the others watched her in silence. She shot a few furtive glances over at Quinn.

"Thanks for the call, Minh. I guess we'll probably be seeing you soon. I don't know if it will be tonight or tomorrow, but we'll be down there before long. Bye." She hung up the phone and turned to Quinn and Shawn.

"I have some rather extraordinary news," she said.

"What?" Shawn asked.

"It seems that Ron Park has emerged from his coma, and he is awake, alert, his breathing tube is out, and he is speaking," she said.

Everyone looked at her with absolute astonishment except Quinn. "He was taking the polymer," he said.

Chapter 26:

Quinn and Shawn packed up and checked out of the Silverado. They drove south to Palo Alto and met Minh Tran and Joshua Mortensen outside of the main entrance to Stanford Medical Center.

"How is he doing?" Quinn asked.

"He's pretty distraught. It isn't like him to show much emotion," Minh said. "But he's been destroyed by the death of his wife, even more than I would have thought, what with their recent talk of divorce and all."

"Maybe we shouldn't go in right away," Quinn said. "Maybe we need to give him some more time."

"No, he wants to speak with you, Quinn. They've told him about the levels of poison and that he's a medical miracle," Minh said. "We told him it's the herb he's taking from the Silverado. We told him about your invention. He specifically asked for you."

"Okay, we can go up for a little while. We have a meeting with Agent Snow at five o'clock up near San Francisco. He's done some more homework and wants to discuss his findings with us. He checked on the Barbara Garcia woman and has uncovered something, which made him reconsider my status. Now we have some more information too. Shawn and I'll have to leave by four o'clock."

"Sooner than that if you want to drop your stuff off at our house," Joshua said.

"We'll drop it off later. This is an important meeting," Quinn said.

They made their way to the Medical ICU. The Unit Assistant showed them to Ron Park's room. It was devoid of any cards, flowers, and anything else suggesting that anyone beyond those entering the room cared at all about him. The only other person in the room was Jeff McLeod, Joshua's mercenary friend. He sat silent and unobtrusive in the corner.

Park was unshaven, hair in disarray, and with bloodshot eyes. He looked like he'd been crying.

"Ron, you remember Matthew Quinn," Minh said.

Ron thrust his arm out to shake Quinn's hand. "We meet again, Dr. Quinn. I understand I owe my life to you. I only wish the cocktail was potent enough to have saved Virginia."

"We're so sorry that she didn't make it. We believe that the police are close to solving her murder."

"Yes, I was told that originally Henri Paradis was arrested, but has been released and now his brother is under arrest for poisoning me. They think he also killed Virginia?" Park asked.

"Virginia died of an air embolus. It looks like she would have survived the amanita mushroom poisoning. But there is no information about how or who may have delivered the air embolus. We don't think Alfonse had access to the kitchen at the Silverado, so we think he's been framed, too. Shawn and I are meeting with a federal investigator later today, and we think there are other people involved, further complicating the situation," Quinn said. "Is there any reason to believe that the family of slain mob-boss Vladimir Michinski would want you and Virginia dead?"

Park scowled, his forehead in deep-etched furrow, as he appeared to be trying to remember something. "Michinski? That name rings a bell somewhere. I've come across it recently, but I can't remember the context."

"He was a heroin dealer and mob kingpin who used to operate out of San Francisco and Oakland. He was killed almost four years ago. We think his daughter, who was also reportedly killed, actually survived and may be involved in your poisoning and the murder of your wife."

"No, that's not the context. Where did I come across that name?" he appeared agitated, his skin flushing.

Quinn's eyes reflexively went to the cardiac monitor, which showed his blood pressure at 150/100 and his heart rate at 135. "Relax, Mr. Park. You'll think of it. Give my buddy

Shawn a call if you remember. We believe that whatever remains of the Michinski empire is somehow involved in the attempt on your life. We have some evidence to support it, and we are hoping that this thread will lead the police and the feds to some more concrete answers."

"Let me know, please?" Park said. "And I'll call you when I remember where I came across the name Michinski."

"Thanks," Quinn said. He and Shawn nodded to Minh and Joshua. "Are you two staying here with Mr. Park?"

"Yeah, we'll keep him company until he is ready for discharge." Minh said.

Quinn leaned forward. "Joshua, I'm glad you two decided to keep Jeff here. Ron still isn't safe. Given the air embolus, and what the Michinski people did when they kidnapped Tasha, I'm glad he's here to provide some real protection."

Joshua nodded soberly.

Quinn and Shawn left the hospital and headed up the peninsula to meet with agent Snow.

"We're going to meet him at Lake Merced," Quinn said.

"Why there? Why aren't me meeting him downtown," Shawn asked.

"I got the feeling he wanted to keep our meeting on the down-low," Quinn said.

"Why?"

"He sounded like something changed. He believes me now. But he wouldn't talk to me on his office phone. He called me back on his personal cell-phone after he left the office. He told me that he didn't want anyone else to know he was meeting face-to-face with us. He also told me who was tailing us today, and told me how to disable the new GPS they installed."

"Did you?" Shawn asked.

"Yep, this morning, while you were loading the car."

"This sounds like a lot of cloak and dagger stuff. Pretty cool," Shawn said. "Do you think he's worried about the feds, his colleagues, or this mob boss's daughter?"

"I don't know," Quinn said. "But either way it's bad."

"I think I'd rather face the feds," Shawn said. "Mobsters are ruthless."

"You don't have to tell me," Quinn said, looking down at the stump of his right pinkie. "But then again, these feds nearly killed me just a few months ago."

* * * * * *

They arrived at the lake and parked. It was windy and raining, and the lake was deserted. They parked Quinn's still banged up Audi TT, which was leaking badly through a poorly duct-tape rapair of the soft-top, and got out.

"He told us to get out and walk, he would join us."

"More cloak and dagger," Shawn said. "This guy is scared. We should be too." They walked a hundred yards down the sidewalk, the lake on their right.

Quinn froze. "Look at that Chrysler with fogged windows," he said. "I bet that's him."

"No, that's a deserted car," Shawn said. "Look, it's probably stolen, one of the windows is broken and the plates are gone."

"But it's fogged up and there's still some steam rising off of the hood. It hasn't been here that long," Quinn said. "Let's have a look," he said.

The two approached the vehicle. Slumped over the steering wheel was agent Snow, a single bullet hole through his temple.

"Oh, no," Quinn said, panic rising in his chest.

"We got to get out of here now," Shawn said.

"Move!" a gravelly female voice said behind them. Quinn turned to see a beautiful Latina woman pointing a chrome-plated snub-nosed .38 caliber handgun at them.

It wasn't Josephine.

"Who the hell are you?" Quinn asked.

She turned and fired a shot into Shawn' thigh.

"Aargh!" he yelled involuntarily wincing and crouching in place, his hand applying pressure to the wound.

"Ask another question and he'll be shot again," she said, rain dripping off of the barrel of her smoking gun.

Quinn helped Shawn into the back of a Mercedes sedan. He sat down, wondering why she did not bother to tie either one of them up. As the dart landed in his neck he had his answer. The last thing he remembered hearing was Shawn's voice: "You bitch!"

* * * * * *

Quinn awoke tied to a chair in an old dingy stone building with rotten oak planks, the smell of oak, mildew, and stale wine in the air. He looked around, and found his friend gagged, wide-awake, lying on a hard wooden table, all four limbs bound. He was stretched into a spread-eagle position. His pants leg was torn off and a bandage was tied around the bullet wound in his thigh. He was moving his hands in frantic silence, trying to get loose. Where in the hell were they?

He heard two voices in an adjacent room, echoing in the stone building, which could have been the inside of a barn.

"I'm done, Barbara! I'm out of here and either of you so much as gets within a mile of me, I'll release it, I'll go public, and you two will lose this game you're playing"

"Honestly, Todd! How long do you think your petty little scheme will last? Your information is already obsolete. You screw with us at your own peril. You have blood on your hands, too. That piece of work with your business partner in the vineyard was sloppy and stupid. You panicked. We could have silenced her more gracefully than your botched job. If we go down, you go down too, only you'll fall harder," a woman said.

"I don't want you to fail, I just want out," he said. Quinn wondered who the man was. He sounded pathetic, weak.

"You make me sick! Get out of here," she said. This was followed by silence. Then an old oak door opened and the same woman who shot Shawn in the leg walked in and eyed the two men.

"Welcome back, Dr. Quinn," she said. "You are as much a lightweight as your friend is a heavyweight. I thought you might never wake up. You've made this rather inconvenient for Catherine and me."

"What do you mean?" Quinn asked.

"I need to know exactly what you've discovered up here in the valley, over at the Silverado, and on your trip down the peninsula to that herbal supplement processing warehouse."

"I don't know what you're talking about," Quinn said.

"You have quite a reputation for having brass balls and a really high pain threshold, Dr. Quinn. What about your friend?" she asked.

She took out a small dagger and cut off Shawn' bandage. He looked on in silence as she drove her knife into the bullet hole and twisted the blade. Shawn lurched, his face deep crimson, an involuntary scream erupted from him as he nearly spat out his gag. She smiled, taking pleasure in the maneuver. She pulled the knife out and fresh blood erupted from the hole as Shawn gasped for breath. Quinn looked on in horror as his friend suffered.

"After I kill him, I am going to start cutting off your other appendages. You already lost a pinkie finger, right?" she asked.

Quinn looked at her, defeat washing over him. "What if I tell you everything I know?" he asked.

"Maybe you'll live," she said. "The irony, Quinn, is that we never intended to have to kill you. You dying would be rather inconvenient for us, as it turns out. But if that federal agent would've said anything to anyone, well, that really would have been a problem. Lucky for you he didn't, or you'd both be dead."

"Why is that," Shawn said, catching his breath after managing to dislodge his gag.

"Your life, however," she said, turning and plunging her dagger into Shawn' uninjured thigh, "is totally irrelevant to us. So do me a favor, and shut the hell up," she said leaving the dagger buried to the hub in Shawn' quadriceps.

He was apoplectic.

She turned back to Quinn. "You have one chance to save your fingers, toes, and genitals, Quinn. What do you know about Catherine and me?"

"I know that Catherine is really Vladimir Michinski's daughter, that she probably poisoned Ron Park's wife with the mushroom risotto at the Silverado. I am guessing that one of you gave her the air embolus at Queen of the Valley, which killed her. The two of you also poisoned Ron Park, trying to kill him, and framed the Paradis brothers for both of those murders. You're making my old polymer at the warehouse in Burlingame and selling it at the Silverado as an herb. Somehow you've convinced the feds it's me doing it. I think that you're working on something else, some new way to make the drug, and that you two have plans to poison someone else at the Silverado, but I don't know who."

"Why was it that Catherine's dolt of a father had so much trouble extracting information from you?" she asked. "I plunge a dagger into your friend and you turn to mush? Come on, Quinn. I'm disappointed."

She walked away from Shawn and got very close to Quinn.

"Why frame the Paradis brothers?" she whispered.

Quinn looked at her blankly. "I don't know," he said.

She stared at him, trying to decipher, he figured, whether or not he was telling the truth. She moved to within an inch of Quinn's face and whispered. "I've got news for you, Quinn, we've already poisoned our second target," she backed away, here piercing gaze burning right through him.

"Me?" Quinn asked. His eye momentarily leaving her gaze and looking at the table Shawn was on.

Oh my God!

"The wine at the Silverado? The Prisoner?" Quinn asked, trying to keep her engaged.

"A good guess," she said back to him before turning back to Shawn, still stretched out on the table. She reached down to the knife still imbedded in Shawn's thigh and gave Quinn an evil 'watch this' sort of look as she grasped it and pulled it out.

Just as she freed the blade Shawn bolted upright, his arms free from the ropes, and boxed her hard on both ears. Stunned, she staggered backwards, dropping the knife.

Quinn saw an ooze of blood from her left ear, and knew Shawn had broken her eardrum. In a flash he grabbed the knife and cut the bonds to his feet. As she came at him he swung the knife sideways, blocking her arm from the left and attempting to plunge the blade into her neck from his right.

The knife penetrated, but not her neck. She took the blade in her forearm, and then connected with Shawn's solar plexus with her other fist. As he doubled over she reached for the knife.

Sensing danger, Shawn bolted upright off of the table. His wounded legs buckled under him as she pulled the knife from her left forearm and lunged with the blade in her right hand.

Shawn dodged the lunge, and hit her twice in the head. He was getting his legs back. She reached back to the small of her back but as she came around with the gun Shawn kicked as hard as his injured legs would, and the gun cracked, a single shot going wild as the gun flew across the room. She lunged at him again with the knife and he caught her arm, bending it backwards until the knife fell from it. He kicked the knife over toward Quinn, who struggled to free himself from his bonds and the chair. As Quinn struggled for the knife, her elbow connected with Shawn's chin, sending him staggering backwards. He righted himself as a ferocious scorpion kick connected with his face, sending him flying backwards onto the ground.

She was on him instantaneously, foot to his throat. His legs came up, but she used her other leg to block the kick, leaning still further on his compromised windpipe. As Shawn turned an alarming shade of purple, Quinn freed himself with the knife, and entered the melee.

Barbara knew Quinn was a skilled fighter. She backed off Shawn and gained her balance. Quinn helped his friend up and gave him the knife, making sure she could not get behind him to where the gun had disappeared in a pile of rubble. Now it was two against one.

Quinn attacked, blocking two fierce kicks as he tried to take her off balance with a foot sweep and a secure grasp of her clothing. But as he got within striking distance, she jabbed him at close range in the solar-plexus sending him into a paroxysm of coughing, then with the ball of her hand, smashed him in the nose, breaking it with a loud crack.

Quinn regained his composure as one of her legs shot out and struck Shawn in the chest. With one foot off of the ground, Quinn's second foot sweep found its mark and she went down hard on her back. He slid down to do a leg lock around her head, but as he positioned his legs, she bit into him, managing to secure a large chunk of Quinn's inner thigh in her mouth.

Fighting the urge to pull back, Quinn squeezed with every bit of his strength against her neck as she viciously tore through his flesh. Shawn approached and engaged her legs, which were effectively keeping him at bay. Quinn, reeling in pain, looked at the woman, whose mouth was fully occluded by the flesh and muscles of his inner thigh, and saw her flaring nostrils. Blood was flowing around her lips in impressive amounts. With one hand outstretched to keep her pinned, he still had one free hand, which he used to plug her flaring nostrils. Her eyes widened in panic; it was just a matter of time.

She kicked, bit and fought with ferocious desperation, flailing, writhing, and trying to get free. At last Quinn felt her jaw slacken as she attempted to get air. Rather than let her get away from his vice-like leg grip upon her, he squeezed tighter, not letting her pull her mouth out of the bite.

"Live by your attack, and die by it, bitch!" he growled. A moment later she was limp, and unconscious. Quinn extracted himself from her, and he looked incredulously at Shawn, who was as beaten and bloody as he was.

"Well, no one will ever accuse her of being a wimp!" Quinn said. He got up and held pressure on his khaki pants, which were turning crimson where her teeth had bitten deep into his leg. He and Shawn, bloody, bruised and beaten, but free, tied her up on the same table where Shawn was restrained, and exited the building into a wooded area, which cleared into a well manicured vineyard on a sloping hillside.

There was the Mercedes that they were taken in with, and to Quinn and Shawn's surprise, Quinn's red roadster was parked next to a rusted, dented, circa 1975 Chevy truck. Quinn's car was locked, and up on cinder blocks. Two of the tires were removed. "So much for a getaway in my car," he said as Shawn darted towards the car. He took the knife and cut into the tarp of the rag-top. As Quinn protested, he opened the car, reached in, and pulled out his compound longbow and arrows.

"Ha!" he said smirking as he limped back toward Quinn. Quinn felt notable relief that they now had a weapon besides a knife, which would do little good against any firearms. He limped to the truck, looked in the cab, smiled again, said, "You drive, Quinn! The keys are on the seat."

Quinn got into the cab as Shawn made his way to the other side, keeping the bow and arrows on his lap.

The old truck roared to life as Quinn turned the engine over, and they started down a serpentine drive heading through the vineyard.

"Where the hell are we?" Quinn asked.

"I don't know but someone's coming," Shawn said.

Quinn saw a small dust cloud ahead, billowing around a small silver sports car in the distance.

"Friend or foe?" he asked.

"Foe, until we know otherwise," Shawn said. "Be careful as we go by."

As she approached, Quinn saw the dark hair, the sharp features, and made the connection.

"It's Catherine," he said. Before Shawn could reply, Quinn gunned the accelerator of the truck and veered toward the Porsche, connecting with it and sending it sideways into a tangled mass of grape trellises. He didn't look back, accelerating the truck as fast as he could. There was the crack of a gunshot, and then another, and an instant later, the back window shattered, raining down a shower of safety glass. A glance in the rear-view mirror showed Catherine standing in the road, a revolver trained on the vehicle.

"We lose a tire, we're done out here, pal," Shawn said.

Quinn nodded, they were now three hundred yards from her and the truck was still operational. Quinn spotted an old wooden gate and made for it. The truck crashed through it easily, splinters of dry wood exploding over the hood, and at once they found themselves on the winding, hilly portion of Spring Mountain Road.

"I know where we are!" Quinn said.

"Get us down into St. Helena and to the police," Shawn said.

A moment later something slammed into the car from behind. Quinn nearly lost control of the vehicle, swerving to avoid heading down a ravine into a small creek. After he righted the truck, he glanced in the rear view mirror at a late model Range Rover, which was barreling toward them again.

"Jesus!" Quinn yelled, accelerating the truck. Shawn hung his torso out the window with his bow but didn't fire. Quinn took the corners fast, tires protesting with screeches, joined by the groans of fatigued metal on pressure points under the truck. The old pickup pitched wildly on its wobbly suspension.

"I can't get a shot at him!" Shawn yelled and retreated into the cab.

The two of them rocketed down the mountain and found themselves in the residential beginnings of St. Helena, where suburban homes and old Victorian dwellings were intermixed with vineyard plots. Shawn let out a whoop.

"What?" Quinn asked.

"Up around the bend. You have to get a couple hundred yards ahead of him," Shawn said. "The road loops around that vineyard like a huge U. Let me out, take him around the bend, and I'll run across the vineyard, fire off a shot, and disable his car. You stop, I'll get in and we'll hightail it out of here."

"How are you going to run? Look at your legs."

"Let me worry about that."

"Okay," Quinn said, desperately wondering how he was going to be able to create the required space between the cars. The Range Rover was newer and had more horsepower than the old truck. He slowed, hoping that the Rover would come along side and he could try to force it off the road, but it hit him again from behind sending him into a tailspin. Quinn righted the vehicle and hit the accelerator, creating about twenty yards of space.

"Shawn I don't think I can give you enough room!" he said.

"Just give me as much as you can, make sure that bastard doesn't run me over!" Shawn said.

As the Rover approached again, Quinn surprised the driver by slamming on his brakes, letting the SUV slam into his back with an ear-splitting grind of twisting metal. The other driver was startled by the move and hit his own brakes. Quinn slammed the accelerator onto the floor and made about sixty yards of space between the two.

"Good work," Shawn said. As Quinn slowed to make a left turn to face east toward the valley floor, Shawn bailed out. Quinn saw him roll twice, and pop up onto his feet, struggling for a split second before disappearing behind a canopy of grapevines and heading south on foot. Quinn tried to keep as much room as possible between himself and the Range Rover, but saw it closing again. As he made the second ninety degree turn, a right which sent him southbound on the roadway he fishtailed wildly, nearly losing control of the old truck. He heard the crack of a gun and his front windshield shattered. The safety glass turned everything opaque white. Quinn winced and held his head out the window to be able to visualize the narrow roadway. He imagined the back of his head with a large bull's eye on it.

It'll be a hard shot while driving.

Two more shots came, the first hitting metal, the second ricocheting off of the pavement. The bastard was aiming at his tires now. He began swerving back and forth, trying to make the shot more difficult. He made the third turn, heading west, toward the saddle between Spring Mountain and Mt. Veeder.

Come on Shawn, where the fuck are you?

The Rover was approaching fast and before Quinn could get to the end of the U shaped roadway, another shot took out his left rear tire. The truck dragged hard, as if someone had attached a piano to the rear fender. Quinn struggled to keep control of the auto and to keep it moving. When he regained control, slowing for what he thought was the coup-de-grace from the Rover, he glanced in the side mirror and saw that the Rover was similarly disabled. His eye fell upon the arrow sticking out of the front passenger side of the Rover. He kept the truck rolling on the flat, at about ten miles an hour, when the Rover stopped and the driver got out. Standing, the man from the Rover fired his gun and Quinn's second tire went flat. The old truck ground to a halt on the roadway.

Where the hell are you, Shawn?

Quinn ducked down below the windows, prone on the bench of the truck cab. He was a sitting duck. He heard footsteps approach, and was waiting for the business end of a gun to be pressed against the back of his head when he heard the familiar whoosh, an ominous thud, and then what could only be the collapse of their pursuer onto the pavement. He chanced a peak out his window and found a very dead Todd Sandoval lying on his side below the driver's side door, the butt of an arrow protruding from his chest and the business end sticking out his back and through his heart.

As Quinn opened the door, Shawn and his bow emerged from the canopy of grapes.

"Quinn, you okay?" he asked, looking down at his deceased prey.

"Fine," Quinn answered. "Todd Sandoval from Terroir Unlimited. He helped me buy my land on Mt. Veeder. Hell of a shot, Shawn."

"Thanks," Shawn answered, breathless. "Check his ass."

"What?"

"Check his ass," Shawn said seriously. "If you listened to that conversation up on Spring Mountain, I am almost certain he's the one who killed Arianna and tried to do us in during our midnight walk through the vineyard."

"Okay, but we have to call the police," Quinn said, kneeling down to check for a healing scar on the dead man's backside. "You'd think if that was him that night in the vineyard, he'd have learned to respect you and your lethal compound bow."

"Police are on their way already," Shawn said as Quinn registered the distant whine of approaching sirens.

"I guess some people don't learn," Quinn muttered to himself. "Shawn, you were right, there is a healing wound in his right butt-cheek." Looking around he found Shawn had wandered away. He stood up and walked over to the Range Rover, where Shawn was busy rummaging through the front passenger storage compartment. "Hey, be careful, we don't want to end up being suspects."

"Quinn look at this," Shawn said, ignoring Quinn as he handed him a wine glass wrapped in tissue. "What do you think this is?"

Quinn looked thoughtfully at the glass after unwrapping it. "I don't know, but I think it's a tasting glass from Wine Magazine.

"How can you tell?" Shawn asked.

"Look, it has a date on it, and a number etched in the bottom. Remember I watched Park and his wife taste at your winery while you were sleeping it off."

"Don't remind me," Shawn said. "What would he be doing with one of those? Look, it's still dirty."

"They store all of those at the magazine headquarters," Quinn said with a faraway tone in his voice.

"You think this glass should have been destroyed with the rest, in the explosion and fire?" Shawn asked.

"I don't know, Shawn," Quinn said. "But I know who might. We have to bring this to Ronald Park."

"What was she saying, that hot chick who tortured us?" Shawn asked.

Quinn turned to him incredulously.

"Seriously man," Shawn continued. "She was having an argument with him. Maybe it was about this glass."

"Well this glass couldn't have been poisoned. We know that the poison was in the Heitz and the Stag's Leap."

"So what was so important about this glass?" Shawn asked.

"Maybe nothing, but we have to bring it to Ron Park to be sure," Quinn said, tucking the glass into his coat pocket as the police arrived.

Chapter 27:

After getting treatment for their wounds, Quinn and Shawn were taken to the police station. It took all day long for them to explain what had happened to the astonished Sherriff Hernandez, who was pleased that finally, neither of them was intoxicated during this interview. After they described the place where they were held, Hernandez lit up in recognition.

"I think that's the Chevalier property up on Spring Mountain. It is a part of another vineyard now, but used to be its own winery back in the nineteenth century. I think there is an old abandoned building on that property."

He sent two officers there, and they reported back that the place had been cleared out very recently, and that there was blood at the scene, and evidence indicating a struggle, including knocked over trellises and vines. That evidence, coupled with recovered gun in the deceased's hands, the wound on his backside, led Hernandez to release Shawn, concluding that he had killed Todd Sandoval in self-defense and in the defense of his friend Matthew Quinn.

Upon release, Quinn called and relayed the story to a particularly distant sounding Josephine Rodriguez while Shawn called Tasha. They told her the story and she was surprised to hear that they were face to face with the Latina woman named Barbara, and she was not Josephine. At her request, they returned to Palo Alto and the Stanford Medical Center. As they drove a rental car down to the South Bay, Quinn engaged his friend.

"I am so sorry about all of this, Shawn."

"Why?"

"You've been shot, stabbed, tortured, had to kill someone in self-defense, saved my ass a couple of times, and this whole mess doesn't even have anything to do with you," Quinn said.

"Well, we're going to be silent business partners, and that makes me involved," Shawn said, smiling at Quinn.

"Boy you are something else," Quinn said.

"It'll make a hell of a story someday," Shawn said with a smug grin.

Quinn and Shawn were shown into Park's private room on the Medical-Surgical ward of the hospital. They passed Joshua's friend, Jeff, sitting patiently in the hallway, and found Minh and Joshua in the room with Ron Park.

"You are continuing to improve, congratulations Mr. Park," Shawn said.

Park made eye contact with both Quinn and Shawn. "I think both of you should call me Ron."

"Well, Ron, it's great that you are out of the ICU," Quinn said. "You've made an amazing recovery."

"Thanks to you," Park said. "I'm glad you came here. I remembered where I heard the name Michinski. I thought you should know," he said.

"Really? Where did you hear it," Quinn asked.

"Well, Virginia and I were completing a book, a history of Napa Valley. And it turns out that after the war, an elderly woman by that name came into Northern California from Eastern Europe. She purchased a large plot of land straddling the Rutherford district and St. Helena with the help of the Catholic Church. She had been held prisoner in a Nazi concentration camp in Poland with her son, and came to America after the end of the war. She held it until the late 1950's and then, for reasons that aren't clear, she died suddenly and her descendants conducted a fire sale, and the land passed to the father of Henri and Alfonse Paradis. Her son was the late Vladimir Michinski, the infamous crime lord of San Francisco and the East Bay."

Quinn was stunned. The Michinski family had a past in Napa Valley? He gave a knowing glance to Shawn. "Catherine wants Grandma's land back," he said to Shawn. He turned back to Park. "Were you told about the explosion at your magazine headquarters?" Quinn asked.

"Yeah, I was grateful to hear that no one was hurt. This is all just too much. It's wine, and I don't care how good wine is, you don't kill people over it. Now someone's bombing offices, and…." he stopped suddenly, his eyes welling up with tears.

Minh sat down next to him and put a sympathetic hand on his shoulder. "It's alright Ron, just relax."

"It's just that, when I started rating wines, I never imagined that what the critics said would carry so much weight. That wineries would rise and fall based on what I thought about their product. I never imagined that what I wrote would make it dangerous for me, would lead to the death of my wife. This was about helping people pick out a good wine, not about destroying wineries and killing people." He pulled himself together. "Anyway, I was relieved that the explosion and fire didn't kill anyone."

"I wonder if it was even meant to," Quinn said.

"What do you mean?" Park asked.

"Well, you keep extensive records, including the storage of single use wineglasses for your tastings, right?"

"We didn't always do that, but when the scandals hit the other publications, we started doing it to protect ourselves. We went public about it about a year ago as part of our campaign to sell ourselves as the last honest place one could get truly unbiased blind wine ratings," Park said.

"Well, what if there was evidence there that needed to be destroyed?" Shawn asked.

"I'd say they succeeded," Park said.

"Maybe not," Quinn said and produced the wineglass.

Park took the glass and looked at it, frowning. "Well, this is etched and dated, and it certainly looks like one of ours," he said. "I can't tell you what wine it is, but we could look that up, we have all that information on a secure server."

"Both of us were wondering if you'd take a closer look at it. It looks like there is more than dried wine residue," Quinn said.

Park looked puzzled, and reexamined the glass. He then buried his nose into the old dry glass, pulling away from it a second later.

"Get me a glass of warm water," he said.

Shawn got up and returned with a small Dixie cup of tepid water. Park carefully poured a few drops into the glass, and then turned the glass to dissolve some of the residue. Then he smelled again, wrinkling up his forehead as he inhaled deeply. He then put his finger in and pulled out a small drop of liquid and touched his tongue.

"It's wine, but there's something else here, I don't know what. It tastes like a mixture of malic and oxalic acid, and liquid smoke. It doesn't really matter, though, because it is not clear that whatever contaminant is there was there when I tasted this."

"That's interesting," Minh said.

"Why?" Park asked.

"Because those scents and flavors might be in wine naturally, but if added to a balanced wine, might push it out of balance," Minh said.

"Minh is correct," Ron acknowledged, looking at Quinn and Shawn.

"What wine was tasted?" Quinn asked.

"I can find out, but I'll have to make a phone call," Ron said.

He reached over to the side of the bed and picked up the phone. After a brief conversation, he registered a look of surprise. He hung up and turned to Quinn.

"Well that's not what I expected to hear."

"What?" Quinn asked. "Which wine was in that glass?"

"Henri Paradis's reserve Cabernet blend," Park said. "I have to retaste that wine. If the glass was tampered with prior to my tasting of the wine it means…." He stopped suddenly, shock in his eyes, followed by a pained look on his face.

"What? Who could have done this?" Quinn asked as the others looked on in silence.

"Only Virginia," Park said in a whisper. "She's the only one who could have tampered without the observers knowing."

"Why would she want to influence the tasting of Paradis's reserve blend?" Shawn asked.

"I don't know," Park said looking ashen. "I can't think of any reason at all."

"Is it possible that there were others?" Quinn asked. "What about other vintages?"

Park was silent, looking down at his bed. "I guess it is possible, but we'll never know, all of the other glasses have been destroyed. She wouldn't do that to me, she couldn't do that to me!" Suddenly he got up out of bed, and walked with purpose into the bathroom.

"Hey Quinn, I thought these were double blinded, didn't you participate?"

"Yeah, they are, but if I watched the shrouding, and then kept my eye on one or two bottles, I could maybe keep identification of them in my head, and know when I poured them if I was Virginia, but not more than one or two. It would be like counting cards with a six deck shoe in Vegas."

"Joshua, can you find some clothes for me, I am getting out of here now," Park said, reemerging from the bathroom, his hair combed hastily backwards.

"You can't go, you haven't been released," Joshua said.

"I'll sign myself out. I'm going up to Napa." Park reached into his bathrobe and pulled out a cellular phone, hitting a speed-dial.

"Deirdre, have someone from the magazine meet me at the Paradis winery. Call the winery and have them prepare bottles from each of the last three vintages, each pulled from the cellar and sealed by the winemaker with his signature over the seal. I want to retaste everything since they cleaned up the TCA problem. Make sure there is nothing wrong with the chain of custody of those wines. Shroud them and put in a dozen wines from the same years from other local wineries from Rutherford and St. Helena. Prepare monitors, and make sure the tasting is completely blind. Inform Mr. Paradis that there may have been sabotage. Someone may have been tampering with his wine prior to tasting, and that I wish to retaste it. I must do this today."

"It's getting late," Joshua said. "Do you want to wait until tomorrow?"

"We have to get to the bottom of this now," Park said. "Can you two drive me up to St. Helena?"

Minh nodded and left to bring the car around. Joshua turned to Shawn and Quinn. "Are you coming up with us?" he asked.

"We'll follow you. We have to know too," Shawn said. He turned to Quinn and said, "Something tells me I am going to lose that land back to him before I ever plant a vine on it."

Quinn shrugged. "This whole thing is tied up with my polymer and Vladimir Michinski's daughter. They were out to get me, and now I think she and her hench-woman were also aiming to get Grandma Michinski's land back from Paradis. I wonder if she was using my polymer to raise the capital to go after that land."

"It seems like just too much of a coincidence that she is going after him and you, and that we ended up buying his land," Shawn said. "But now we have a motive for her going after both Henri and Alfonse. She didn't have it in for Park, but she obviously had some leverage on Park's wife, if she is also behind the tainting of the wine."

"If the wine is tainted," Quinn cautioned.

"Right, but Quinn, if it is, what better person to kill than the one who was manipulated into destroying Paradis, and the only one who might be able to save him?"

"Plus, if Park were dead he wouldn't have been able to retaste those wines," Quinn said.

"The biggest irony is that it was her and her illegal operation that saved Park. It's your polymer, but she is the one responsible for him having access to it. It is totally amazing," Shawn said.

"There's some light at the end of the tunnel, Shawn. This is all beginning to come together."

"If we get you cleared, you get all that frozen money back, maybe we can go in on a project together, officially together, I mean," Shawn said, his face lighting up.

A half an hour later, they were on the road heading back up to Napa Valley. They would meet the monitors and the rest of the tasting team, along with Henri Paradis in his tasting room at 10 pm.

"So if Park retastes the wine and it's schlock, the whole concept is blown," Shawn pointed out. "We need evidence, we need to prove that she is the owner of that production facility in Burlingame."

"The wines are going to be good, I'm certain," Quinn said. "As far as Catherine and her plan go, her decision to begin marketing it as a natural health food supplement made it unregulated by the FDA. You have to hand it to her. She's one smart bitch. She's playing a lot of people."

"Why frame Alfonse? Was she trying to destroy him too?" Shawn asked.

"At first I thought he might be in on the whole thing, but now that he's been arrested, I think she knows enough to ruin him so that he'll force the sale of the special plot, the one that makes that unbelievable wine. He has a fifty percent stake in the legendary family plot. Maybe she wanted to get him desperate enough so that she could force them both to relinquish that land, which would otherwise be that last thing either would do. Maybe she wants to be the next baroness of Napa Valley."

"Seems ridiculous, she's already a tycoon," Shawn said.

"Right, like all of these other tycoons in the valley. She probably has to do this to feed her ego," Quinn said. "That's why I did it originally."

"Well, if you're right, she's formidable," Shawn said.

"Just like the rest of her family," Quinn said, the remnants of his right pinkie finger twitching slightly.

Shawn' phone rang. He looked at caller ID. "It's your friend from UCSF," he said, handing the phone to Quinn.

"David, how are you?" Quinn asked. He listened intently. "Wow! She did it, Unbelievable! Keep the cultures, freeze-dry some of them, and I'll come by and pick them up. Thanks again, David. I owe you one," Quinn said.

"What?" Shawn asked. "She genetically modified the yeast to make your polymer?"

Quinn nodded. "Yeast grows all over a vineyard. Wine is one of the most chemically complex beverages in the world. It's a food, and is regulated as such. She would have to inoculate a vineyard maybe only once," he said.

"And her beverages become the elixir of eternal youth?" Shawn asked.

"Uh-huh."

"Talk about cult status! Drink my wine and live forever. People will pay a hefty premium for that."

They arrived at the winery of Henri Paradis. Park, in spite of having sold the publication, retained considerable influence with the employees of the magazine. When they arrived there were about two-dozen people, including several members of the Napa County Sherriff's department, and reporters from the Napa Valley Register, The Sacramento Bee and the San Francisco Chronicle. Park waited for everyone to gather around him before entering the building.

"I want to thank all of you for helping bring this very important meeting together." He spoke as if he had a lot more to say, but after his first utterance, the large door to the winery workroom opened and Henri Paradis walked out with Josephine Rodriguez, and greeted Ron Park.

"Mr. Park, it is a pleasure to have you," he said without any emotion. "If you'll come inside, we've set up a table for you and your people." With that they went in, immediately noticing a table made up of an old wide plank of mahogany stretched out between two oak barrels. Park nodded his assent, and the people from the magazine began setting up the table with marked, etched glasses, and shrouded, still unopened bottles.

Quinn tried to make eye contact with Josephine, but she didn't return his gaze. She was busy observing the affair as it unfolded. She looked nervous.

Park looked directly at Henri Paradis and asked where his winemaker was. As if on cue, Paradis' son-in-law and winemaker Andrew Wooten, who seemed to have a difficult time controlling his disdain for Park, appeared and presented the three bottles. With a silent motion of his head, Wooten gave the wines to an assistant, who quickly shrouded and brought the wines to be with the others.

Park sat down and the whole thing came together, the wines were shuffled and placed in random order. A pretty red head with long legs and a red satin dress came and sat down. Three official looking observers took their seats so they could observe the tasting with an uninterrupted view. Before sitting down, Park turned to Henri Paradis and his winemaker.

"You two should stay, keep an eye on what bottles are yours, and make sure no one has done anything to them. When we are finished, you can taste them yourselves, and be certain that they are as they should be."

Paradis nodded and said nothing. Quinn watched as Andrew Wooten kept an eagle eye on his wines. Park sat with his back to the wines as they were corked and labeled with numbers. Following Wooten's eyes, Quinn surmised that Paradis' wines were numbered four, seven, and ten of the dozen wines to be tasted.

Park sat down and the tasting began just as the one had in Shawn' tasting room, there was silence and all eyes were on Park. When he came to the wine labeled number four he smelled, swirled and smelled again. "St. Helena, east of the highway," he muttered to himself. Andrew Wooten looked as if he were about to burst. Park tasted, his eyes closed, swishing the wine back and forth across his tongue, he moved his head back and forth, in deep thought. He finished, spit the wine out, and wrote his note in silence. The rest of the tasting was completed over about an hour. After tasting the last wine, Park finished writing, and turned to his assistant, handed her the legal pad he had written on, and stood up.

"Mr. Paradis, I don't know for sure which wines were yours, but I do owe you an apology, as I did not rate any wines tonight below eighty seven points. We do not, as a rule release wine scores at the end of a tasting, but under these extraordinary circumstances, tonight I'm going to make an exception. Gail, you may unshroud the wines at your convenience and read the scores of the wines belonging to Mr. Paradis."

The redhead stood up and nodded at her two assistants who quickly pulled the shrouds off of the bottles. The last three vintages of Paradis' wines were indeed number four, seven and ten, number ten being the barrel sample of the reserve Cabernet tasted just a few weeks earlier. She smiled, seemed totally at ease with the crowd, including some photographers who came in during the tasting.

"Ladies and gentlemen," she began, "wine number four: The appearance is garnet in color. The nose on this wine is of nuanced vanilla, crushed berry fruit, mineral and sage. The mouth feel is refined and balanced, with silky tannins and a lively zip. The wine glides across the tongue layering out lush blackberry and crème-de-cassis, mocha, and hints of brown spice. The mid-palate is thick, with vanilla and berry fruit dancing in harmony, and the finish lasts for minutes. 97 points."

The crowd immediately erupted into a loud murmur. Paradis' face remained unchanged, but Andrew Wooten was flushed and let out a long exhale. Quinn again tried to make eye contact with Josephine, but she remained focused on the woman reading the notes.

"Wine number seven: Deep ruby in color, nose of scorched earth, coffee, and sage, with old oak and brown spice. The mouth feel is medium to full bodied and impeccably balanced, with velveteen tannin structure, but a powerful backbone. The wine reveals classic Napa cassis and ripe boysenberry with hints of crushed raspberry. There is spiciness to this wine, which sets it apart. There are seductive layers of coffee, bittersweet chocolate, and nutmeg building to a crescendo on the hind palate, a magnificent wine. 98 points."

Henri Paradis' face broke into the smallest of smiles, and he gently pat the shoulder of his winemaker, who appeared on the verge of ecstasy, but was holding in any noise, although Quinn thought, just barely.

"And finally, Mr. Paradis's pre-release barrel sample: This wine is inky dark in color, and uber-extracted. This wine has a reticent nose, with hints of crushed granite. The mouth feel is very full-bodied and wound up tight. Tannin structure is less austere on the palate, and the wine is perfectly balanced and age-worthy. Cinnamon oak and ripe blackberry flavors give way to layers of vanilla bean and coffee extract. The wine is monumentally complex and layered. There is so much going on with this wine it is almost surreal: sage, cinnamon-toast, cassis, and wet rocks on the mid-palate, and a finish of roasted vanilla, smoke and raspberry all wound around a tight core. This is a benchmark wine, one that should evolve and improve for decades. 99 points."

The room thundered into applause. Park smiled and nodded at Henri Paradis before slipping out the door.

Paradis got up and approached Quinn, Andrew Wooten in tow.

"I believe you two have given me my winery back," he said, his smile radiating warmth.

"In my case, literally," Shawn said with a faux grimace before shaking the Paradis and Wooten's hands.

"I will be forever in debt to both of you," he whispered, and turned back to the crowd, which had mysteriously grown much larger. Quinn looked around for Josephine, and found her looking subdued in the corner.

Quinn approached and she looked at him ruefully.

"Good day for Henri Paradis," he said jovially.

"Quinn, we have to talk, but not here," she said matter-of-factly.

Chapter 28:

"What?" Quinn asked Josephine when they reached a quiet place. She looked entirely more serious and subdued than she should have under the circumstances.

"Matthew, I haven't been completely honest with you," she said. Quinn's heart sunk.

"What do you mean?" he asked.

"Remember when we first met?"

"The accident?" Quinn asked. "Just barely. Please tell me you aren't in with the feds."

"Quinn, I am not in with the feds, or anyone else, at least, not exactly," she said, her voice trailing off.

"You are confusing the hell out of me."

"I, that is to say, our meeting wasn't entirely an accident," she said, looking pale as she spoke.

"You ran me down on purpose?" Quinn asked, confused.

"No, I had no intention of running you down, but I was, at the request of my sister, looking for you," she said earnestly.

"I have no idea what you are talking about Josephine," Quinn said. "Your sister told you to look for me in Berkeley? Is she a federal agent?" Then he realized who her sister was. "No, she isn't is she? But I've met her before."

Josephine continued. "Barbara was estranged from the family after we both graduated from college. She was so angry that the Elder Paradis did not bring my father into the business and make him an owner and partner after all that they'd been through. He'd verbally promised that, our father had said. When the elder Paradis died and Henri took over, she hoped he would honor the deal. Well, there was no deal. She hated our father for not wanting to fight over it, and then when I did some pro-bono work for Paradis she vowed never to speak to me again. She went her own way. She disappeared for about three years. I heard from her for the first time the morning we met. We were supposed to meet for coffee, but she asked me to make sure that you were found and okay."

"She wanted me to be okay?" he asked.

"She told me that you were important to her and that you were in trouble. I had to make sure you were either okay, and if not, to get you to a hospital safely. She insisted that I not ask any questions. I really wanted to reestablish contact with her, so I listened. I was actually scanning the road looking for you when you rolled out of that ditch. I was looking on the other side of the street and didn't see you until it was too late. It was never my intention to hurt you, Matthew. You have to believe that."

"What was your intention, Josephine," Quinn said, sounding every bit as icy as he was feeling at the moment.

"My intention was to find you for my sister, and make sure that you made it to a doctor. She knew that you were there, and that you were hurt, but she didn't want to be seen by you."

"The girl at the Silverado, the one I heard and partially saw in the spa after hours, was that your sister?"

"I think so," she said. "We haven't spoken since she told me to stay away from you."

"She told you to stay away from me?" Quinn said.

"She said you were damaged goods, too damaged. And she said you wouldn't be around long anyway."

"Josephine, you realize that she's the one who tortured Shawn. She was the one at the Chevalier property."

"Tasha told me. I never would have thought it was possible, but now, I don't know," she said.

"What is her relationship with Catherine?" Quinn asked. "Are they business partners, or did they meet at some hate-club for Henri Paradis? Is that how they are mixed up with me?"

"My sister's gay. She doesn't talk about it. I think the two of them are in a relationship," Josephine said.

Quinn nodded. He looked at Josephine intently. "Well, your sister found a sister in arms with Catherine Michinski.

We just found out that Catherine's grandmother lost all of her land in Napa in a fire sale to Henri Paradis's father over fifty years ago. If your sister's desire was to take a bite out of the Paradis family, she found the perfect co-conspirator. That means she's tied up in the murder of Park's wife, the attempt on Park, and two attempts on Shawn and me.

"This whole event is surreal," she said, shaking her head. "Barbara is no stranger to crime. She did time in juvenile hall for breaking into the school to change her grades. She was kicked out of college after hacking into the mainframe. She also did time for hacking into some large banking sites. She's a computer and programming genius, a first rate hacker, but somewhere along the line, she lost her sense of right and wrong."

"The whole thing ties me and my damn polymer to the near-downfall of one of Napa's finest statesmen, all orchestrated by Catherine Michinski and your sister. Your sister is Barbara Garcia? Was she married once?"

"No. She took our mother's maiden name when she became estranged from my father. She should have no feud with you or Henri Paradis, to whom she owes nothing but a debt of gratitude. I need to speak with her."

"Josephine, that woman, whether your sister or not, is dangerous, brutal, and cold-blooded. She shot and stabbed Shawn with no goal but to inflict pain. If I didn't know better, I would have thought she was enjoying it," Quinn said.

Josephine squeezed her eyes shut as tears came out. "Quinn, she's my sister. I have to believe she is capable of redemption."

"What is your plan?"

"I am going to set up a meeting with her. I'll get her the best lawyer in the region. I know just the man. He'll be able to get her a deal if she comes clean, and helps clear your name. As far as I am concerned, that's her only path to redemption."

"And if that doesn't work?" Quinn asked. "What happens if she refuses, or turns on you?"

"I don't know," Josephine said. "But I have to give her the chance."

"Good luck," Quinn said. His stomach churned as she left. Shawn walked up to him from behind.

"It's her sister, the one up at the Chevalier property?" he guessed.

"Yes. I'm worried that this is the last time I am going to see her alive. And I think I'm falling in love with her."

"Then, my friend, we need to make sure that this isn't the last time we see her," Shawn said. "Let's follow her."

Chapter 29:

The next morning Quinn and Shawn got up early and cased Josephine's home in American Canyon. At seven thirty she got into her BMW and drove towards Napa. They followed at a distance.

"Shawn, in the books I read, the person being tailed always notices. Don't you think she'll notice us?"

"Maybe," Shawn said. "I don't really give a damn, though, as long as we're around if she needs us." They were about five cars behind her, and she didn't appear to be in a hurry. She turned into the Silverado Springs Resort.

"I don't like that we're going here," Quinn said.

"Well, the first time you saw her sister it was here, wasn't it?"

Josephine parked her car and walked into the resort. They parked and followed, keeping a little too much distance for Quinn's comfort. When they entered the resort, Josephine was nowhere to be found.

* * * * * *

Josephine had managed to contact her sister, and insisted on a meeting. Barbara had sounded irritated after the call last night, but at last agreed to the meeting. She asked her to meet at the spa at 8:30 in the Supervisor's office an hour before it opened for the day.

Josephine arrived at 8:00 and let herself into the spa area, successfully soliciting the help of the custodial staff to unlock the spa. She let herself into the back area with the offices, and found nothing immediately incriminating in the first two she looked through. She came to the supervisor's office. It was locked. She looked down at the end of the hall and saw a door marked storage. She wondered if this was the office where Quinn first saw Barbara. She had to get into that office. She reached into her purse and produced a screwdriver and a small hammer. She calmly approached the hinges of the door and removed the pin from each of the hinges. The door wedged slowly, but once she had it off the hinges, she was able to remove the door with little difficulty. Inside now, she looked around, unlocked the door, and reattached it.

She sat at the desk in front of a computer. Realizing that there was little else in the office, and nothing in the desk drawers, she turned it on. Barbara was one of the user names, she selected it, and the password request came up. Josephine thought for a long time before hazarding a guess. She thought about her sister, and what was important to her. She remembered a cocker spaniel her father had gotten for Barbara. One day when the girls were playing in the vineyards, Honey, that was the Cocker's name, was bitten by a rattlesnake. She died that night, and Barbara was devastated. Josephine remembered it was the fourth of July and there was a large fireworks celebration and a party at the vineyard and winery that night. She stayed in with her sister who cried all night. It was her strongest childhood memory of her sister. She tried several incarnations of the dog's name unsuccessfully before trying "Honey0704" and to her surprise, she was granted access.

She scrolled through the documents, and immediately zeroed in on a PDF file labeled 'Silverado Chain of Ownership'. She clicked it and it opened. She scanned the file quickly as she was accustomed to, having learned the skill in law school.

Her heart sank when she realized that through a convoluted chain of trusts, the ownership of the Silverado was a trust belonging to none other than Matthew Quinn. The property was more than 90% leveraged.

She found another file, labeled 'Accounts'. In it, was a list of no less than seven off shore accounts, each with between two and fifteen million dollars in it. All of them were trusts, and all of them belonged to Matthew Quinn. Her heart sank further.

Now, furious and no longer intent on helping her sister, she continued scanning the documents, and found another, labeled "production." It showed that the laboratory and production facility in Burlingame were leased to a corporation, and on the board of trustees was Matthew Quinn. Josephine knew that there was enough material here to put Quinn away for the rest of his life. Josephine was crestfallen that her sister was utilizing her considerable tech skills to frame Quinn.

The door lock clicked and opened, her sister flashed a look of surprise, but for only a second.

"Well," she began, "Good morning, Josephine. Fancy that you should have broken into my office, and it appears, accessed my protected files. It's a crime, but then again, you knew that didn't you?"

Josephine steeled herself. "And you, how did you get yourself mixed up with Matthew Quinn? Why would you use your financial and computer knowhow to set him up like this?"

"Remember your botched favor in Berkeley?"

"Yeah. How did you get involved?"

"Quinn is nothing to me. He was going down whether or not I got involved. I just provided some of the financial knowhow to trap him. I did it as a favor," Barbara explained.

"The real target was Henri, wasn't it," Josephine said, but she knew the answer already.

Barbara's mouth tightened into an angry smile. "You should be ashamed. After his father died and Henri failed to honor the pledge to our family, you should've been as angry as me. You should be helping me," Barbara said.

"How long have you been after him?"

"After his ill-fated attempt to expand into Tuscany and his commitment to the college, I knew he was weak. We arranged to contaminate his winery, and he lost two vintages to cork-taint," Barbara said with an evil smile that was close to a sneer.

"You caused the TCA contamination?"

"Since it can happen for no reason, no one suspected me. It was easy," Barbara said. "We then got leverage on

Park's wife. We knew what she wanted and were able to manipulate her into tainting Paradis's wines at the tastings. We took advantage of the scandals and his growing influence on the industry. With that, we were able to make Paradis more and more desperate, until he started selling land. We have him exactly where we want him. Now he's finished."

"But Barbara, why Quinn?"

"My girlfriend," Barbara said as though that explained everything.

"He's done nothing to you," Josephine said. "What kind of twisted morality play is this?"

"He killed Catherine's father and brother, and destroyed Catherine's family," Barbara said.

"And she stole his invention, and has made hundreds of millions of dollars peddling his polymer." Josephine said. "And there are several witnesses which corroborate his side of the story. Quinn and everyone he was with were acting in self-defense against her father, who was a drug kingpin."

Barbara paused, looking intently at her sister. "So you know about that," she said. "Well, it turns out that Michinski and his son survived the confrontation with Quinn."

"They're still alive?" Josephine asked.

"No, but they had to be dispatched by Catherine," Barbara said.

"She killed her own family?"

"Yeah, and made it look like she died too. It's too bad that you know that now."

"Why is it too bad, Barbara?" Josephine asked. "Are you going to kill me, your own sister?"

"I just can't let you walk out of here with that information," she said. "You know too much."

"So that's how it is, Barbara? You would kill your own sister over this?" Josephine asked rhetorically. "Why not? Your lover killed her family." She fought back tears as she understood fully that her sister was beyond redemption.

"I would kill anyone who got cozy with the man who betrayed my father," Barbara said.

"As I recall," Josephine said, "our father was at peace with the plan going forward, and you disowned him as well as me, and even changed your name to mom's maiden name out of disgust for him. Is that the kind of loyalty you prize? You are the one who betrayed dad." Barbara flinched, and Josephine knew she had struck a nerve.

"You are so weak!" she spat. "Get away from my desk!" she came around to the side of the desk where Josephine stood. Josephine stepped back, her sister's look and posture suggested more of a threat than Josephine was prepared for.

Barbara looked at her like a feral animal, and turned briefly to the computer. She leaned down and typed something, and the screen began flashing and moving very rapidly.

"You're erasing everything, covering your trail?" Josephine asked.

"The feds have all they need. Agent Snow is out of the way, and no one else has put this together. As we speak, the feds are getting a warrant for Dr. Quinn's arrest. He'll rot the rest of his life in a federal prison, convicted of patent infringement, illegal distribution, and tax evasion. Not even a slick lawyer like you could get him out of this. Those links are iron-clad. I made sure of it myself. The feds have irrefutable proof that Dr. Quinn not only owns the Silverado and leases the lab in Burlingame, but that he has millions of dollars in off-shore accounts."

"Whose money is really in those accounts?" Josephine asked. "Not yours or Catherine's."

Barbara inched toward her. "I went to work for Alfonse. He's become a sloppy businessman. It was so easy to embezzle money from him, some for me, some for Catherine, and some for those off-shore accounts. Now, all that money belongs to your sweet, innocent, dying boyfriend, Matthew Quinn. Alfonse didn't even realize it until after Henri was arrested. His business worth had dropped by over ninety percent. Alfonse is as big an imbecile as Henri. He hired me because he knew I hated his brother. I love the irony. He helped bring his older brother down, only he went down with the ship too."

"And you poisoned Park and killed his wife?"

"Well, we were worried that the bitch wasn't going to die, so we had to make sure she did."

"Did you or Catherine give her the air embolus?"

"Does it matter?"

"It does to me."

Barbara paused. "Catherine did that. But I am the one who poisoned Park with Henri's cyanide and then planted some at Alfonse's place."

"Barbara, you're a step slow," Josephine said with a forced calm.

"Oh, am I?"

"Yeah, you are," Josephine said, taking the offensive. "Here's some irony for your evil-genius intellect to chew on. You and Catherine underestimated Matthew's polymer. Ron Park survived the cyanide and the fentanyl because of the drug. He found out his wife sabotaged Henri's wine. Todd Sandoval betrayed you and Catherine, even after he died. He got his hands on one of the tainted glasses, Quinn found it, told Park about the tampering, and he retasted Henri's wines from the last three vintages last night. He wasn't supposed to live to ever retaste those wines. He did, and he rated them ninety-seven, ninety-eight, and ninety-nine points. It's front-page news. The demand is exploding after less than 24 hours. Both back vintages sold out already. Henri is buying back his land from Shawn and is working out a deal with Alfonse. Henri's back, and it's all because you and Catherine stole Quinn's incredible invention. You failed, Barbara. Henri is being viewed as both a hero and a victim. He's larger than ever, larger than life. His wines are cult status now."

Josephine looked at her sister as she coiled like a snake. At once Barbara lunged at her, exploding with fury. Josephine attempted to dodge, but was struck hard in the side of the head. She knew she did not have the same combat skills her sister possessed. The room spun from the impact. Before she could put a hand out to balance herself, she was struck again, in the solar plexus by a ferocious kick. She staggered back into the wall and slid down. Barbara approached and let Josephine stand. She assumed a kung-fu position and smiled, taunting her sister.

"It doesn't matter. After I kill you and your boyfriend goes to prison, I am going to kill Henri, his daughter, and her husband. His land should belong to Catherine anyway, and by extension, me. We were the rightful owners, both having had the land taken from our families by the fucking Paradis family!"

With that she moved forward, Josephine moved backward, cowering, hoping that somehow she could get to the door. If she ran, she could get away. That was the one thing she knew she could do better than her sister. Josephine expected another blow by kick, but instead Barbara closed in on her, instantly it seemed.

She was taken by the lapel, turned and with shocking velocity, was thrown over her sister's hip, and onto the desk. She collided with the computer, and the screen, the keyboard, and Josephine toppled onto the other side, the oversized LCD screen landing on her chest, knocking the wind out of her.

She picked it up and as her sister approached, holding it up as a shield. Barbara's foot crashed through the screen and hit her neck. The blow nearly caused her to black out. But she managed to stay conscious. She jerked the broken screen to the side, sharp chards of LCD plastic digging into her sister's leg.

Barbara grunted and moved to liberate her leg from the computer screen. Josephine rolled onto her stomach and spotted at her purse, right below her nose. She reached into it as the screen hit the ground beside her.

She managed to get to her knees, and then took a vicious kick in the gut. The triathlon conditioning and core strength she had worked on so diligently helped her partially withstand the blow, but she was nearly incapacitated. She staggered to her feet, one hand still in her purse. Barbara lunged at her, blocking her right hand as it attempted to stop her advance, but as Barbara closed hard upon Josephine, her eyes opened wide, in shock. She was right in Josephine's face, nose to nose, staring right into her eyes, looking more fierce, feral, and frightening than anything Josephine had ever seen.

"You fucking little breeder slut," Barbara whispered as she backed up two steps.

Josephine started crying.

"I'm sorry, Barbara, I am so sorry!" she said, and she meant it.

Barbara looked down at her abdomen, and saw the hub of the screwdriver sticking out, the rest of the tool buried in her taught, sinewy abdomen.

"Sorry my ass," she said, reaching for the screwdriver and pulling it out.

"Barbara, no! Don't!"

It was too late.

Barbara stepped toward her, holding the bloody screwdriver like a switchblade in a fight, but on her second step, she staggered, blinking. She stopped and shook her head. A moment later, she dropped the screwdriver, put her hands on the desk, and then collapsed. Her heart stopped thirty seconds later.

Josephine sat down, cradling her dead sister's head in her lap, sobbing uncontrollably when Quinn and Shawn burst into the room. They looked around, saw Barbara with a large crimson stain covering her swollen and blood filled abdomen and an open-eyed death-stare at the ceiling. They looked at Josephine who met their eyes through her tears and sobs.

"Matthew, listen to me," she began.

"Oh Josephine, I am so sorry," Quinn said. "You need to get to a doctor, and we need to call the police!"

"No!" Josephine shouted. "Give me a minute to explain."

"Josephine, you don't have to explain anything," Quinn began.

"Shut up and listen to me!" she shouted desperately.

Quinn shut up.

"My sister is a computer hacker and a financial genius. She knows how to launder money, create dummy accounts, untraceable transactions, everything. She's like Minh Tran without a conscience. She went to juvenile hall as a teenager for doing things like that, hacking into the school's computers, the local bank branch, stuff like that. She seemed to straighten out, and went to college. There her learning exploded. But she was kicked out. Anyway, they framed you, Quinn, the whole thing."

"Josephine, we know that, and we can show that it was them, not me," Quinn said. "I am going to clear my name, and Shawn and I are going to make some kick-ass wine together. We got them. We won!"

"Quinn, you own the Silverado and the production plant in Burlingame is leased to you," she said.

"That's not true."

"Yes, it is. You just didn't realize it. You also have tens of millions of dollars in off-shore accounts in the Cayman Islands, in Switzerland, and the Azores," she said.

"Josephine, no I don't," Quinn said. He turned to Shawn who gave him a very pained stare. Both turned back to Josephine.

"Your sister, she set these up, and made them impossible to trace back to her and Catherine?" Shawn asked quietly. Quinn let out a long exhale as he backed into the wall. He slinked down to the ground as his legs collapsed under him.

"Yes. She funneled money from Alfonse Paradis into the accounts. That is why he's bankrupt, not because he was a bad businessman. She's already forwarded the evidence to the feds, and erased her trail. They are preparing to arrest you, Quinn," she said.

"And when they test me this time, I will have the polymer residue in my blood," Quinn said. "Catherine gave it to all of us in the wine."

"Quinn, you can't win this case. How would you vote if you were a jury? There are millions of dollars in off-shore accounts with your name on them, they can prove you own the distribution and production facilities, coupled with the fact that you are the only one alive with the knowledge to make the polymer. With a positive blood test, you'd be convicted in a heartbeat. Catherine is still a ghost. If we can't catch her, we'll never be able to prove she's alive."

"They'll never try me," Quinn said in a quiet, defeated tone. "They'll just hold me without trial until I die, or they'll kill me. That way the polymer's existence won't ever be brought to the attention of the public."

"Quinn, you have to get out of here," Shawn said with urgency. "We have to get you out of here, out of the country, now."

Josephine looked at Quinn. She wiped the tears from her cheeks.

"He's right, Matthew. Get out of here, and don't come back until we've figured out a way to get you exonerated or pardoned." She turned to Shawn. "Shawn, get him out. Call your friends in the South Bay, have them figure out a way to smuggle him out of the country. They're resourceful and well connected. They'll know what to do. I'll stay here and deal with this," she said, nodding towards the destroyed office and her dead sister. She was no longer crying.

"Matthew, this is not the end," she said to him as he pushed to a stand. "I'll find you."

Quinn looked into her wide-open and unashamed eyes. He paused briefly, then grabbed her and pulled her toward him, hugging her so hard it hurt.

"I love you Josephine. I wish it turned out differently." He released her, looking into her eyes, eyes that showed more strength than he had ever seen before. He was overcome with emotion, felt himself on the verge of tears, but he knew now wasn't the time. He broke eye contact, nodded curtly and turned to Shawn. In a moment they were gone.

Chapter 30:

Shawn stopped at a 7-11 on the way out and purchased a prepaid cellular phone. He handed it to Quinn who used it to call Minh. When Minh answered, Quinn put the phone on speaker.

"Minh your phone is bugged. Meet me where you picked me up that day four years ago when we went to the university," Quinn said.

"Which one," Minh asked.

Quinn paused. "Minh, your head's in the fog right now. Get your head out of the fog."

"Got it. We'll be there," he said.

"You'll be tailed," Quinn said. "They mean to take me."

"We'll work it out. I'll smooth out your journey. See you soon," Minh said.

Quinn hung up the phone.

"What did that mean?" Shawn asked.

"Several years ago, when I was on the run, he brought me up to UCSF and we were nearly caught. We rendezvoused at Stowe Lake in Golden Gate Park. The police knew about that. What the police and the feds probably didn't know is that a few months later, we needed a final piece of information, so Minh broke me into the science library at Stanford, his alma mater, and we were almost caught again by campus police. We split up and met at the tennis courts near the golf course on Stanford's campus."

"So we meet him at Stanford, then what?" Shawn asked.

"We go someplace safe, and try to work the rest of this out," Quinn said.

"He said he'd help you get down there, how is he going to do that?" Shawn asked.

"God only knows, but the kid is as dangerous with a computer as Josephine's sister."

The drive from Napa was unremarkable, each of them stiffening up when they saw a police car. But either the APB had not yet been put out, or else the police were too busy to notice. They arrived an hour and a half later at the tennis courts. They saw Minh, dressed like a student, with ratty jeans a t-shirt, and a backpack, with wrap-around sunglasses. He sauntered up to them. "Park the car and follow me," he said. Shawn and Quinn did what they were told, following Minh to a beat-up 1967 Mustang, with rust eating through the wheel-wells.

Quinn smiled as he got into the car. "Not too becoming for a rabid environmentalist, multi-millionaire venture capitalist in Palo Alto," he said. The engine coughed and sputtered before coming to life, sending a large plume of blue smoke out of the dual-exhaust tail pipes.

"That's just the point. I drove the Tesla to my buddy's office over at Oracle. I know a couple dozen people over there. I had my buddy drive my car out, wearing my clothes. He's Vietnamese, and we're about the same size. I came out in a limousine with tinted windows. That took me to Joshua's cousin's house. He restores old rust buckets like this one. He let me borrow the ugliest one, and like that, we're clear!"

"Solid work, pal," Quinn said.

"Hey, I didn't get where I am by being stupid," Minh said.

"They probably bugged you, did you two swap socks and underwear," Shawn asked.

"No need," Minh answered smoothly. "I prefer going commando."

"Too much information," Quinn said. Shawn just laughed.

They drove silently until they reached Capitola, a small town on the Central coast, south of Santa Cruz. They came to a small house about a half-mile from the marina. The garage swung open and they drove right in. Joshua was already there with Jeff McLeod.

When they went into the house, Joshua spoke. "Matthew, Shawn, you remember Jeff?"

Quinn nodded and shook his hand.

"So they have an arrest warrant for you," Minh said.

"Yes," Quinn said. He told them the whole story, including what they learned from Josephine.

"Jeff, can you help Quinn?" Minh asked.

"We've been more prepared since that last episode, Matthew," Joshua said. "We barely got the cash together to get Tasha back that night in Oakland. We weren't going to get caught with our pants down again."

"I'm the contingency man," Jeff said.

"He's totally up-to-speed," Minh said.

"How, exactly does one become a contingency man?" Shawn asked.

"I'm ex-military," Jeff said. "Navy Seal, Annapolis '95, special training in undercover-ops, spent eighteen months in Bosnia, and did two tours in Afghanistan. I got men into and out of the caves at Tora-Bora, and twice got within a hundred yards of bin Laden, and managed to get back out again. I didn't get him, but two of my protégé's were present when we finally did get the bastard."

"If you're that good, why aren't you still in Afghanistan?" Quinn asked. Jeff looked at Minh and Joshua, and instantly Quinn knew the answer.

"You've got to be joking! 'Don't Ask Don't Tell?' They bloody kicked you out? Within a stone's throw of bin Laden twice and they kicked you out? Jesus Christ, our military is stupid sometimes," Quinn said.

"Ancient history, now. I could get reinstated, but I've decided on a different career path. These boys have supported me, and still do," Jeff said. "My loyalty to them is as great as it is to my country, greater in fact. I know what the feds are coming at you with, Quinn, and I support your innocence. I'll help get you out. I am going to step out now." He turned to Minh. "Minh, Joshua, make your way down to the beach in four hours, just like we discussed. Take the dingy out to the last buoy. There is a small cabin cruiser there. Take the boat out and make your way toward Pebble Beach. Drop anchor about a mile off the coast and wait. I'll meet you there." He walked out the back door and disappeared. Dusk was falling, and a layer of fog was rolling in off of the ocean.

The four of them sat around the table in the kitchen. Joshua walked away and returned with a bottle of wine.

"For old times, sake," he said, producing a bottle of Pride Reserve Cabernet. "Still on the young side, but these wines almost always drink terrific," He said. They were subdued as they drank. Quinn remembered four years ago drinking at Pride with Tasha. Quinn thought as he drank the wine, how much his state of mind affected his affinity for it. He had had the wine before, but it just didn't taste as good with all that was hanging over his head. He refused a second glass. Shawn looked at his watch and got up to leave the room. Quinn watched his silent exit. He returned with a knowing smile.

"You look like someone just shot your dog, pal. But I got a plan for you. Here's a supply of your most praiseworthy invention. Take it and undo the damage done to your ticker and lungs by the feds. You'll feel better."

"No, I won't," Quinn said.

"Didn't anyone ever tell you that living well is the best revenge?" Shawn squawked. He broke the seal on one of the jars, and pulled two capsules out. He grabbed the last of the Pride Reserve and poured it into Quinn's glass.

"Open up!" he demanded. Quinn opened his mouth and Shawn tossed the capsules in.

"Now, drink this wine and swallow your elixir, you stubborn, skinny asshole!" Quinn took the pills, the first time he ever knowingly and willingly ingested his polymer.

"You're right, Shawn. They stole back their money, so it's my right to steal back my polymer, isn't it?"

"That's the first sensible thing you've said all day," Shawn said. "Now let's get you the hell out of here before someone finds out where you are."

When the hour approached, they walked in silence to the beach and the boat. Quinn did not know what the plan was, but didn't much care at this point. He was still free, and would try to stay that way. God willing, he would stay alive and healthy enough to see Josephine again.

When they reached the beach, they made their way to the pier, stepped onto the dingy and took it out towards the cruiser. Quinn saw lights on in the cabin of the boat.

"I have one more surprise for you, Pal." Shawn said.

Quinn looked at his friend, confused. Just then, the door swung open on the fishing trawler, and Tasha and Josephine came out to greet them. Josephine approached him silently and leapt into his arms, smothering him in kisses, holding him tight.

"I am so sorry sweetheart," he heard himself say. "I'll get it all reversed, get myself well again. I don't want to miss out on you, on us."

She grabbed his face, her forehead pressed against his, looking him in the eye.

"I'll devote every resource in the world to getting you back, getting you free, getting you here, with me," she said.

He saw a fierceness that was at once beautiful and frightening.

"I love you, Matthew Quinn, and no one will deny me you."

His five friends drove Matthew Quinn out past Monterrey Bay, and down towards Carmel and the famous golf courses which lined the shore. At the requisite point, they dropped anchor and waited in silence.

Six more hours passed without anything happening.

"Do you suppose something's happened to him," Shawn asked.

"I'm starting to worry," Minh said. "He's never late."

"You men never have any patience," Tasha said. Josephine nodded silently, her hands silently stroking the back of Quinn's neck.

“If we are caught, there’s not to be a fight. I go quietly,” Quinn said, looking at his watch. “Jesus, it’s after midnight!”

“Quinn, if you’re caught here, we’re all caught,” Minh said. “I set up a virus and jammed all the lines and terminals used by law enforcement. It was a nasty virus, the first one I made since high school. If they find us together, they’ll figure out it was me and I’ll go to jail for industrial espionage,” Minh said.

“Why would you do that, Minh, endanger yourself like that?” Quinn said, feeling sick to his stomach.

“Easy, for you, pal,” he said. “We helped put you into this situation. We’re guilty of taking your polymer. We made a profit off of it when you sold it, so we’re wrapped up in this, and we owe you something. I needed to make sure the cops were not looking for you two when you drove down here. My virus did just that. I have no regrets,” Minh said, and flashed his toothy smile at Quinn.

Tasha got up out of Shawn’s arms and hugged her brother.

“You’ve got a great heart, Minh,” she said, “a nasty talent, but a great heart.”

“Yeah, I’m going to direct my nasty talent to seeing if I can trace Barbara’s untraceable computer shenanigans. In my experience, nothing is untraceable. It doesn’t matter how good she is. I’m better,” Minh said.

“And so modest,” Tasha said. “Ladies and gentleman, my arrogant little brother.” But she looked proud of him as she said it.

They heard the rumble of a diesel engine approaching.

“I think that’s him,” Joshua said.

“Or the Coast Guard,” Quinn said. Josephine looked at him ruefully.

They went up on deck and saw a seaworthy wooden fishing trawler approach. They shined a light on it as it pulled alongside and threw a rope over. That is when they saw the telltale damage of bullet holes in the hull of the boat, and splintered wood and bullet casings on the deck. Jeff emerged from the cabin, a large crimson stain on his jacket, near his collarbone.

"Sorry I'm so late," he said.

"Jesus, Jeff, what happened?" Joshua asked.

"In spite of our efforts, the feds came at me hard. Best I can tell they were unable to inform the Coast Guard.

"How do you know?" Shawn asked.

"I didn't give them the chance," he said as he dropped his gaze.

"Do we want to know?" Minh asked.

"No, you don't," he said matter-of-factly. "This boat came out of the Golden Gate with no serial numbers on it, no name, and nothing to identify it. Now it has a name, and serial numbers. I wasn't able to clean up the rest of the mess. Quinn, you'll have to do that yourself, there's wood putty and paint. The repairs should be straightforward. I took out their radio equipment when they were still a half-mile away. And, no Tasha, I did not wound any fellow American servicemen. I just destroyed their boat." He turned back to Quinn. "You should be free and clear, Quinn, but you've got to go now. In the next several hours, they'll find that crew on what's left of their disabled vessel. Then word will get out and they'll go after you. The further you are away from here, the better. Head out to international waters, and then go south, don't tell us where, and if you have any needs or any troubles, call this number. He jumped onto the boat Quinn and the others were on and handed him a card with nothing but a phone number on it.

"How far can I get in this thing?" Quinn asked. "I mean, how far until I have to refuel?"

"It's a diesel, and there's a five hundred gallon tank. It's full. There are several drums in the back, each of them a hundred and twenty gallons, and they're also full. There is a siphon and the fuel tank is well marked. There are clothes in the cabin. It cruises nicely at about thirty nautical miles an hour. Run it day and night, you can get more than 4000 miles from here before you'll run out of diesel. If you don't stop, you'll be south of the Equator before you need to refuel. There is a full arsenal in the hull if you need it, and a month's worth of dried food. Minh and Joshua made sure there's plenty of water and wine. Stay away from the Panama Canal. Good luck."

"Just like that eh?" Quinn said. "I guess this is goodbye forever," Quinn said.

"Not forever, pal," Shawn said. "Don't underestimate Tasha and me, this toothy little genius over here, or the power of S and M wines!" He smiled a genuine smile and hugged Quinn.

"You'll be alright Quinn," Joshua said. "We'll get you out of this before too long."

Quinn turned to Minh and Joshua.

"In a thousand lifetimes, I could not repay you for your friendship and loyalty. Thanks guys." Quinn turned to Jeff. "I am sorry you got hurt, but thanks for everything. Thanks to you I actually might have a shot at this."

"I'm well paid for my work, Dr. Quinn. This is nothing but an occupational hazard," he said, rubbing his shoulder.

Quinn turned to Tasha.

"I'm glad you're my friend. The best thing you could do for me is to take good care of Shawn. He doesn't always take the best care of himself." Shawn scoffed behind her. "The world balances itself out, doesn't it?" he said to her. She nodded silently, a single teardrop making its way down the side of her nose. Quinn released her and turned to Josephine.

Before he could speak she covered his mouth with her hand. "You owe me!" she said, sticking her finger into his chest. "You take those damn pills. Take them every day. Take them for me. You owe that to me, to us. You have to live. I'll do my part and we'll pick this apart and get you cleared. You make damn sure you do your part. I'll find you." She finished and kissed him hard on the lips, pulling him aggressively toward her. Quinn embraced her, wishing he could stay with her forever, wishing she could come with him. But as selfish as he was, he wasn't that selfish.

Where he was going was terra incognita. She deserved a stable situation. He had to find a way to give her that.

Jeff nodded in silence as Quinn climbed on board the fishing trawler. As he untied the ropes holding the two boats together, Minh tossed a duffle bag onto the deck. "That's yours. For whatever needs arise!" he shouted. Quinn knew what was in the bag, but opened it anyway. There was a Canadian passport and stacks of non-sequential euro notes in the bag totaling perhaps two million euros. He opened the passport. It had his picture and the Canadian seal upon it. "Jim McGowan, again?" he asked.

Minh shrugged. "Have a safe trip south, Jim." He smiled, all-teeth.

Quinn made to protest, but thought better of it, nodded and bowed a thank-you to his friend, and blew a teary eyed kiss to Josephine. He was choked up as he went into the cabin. The engines fired up, and the trawler and Quinn headed away from his friends and his new love. They disappeared behind him into the darkness and gloom. It was almost two in the morning and he was headed south-southeast. He slowly accelerated to thirty knots.

Terroir/Myette

Chapter 31:

Three days later, Shawn and Tasha walked into the law offices of Stearns, Webber, and Sloan. They found Josephine in her office with Henri Paradis. She was dressed in black. She greeted both of them warmly.

"Shawn, thanks for all of this, and for coming up here," she said. He smiled and they embraced. "Tasha, thanks for coming up here." She gave her a girlfriend-hug and pecked her on the cheek.

"Well," she said, stealing a glance at Henri, "we're both so pleased that you had the ethical foresight to allow us this buyback opportunity."

"It's Matthew Quinn you should thank," Shawn said.

"And where might he be?" Henri asked, as the corner of Josephine's mouth turned up just slightly.

"God only knows," Shawn said. Tasha was silent.

"Well, I hope the wind remains at his back," he said. "Shall we get down to business?"

"Certainly," Shawn said. "Where do I sign?"

"You know it's not that simple. We'll go over the basics here, and then you'll go over to the title company and sign over the papers," Josephine said.

"What happened to the charges against your brother?" Shawn asked, looking at Henri.

"They were dropped," Henri said. "And he has had a change of heart. What with all of the death and suffering that has happened in the last several weeks, we all have examined a lot of our personal shortcomings, our personal hostilities. This is not what our lives were supposed to be about. We're trying for a new start. He's lost his empire in the Central Valley. He's interested in settling with me and in jointly replanting the family plot. It will be a fifty/fifty venture, and with any luck, we can harvest our first grapes for wine in three or four years. Maybe we'll have a release in six years or so. I'll be nearly eighty then, but it'll sure be something to look forward to.

What are you going to do, Shawn? I can keep my eye out for a plot of land for you."

Shawn smiled and put his arm around Tasha.

"I am going back up to Fairplay. I'm going to see if I can maximize my potential there. Maybe we'll be able to compete with Napa someday. Not with Cabernet, but with our own grapes, maybe Syrah or Grenache. Tasha is coming up to see what life is like in the foothills. Someday Quinn and I will pursue a joint effort down here, but it won't be any time soon. The time just isn't right at present."

Paradis nodded and smiled warmly. "It'll all work out in the end. The foothills, they remind me of Napa back in the seventies, just getting onto its feet. The best days are ahead for the Sierra, I'm sure of it."

"We'll see. Thanks. And, will we see you two later today?"

"I don't think it would be right for me to be there, given the circumstances," Henri said. "I have to respect how she felt, regardless of her actions."

"Are you okay, Josephine?" Shawn asked.

She turned to him and stuck her jaw out. She paused, a flash of real pain on her face. She nodded definitively. "I'll be okay. It was…." she broke off, tears welling in her eyes.

"I'm sorry," he said. "We'll see you at the memorial."

She forced a smile, and bid Shawn and Tasha farewell.

Two hours later, Shawn and Tasha met Minh and Joshua at the cemetery. Jeff was there also.

Minh spoke. "We asked Jeff to provide some logistical support here for us. We figured Catherine's likely to show up, and we didn't want her to turn this into a bloodbath, at least not without some firepower on our side."

"He's a good guy to have around in a pinch," Joshua said.

"Well, she'd be crazy to try anything," Shawn said. "But then again, she'd be crazy to do half the shit she's done."

"Isn't she wanted in questioning for the murder of Virginia Park?" Tasha asked.

"They aren't actively pursuing that," Minh said, coughing into his hand. "Her alias, Veronica, has reportedly disappeared. Besides, they said something about the most important witness being missing also." He looked away.

The ceremony began, and they listened in silence. On the other side, a woman with dark sunglasses, blond hair, a black veil, and a black pants suit approached. She watched the funeral silently and alone.

Shawn leaned toward Tasha. "That's her. That's Catherine. New hair, but it has to be."

The funeral ended without so much as a shot fired, with most of the Eulogy given by Josephine. After the ceremony, everyone left to return to his or her respective home.

* * * * * *

Christine Miller returned to her new vineyard and estate. She had abandoned her Eastern European roots with this alias. She was scheduled for another round of plastic surgery next week, and would keep wearing blonde wigs after today. She had to admit, Matthew Quinn had good taste. The vineyard and house atop Mt. Veeder was beautiful and picturesque. It wasn't the plot of legend that she had sought, but it was great nonetheless. Good earth, good vines, and great wine. And soon, very soon, there would be something else, something magical.

She watched the news as the feds closed down and mothballed the Silverado Springs Resort, retaking the property of the fugitive Matthew Quinn. They also shut down the laboratory in Burlingame. It needled her some, but she would get over it. She knew she had gotten more from Quinn than she had lost to him. She didn't give a damn about her deceased father and dim-witted brother. Their actions had cost her more of the family fortune than Quinn. Quinn was just a convenient scapegoat.

She didn't know how she felt about his escape. Maybe his escape would keep eyes off of her, and as an expatriate, he could do little more damage to her or her fortunes, but she craved revenge upon him for thwarting her plan to destroy the Paradis family, and she wanted revenge on Josephine for killing Barbara.

She had loved Barbara. If she was ever in love, it was with Barbara. She was beautiful, wickedly intelligent, deadly, and so very angry. It made her the sexiest woman alive to Catherine. Her death was the worst loss she had ever suffered. Revenge would be methodical, logical, and would occur only when the time was right. She would make them all suffer before they died, and she would profit by it. She wasn't sure how, when or by what means, but the gay millionaires, their slut sister, her bastard of a boyfriend, Barbara's fiercely sexy cold-blooded sister, and yes, Quinn himself, would still suffer more. That fellow at the funeral standing in the background: who the hell was he? It didn't matter. He would pay, too. She had a fortune and a veritable army. She could stay on her vineyard atop the mountain, and watch as her enemies were eliminated, one by one.

Of course, there would also have to be revenge upon Henri Paradis. She had failed there, thanks to Quinn. But time was on her side.

Catherine wandered out to her vineyards, and watched as the small tractor drove between the dormant grapes, delivering a fine mist of yeast to the soil around the vineyard. This was not just fermenting yeast. It was the product of three years of scientific work. Why try to make the miracle in an industrial plant when a small single celled organism can do all of the work for you?

She was proud of her accomplishment. In three years, her wine would be the elixir of immortality, and it would command astronomical prices, prices that would put the cult wines to shame. Like the herbal concoction before it, its ingredients would be completely unregulated, in fact, just fermented juice of grapes. The medicinal properties would be just a "natural" byproduct of the biodynamics, the *terroir* of her soil. It was too easy.

Terroir/Myette

www.ingramcontent.com/pod-product-compliance
Lightning Source LLC
Chambersburg PA
CBHW062028170626
46813CB00001B/328
9780615627007